Be My Knife

Also by David Grossman

Be My Knife

David Grossman

Translated by Vered Almog and Maya Gurantz

Picador
Farrar, Straus and Giroux
New York

www.picadorusa.com

Picador® is a U.S. registered trademark and is used by
Farrar, Straus and Giroux under license from Pan Books Limited.

For information on Picador Reading Group Guides, as well as ordering, please
contact the Trade Marketing department at St. Martin's Press.
Phone: 1-800-221-7945 extension 763
Fax: 212-677-7456
E-mail: trademarketing@stmartins.com

Library of Congress Cataloging-in-Publication Data

Grossman, David.
    [She-tehi li ha-sakin. English]
    Be my knife / David Grossman.
        p. cm.
    ISBN 0-312-42147-8
    I. Title.

PJ5054.G728 S5413 2002
892.4'36—dc21   2001033645

First published in Israel under the title *She-tehi li ha-sakin*
by Hakibbutz Hameuchad Publishing House, Ltd.

D10 9 8 7 6 5 4 3

When the word turns into a body
And the body opens its mouth
And speaks the word from which
It was created—
I will embrace that body
And lay it to rest by my side.

—"Hebrew Lesson #5"
  Chezi Laskly, *The Mice and Leah Goldberg*

Contents

Yair

April 3

Miriam,

You don't know me. When I write to you I don't know myself very well, either. I tried not to write, I did, I've tried for two days, but now I've broken down.

I saw you at the class reunion a few days ago, but you didn't see me— I was standing over to the side. Maybe I was standing in your blind spot. Someone said your name, a few boys called you teacher, and you were standing with a tall man who must have been your husband. That's it, that's all I know about you—and even that's a little too much for me. Don't worry, I don't want to meet you in person or interfere with your day-to-day life in any way, but I would like you to agree to receive my letters. That is—to let me tell you about myself in writing every now and again. Not that my life is so interesting (it's not, and I'm not complaining), but I want to give you things I can't give to anybody else. Things I didn't think could be given, or that I ever would want to give to anyone. You know you're under no obligation, you don't have to respond (and I'm almost sure you won't), but in case you feel like giving me a little sign that you are reading, I rented a post-office box just for you. The number is on the envelope.

There's no point to this if I have to explain it, so you don't have to bother responding, because then I was wrong about you, clearly. But if you are the woman I saw hugging herself, with a slightly crooked smile, I think you'll understand.

Yair W.

April 7

Dear Miriam,

Ever since I got your letter, I haven't done a single thing—I can't—can't work, can't live my life, I've just been running circles around you, howling out your name. If you were here right now, I would hold on to you with all my strength; everything I'm feeling would tear us both to pieces (don't worry, I'm not terribly strong). And what's more, I promise to answer every question you asked; you deserve only the most honest answers just for writing me at all—and for writing what you did! You agreed! You weren't scared off by my restrained suicide note (which left two deep rings of tooth marks on the inside of my cheek). First, though, before anything else, I must tell you how we really met, you and I, and I don't mean the class reunion last week (you answered me! In one day! You didn't laugh at the lunatic who suddenly erupted at your feet). The reunion belongs to real life. What has reality got to do with us? What room, do you think, will it make for us?

Where to start—if only I could start from all sides at once without feeling as though every word has too many letters, takes up too much time. I feel as if someone is perched on the point of my pen, turning Hebrew into French—I never imagined how hard it could be to explain, to force that feeling apart into words. You wrote that I reminded you a bit of the boy with the thousand-league boots; well, I wish I could just leap over the stage of logical explanations, so you could know everything right away, so you could take me, all of me, I could exist in you—open my eyes and see you smiling at me, saying, "It's all right, don't worry, begin." (I'll stop here. I have a feeling that every additional word will hurt my case with you. It's your turn.)

Yair

April 7

(Just a few more words.) I sent that letter, came back, and still couldn't calm down—why should I?—oh, Miriam, please pay no attention to this fool who's been smiling uncontrollably since this morning. He's so happy. He wants right at this minute to take off his clothes, strip off his epidermis, everything, and stand before you bare, right down to the white kernel of his soul. I wish I could paint for you, bray for you, neigh, bark, even whistle for you everything roaring inside me (which reminds me—when I was about twenty, I looked for ways to be a secular version of one of the Righteous Thirty-six. This led to a plan to, at least once a week, sit down on the bus behind a solitary woman, preferably a woman in black widow's weeds—but you can't be picky—and, without letting her see me, quietly whistle a love song in her ear that could trip through the outer shell, into her inner ear, and touch everything that was asleep, despaired of, congealed) . . .

I'm not at all scared that we're strangers, by the way. On the contrary, tell me, what is more attractive and provocative than the possibility of taking something very precious—the most precious thing—a secret or weakness, or a thoroughly implausible request like the one I made of you, and deliberately placing it in the hands of a total stranger? And then to be tormented by so much shame and disgrace for allowing the beggar in me such a transparent delusion, so that for three days and three nights I spent every moment in self-imposed solitary confinement, a trap . . . then, just as I was about to give up, stupid, spiteful, gloomy, and gray, all of a sudden your white hand—

Look, maybe you can't see what excites me so terribly, but your warm, radiant letter, especially the P.S. at the end, that one line—it was as if you came and led me by the hand from shadow into light. That's how I felt, that you had given me your hand and led me across a watershed of light, it was so simple, as if it was completely natural for a person to do that for a stranger.

(And now, a cold wave. Of all the times, now, just at this moment, and why? Because it was good? A cold wave rising from my stomach, a cold fist rolled up into a ball just under my heart—get acquainted with it.)

Again, please understand I'm really talking about letters only, not a meeting, never a body. No flesh, not with you, your letter made that so clear to me: only words. It would ruin us, being face-to-face, it would immediately take us down into familiar territory. Also, of course, we will keep this strictly secret, we won't let anybody in on it, so that no one from the outside can use our secret words against us. Only my words meeting yours, so we can feel the rhythm of our breath slowly becoming one.

It makes me so tired to write this way, not a usual fatigue, but after every few lines I really have to stop to take a breath, calm down.

Evening. I took a break. Recovered a little. It has been exactly ten hours since I found your white envelope in my box, with my name on one side and yours on the other (maybe I didn't need any more than that at first). And inside, on half a sheet (were you in a hurry?), your answer. I couldn't truly grasp what I was reading in that first moment. It was as if a dazzling glow radiated out of every word, even the most nebulous ones. The way that, if you plumb the depths of the word "I," there's a moment of understanding; and then a kind of dark gloom started to spread out from the center and draw me inside. Then, when I got to the P.S.: your thanks for my unexpected gift (you're thanking me!), and your heart, suddenly filled with yearning for itself as a child—well, there's nothing else to say at that moment, is there? The most significant thing has already been said.

Listen, though—I once read that Our Sages of Blessed Memory had the idea that we have one tiny bone in the body, above the end of the spine—they call it the "Luz." You can't kill it, it doesn't crumble after death and can't be destroyed by fire. It is from this that we will be re-created at the Resurrection. I used to play a little game with myself—I would try to guess the Luz of the people I knew, divine the final thing that would be left of them, that indestructible thing from which they'll be reborn. And, of course, I searched for my own Luz as well, but nothing within me met all the necessary conditions. So I stopped asking and looking, I gave my Luz up for lost, until I saw you in the playground. All of a sudden that forgotten thought arose from the dead, and along with it the sweet and crazy notion came to me that maybe my Luz isn't in me after all, but in someone else.

April 7

Me again. It's just before midnight, and this is the third letter today. Don't worry, you have no idea how many letters I *haven't* sent you today, because this is the first day we've shared, this day that your letter came to me and I answered. I can believe—until your next letter arrives, at least—that you are reading me exactly as I'm writing to you, half asleep,

6

half daydreaming (I actually danced as I walked through work today), so I can murmur "Water, water" to you in my thin voice. My voice gets reedy when I think about you, Miriam, water, trickle water on me. I don't know why. Maybe because without the rough *r*, your name is *mayim*, water. And maybe because there can be no fertilization without liquid, I feel in my bones that we two need to be surrounded by lots of water, by waterfalls and rivers, simply so we can begin to exist.

Did I exaggerate? Did I get carried away? I felt you flinch (really: your body made a face), or maybe I used some especially bruising word? You must guide me, explain to me where you hurt and where I have to be gentle. Or did I just flood over today and tire you out?

Because writing to you does exhaust me, as I told you. I have never felt so dizzy from writing. Five lines, ten, and I really start to feel dizzy. It's nice, too, though, it reminds me of how I felt as a child, the first time I went out into the world after a long illness. Listen, maybe we should decide from the first that this correspondence won't go on for too long? Shall we say a year? Or until it becomes unbearably pleasant? Because if my body is telling me the truth right now, and as we know, the body doesn't lie—

Oh, doesn't it, though? How many times have I lied with my body? How many times have I kissed and stroked, closed my eyes with a sigh and come like an explosion, and not meant anything special by it?

How many times have you?

Miriam, if what I feel for you is true, even a year might be too long for the two of us. We won't last longer, and we'll sow destruction in our wake, and it seems to me that we both have something in the world, outside ourselves, to lose. So I thought, All right, it's stupid, but maybe we'll decide on this from the beginning. We'll set some date, or wait until something specific occurs in the world, an outside event that has nothing to do with us but can be our private sign on the general calendar. What do you say, does that calm you down (it does give us some sort of framework)? That way, we can also know from the beginning that our separation is out of our hands and that we have to make everything happen before then. To be all or nothing, what do you think?

You're gone again, you've cooled off and pulled back all of a sudden. I know I've been writing total nonsense, that I've ended our story before it could even begin, but wait! Don't make up your mind about me! Listen: it would be so easy for me to rip up this page and write everything over again without those miserable lines—to prevent the moment when I lose you to my own fear.

You see, I let it stand. Exactly as it is. I didn't erase a thing. Because the moment you answered me, I decided that everything that happens in me because of you will be yours. Inscribed in my body, and in yours. Every thought and desire, lust and dread, every baby, fetus, or abortion created in me will be yours. This is the core of my pact with you, and only with you: I hereby relinquish all my wooing masks, along with my self-censorship, all of my defenses—

(What a relief, just to write those words.)

Except that I just read what I wrote.

I wish I could write to you in some other way; rather, I wish I were a man who wrote some other way. So many thick words, when, in fact, it could also be so simple, couldn't it? Just "My dear, tell me where it hurts." So I will shut my eyes tight and write quickly: I wish that two total strangers could overcome strangeness itself, the mighty, ingrained principle of foreignness, the whole overstuffed Politburo sitting so deep in our souls. We could be like two people who inject themselves with truth serum and at long last have to tell it, the truth. I want to be able to say to myself, "I bled truth with her," yes, that's what I want. Be a knife for me, and I, I swear, will be a knife for you: sharp but compassionate, your word, not mine. I didn't even remember that such a delicate, soft tone was allowed in the world, of a word with no skin (if you say it aloud a few times, you can feel salty hard earth as water starts pushing through its veins). You're tired, I will force myself to say good night.

Yair

April 12

Miriam,

I knew it, don't say I didn't know and didn't warn myself.

Is that truly what you felt? And to that extent?

Well, as you can probably imagine, I didn't much enjoy that slap in the face. Giving with one hand and then taking with two, Scheherazade entwining herself with the idiot Sultan . . . This morning I couldn't bear the suffering and express-mailed your first letter back to myself.

8

Though you do understand, don't you? It was all out of the fear that—after I succeeded at tugging at your sleeve and keeping you for a moment by my side—my faint charm will expire and I will never have a second chance. And you must, must believe me—my true self will be revealed only in a second look, or a third. Under no circumstances in the glance you are giving me now.

Anyway, Miriam (you have a warm name, it flows and checks in the same moment), stay with me just a little while longer, just until this unwilling seizure ends—you can scribble a few more desperate little notes about me in your diary in the meantime. Still, let me stay longer, during your lonely sleepless conversations with yourself, or with Anna (a friend of yours?), or with your cat and dogs. And then, maybe, not everything will be lost for us. After all, you did ask, it seemed with genuine concern, what it is that terrifies me so much, and how the same person who could dare make a wish so great from his life could also be so frightened of it.

You can explain that to me. Please.

Should I tell you how many times I have read your two letters? Do you want to laugh? At every hour of the day and night, in whispers and aloud. In the steaming water of the bathtub, over an open gas flame in the kitchen, and in the middle of a work meeting, my brow furrowed with seriousness, surrounded by ten people. My ridiculous attempts to be with you in every state of matter. I went to the toilets in the Central Bus Station of Jerusalem, especially for the pornographic scrawls and obscene graffiti, so they would blister and peel with shame when they heard your earnest words, the way you write without games, without pretense; even when you're disappointed, you write without protecting yourself even one little bit—just like that, you come to me, giving me your trust. Without even knowing me at all.

Should I tell you more about myself? What is there to tell?

Something in your writing reminded me—I once thought of teaching my son a private language. Isolating him from the speaking world on purpose, lying to him from the moment of his birth, so he would believe only the language I gave him. And it would be a compassionate language. What I mean is—I wanted to take him by the hand and name everything he saw with words that would save him from the inevitable heartaches. So that he wouldn't be able to comprehend the existence of, for instance, war. Or that people kill. Or that this red, here, is blood. It's a used-up kind of idea, I know, but I loved to imagine him crossing through life with an innocent, trusting smile—the first truly enlightened child.

I don't have to tell you of my joy when he began to speak; you probably remember the wonder of a child first naming things. Although every time he learned a new word, one that is also a little "theirs," everybody's, even his first word, a beautiful word like "light"—my heart curdled around the edges, because I thought, Who knows what he is losing in this moment, how many infinite kinds of glamour he felt and saw, tasted and smelled, before he pressured them into this little box, "light," with a *t* at the end like a switch clicking off. You understand me, don't you?

Oh yes, of course you understand the edges of your heart curdling. You might even be a modest expert in your way. I knew it from the first look. And I have, as well, apparently succeeded at dampening your spirit and curdling your heart in no small way.

But was it really that bad? Really, truly? As if you had lost a precious thing that you yearned for up until the moment you had it?

At least tell me what that precious thing was, so I'll know what was almost in me.

Yair

April 16

You are right, of course, and I absolutely deserve a scolding (but not for a moment have I thought that you were made only of words). Who could imagine that you also have such a thin, biting, cutting sarcasm to you—I saw a hint of it in your shoulders and your back, something pinched and embittered, as if preparing for the next blow—or am I completely wrong?

Or is it all my fault? Tell me, am I the thing pinching your spine? I know so well how I do it to myself, I just wish I wasn't doing the same thing to you . . .

Listen: today, across the street from my workplace—an industrial area, midmorning, at the harsh peak of light—I saw a blind man sitting at the bus stop. He had a bowed head, a stick squeezed between his knees. A bus stopped, and another blind man got off it. When he passed in front of the one on the bench, they both immediately pulled themselves up erect and their heads came together. I stood still—couldn't move. They groped and discovered each other, and for one moment it seemed as if they were tied together, clinging, frozen. It lasted no more than a second, in total silence, and after that moment they detached themselves and went their separate ways. But my skin was covered in goose bumps, the hair on my skin stood up in your name all over my body, and I thought, This is the way!

So come on, come closer, I want to give you something real and intimate, don't run away, don't stiffen up, something very intimate to offset the "anonymity" you slammed at me, sitting on your porch as if you were in a full courtroom (a purple leaf fell, trapped between the page and envelope of your letter, and got squashed a little bit over your "intimacy-anonymity," blurring both words). Flex your muscles, Miriam, we said it was all or nothing.

When my wife and I were first dating, we took a trip to Mt. Carmel one Saturday morning. And we passed through a little patch of forest. It was very early, just a little bit after dawn. We talked, and we laughed. And I—who usually despise what is called the Beauty of Creation—could suddenly no longer contain within myself the wonder around me, and immediately stripped down and started running between the trees, naked and yelling and dancing. And Maya (we'll call her Maya between us, and you are also welcome to choose names for your dear ones as you wish) was astonished and stopped—maybe she was just put off by my nakedness, which she saw out in the open for the first time—and it isn't that lovely in the dark—and I heard her calling to me, quietly, begging me to stop. It was too late—I was already drunk with nature, and I leaped at her from all directions in a kind of a wild bridal dance, which looked pretty ridiculous, I guess. I invited her to join me and felt—for just a moment—that she wanted to—you see, I had never agreed to dance with her before, not at parties, or among people, and suddenly, here I could do it naked—I was possessed, I didn't do it on purpose. Just imagine, dancing and naked, corks popping with happiness. Perhaps it is impossible to be unbeautiful when you're happy. And Maya almost gave herself away, I felt it roaring inside her, roaring to me; she almost uprooted herself—but, at the last minute, stopped. Why did the policeman in your dream demand that you file charges against me for writing threatening letters?

(And how it revived me all of a sudden when you told the nosy idiot that they actually look to you like letters threatening my own life. And maybe that's why you're staying with me.) And I was dancing in the forest. I wish I could dance like that now, at this point in my life. I danced, because in some wonderful way that cold wave of doubt failed to emerge in me—

It did emerge. Of course it did, my gears work with clocklike precision, injecting venom from my glands into my bloodstream as soon as my heart expands for any reason. But that time, it just made me dance even harder. I don't know why, perhaps I felt as if I was making the right mistake for myself, for once; and even after Maya had already turned back and gone and sat in the car, I couldn't stop, running between the trees, dancing, the smell of the pines became so pungent my eyes watered. I was naked, surrounded by voices all around, birds and faraway barks and the buzz of insects; I smelled the earth and the caves and the ashes of summer bonfires, and I felt as if a huge cataract that had been covering me was peeling off my body. Only after I had simply collapsed from exhaustion did I gather my clothes and go back to the car. Her face was pale, and she didn't look at me; she asked me to put my clothes on because people might come by and we'd better go home right away because her parents were waiting for us to have breakfast with them. And suddenly her voice broke and she burst out crying. I started sniveling, too, I understood that this was the end of our young love. And I thought I couldn't stand breaking up with her, because I had never loved someone this way, with the same joy and simplicity and health as I loved her, and as usual, I had spoiled it from the beginning by exposing myself.

So we sat in the car, each one to himself, and we actually wept quite bitterly, she's dressed and I'm naked. Our crying brought us closer, we nudged each other and laughed, and I started putting my clothes back on. And she helped me, dressing me, garment after garment, buttoning me, rolling up my sleeves. And I kissed her and licked her tears throughout, because I understood that she was crying over me but not leaving—mourning me and staying—and my heart swelled with gratitude. I knew I would never do anything like that to her again in my life, and I decided to protect her from myself from that moment on, because she couldn't live defenseless in the same world in which I was doing such things. She laughed through her tears and said almost the same thing, that in order to defend her from me I would simply have to stay with her always. That was half a joke, but also a profound truth, the fatal logic of two, of a couple, and you ought to know that this kind of logic sometimes reveals itself to a couple only after a complete life together (I saw the man you stood with or next to). But we peeked into it somehow from the very first moment.

I haven't thought of that moment in years. I was always a bit appalled to remember myself dancing the way I did. And the rest got blurred right along with it. We were just frightened children; but in spite of that, in a flash, we managed to establish a complex life contract with each other. We warned by law and were warned by law, and I am amazed to understand now how within one second we focused our gazes in such a manner that from that moment on they would turn only at the right angles needed to ensure that our love would always win, at any cost. And we also agreed on the cost. And we have never spoken about it, never. How can you suddenly speak about that in the middle of life, tell me.

Tell me.

I shouldn't have told you about that, should I? What have you got to do with the married life of a person you haven't even seen? I already feel the coldness of that mistake. Here I am, again, a clown—this is probably what it looks like to you, some man throwing everything he owns up into the air, and of course everything is scattered around him on the ground. Never mind, people love clowns—that is what my couple of great educators taught me (but consider, on the borders of your mind, think of me, let's say, like a man with a huge burn on his face deciding to enter a room full of people). Perhaps your way of thinking dictates that I should have waited until we knew each other a little better before telling you such a story, yes? I think along the same lines, but with you I'm not doing things according to my reflection but according to my distortion. And, at the same time, I don't want to wait, because our time together is different, spherical, every point on it is at the exact same distance to the center. And I won't apologize if I'm embarrassing you; this is not salon chatter. It is murder to erase one word to you—and everything I said here—I didn't plan any of it—and I will not erase a word!

April 16–17

Can't sleep. I wish I could already know how the letter I wrote this morning makes you feel. And whether you'll continue to write to me after you read it. I am almost certain you won't. You'll consider it rude of me to expose such aspects of my life. Well, I am quite pleased with myself for sending it anyway. Even with the full day of self-torture that went with it. And you were right that I'm looking for a partner to join me on an imaginary journey, but you were completely wrong when you said that I might not need a real partner. Exactly the opposite: I need a *real* partner for an *imaginary* journey. As I'm writing these words, my heart thumps in a physically very real way, and in general, my heart beats true only when I imagine—now—again—thumping. Did you know there is such a bird, a thumper-bird, a parpur?

If you touch its chest—once—gently—its heart stops beating and it dies. One mustn't make a single wrong move with this bird, because any tiny mistake sends a delicate impact to its heart and it just stops beating. If I could only buy such a parpur, two actually—no: I would buy a flock and let them fly here, above what I'm writing you, so they could be living lie detectors, like the canaries that used to be sent into mines to discover gas leaks. Imagine, if you will: one false or inexact word, or one that is rude, or just indifferent—and a dead bird falls on the page. Then you'll see how I write to you.

By the way, I forgot to tell you that you offended me when you thought I might have mistaken you for someone else I saw that night. And I was even more offended by your difficulty in deciding which you would prefer—that I was mistaken or that I was right.

But you know what really broke my heart? When you described yourself to me to make sure. Because of how you somehow diminished yourself into one single sentence, in parentheses on top of that ("Quite tall, long curly messy hair, glasses . . ."). If you really feel yourself to be in parentheses—at least let me squeeze into them as well and let the whole world remain outside. Let the world only be the element outside the parentheses that will multiply us on the inside.

Y.

P.S. Anyway—even though this journey isn't exactly smooth right now, rough going and twisting and turning from the beginning, I have to tell you something. Do you have any idea that my pupils dilate when I see a word of yours in another place, even when I stumble upon it in a newspaper or in a TV commercial . . . because certain words are so obviously yours, your soul prints, and coming from any other human being they sound like speaking equipment, fragments of language, no more than that. And until there was you, I never imagined that meeting a stranger's language could be as exciting as the first touch of her body, and her smell, and the texture of her skin and hair and beauty marks. Do you feel the same way?

April 21

But how will I bring us together, to meet? You and me, how will I bring us together? Your letter arrived. It's on the table, blanched as a corpse. White reflects all the light beams, doesn't it? I will open it soon. Let me enjoy the doubt, let me spread a little optimistic color . . . have I already told you that I keep seeing us submerged in green? Green keeps flashing through my mind when I think of you. Great, wide green. Here, the endless depths of an ocean; there, a dense European forest; there again, maybe just a large lawn (I should have warned you my dreams usually end grasshopper-high). You're sitting in the grass reading a book, and I, let's say, a newspaper. And there is a wide space between us, a huge lawn: two strangers, and how do you bring them together in an embrace instantly, without having to go through all the in-between stages and without reciting all the sentences that millions of men and women have chewed the flavor from, before them?

By the weight of it—one page, not more. I thought of writing what is written in there myself as preparation. But you forbade me to make my own decisions about what you think and feel. So maybe I'll write about a little daydream playing in my head for a few days now, a daydream about us. I wonder what you will think of it, this picture, quite a silly one of me and you and how we were deep in thought, reading—but because we were the only ones there on the grass, we became sharply aware of each other's presence. I was wearing jeans, as usual; you were in a black dress, a little loose and caressing your body from head to toe, and covered with stars and bright moons. If I'm not mistaken, there was also a delicate, breathing green scarf covering your shoulders. This is how I saw you at the reunion (a scarf? or a long silk shawl? every detail is important to me now). "The only thing I remembered was the green gown she wore," this is how the Seducer met Cordelia for the first time in *Diary of a Seducer*, and maybe this scarf is the source from which all my green springs.

The green that, in a blink, was turned off by your husband's huge gray sweater, which he threw over your shoulders when you shivered. Do you remember that? Because I clearly remember some kind of quick attacking motion from his side that shocked me, while I stared at you, when I was still unaware of how I was staring at you. And he—that "he" from whom you by no means intend to hide our relationship, only because it would never occur to him to investigate what you do and with whom—suddenly, from the altitude of his titan's height, he threw the sweater over you like someone tossing a lasso over a runaway colt.

But what really made you shiver? Quite tall, long curly messy hair, glasses . . . if those annoying parentheses hadn't been there, I would have laughed: is that how you see yourself? Only that? Why didn't you write about your magnificent stance, erect and soft at the same time; and about your radiant cheeks; and how is it that you didn't mention that your face has a kind of naïveté, light-complected and freckled, a bit anachronistic—don't take offense—like people from the fifties . . .

And why didn't I immediately write words like the gold of the grain and farmland and butter. That you have a face that from a first or an indifferent or unkeen look seems almost modest compared to that wonderfully expressive body—I hope I'm not offending you—the face of a decent, good little girl, the handsome, responsible face of a class president. And suddenly the eye is hooked by something unexpected, the dark mole under your lips, the mouth itself, wide, trembling, and restless, which seems as if it has its own inner life. You have a hungry mouth, Miriam; tell me if anybody has ever told you that and I will immediately find another word—under no circumstances will I splash about in their words.

I swallowed your face that evening. I saw you for maybe five minutes, but for those five complete minutes you were branded into me, and I know your face by heart and by my heart in your mouth, and after you've heard all this, you will have to decide if that "queer moan" came truly because you thought I had mistaken you for another woman. Or if, perhaps, you moaned because she was you after all, because my fortunes chose you . . . I will not help you waver, it has been three weeks since then and every new woman I see—no sooner do my eyes fall upon her than my mind returns to your image. Oh, how your face moved me. I, who always start from the body. But I didn't neglect the body, God forbid—I think you tried to blur its lines with yours ("quite tall" . . .)—my pen is already shaking in my hand with the thought that soon I will write your body, the beauty of your body and its generosity underneath your clothes. And also the slightly rigid roundness of your shoulders, I don't forget it, as if somebody is taking refuge in you and you are defending him.

And how you lowered your head, and how your body shivered a bit underneath that dress, and how, as if within a dream, in slow motion, you hugged your body to yourself as if you were sorry for it—it sounds strange, but that's how it seemed, as if you felt sorrow and compassion for it. And with one look I knew things about you—I'm probably annoying you again, arrogantly telling you about yourself with no hesitation—but I simply knew. Your face was open and disarmed at that moment, I have never seen a mature, grown human being so peeled of her epidermis. You could actually see every emotion passing through you immediately written upon your face—you're incapable of hiding anything. Do you know how dangerous that is? And where were you for that life lesson?

(Enough! I can't hold back anymore. Come, scowling, stern-faced messenger, come, you astringent pink slip, let's hear what you have to tell us.)

April 22
Miriam,
Before everything:
In the supermarket today, this evening—a child I didn't know asked me to give him three bars of chocolate from a high shelf. I reach my hand up to the shelf—and in the blink of an eye he is transformed into a sick child in whom an unknown disease resides, who has been taken care of and worried over for a few months. And now it seems he's going to be fine, he's on the road to recovery, and he suddenly starts gorging himself on chocolate, a chocolate attack; he's sleepless, gets out of bed at night, bingeing, and can't be stopped. And you don't feel good about taking away that one little pleasure when he's been going through such a difficult treatment—but the thing is, that child knows something. More than everyone—more than his parents, his doctors, even himself—he has some kind of internal premonition and is equipping himself with choco-

late for the long, cold journey that awaits him—I handed him the chocolate bars and he ran off happily.

Such a flicker of nonsense came to me as I was reaching up to the shelf, and I swore to remember it so I could tell you about it, I even scribbled it down on a little note. So what? I have ten of these a day, and I lose ten for good, and truly, it isn't an especially grand flicker, but if I hadn't written it down for you, I would have forgotten it, too. And that's a shame; still, it is a shame that even such a tiny flicker would die before it was born, for it is a living fragment of the soul. Of course, every person has hundreds of these, but no one would have come up with this stupid idea. And even if it did occur to someone—who is capable of telling another person about such a flicker? Have you ever heard somebody telling another person about his flickers?

And where did I find the nerve to tell you about such internal foolishness, something undoubtedly no more than a crackle of static from my brain?

Perhaps from your sudden understanding that if you stopped writing to me now, only because I drive you to distraction here and there, you might never forgive yourself for the rest of your life.

Look, Miriam, I've been reading your short letter over and over. Maybe I don't dare to understand it all the way through, but I think it says here in your miniature handwriting that it is clear to you if you turned your back on me now, before you even truly met me, you would feel as if you were denying the essence of your faith.

And I already know, by the way, you shouldn't have had to explain in such detail that this "essence of faith" has absolutely nothing at all to do with me—that it is completely between you and yourself, perhaps it is even, as you said, the Thing between you and yourself. But I'm also reading the strange cluster of strange letters you added to the bottom, that it sometimes gives you the shivers—that a stranger could notice in one quick glance that Thing between you and yourself, and without even knowing you, call it by its private name.

Yair

(Tomorrow already)

I mean, if I could only put some of these together, these soul-fragments, maybe I could see them as one complete mosaic and finally understand something, a kind of *principle* that holds me together. Don't you think so? I'm talking about the things that have no first names, that accumulate on the bottom of the soul through life, layers of sediment and ore. If you asked me to describe them to you—I would have no words, only contractions of my heart, a passing shadow, a sigh. Someone hugs herself in the middle of a group of people and suddenly you are filled with yearning. Someone writes: you introduce yourself as a "stranger." But a complete stranger could not write to me this way . . . and immediately my throat closes up. One drop leaking out from my loneliness gland. No more than that. But what is more real and important than that? Once, during a guard shift in the Sinai, Rilke explained to me that, in the depths, everything transforms itself into a law. Very nice, I told him, how reassuring to think that somewhere everything is tied to some kind of meaning, but this insight doesn't satisfy me anymore, Rainer Maria, my time is ending fast and even if I live for another thirty years, I will see only another thirty-one saffron flowers. Adds up to a pretty small bouquet, and I would like to see this constitution drafted before my own eyes, for once. Do you understand? The *constitution*, and I want an organized tour through those mysterious "depths," and I demand to know the private names of all the forms mentioned above, to call them by their names at least once, so they will answer me and finally, for once, be mine. Just not this permanent, consistent silence (that is in this instance, for example, with no describable cause, amid the daily mob, shattering my heart).

Y.

By the way, don't try so hard to remember who I was among all those people surrounding you that night. It is truly unimportant, you didn't notice me at all. But if you insist—not tall (even perhaps shorter than you, I hope you don't mind, it doesn't matter in writing), skinny. Not a lot of investment was made in my material production, perhaps not too much thought, either. Not an Adonis, exactly, if you ask me, that is: not unugly. Now do you remember? A slightly gloomy face, a fair straggly beard? Pacing pointlessly and restlessly between the groups, and not sticking to any of them? Do you remember anyone like that? Some kind of hybrid between a sulky marabou and a Jew? In short: spare the effort, you won't be able to remember, because there's nothing here to forget.

April 28

You don't feel sorry for me? Really?

No pity?

But what is so terrible about being a little bit of a teenager when I write to you? I'm a teenager and a complete baby, an old man and a newborn. I exist in so many moments of life when I'm writing to you, and I wish you, too, would have given me a little of the flame that you allowed yourself for a few moments (Only a few moments? Really, now?) when you went through that same horrible spell of adolescence. And how is it ever possible to pass through the tunnel of these dark years without a bit of yourself catching fire, why do you restrict yourself in your burnings today as well? All your ages, Crazy Yair Buys Everything, the entire stock of your thermal market, because understand this: the place I want us to reach doesn't have enough vitality and energy yet. And if I distance myself from it, and look at it from the outside, it cools off for me, too. And when you doubt it, even with a tiny single remark, it freezes immediately. Do you think creating something from two people is easy?

Since yesterday, I've been trying to understand what happened to you between the last letter and the one that is here. Which outside voice did you listen to? (It was Anna, wasn't it? Then you told her. I am certain you have no person closer to you than she. She's already turned me into a joke, hasn't she?) Because if you didn't, how can you explain your sudden withdrawal, demanding—with a kind of unnatural coldness, anxiously, tight-lipped—that I finally tell you about myself, about the self that is visible to the eye.

I had hoped that we had already gotten past that. That you understood that my daily self is none of our business. Who's even interested in that self? And what does it matter if Yair Wind is not in the phone book? He is not in that book! "Visible to the eye?" I told you, you didn't even see me that evening, I was standing in your blind spot. Write to your blind spot. Look deep inside and you'll see me signaling to you with two hands within it, within the pupil of your blind spot, Miriam, please—

Did you notice, I'm not even trying to argue with your feelings: until I started writing to you, it was true, a precise description of me, all the symptoms of my disease. Even the "eloquence" that to you is always suspiciously smooth. I think I know what you're talking about, your senses or your suspicions aren't so strange; that I am capable, almost without noticing, of depositing my poignant weaknesses into the hands of complete strangers, a strange and embarrassing trick of seduction, you say, and as if we're not really dealing with lives at stake . . . I'm reading these precise, razor-sharp definitions and thinking, She is analyzing me as if she had never been excited by me, and she gets excited by me as if she is incapable of analysis. So who is she?

And I have no intention of calling your home, thank you. And I was quite astonished that you became so enraged over my innocent proposal last week that you call your dear ones by whatever names you like. They have real names (I know) and you don't intend to invent them all over again for me (of course) and why can't I believe in the possibility of a simple, natural, open relationship between two human beings? And I was already so sure that by the end of this tsunami you were going to hang up the letter in my face forever and would never, ever in the world, ever again—and then you give me your home number?!

I won't call. Out of the simple reasons of the "Sanctity of the Bond" (somebody might be at home and hear), but mainly because even a voice is too real for the hallucination I want to have with you. It can be created only with written words, and a voice might pierce it, and then the whole world of reality will flow inside. The details and the numbers and the little sweaty molecules of life; certain subjects are too closely related to subjugation, within a second the entire ruling mob will flow through in a great tsunami and put out every spark. Why do you insist on not understanding this?

It doesn't matter, you're incapable of faking it for even five lines: protected by your fortress of little disagreements and explanations, all so logical—as long as I play these childish spy games or stick to the foolish idea of a "guillotine" that will come down on us out of nowhere in a few months, you are unable to trust, with all your heart, in even the "sincere and emotional" things I'm telling you. On the other hand, you do not like the corner into which, because of my illusions, you are slowly pushing yourself, the corner of a closed-off critic, a cold person. And in this manner you continue to stone me through at least another three corseted "I do nots," in the voice of a teacher with a banana-shaped hairdo—but suddenly your lips trembled and a little "I don't" escaped, little and law-breaking. "And I thought you could already feel that I don't get scared by true passion in my feelings and relationships, on the contrary, on the contrary . . ."

See how each time I reach this punkish "I don't," my heart clenches with pleasure, each time, again (as if you had rolled down one silk stocking for me).

No, tell me, honestly: Was I wrong? Was I wrong about you? Now, again, for instance, a gray wave rises and fills the pit of my stomach, maybe I was wrong and am actually tormenting you, because it is obvious that whoever isn't in tune with the string I offered you will hear only the squeaks, the tin squeaks of my mailbox, or the little bureaucracy of adultery to which I exposed you above, the Sanctity of the Bond that undoubtedly sickened you.

And of course, I had been thinking about whether I should take it out, or put it a bit more delicately, but I left it in, as you already know, because I want you to know about me—to know me, naked, in the little clerical work assigned by my miserable fears, and in my stupidity and in my shame, and in my ignominy. Why not? My "ignominy" is also me, it wants to be given to you, too, like my pride, with same amount of power; it wants, it needs, terribly.

You know, sometimes when I'm writing to you, I have this utterly odd feeling—a completely physical one—that before I could ever actually speak to you, I would have to watch all my words leaving me in a long line, traveling all the way to you to turn themselves in.

This word—"ignominy"—I have never written it before. It is here now, and it smells like a very old, very used slipper (actually, it smells of a home).

Here, just because of a moment like this.

It is frustrating to me that you are again clinging to the corners of the altar of solid logic—which is indeed a useful tool in life, but we are not in life, Miriam! This is the very secret I've been whispering in your ear for a month: we are neither of us alive! I mean, nowhere are the regulation rules of relationships in play, certainly not the usual system of law of men's and women's relationships. So where are we, anyway? What do I care where! Why name it? In any case, the name will be "theirs," a translation. And I want a different code of law with you, which states that we will, both of us, set our rules and speak in our language, and tell our stories and believe in them with all our hearts. Because if we don't have a single private place like this, in which all these beliefs become truth, even if only in writing—then our lives are not lives; even worse than that, our lives are just life . . . Will you sign it?

Y. W.

May 7

Finally.

And I had already despaired and almost given up.

It's a shame that we wasted more than a month, and you are right, we didn't only "waste" it—but we won't give up, and we won't feel remorse for anything. And now (a little late, of course) I am practically horrified by my egocentricity. I didn't even take the time to consider what you need to give up in order to get close to me and to believe in me and in those rules of mine. I burn toward you so much that I was certain I could melt everything else away, logic, life circumstances, even our shared personality . . . It really is a wonder, then, Miriam, only now can I grasp what a wonder it is how you suddenly decided (so decisively, with your lips and your chin!) to throw all definite and logical explanations into the deepest pit in the fields around your home in Beit Zayit. And to come, even though . . . and, even though, allowing me to put your life in my hands.

My unfamiliar hands that are shaking a little now from the weight of the responsibility.

And how will I thank this mysterious friend of yours, who with a few words turned your heart toward me? But what exactly did he tell you about me, and who is he? A man with torn eyelids—and no other details, you didn't explain anything. That's fine, take it slowly, I'm getting used to your abstracted manner of speaking, when you seem certain that I understand, or when you don't even care and you let yourself mumble freely, and then I know your soul is relaxed before me and that you are speaking to yourself in a reverie, a waking sleep . . .

Anyway, don't forget to thank him for me. Although it confuses me a little to know that you have such a close male "friend." And that you can have such detailed and open conversations with him. And I'm holding myself back so as not to ask you what you need me for if you have such a person, who succeeds in making you speak no matter what your mood, and who is always with you when you fall into your Josephan pit, abandoned by the world.

Do you think you'll ever want or be able to tell me what it's like in there, too?

And who throws you in there so easily (again and again and again), and who is not coming to pull you out?

And what happens to you on those days of damnation (did you really mean that word?), when you are the pit itself after even Joseph himself left it?

Strange, isn't it? I guess I don't really have any clue as to precisely what you meant, and I suppose that the two of us are giving the names "Joseph" and "pit" to two completely different things—even though I sometimes say a sentence of yours aloud, or just a combination of words, and feel an internal stitch being torn through the whole length of my soul.

Write to me. Tell me. It's a shame to lose a single day.

Yair

May 8

I sent you one yesterday (did you get it yet?). But the conversation somehow continues into today: somebody called to make a business appointment with me. He wouldn't come to where I work, and furthermore insisted that we meet in front of a department store (I meet more than a few crazy people in my line, but sometimes they do have interesting material). I asked how I would recognize him. He said he would wear black corduroy pants and a plaid shirt and—suede shoes . . . I stood there in the sun for almost an hour and didn't see anybody who fit the description. And then, when I'd finally got fed up and was ready to leave, I looked down the block, and by the phone booth I saw a dwarf, the smallest dwarf I had ever seen, twisted, with a bent body and grotesque face. He was leaning on two tiny walking sticks and was dressed exactly as he had promised (and I couldn't go near him).

Afterward I thought, In my pocket I have your letter with that sentence that on the first reading seemed a little incomprehensible and abstract to me, about the kind of sorrow that you can't share with anybody. It is exactly enough for one person.

May 11

Yes, of course, my dear, my marvel, with all my heart, what do you think? . . .

There is suddenly more room between us. I actually felt your breath coming from beyond the page—your shoulders loosened up a little.

Also because of the colors and the blooming and the smells that burst like a grand waterfall onto your pages. Until now you wrote almost entirely in black and white, and the fact that there were finally two there, two pages (you're right: with two wings, you can finally take off and fly). And I find it wonderful that you chose to bring me to your home, not on the main road by which everybody comes, but from the distant dam of Ein Karem. And through the valley. And, it seems to me, past every flower and tree and brier, passing lizards and grasshoppers and stilts. I haven't been led this way for years, like a sheep to pasture. But who could resist your charm, when you suddenly wake up and laugh, running in front of me, stroking every dandelion and mallow and every olive trunk. And look at the sage, how abundantly it flowers, and how generously it gives off its scent . . . Not to mention all the tordylium and pearl grass— tell me, who taught you all these private names and their smells, and the texture of their leaves and how to crush them, and the gallnuts and fritillary?

It's a good thing that I'm a quick reader. Even so, I could hardly keep up with you as you climbed and scaled the rocks. What are you running for? I didn't imagine that your big soft body could move this way, like a lioness, you wrote, surprising . . . and a strong vital smell hovered above your words, the smell of sweat and earth and stamen. You are wonderful when you rejoice, when you're rolling around in a field of poppies or throwing oat flowers at me (I'll be throwing them back at you soon! Did you play that game, too—How Many Kids Will You Have?). A white-and-yellow daisy got caught in your hair. And for a moment I shrank with the misery of an amputated hand, because I couldn't untangle it from your hair, and I couldn't give you a boost to climb over the terrace. And all the scratches and stings I didn't get, your sweat, which I didn't get to lick—I'm only writing it and missing it. It's a good thing you stopped in the village to chat with kindergarteners, all lined up. It gave me a moment to breathe. I noticed that you made certain not to tell me if one of the children belongs to you (by your description, one could think they were all yours). And generally, in your last two letters, it seems to me that you're teasing me with riddles, hiding and reappearing, smiling secret intimate smiles. And it's wonderful. I'm barely alive, but keeping up, through your secret passages between the houses and fences, all the way to the gate of your house, blue speckled with rust—why rust? maybe someone isn't doing his job keeping the house up properly? Well, I didn't say anything, and who can even think about that when you are spinning around to face me in a swirl of imaginary skirts, and for one moment, within the motion of your spin—I don't know if you felt it—you came and spread out in all of your ages in front of me, and your brown eyes shone like the few words you whispered to me and like (oh dear, I feel a simile coming on) two pits in an opening loquat: would you like to come in?

Yes, of course, my dear, my marvel, with all my heart—what do you think?

(Morning)

Tonight, in the middle of a deep sleep, it came to me—could it be that he is the same friend whose diaries you read every few days, so that you can know what he was doing on the same day a few decades ago? Who—as you already told me in your second letter,—is your morning prayer?

Please don't be angry with my attempt to discover which private conversation of yours I slipped into. I was only playing a little detective game, and in the middle of the night I jumped out of my bed and checked a few dates and flipped through some pages, and here you are, on exactly the same day you suddenly returned to me, on the fourth of May. I found that this is what he wrote in the diary from 1915:

"Reflection on other people's relationship to me. Insignificant as I may be, nevertheless there is no one here who understands me in my entirety. To have someone possessed of such understanding, a wife perhaps, would mean to have support from every side, to have God."

And even if my wild guess was completely wrong, even if I stepped into a too-private place, I would like to give you something in return, from the same day, from the same man:

". . . Sometimes I thought she understood me without realizing it; for instance, the time she waited for me at the subway station—I had been longing for her unbearably, and in my passion to reach her as quickly as possible almost ran past her, thinking she would be at the top of the stairs, and she took me quietly by the hand."

Y.

May 16

You're such an enigma.

You don't have to solve me, you tell me, just be with me. Here I am—and I am with you, as you walk through your yard, a little paradise you've created for yourself (when I climb the stairs to the porch with the bougainvillea shade, I finally recognized the purple leaves from the anonymous-intimacy letter). You had already flown inside. I was still in a bit of shock from that move—and then flooded, I was simply flooded with light and warmth, and also with the huge array of colors, the jungle of giant potted plants, the wool carpets and embroidered pictures and the piano and the walls crammed with floor-to-ceiling bookshelves. I instantly felt safe. Even the clutter seemed familiar to me.

So that's it? I'm inside, inside your home. You have a generous home, not just generous—like a river practically overflowing. And a little bit like the Old Curiosity Shop, just as you said. I learned it by heart, I even sketched it out on paper, so I could know just where the wall with the photographs is, and on which window the orange-and-red stained glass hangs, and where the blue glass vases from Hebron sit, and how the sunbeams break through them in the morning and fall and spread out on the embroidery with the filigree (what is that, exactly?), but mainly I saw you, your words, you suddenly wrote like——did you notice?

Do you understand what I am talking about?

This is in no way a criticism of you, it's just a question, or let's say the unwilling cock of an eyebrow: because you were extremely happy on the way from the dam, you rejoiced and I couldn't help but get excited along with you. And in the house, how can I explain it? It seemed to me that, for a moment, you were somehow aflame . . .

Quickly—quickly, moving from room to room, nearly breathless, agitated in a way not at all in your usual rhythm, and when I think about it now—not at all in your tone either, not your verbal muscle tone. It was as if you frightened yourself by bringing me into your privacy so suddenly. Or perhaps you only wanted to show me that anything I can do you can do as well?

I'm such an idiot. What am I complaining about, I wish I could do that, too. Be as happy as a child, standing for the first time in front of a picture that has been hanging in the living room for years, or over a jar of pickles—be awed by a "large, pregnant" piece of pottery . . .

I feel so relieved that I can now lean back and let you know—that almost from the start I felt a little ashamed before you, and mainly—too much of something (exaggerated and bubbling, et cetera, et cetera). Perhaps it was because you seemed so reserved to me that night, so self-sufficient, there was something so clear and crystal and ascetic about you, almost scolding me without even knowing me. And suddenly this crowded house.

On the other hand, don't be mistaken, it also relaxes me to know it, it proves another little one of my proofs about you and me. Perhaps not a very grand proof in itself, perhaps you won't be happy about it, I'm not very proud of it myself, but suddenly it was because I found it in you as well—

I hope you're not offended. Truly, this is not a critique of your taste. I wish you to understand that it is not "taste" or "tastelessness" that is important to me now. Only the signs of our alikeness in everything, big or small; and the delicate, mysterious affair that we shall call "the right measure" I mean—a likeness like the one that exists, say, between two cups, broken in exactly the same place.

Yair

May 20

It is, of course, impossible to write down all those moments throughout the day. But I liked the fact that you used the word "date" to describe it. We're on a date.

This morning, for example, in the daily traffic jam right before Ganot Interchange. A large Volvo driving in front of me with a little boy sitting in back who was waving hello to all the drivers. There were five of us in the cars around him, and none of us moved a facial muscle; we didn't give him a single sign of being seen. The boy smiled hopefully for a little longer. There was something shy and fragile in his smile.

My dilemma: If I was to wave back at him, he would immediately recognize that I am only pretending to be a grown-up. That I am the weak link in the chain tied around him. At that moment, he might start making obscene gestures at me, thus making me the joke of the jam. I could see in the vulnerable line of his mouth that he wouldn't miss an opportunity to gain this kind of strength.

I consulted you (that is to say, we had a date). I accepted your opinion. I smiled at him. I waved to him. I saw how his smile grew bigger with happiness, almost in disbelief that such a thing was happening to him . . . He immediately told his father, the driver, who looked at me through the rearview mirror for a long time. I looked away and saw what the other drivers were thinking of me.

I also thought that if there had been a woman among us, she could have smiled at him and dismissed me from that duty.

So again, for the second time today: Good morning to you.

I am amused by your way of not answering my direct questions immediately. (Such as what I wrote about your home.) And I already know that in two or three letters I will get an indirect answer, or sometimes I won't get any. I suppose this is your way of determining a path and rhythm for yourself, not letting me take the reins . . . But you asked a question, and contrary to all the hemming and hawing that came before it, I can respond quite simply: I certainly want another child. Another three, maybe. Why not? To walk down the street like a mother duck with her living, quacking train—that is the peak of prosperity. But in the present situation, since you're asking, even one more will do.

Do for what? It's hard to say exactly.

Perhaps—turn us into a family. Because we are not one yet.

Well, that surprised even me. I'll send it anyway.

Y.

It's not that we don't live together well, the three of us (I have to make you understand), but somehow, in the meantime, we are just three people who are getting on just fine, even in love with one another, in deep friendship (but—as you know, a triangle is always a very shaky geometric construction).

(Almost midnight)

And I wish I had a girl. There is nothing I would rather have. A soft little girl. A little honeysuckle. It's also the thought of seeing just what kind of girl would come out of me; a legitimate feminine version of myself: and to see how all her parts coexist, elbows and breasts. And perhaps she, somehow, just by being, will know how to settle that old quarrel of which we have yet to speak, you and I.

And there is, of course, also the will to know, in that way, through a little girl, the half of Maya's life I don't know.

Maya—that really is her name. To love her all over again, from her genesis, as she grows up and matures—does that sound strange to you?

If I only had a girl. I would name her Ya'ara, Honeysuckle. This little honeysuckle, look, my nymph gland is starting to leak uncontrollably. A girl with dark, soft hair crowning her temples, and green-eyed like Maya, and red-lipped, and how she bubbles over with happiness—because she will be happy, you'll see, almost anything in the world will be cause for her to rejoice.

But how will I know how to raise her without what is in me seeping into her, that which has already covered Maya's innocent, open face with vague, tired skin, and has already sucked dry one child who used to be a glimmer of light.

There, I wrote it.

So yes, if you're asking, the thought that I might not have another child kills me, and Maya is not willing yet. She probably has good reasons to hesitate, and I am compelled to be satisfied with suspicious, yearning looks at little girls in the street. I used to yearn for their mothers, and now . . . Well, I didn't think we'd be speaking about such matters at all! I was certain that, at this point, we would already be celebrating in a realm of passionate hallucinations. That I would write you, for example, that even the smell of my sweat becomes sharper only by imagining that, in a little while, your fingers will be pressed to this page. And that even your telephone number, with the concave between the breasts hinted at in the 868, excites me. But I'm glad I can tell you about the rest—to describe the fat little legs my girl will have (when she wears her yellow dress!), and her naked peachy body when she showers in the sprinklers in the yard—

Down, heart, down!

Y.

May 25

Walking on a tightrope?

I thought—a clown. But apparently there are more jobs in the circus. Does it really look like that to you?—that I suddenly came running, pushed the end of a rope into your hand, and said, "Hold it!"?

You made only one little mistake: you said that it's unclear to you just how I managed to convince, or at least plant the doubt in you, that if you let go I'd fall. But it isn't a rope, Miriam—it is scarcely a string, a word-web (and if you do let go, I will fall).

And before everything, you have to understand that I have no wish to tell stories to other people. It's only you that I want to write to, and it is only in your honor that this urge was suddenly aroused in me, just like that, with no warning, in the middle of life. Because I haven't ever known this kind of passion, up to even the moment before I saw you; maybe when I was a child writing school essays, funny sketches, etc. And that earthshaking theory that suddenly came to you in the middle of the night and kept you from sleeping (it's about time!) absolutely does not apply to me. I honor books too much to write one myself—it would be disrespectful. So don't worry that what you imagined about me, even wished on me, might be salt on my wound: I have no wounds, and if there is one—it isn't even open yet.

It is only in connection with our relationship that I will, with great caution, put to use that word which is, yes, fatal to me as well: I hope I will, at the very least, learn how to be a true *artist* of this connection between us. I wouldn't dare ask for more than that.

Do you remember saying, not long ago, that in trying so hard to invent you I might not be able to find you? Well, I think you are starting to understand that in order to find you, I have to invent a little . . .

Here, listen, this is how it was: the two of us, on that huge lawn, and everything around us was green, every shade of green was there. I am actually imagining the big lawn of Kibbutz Ramat Rakhel on the edge of Jerusalem, on the desert's bank, do you know it? You are allowed to go there and see. Invest some effort in me, why don't you. Because I went there, yesterday, after getting your letter. I read it in front of the desert. I read it silently and aloud. I tried to hear your voice, its tune. I think you speak slowly—in your writing I can hear you lingering (a favorite word of yours!) on each and every word. There is something ripe and full about your speech. And I feel how it focuses me, as if it is carving something out of me—I wish I knew what it was. Sometimes I feel as if you know exactly—a lot better than I do—what you are aiming at there, when, for example, you say that you think I have this kind of fifth column in me and that, for some reason, I insist on being loyal to it, above all . . .

Or what you mumbled at the end, when you were already half asleep; it wasn't a very fatal mumble, but full of sweetness: look at how I'm writing to you, as if I've been used to chatting with you in my kitchen at night for twenty years.

Can you already understand what I am creating you from?

It is because of light little pats on the back like those that, yesterday, on the grass, in front of the desert, I gave myself up to the addiction of us. I actually saw us there, you and me. And how we slowly lost our concentration on what was written. A light breeze was blowing, and my newspaper rustled, and the pages of your book began to flip. I am talking about five in the afternoon, the sun still shone, and we both felt so fair in the light, nearly transparent. If one other person had walked by, the magic would have vanished, but it was just the two of us, and before we exchanged even one word, we were already entangled in the webs of our separate stories. You have your own story, and so do I, and it is amazing to feel how they are already rapidly weaving together. The way stories always do. Why, sometimes, in an ordinary moment on the street, you can feel your soul torn apart as it is stretched and pulled into the story of someone just passing by. Usually, the stories die instantly as well, having also been ripped apart, without those involved ever even knowing what they lost. A minor heartache remains, nothing more. Then quickly disappears. It lasts a couple of hours for me, though, sometimes, this kind of melancholy, as if I had undergone some kind of little spiritual abortion, the death of the story.

(Are you with me? I felt I was losing you for a moment. Just at the height of our closeness, you shrank and withdrew. Perhaps I flooded over my banks once again? Or said something offensive?)

Say: did you really put on the *Zorba* soundtrack and dance the sirtaki in your living room? With me and Anthony Quinn? But why are you telling me only now? Why didn't you give me that right after I told you about my dance in the forest?

At least you said that a dead parpur fell on your page when you hid it from me. Go easy on me, go easy on me, open your white-knuckled fists just a little. It's a shame you didn't send any of those pictures of that clenched girl (you were probably the tallest girl, always standing in the third row of the photographs). It is even more a shame that I am not by your side when you wake up every morning, to unfreeze your fingers and stroke your knuckles. What are you holding so tightly in there?

And what does it mean that you were "the good queen of the class" (is there an evil queen, too?).

But enough heaviness, come, let's have our date: suddenly, at exactly five o'clock, when we still were keeping our distance, a bizarre, terrifying noise sounded—try to imagine a rusty zipper suddenly being ripped open, running through the belly of the earth, across the entire lawn. And our glances flew right and left, frightened; and your eyes, big and brown and lovely, grasped hold of mine for a moment. And we pulled ourselves up straight, and stood, as if by the force of our gaze alone (Is that clear? Is this picture clear to you? I want you to see into my imagination, see it exactly!). I see you bending and stretching your long legs in an irresistible motion under your dress, your chiseled ankles, and you're standing dizzy and loose like a gazelle, an uneasy gazelle, for just a moment—what really terrified you so when I wrote that we are both of us not alive? What's hiding in this, *Oh, Yair, where do I start?* Just start. It will come by itself (you sighed a lot in the last few letters, did you notice?). Why, you are so alive to me, in the bounty that bursts from your full body, and generally, in your fullness. The fullness of you touching anything, the way you embroider me silently, string after string in your every living day, what are you talking about, you are so alive!

And me. At the edge of the huge lawn, the would-be buck, but not very virile, no, not terribly endowed with horns, not very muscular, my thighs—just a clerky, narrow-chested, balding buck. This constant balding, how humiliating it is—and I too am looking, awestruck, at the source of the noise, the destruction of the peace I had been savoring before I stole a glance at you. But are you at all interested in the continuation of the story now, after I have been pictured to you? Tell me the truth—if you are getting entangled in this kind of false romantic relationship, wouldn't you prefer a real buck?

All right, all right, I know I mustn't ask you questions of this kind. How you raged when I described myself as "not un-ugly"! You don't give an inch in these things, do you? Not even as a joke: you don't even know people to whose essence the word "ugly" applies? Really? Well, that could be. But you also refuse to accept such a thing as the regulation rules, the laws of men's and women's relationships . . . Tell me, how many years will pass before I succeed in opening your eyes?

And that other matter, the one you mocked me for calling the Sanctity of the Bond—

I had better shut up, hadn't I?

Come, look there, be with us—we were surrounded on all sides by this whistling whisper in the earth. We were both thinking of venom, the desecrated Garden. I don't know if you know this feeling—something strange but also too familiar suddenly spreads through all living tissue in a blink—listen with me, listen well, whispers and whistles, encircling us like the excitement of obscene, ignorant gossip (srsrsrsrsrsr) . . . maybe this is why our hearts twitched in sudden fear, with guilt. Even your heart, Miriam, your pure heart; which no one in the world will ever scrutinize to discover what you do and with whom—admit it, admit how quickly the internal serpents bite, don't they? They punish us for even the most heartfelt wishes, for sweet fantasies, and immediately I hear my father's lips cluck, as when he told my mother how he caught the general deputy, his boss, kissing some woman soldier in his office—

Enough, I am tired. I was deserted by the good spirit. See how hard it is for me to imagine a beginning. So many rocks and so much mud blocking the tunnel.

(I will continue later.)

Y.

(Night)

And suddenly, at that moment, the riddle within the earth was cracked. And a thousand jets of water took off from hidden sprinklers (well, it's the best I can do), and the two of us screamed with a single shock, and we ran, who remembers where—just not, however, to the one logical place, not outside; what's waiting for us there, anyway? And we smiled, and purposely made a mistake, we were attracted to and aimed at the wettest and most flooded spot, where all the jets of water became one, and we finally bumped into each other, surprised. And we held on to each other tightly, the poor refugees of a flood entwined, yelling much louder than was necessary—"We have to get out of here!" "At least give me your book so it won't get wet!" "But we're both in the same water!" and making a lot of noise together, but not actually moving anymore. Stopping slowly, and looking through the water that's turning your lips a little blue, and shining in light flecks in your wonderful hair, brown and full and untamed, with a few thin silver strands (never dye! this is the last request of a man condemned to you: let it slowly turn silver!), and breathing too fast, and laughing at our stupidity, the way we were caught and got soaked like children, practically two children, and gargling the water filling our mouths. Our mouths are swimming with drunken words. See us in the splashes of water—we're so shiny and clean, like two bottles, two bottles that survived with the messages still inside. Meanwhile, what do you notice about our outsides; for example, you are older than me, not by a lot. I think the gap in our ages bothers you a little, but I was never your student—I suddenly hear myself telling you that, and there's no logic to it—only the urgent need to tell you immediately, in the water, that in front of almost every person, always, sometimes even with my son, I feel as if I am somehow the younger one, the one more lacking in experience, more milky, and you listen and immediately understand me, as if it is obvious that this is the first thing a man tells a woman when he meets her in water.

Listen, I have never written anything so odd, my whole body actually contracted and shook . . .

Where were we? Don't stop now, don't lose these inner tremblings; our breath, it slows slowly, but we still don't move apart, we're still touching, and looking into each other's eyes; it is a quiet, direct look, completely simple, in the midst of all the complications of situations like these; it is simple, like a kiss you give a child who comes to show you a fresh wound. It is heartbreaking, the thought that you can see into a grown-up person that way.

We're not laughing anymore. There is a long silence. Almost scary. Want to detach and cannot. And in your eyes and mine, more and more curtains are parting, revealing the depths, and I am thinking how similar a moment like this is to a moment of disaster—nothing will ever be the same. And we're terribly exhausted, holding each other to keep from falling, and see our story in a sort of strange and sad clarity. The words are not important anymore, and the language doesn't matter either; it could be written in Sanskrit, hieroglyphics, the hieroglyphics of chromosomes: see me as a child, see me as an adolescent, see the man I am. See what happened to me on the way here, how my story faded—where do I start, Miriam. I always think that there is no fragment of innocence left in me. Yet I came to you in innocence—from the first moment I began writing you, my words to you came out of a place completely new to me, like sperm kept for only one particular loved one, and the rest emerging from some other part of my body. But you probably want to go to sleep now, and so do I, even though I don't have a chance tonight, not anymore. Another moment, then. Help me to calm down, give me your hand, even a finger will do for me now; I need that now, right now, for you to be a lightning rod for me.

(Is that too much to ask from one person? At least stay until the ash from my cigarette falls.)

Say, did I read you right? That a triangle is not such a shaky structure? And in "some contexts" it might even be a solid, satisfying structure? Even enriching? And also very fitting to human nature, "at least to my nature," you wrote, and great curiosity was roused among the brief and concentrated audience of your words . . .

Under the condition that it is equilateral, you added immediately, and all involved know they are sides of a triangle. (Are you scolding me? What have you already heard about me?)

It's too late to go into this now, and the ash is shaking tremulously at the end. I'll wait patiently for your answer; but know that I am amused to see how in a few strokes of your pen you have created a new and pri-

vate branch of science—poetic geometry. It is a pity, though, that you
didn't explain to me how it applies in life, this wonder you are wishing

(it fell)

May 30

I can't get enough of looking. The photo of the shadow on the hills
opposite and the jets of the five o'clock sprinklers wearing all their shine,
and mainly the bottle (what a photo!), the broken bottle on the rock . . .

And that you got wet, Miriam, that you simply got up and walked
into the cold shower, and stood in it for so long (I, by the way, couldn't do
it; in cold water I turn blue within seconds). What did you say at home
later? How did you explain it? Did you bring clothes to change in, or did
you just jump into the water without thinking?

This moment doesn't stop echoing in me, my written words splashing
into living water. I have no skin left on my body from all the showers I've
been taking the past few days; just don't let go of my hand, let us continue to
dive deeper and deeper together. Let us be in that place in which we will
both be filled with the strong excitement of nakedness—because the water
makes our clothes stick to our skin, so the shape of our bodies is revealed,
your full, round breasts suddenly pop under a wet white shirt—and both our
faces are washed and cleaned of all the fatigue and strangeness and indifference, and the denial of the essence of faith. All the adult epidermis that has
scabbed over us throughout life. And I who could read what you were trying
to make flesh, when you danced the sirtaki in your living room—you were
telling me that you wouldn't be rushing to dress me over at Mt. Carmel, that
if you had seen the beauty I saw, you also perhaps would have joined me and
danced in the same way. But I know! From the moment I saw you I felt the
strength of that will in you; and don't get me wrong, I'm not talking about
the nakedness of passion right now—but about a completely different kind
of nakedness, one you can hardly stand in front of without shock and a quick
escape into clothes. The nakedness of peeled skin, this is what I'm looking
for now; it is becoming clearer to me from letter to letter (nakedness—like
one of the words you wrote on the back of the bottle photo).

And you couldn't even know this, but since I was a teenager, for years
the thought of running naked in the streets has driven me crazy. To expose yourself—not to shock people, no, just the opposite. To be the first to

do it for everybody else—imagine it, to take off all your clothes and jump in between people, bare (I, who am ashamed to take off my clothes on the beach, who can't stand it when people see me putting a letter in a mailbox on the street—something terribly intimate is revealed in a person who sends his own letters, don't you think?). That same I would die to be, even for a moment, a flicker of one soul in the fog of others' indifference and strangeness, to yell one clear wordless yell to them, only my body gaping.

And perhaps, after three or four such appearances all over town, maybe another person would join me all of a sudden—would you imagine this with me? Someone who will somehow have to ground my excitement into his own body. I can imagine the first one to catch it will be a madman, but after that, there will be others, I'm sure. And the first of them will be a woman, she will suddenly tear off her clothes and smile with relief and joy; people will point at her and laugh. She will suddenly begin to remove her armor of delicate fabric, and they will go silent at the sight of her body, and understand something. A long silence will pass. And suddenly, at once, that built-up electric tension, the exertion of hiding and covering and disguising, will discharge in a great explosion over their heads and a great storm will roll in. A woman, and another woman, and another man, and children, a lightning storm of naked bodies (I always like to imagine that moment). And immediately, the Modesty Squads will show up, special police officers with solderer's glasses will speed through these centers of obscenity, equipped with thick tarps and asbestos gloves—because catching a naked person with bare hands is repulsive (I always think, a naked person will cut through dressed people like a knife; the clothed will shrink back as if from an infectious disease or an open wound). Think of it—people without clothes, there's no point in pretending anymore, you can't really hate a naked person (go fight a naked soldier). And you wrote that one word, "compassion." That's what makes my heart stretch out to you, that you can suddenly, during the simplest of everyday talk, light things up with a word.

So, yes, Miriam, it will be so simple and honest and natural—the compassion in nakedness. (One minute, I hear a key at the door. Have to stop

(False alarm. The cleaning lady.)

But in the meantime, where were we, what are all my noble thoughts worth, in the meantime the entire world is dressed and armored and there is only us, hugging and wet and shivering from the cold, or from whatever makes you shiver. And my eyes were in your eyes, and the true weight of a woman's body was in my body, an alien soul fluttered freely in my soul, and I didn't contract and spit it out like a pit stuck in my throat; on the contrary, I inhaled, breathed her into me more and more, and she enfolded my body within herself, and I understood the beautiful expression "the creatures of my torso" for the first time . . .

And later (I'm a bit drunk on thoughts, do you mind?) both of us, hand in hand to my car, cheerful, but just a little cheerful, if only because of the dry knowledge, which had waited patiently and with vengeance outside the Isle of Water that we were for a moment, and is starting to sneak into our heart (that is also a great photo, the one of all the splashes of water coming together into a trunk of blue. It's hard to believe that you haven't held a camera in your hands for seven years). And next to my beat-up Subaru (yes, of course it's a Subaru), you let me dry your beautiful thick hair with the old towel that had been rolled up in the car. After I shake off everything that has clung to it since it was new: the grains of sand from family trips, twigs from the last Independence Day bonfire, and the stains of chocolate pudding and chocolate milk wiped off one particular small mouth, a quarter to five years old. If you really want the dirt on me—this same bold towel of mine treasures all manner of perfectly good stains from my life, my life which I like a lot, but—I wish now you could understand more—how my soul is constantly torn in two, help me! A devoted family man, and one capable of writing you such letters, and to whoever solves that correctly is promised eternal peace of the soul, even a temporary one will do.

And your forehead is revealed to me again, out of the wild of your hair, and your brown eyes, wide open and serious and questioning me under your full eyebrows—and your eyes are terribly sad, I wish I knew why, and, anyhow, in every letter I feel how in an instant they are so ready to illuminate, to rise—your Giulietta Masina eyes (at the end of *Nights of Cabiria*, do you remember it?), and you're asking me again with that look—Who are you? No idea. I want to be whatever your eyes will see in me, yes. And if you are not too frightened to look—then maybe I will be.

And I hold your face gently in my hands. I've already said that you're a bit taller than me, but when we are together we fit, and it doesn't look ridiculous. I feel your warm face in my hands and think that almost all the other faces I meet in my everyday life are made up of expressions that are only fragments of quotations of others' expressions. But your face— and then I pull you to me and kiss your hungry and thirsty mouth for the first time, placing my lips exactly on your lips, soul to soul, and your mouth is very warm and soft, and you pull your upper lip a bit higher— you have that motion in you, I've seen it—and I of course will wonder for a moment if maybe I could sleep with you before I know your name— don't forget that I'm still a man and have this rooster's dream (which has yet to come true). But then, just because, against my self and my stupidity I quickly ask, What's your name? And you say, Miriam. And I say, Yair. You murmur, with a cold, shivering smile, that you have a very thin skin; and I listen, with care, to what you whispered to me in that smile: that I have to treat you gently, not rudely, not as a stranger, not touch you with the same five sausage fingers that the world has probably sent to you more than once. More and more I fear this is what it has done to you. And my soul will yearn for you when you speak. When I write to you— even at this moment—my soul emerges from me when you smile, when you tremble, when you approach my body—because unlike most of the women who have approached me in my life, I know you will immediately press yourself to me with your all, with your wholeness, because you are so alive. And I mention this tiny fact to myself that has always attracted my attention; because, you see, women always held me in the beginning with only half their bodies, their half-body into my famished body; just one breast, to be precise (but I don't know how they hold other men). And you, from the very beginning, break this little feminine law and announce with your body that you are loyal and committed only to the man I am and not to the force of all the women behind you.

I already know how I will feel then, it is written in all my cells, how in that moment, finally, a new warm emotion will gently till the ground of my heart. I want it so much—and you? Write me what is happening now in your heart, which was filled with a longing for its young self. And all at once you pull me to you, harder, and kiss me with all your soul and all your heart, as if they will give and pour out into me; your entire being, created and encoded within your flesh, will open and be solved in me, bit by bit, until the whole thing melts, that Thing between you and yourself—that is now a little bit of the Thing between you and me. It is melting and fusing into one within my mouth and tongue and nose; and only then, we might be able to detach ourselves a little bit and look at each other with craving eyes, and I will whisper, breathlessly, "Oh, Miriam, look, you're all wet, how will you go home?"

(I hope I dream about you tonight, I want to scream out your name in the middle of sleep, and then the secret will be out and I won't hide you anymore! You are a woman who must be revealed!)

Yair

June 5

Miriam, salutations:

About six days ago I sent a letter to you at school, as usual, and have not since received a reply.

I suppose it is just a matter of time. Perhaps you are busy toward the end of the school year with the report cards and all (already?), but I still thought I'd check to see if you sent any response. I am in a bit of a stupid state right now because of the ever-present possibility that you, for some reason, have decided not to answer me and to disappear. Maybe because of my last letter. Maybe because something in your life suddenly changed. But I am certain that even in such a case you would have written, wouldn't you?

I just started to worry a little bit—because I bring my letters to the mailbox at the school gate (perhaps you've already noticed that there's no postmark), but maybe the internal mail system has problems and the letter never reached your box.

If so, whom did it reach?

Or perhaps there was something else that made you angry. I'm trying to think aloud—perhaps it is your claim that I am, again, slowly reassembling reality into a series of words and being completely satisfied with them, unstitching you here, embroidering you there.

Well, as you can see, I am starting to make a mess, so please—so I can at least know how I figure in the hierarchy of your department of affections. Just do me a favor and don't hesitate to write the whole truth; I mean, I can certainly understand, if that miserable letter did reach you, that you've decided that you don't want to have anything to do with such a person. Here, I even wrote the words for you, to save you polite contortions, you don't need to worry about me or to pity me—I am a lot stronger and tougher than it may seem to you (it really is hard to break me).

Here, I'm inviting you to tell me everything you felt when you saw how I allowed myself to expose myself like this in front of you without knowing almost anything about you. Without a single thing connecting the two of us in reality, I suddenly jump and expose the armpits of my soul to you in an obscene striptease. Isn't that what happened? Isn't it? Admit it, why not, admit something for once!

I mean, you stood at a distance in such a way, screening me with your arms crossed, with questioning suspicion, a bit frightened, and a bit amused with this one-man band that just marched through you. While I was completely dizzy from your last letter, with the photos from Ramat Rakhel. Perhaps you forgot the intimate things you wrote there, even the tiny fact that for the first time you wrote the word "us." Yes, we are both people of words—and then your sudden realization that, perhaps, I am a person who actually suffocates inside words. Do you remember? (Because I remember every word.) Meaning that perhaps I feel a little "claustrophobia in 'their' words" and that perhaps, because of this suffocation, I sometimes gasp out this way, swallowing . . .

This is the kind of relief I felt, as if you had come, giving me permission to breathe differently; and then, out of fugitive happiness, without shame, without guarding myself, and excited, and intoxicated from you, and from us—

Listen. It's a waste of ink. I'm letting you go.

June 6

One little addition, even though: just for you to know that if this is how you saw me, you were not alone. You might not have noticed but I was standing right there beside you from the first letter I wrote you, with my arms crossed high on my chest. What were you thinking? I was standing there on the side, too, of course I was, screening this eruption of mine exactly as you were—anyway, it's important for me to tell you. All the rest is unnecessary, isn't it?

Then why can't I stop?

Write to me, anything that comes into your mind, just don't leave me this way; I went just now, again, for the fourth time today, to the mailbox.

Enough of this, come on, you owe me at least this, that we should stand together for a moment, shoulder to shoulder, and look at it, and condemn it together for the last time, that internal organ of mine that suddenly burst out and made exception, a glandular dance.

Stop! Two hand claps of the director and set change: let's be, for one minute, like two camels, of all things; camels suit me right now, so why not? It came to me, I'm sharp and original even in my roughest moments—a camel-couple with long, humorless, camel-y faces, a pair of mature camels, a male and a female, sober and chewing on boredom and knowing full well our place in a caravan that's progressing, heel by toe, just as it should. Until, suddenly, one bizarre donkey foal jumps out of the procession. Maybe it just looks like a foal. Maybe it is even a hybrid of a camel and a clown's hat—nature made a mistake—with donkey's ears and a little camel-y hunchback, and this infantile weirdo is breaking into a fool's jig; get back, Miriam! because disgusting rivers are flowing out of all his orifices, grab a coat, a sweater at least (!), so that the shedding layers of his slightly overexcited soul will not soil you, for God's sake.

This is the exact way I see the "performance" to which I've condemned myself before you with that letter; actually, with all of them. From the beginning. Don't know what happened to me. In one moment my heart overflowed and flooded into the wide spaces in my brain. What actually happened? I remember seeing you, there were people around you, there was a lively discussion and you didn't participate. Suddenly your lips sank and you smiled a strange smile, a sorrowful smile, no harder than that, the smile of a person who has found out that very minute that she has lost her last hope, the hope for her soul, no less, but who knows that from now on, this is the way it has to be, and that she will have to go on living with that loss . . . and that was the moment I entered your life. A kind of odd, unhappy moment, but I didn't even have time to think about it, because in that moment I saw my name lying on the bottom of your smile and I leaped. On the other hand, perhaps my name wasn't written there, perhaps I so wanted you to know that I could see it and that you weren't alone that I jumped too quickly. This is not new for me, either; you should know, I have a long gloomy history of such unripe leaps—in work, and in my life, and in family matters, it was already happening in school, and in the army, and in letters to the editor—in any place I felt that something was being held back or blocked; no matter what the reason was, whether because of opacity or cowardice or stupidity or simply because "you just don't do that." In such a moment, I always rebel, on purpose, out of spite (says my father)—not true, when I rebel it's a rescue mission—I thought you understood, it is you who first dared to write the word "wish"—and then I am flooded, at once, you saw it. And damn the name of the laws of nature and society that determine, let's say, that a certain person's soul must be satisfied with only its separate existence, alone, within his own skin.

Or alone, within his own pit.

It's silly to keep on explaining (and I can't stop), but it is always this way. Somewhere, very close, something is building up, someone is begging to burst out already, something that will suffocate if it doesn't crack, and even though I don't know its being, its choked scream is clear to me. You asked me what kind of music I listen to when I'm at home and when I am at work, and especially when I am writing to you. You asked as if you assumed that I am always surrounded by music. I'm sorry to disappoint you, I'm not very musical. I am, in my opinion, dysmusical (all in all, I went and bought the *Children's Corner* by Debussy and I listened to it in my car again and again, and, of course, Emma Kirkby singing Monteverdi, and perhaps someday I'll understand what you said). But I always listen to that scream and immediately understand it, not with my ears but with my stomach, my pulse, my womb, and you hear it, too. You heard me this way, so why, suddenly, don't you hear it?

Oh well, what's the point. Besides what you decide. For me, it's just important for you to know that I understand exactly what is happening inside me now, and what you think of me. Why, it's a regular torture, Miriam, that I am always both, the one standing with a stern face, arms crossed over my chest—and the one who is suddenly gutted and falls and falls, and while falling is still arguing with the stern one, screaming on the way to his doom, Let me live! Let me feel! Let me make mistakes!

But I am certainly, undoubtedly, the other one as well. What can you do? The pursed lips that spit out in disgust, You already know how it will end, you will return to me, crawling, as usual, says he dryly (he has symptoms of dehydration in his tissues). And the donkey foal continues screaming all the while—because, Miriam, maybe he will succeed just once—by mistake of course, because, by imperial decree, such acts of compassion could happen only by mistake. But maybe he will finally hit the target, just once—no! Touch the target, touch, touch one alien soul, actually touch, soul to soul, tissue to tissue. One single time, one soul out of the four billion Chinese in the world (in this situation, suddenly everyone seems Chinese) will crack open in front of him and yield its harvest—

And so he falls and screams in his breaking, reedy voice, which continues to change throughout his life.

Then again, it appears, of course, that around every such scream are ten wise, learned, moderate, and impartial men; and they consult and request to confirm whether we had crossed that bridge too soon—perhaps this was just one of your flimsy ideas (so they tell me, dryly, with dry lips)—one of those ideas that ripen only in nightly darkness and evaporate in the light of day, meaning—just another damaged crossbreed that might be born deformed and defective.

And I . . . you should see me there. Actually, you did see it. This is what probably repulsed you. Because I know exactly how I look in those moments, when I plead with them for no less than to take complete pity on me. Why lie, Miriam? I know, in my deepest depths, that if it was in their power to do so, they would never approve of me either, just as you haven't ("is not entitled to official stamp of authorization," they would have determined). So I run between them, almost hysterical, begging them to consent to see what I am seeing, that at least one of them could see it as I do, because if one other can see it—just another one is enough, you don't need any more than that—suddenly it will exist and be, and be redeemed, and then something in me will be "authorized." But just try to explain something like that to *them*.

And then I can't take it anymore (I am documenting the whole process for you here), and the moment of fuck-it-all arrives. The moment when I finally think, for example, What am I worth if I'm not sending these? My soul swells to you, and I'm flying, just as I flew to you, here, even now, it is me there, flying, continuing to fly to you, to whoever agrees to believe with me, look, laugh. It's me, the weak fuse in the network—every network, every bond, every touch, every tension, every friction—or any possible combination of me with those—and with you. And now, as I watch it sink and sputter between us, I am asking you, again, one final time, to believe in us. Perhaps we will touch a gold vein, by chance—we almost did, already, there were a few moments of light, and I have gotten used to your annoying High Court integrity (and also to your funny confusion of words when you're excited). And where will I again find such a childish, mature woman who is capable of meditating on Adam and Eve's first lovemaking, taking such pleasure in how naturally they discovered what is good to do, and what happiness and delight it is to discover only by way of nature . . .

You see, I remember everything. I may be destroying all evidence of your existence—I'm forced to, by the Sanctity of the Bond, and the rest—but you exist inside me in a way that scares me, because what am I going to do now, surrounded by this entire new existence that doesn't want me?!

Here I am before you: I am the donkey foal. I am the hole in the fence, the crack through which mistakes and treachery—and also bald ridicule—drip into the house. It has been this way since childhood, ever since I can remember myself I have been the hole, how unmasculine. And to whom else could I say such a thing? Believe me, believe that at least—in my moments of flight, moments of gliding, I am the most me, the me that is meant to be. And in a surprising manner, it is a moment full of happiness, generally—it is a full moment, it is everything together, and I wish I had a way to spend my entire life in such a moment.

And then, of course, there is the thump of the landing, and lots of dust around, and terrible silence, and I am sobering up from all that I was for a moment, cautiously looking around. And I start to freeze from the cold that surrounds me within and without, a cold that only clowns and fools know. So it is true that once or twice in my life it so happened that I was a living seed and a brilliant idea, but mostly—no more than spit. And if you want one, I am, for example, stuck in this time in my life like Heine in the grave of his mattresses with forty thousand books and pamphlets and magazines piling up around me. I had an idea, you see? A great idea . . .

That's it. Sometimes you survive a glorious leap like Nakhshon and get credited in the Bible; mostly, you find out that the pool below you was empty. But always—even if you succeed—you're somehow terribly alone when you go back to all the rest, and to their appraising looks, that suddenly seem to you as if they're ahem-ing with their eyes. And my father would say to me, The whole body wants to pee, but you know what to take out to do the job.

This is how I feel now, and it destroys me, I can't stand such a look from you; because for a completely different glance of yours, I decided to jump headfirst, on three, whatever the dangers, "and not less than everything," by the demands of T. S. Eliot's requirements. And now I'm eating myself up for not having been more cautious.

Because I could have written to you a sophisticated, caressing letter, and clouded my intentions, and seduced you slowly, and flirted with ease, and definitely have met body to body, by all the common rules of the adulterous games accepted and in play in the grown-up community. When I think of things I wrote to you, things I told you about my family, or things that, because of you, I told myself about my family, that horrible sentence about three people living together—I feel like castrating myself, tearing out my own tongue!

June 7

Enough, enough. What an unbearable night. (And to think that you might not even be capable of imagining my suffering!) I never told you how it started, exactly; I mean, I told you only so much. I think I've repeated that much at least thirty times by now, but I was only telling you about yourself, about what I saw in you. And I can't have this end without your knowing what was happening inside me in those moments.

So here it is, in short order, and then we can finish with it. One night, about two months ago, I saw you. You were standing in the middle of a large group that had gathered around you, and especially around your husband. A whole flock of respectable teachers and educators, and everybody sighed over how hard it is to succeed in the education racket, how long it takes to see the fruit of your labors. Someone—of course—mentioned Khoni and the Circle, and another tale, about the old man who planted a carob tree for his grandchildren, and your husband—excuse me, your "man" (although it seems to me that he certainly sees himself as a "husband")—was going on about some complicated genetic experiment he's been working on now for ten years. I can't be too precise about the details, because I wasn't really concentrating too hard on what he was saying. Please send him my apologies. The bitter truth is, his story was long and boring. A lot of *facts* in it, something about rabbit fertility, I think, and about the instinct, in times of stress, to draw the fetus back into the womb (?). Doesn't matter. In any case, everyone listened to him, with his infectious self-confidence and that special manner of speaking, slowly, authoritatively. A man like that knows the world will fall silent and listen, raptly, as soon as he opens his mouth. He uses a full range of facial expressions brilliantly, and has the self-possession of a mature male, what with those long cheeks and developed jawline and thick brow . . . By God, you're lucky, Miriam. You got the best male of the herd. Darwin is saluting you from his grave. Of course, the two of you made a wonderful pair, clearly, scaling the high altitudes together—you see how I was still free there, meaning, free to make that mistake?

Then your husband let out a burst of laughter, and that was it: I remember how astonished I was by the strong, manly, *sparkling* laughter that surged out of him. How I shrank from it—as if he had caught me doing something shameful. I don't even know what he was laughing about, or at whom, but everyone was laughing along with him; it was as if they wanted to, for a moment, dance among those commanding rays pouring from his beaming face. I looked at you by chance—perhaps because you were the only woman there, and I was searching for understanding from or protection in you—and I saw you weren't laughing. On the contrary, you shivered and hugged yourself; perhaps his laughter (which you probably love) revived some painful memory inside you. Or maybe it just horrified you as much as it did me.

So they kept talking, all extremely interested; what am I talking about—*fascinated* by the conversation in that way they are all so very good at, but you weren't there anymore. It was amazing—I saw how you sneaked away from everyone without moving one step; you simply took advantage of the momentary diversion to disappear. And I also saw where you disappeared to. Something behind your eyes opened and closed, one flash of a secret door, and suddenly only your body was left standing there, sad, abandoned by you (that I will never be able to tell you about it again, your fair, soft body, butter and honey—). You dropped your head a bit, and held yourself in your hands, as if you were cradling your child-self, and your baby-self, and ripples and furrows of wonder started trembling on your forehead, like that of a girl hearing a long, complicated, sad story; yes, your whole face started sailing upon your face. And I unconsciously felt my heart reaching out to you in the dance of the donkey foal; there is probably still a gap where I am missing a rib from that moment, everything went crazy and so did I.

(Don't worry, I'll be leaving your life in a moment, last throes.) Now I can allow myself to remember how that large group of students swarmed around you immediately afterward—do you remember?

It's strange how I managed to erase it from my memory until now. They practically kidnapped you from the adults for the favor of having a photo taken with you—they almost carried you on their shoulders. And that one moment you passed by me, and I saw you were still daydreaming a little, but starting to make the effort to smile on the outside; it was a completely different smile, public, fluorescent—would you look at how completely I had forgotten about it?

But maybe I didn't forget it. Maybe it was this thrilling peep into your inner workings that let me know, immediately, that you would understand me?

Because it was a moment of "your ignominy." Without understanding it yet, I think I recognized it: this smile, a bit like a contraction. You were wearing an election-campaign smile for a moment . . . What am I saying? You? An election campaign? Yes, yes, I am certainly never wrong about these things. So, even you? Elected over and over again, charming, yes, emblazoning yourself on the eyes of strangers. (And now I'm even sorrier that we won't continue this.)

And I don't know if you felt what came next, perhaps you hadn't yet fully recovered your senses. Your students, a herd of oafs and clods, teenagers, scrapers of facial scruff—how they all started fighting for the privilege of being the closest to you, so they could touch you, suckle a look or a smile from you, announce whatever terribly important problem was troubling them at exactly that moment. It was kind of funny to watch—

"Funny" is not the right word. Pity for the parpur. Because even the man standing to the side had, in that same moment a bizarre, unexpected impulse—it's actually embarrassing to recall—the same wild urge to open wide his fledgling mouth in a madness of sudden, terrible hunger—Me me, Teacher, me me . . .

Enough. Enough. I'm humiliating myself even more with every word. Please, take a piece of paper, write a few words, just one will do—yes or no. I don't have the energy for a long letter from you now. Write "I'm sorry, I tried to get used to it, to you, I really did try hard, but I couldn't forgive your turmoil, your misleading statements."

Well, fine. We are agreed. At least we know where we stand. My heart will probably continue to shout out your name for a little while longer; and eventually, it will heal. Perhaps I'll return to Ramat Rakhel, or some other place out of town. Some place with no people, that can be ours, at least long enough so I can yell out with all my strength, "Miriam! Miriam! Mir-yam!"

Yair

Don't worry, another day, or two, slowly, the letters will peel away, and the only thing left will be my clockwork scream to you—hee-haw, hee-haw!

June 10

It so happened that your letter arrived after I was already completely exhausted. I opened the mailbox, simply out of habit, the same way I've done tens of times in the last week, and your white envelope was there. I stood there, looking at it—and didn't feel a thing. Just tired. Perhaps afraid as well. Because I was hoping that I had already become used to thinking it was over. Frozen for good. And where would I find the strength to undergo all the aches of defrosting?

I read it, of course. Once, and again, and again. I still can't understand how I could fall apart so quickly over a break of a single week. Can you believe it—I felt as if you were gone for at least a month.

As if I was just waiting for an excuse to torture myself.

I've nothing to add today. I'm glad you're back, that we are together again. That you didn't even think of disappearing on me. Just the opposite.

And I'm still angry at you for not taking a moment to consider how much I would suffer. How could you, *you*, not know me? You could have at least sent a note before leaving, or a postcard from the Central Station at Rosh Pina. It would have delayed you by no more than ten minutes and saved me a lot of misery.

On the other hand, I am starting to grasp that if you had the choice, you probably wouldn't cause me suffering.

So, we can fade this letter out on an optimistic note—you probably had no choice.

June 10–11

This is still not a response, not a real response, not the response you deserve for that letter, for the depths that revealed themselves to me as I read and reread it. Mostly because of how you released me gently, rope by rope, from the knots of the trap I set for myself. Sparing me any and all embarrassment over the Gastric Juice Concerto I played for you.

(They really let you leave work? Two weeks before the end of the school year?

And what do they have to say about it at home?

It's none of my business.)

I am, every time, mystified by the contrast between your sound, composed mind, the stable, calm motherhood within you—and the fluid tosses of your head, the unexpected leaps, unexpected even from you. I see you pacing through the oak grove above the Kinneret, erect and serious-looking, and hugging yourself hard, looking for your lost peace of mind, pushing me away again and again . . .

What's that? It's just a smile. I remembered how in your first letters you said, time and again, that it was hard for you to believe that such a storm was created in me from one quick look at you ("And what if I don't have another side to my face, what if you only cut a picture of a woman out of the night for yourself?"). And then you slowly started to explain to yourself that it always begins like that, really—from a single look at a stranger. And now, what you wrote me from there on the rock, that only a "narrow-minded and material" sort of person could consider us strangers—earlier, when I woke up (it's half past three), I sat in the living room, in the darkness, curled up on the armchair. I was thinking about you and me, about what is happening so unexpectedly to us in the middle of our lives, and I was happy that I was, by chance, by myself a little at home, in complete silence. I invited you to be with me, and you came. I usually try not to think about you when I'm here, in my everyday life. I try to keep strictly to the law of the separation of governing bodies. I hesitate whether to tell you when I do always think of you, always—when I'm taking a shower, or when I'm, what to do, taking a piss. Yes, when I see it.

And I tried to figure out, between me and myself, whether I am at all capable of being a lightning rod for anyone—I saw that you were very much troubled by this, but it is difficult for me to give you a clear answer, one that is real, earnest—no one ever asked me such a thing. No one ever asked. And no one ever asked as directly as you, in such a cutting, single-minded way, and with such desire.

I guess they saw the answer in me right away.

But then again—do you remember when I wrote to you that the moment I saw you I felt, for the first time, a strong, clear desire to have another person inside me? So maybe this is an indirect answer to your question. I just asked myself, Is it still so? And I answered, Yes, even more. Much more.

Tell me, how is it that I am not scared of wanting such a thing—how can anyone let another person inside herself, anyway? Seriously, Miriam—tonight I suddenly grasped what an amazing thing it is, quivering with generosity and compassion, that a person can let another person penetrate even just her body! This completely natural thing suddenly seems almost abnormal! And people are doing it without thinking twice (so I hear), penetrating and letting themselves be penetrated—even a fuck is sometimes a cliché—or perhaps, in order to make such an intrusion possible, you must purposely not allow yourself that kind of understanding? Is that it?

Can you imagine—for a moment, I was afraid I wouldn't be able to do it anymore, those familiar swimming motions—do it regularly, I mean.

So, probably out of that slight panic, I dwelt on one of my favorite hobbies: I sat with my eyes closed and relived one of the fucks from my private collection—you are the first person I am telling this to (because you told me about Adam and Eve's first time, perhaps). It reminds me of how I would try to replay complete soccer games in my head as a child—and these days, what to do, fucks, my little adulteries, the most agreeable way to transcend norms, as Nabokov once put it to me during a long ride to the base in the Sinai.

I can't do it with all of them, of course—six or seven at most (it has been a few years since a new one has been added to the collection). The most special ones, the ones during which I was in the rarest and most desirable state of consciousness. Dreaming and awake at the same time, completely drowsy, and also open to receiving every move of her hand and body, and what she said, and how she breathed—and I can retrace the curve of her hips and the location of her beauty marks (where do you have them? I know about the one under your lip—in my opinion, it is actually a microfilm you are smuggling on your innocent face—but where do you have more?). I don't forget a detail in this silent reliving, and don't ask me how—I don't have a clue: I am like those chess geniuses who can remember the moves of hundreds of games by heart. What do you know, Miriam? This might be my hidden genius, my grand crusade (*my art* . . .)?

Now I shall seal the envelope and the pleasure of waiting will begin.

Yair

(Morning)

I still want you to know whom you're dealing with. I think I went easy on myself tonight regarding the "lightning rod."

Because I . . . I use all of my powers to keep myself *balanced*. Not a millimeter less or more than total precise balance. I'm not particularly proud to be writing this, but the foundation that has been laid for my emotional stability is the size of a peanut. Really. You saw what happened to me a week ago. It scares me, how easily I can lose it, collapse in a blink. It's also so easy for me to want to stop existing, give up everything.

And you're asking me if I can be a lightning rod for someone? Me? Why, everyone around me has to always perform at the peak of his health and normality, and yes, of course you were right about something when you wrote about Maya being my "mother-base." Yes, that's the way it is, and you can't shake it. And isn't it nice that all those closest to me keep so strictly to the mandatory entry code of membership that my small club requires.

That's it. I puked it out. The most pathetic in me. Miserable. Spoiled. A soggy mess. But it's important to me that you know. It sometimes amazes me how obedient they all are, how they subconsciously fulfill their requirements. All of them are born healthy, develop to maturity nicely, and are never tempted to fall prey to some incurable disease or defect. Nor do they die suddenly! There's no dying with me! Not even in old age—only after I go will they be allowed to even consider it! Even my parents are probably forced to stay alive only so they won't die during the springtime of my existence—we shouldn't even talk about my father, who for several years has been stuck in the guts of the end of his life, only because of my draconian laws.

You do understand that it isn't only death that has to obey me—any diversion, every break of the blessed routine is forbidden. If Maya, for instance, would happen upon the thought—even approach the notion—of falling in love with someone else, leaving me, leaving me to my pack of jealousy-bloodhounds, it would be the end of me, as simple as that, a five-kilo sledgehammer on the heart of the parpur. That is my unwritten law: whoever wishes to be close to me commits to my soul. Because any common idiot can see how easy it would be to kill me. One look aimed and fired at me will do. I'm not joking: somewhere inside me I am convinced that whoever sees me, even strangers on the street, can, without knowing me, immediately know where it is possible to crack me open with one touch, to negate me with a word. And even though—apparently—all the people surrounding me these days don't do it, don't put me out of my misery for some reason, I don't quite understand, I'm a little suspicious—what are they conspiring over? And you too, yes, you over there, the unseen, the written one—keep us safe, take care of both of us, even in the places where I am at my most pathetic, where I'm only half a man—be doubly strong, you can do it, I can tell, you have the fortitude for that—be our bodyguard (it's interesting that in Hebrew it is "headguard," whereas in English it is "bodyguard")—

I'm not sure I'll send this mess. What did it spring from? I don't know why these streams of filth have been passing through me, after I felt so close to you last night. I'm thinking about what you said in your last letter, about the strange impulse I sometimes have to make myself ugly in your honor, that dream you had about the strange vegetable seller who is putting the rotten tomatoes on top. If it is true, then take this into consideration as well—because I do feel that I have given you something here that I have never before dared to give myself.

I have to send it, right?

June 11
(I didn't have to wait for even four hours. They must have crossed on their way. When you read mine, you'll probably understand how odd it is that you are responding to things you hadn't read yet.)
Miriam,
I think that our meeting in the sprinklers is the wrong story. This is not the way I want to reach you.

Not only because you laughed at me for refusing to believe in the banal wonder of a real meeting between two people, even on a bus, in a bank, at a reunion party, or simply in a vegetable market—but because somehow, really, two strangers sitting in the grass and finding themselves

54

embracing in water—somehow, after your letter, after you said I put too much effort into romanticizing reality . . . I don't know, all of a sudden it seems boorish and forced to me, a water show full of hydrotechnic tricks. It doesn't suit you, nor is it in accordance with the softness with which I want to reach out to you, the quietness that surrounds you, and certainly not what you wrote in the last lines, that surprising explosion that I still don't know what to do with.

Still, it is still extremely important to me that you agree that "sprinklers" are also possible between us, and—that everything is possible between us: we'll have many of these first dates, and each time discover ourselves all over again. Why give up anything? Why give up "everything"? I want *everything* with you. You are the only person I can want everything with. Maybe, only through this excess, this waste, this "everything" can it slowly reveal itself to us—the elemental ore that can be created only between us, that can never be created between any other two people?

Of course you were right that reality itself is also a wonder and a miracle, I too am well practiced in saying such pretty things in a soft, veiled tone—if you'll excuse me—but don't forget that "reality" itself is, when it comes down to it, only a momentary coincidence on the surface of a huge sphere crackling with possibilities that will never be realized. And each and every one of them could have told us a completely different story about ourselves, played us differently. Why shouldn't we come to each other from the least expected places, from the dark side of the brain?

I want to have *ten* different affairs with you! Why not? Each one of them speaking—no, shouting out, for a completely different man in me. Men unfamiliar to me. This is why people try to connect with one another, isn't it? I'm asking you the same question you wrote me, exactly— if I would ever be brave enough to look deep into your eyes and read for you what you yourself cannot read there. I wish I could answer you with full confidence. I don't know (but is this why, in the very first moment, I stood in your blind spot?).

Am I asking too much? Perhaps. But why settle for less? We spend all our lives just "settling" anyway—and I want to touch everything with you, with wide, sweeping, generous motions, as if I knew it was for the last time in my life! And how is it that you were capable of stopping yourself in the same moment that you finally started to give part of yourself, from deep inside you—"my ignominies," you said, as if you were just joking, or trying on one of my words, but suddenly it became serious, didn't it? "And why don't you finally stop calling every insult thrown at you ignominies?!" Without warning, you became furious, but that word—I felt it cling to you, stick to you, as if you had to say it again, and again, and again, to shake it off you, but also to touch it, one more time— "What is the connection, anyway, between insults, wounds, and ignominies?" "Why do I keep feeling some strange pleasure in the way you keep confusing wounds with ignominies?" The more you repeated it, the more you said it, it fused to you, to your body, even closer, harder, and then you—

Explain it to me, Miriam—the war you are fighting that leaves you searching, at the end of some days, so desperately for a clear will to get up the next morning—what are you talking about, exactly? And where on earth did you get this crazy (and false) feeling that you are a person who should not create anything new in this world? I'm the person who keeps changing his face, is the consistently unstable, destructive force between us. Don't forget!

(Or perhaps, now that I'm thinking about it, perhaps it is some kind of illusion you are creating for me, the story you are choosing to tell me about yourself. But why would you tell me such a horrible story?)

Do you understand the kind of state you left me in by not explaining anything?—". . . and sometimes the feeling that every living thing, even the two little kittens Nilly gave birth to yesterday and, as is her way, left for me to nurse, even they are like stolen fire for the moments they are in my hands." And you immediately fell silent. There were quite a few empty lines toward the end of the page, and I didn't know how to fill them—my imagination went wild—and when you returned, summoned in front of me, your face was back to normal and you told me something small and irrelevant—if you'll excuse my teacherly remarks. I think you just wanted to end your letter politely. It is very nice that your son has now devoted himself to an operation so prestigious as counting to a million (a way not worse than any other to waste your life)—you finally told me, clearly, that you have a son—I was starting to worry—but how could you *leave* me like that after mentioning those things?

Enough, enough—let's unclench our fists—our dark secrets are always less terrible than we imagine them—so give yourself to me, without walls, without reservations—write to me, for instance. Tell me—in a completely separate letter—a one-sentence letter—tell me the first thing, the first thought, the first flicker flashing in your mind when you read this letter. (Yes, yes! Now! At this very minute! Write it down, put it in an envelope, and send it, even before your "official" reply, even before dealing with all the complications inherent with me within you.)—

June 14

Boom!

So now it's my turn?

After we come, we'll fall asleep, lying close together. Your back will be stuck to my belly, and I will squeeze my toes like clothespins on your ankles, so you won't fly away on me during the night, and we'll be like a picture from a nature book: a length cut of a fruit. I am the peel, you are the flesh.

Yair

P.S. I didn't believe you would dare so much.

June 17

And when we lie down together, I would like to close my eyes and gently touch the edge of your hairline somewhere under your navel (your belly button), so I can, with the tips of my fingers, feel the place, one of the places, that delicate silky place, where you changed from a child into a woman.

Y.

June 18

One out of turn:

Yesterday I walked down through Queen Heleni Alley. A child, nine or ten years old, was walking in front of me. We were alone. The alley was dark, and once in a while he glanced back and quickened his pace. But even when I walk slowly, I walk pretty quickly. I could feel his fear.

I could remember this kind of fear well. And I wondered how I could put him at ease without embarrassing him. Then he tried to leap away—but he twisted his leg badly, and now he dragged it along behind him, whimpering in pain. This is how we walked, together, at a fixed distance, until we reached the end of the alley. He's limping outside, and I, inside.

Y.

The problem with these quickies, obviously, is that you're hungry again after an hour (although "sometimes, the way you touch me—it is one touch, the same I feel in that spot of pain and pleasure" will do for me for at least a week).

June 19

Have you written to me yet? Have you sent it yet? When does your box get emptied?

(Just a little exercise of my agitation muscles—don't want them to get flaccid. That way you can always recognize me.)

About those final assumptions of yours—you were triply wrong: I am not writing to you from prison. I am not sick and bedridden with some terrible disease. I am not even an Israeli spy for Damascus or Moscow on a brief vacation home before returning to the cold—

I am all three.

What else? Not much.

A lot: your fingers trembling when you find my envelopes in your box in the teachers' lounge.

It's the same for me, what do you think? First I examine with a touch—how thick is the new letter? How much food will I have to savor over the next days and nights—

To answer your (surprisingly weird) question—hands and digital together (but why is that important anyway?).

Oh, I remember something I keep forgetting to ask you: do you have any—this is silly, I know, but anyway—do you happen to have any connection to a Chinese newspaper (completely in Chinese!), a weekly magazine published in Shanghai that I've started receiving lately out of nowhere—I didn't order it.

If you don't, forget the question.

This is not a letter. It is just a nightly humming, a whistle in the dark until you return to me.

(It never ceases to amaze me—how my desiccated life chose to expose a giant breast for me.)

Yair

June 21

An open mouth or a hole in a tree trunk? I'm struggling to decide—but so filled with joy—because *there weren't any words there!*

I didn't know you painted, too. The line and the black and the power of your touch.

I swear by my life: someday I will dance for you. I won't care if we are surrounded by people—I will just look into your eyes and I will dance.

But in the meantime, I need to write, don't I? So then, in honor of your black strokes:

A shrunken black monkey, let's say, scrambling over his mistress's belly.

Does that make any sense to you? No matter. We allowed ourselves the freedom to mumble. To me, it means: the master bought it for her at one of the fairs he passed through in his journeys. The master is always on a journey, the master's journey. The monkey is tame. It was bought for the lady's pleasure, but not for its own. God forbid—do you understand? It always has to remember its place—the place of the replacer, the guard, until the master returns (and perhaps there isn't any master at all).

Y.

And I know you can read my mind at this moment—how you said it was strange to you that I can remember every motion, moan, and beauty mark of the women who were with me—but couldn't find myself in those memories.

June 22

When I'm with people (this came to mind tonight while I was bathing my son)—it doesn't matter if they are strangers or those closest to me—I am always accompanied by one thought: I am impotent to do the one thing all of them do so naturally—putting down roots.

Question: Tell me, idiot, why the hell are you sending these bits of trash? All your trifling thoughts and dime-store philosophies? Why do you have not one crumb of nobility or taste to tame your words, to guide you so that you don't say *everything*?!

Answer: It is the donkey foal in me, and it is the special impulse I have with her, more than with anybody else I ever knew, to say everything, even these dime-store philosophies of mine. It's not even to tell her, sometimes it's to have this flicker fly to her, like an unconscious relative whom you bring to the emergency room and just throw into the doctor's hands you pray will be able to mend him. Tell her about the Möbius strip.

Question: Are you crazy? So soon?

Answer: What do you mean "so soon"? There's no such thing as too early or too late, we're on spherical time, remember? She said she was actually born for this kind of time . . .

Come, lend me a hand, I will now tell you that one of the things I sometimes do is to think of him as *old*. I am talking about my son, about—let's call him Ido. About my Ido.

Maybe it's to inoculate myself (against what—too much love for him?). I picture him old again and again. And it helps. It puts out every passion born of love and panic for him instantly.

Notice: old. Not dead. I have my expertise in that one as well, of course. But dead is probably too simple and unequivocal for the torture I need. My son—old, stooped over, staring absently at the television in some institution for the likes of him, strings of spittle drooling from his mouth. Dead, because the spark lighting his eyes has already been turned off. It's not simple to concentrate on such an image; try it, it requires the operation of extremely strong soul-muscles, the muscles along the spine of the soul, because the soul arches in terrible resistance against it and great strength is needed to force its surrender . . . Where were we?

With my son, with the post-factum infant, my old son, a little man, all crabbed up with brown spots on his hands, infected with one of those diseases of his age, trying to remember something that slipped away—me, perhaps? Perhaps the twists of his memory suddenly rouse thoughts of me? The two of us together in a good moment? When, this morning, a speck of dust got in his eye and I licked it out with my tongue? When I covered all the angles of the shelves in our house with foam rubber the day his head started to reach them? Or just when I loved him, terribly, in my own limited way?

And perhaps he will get confused for a moment and think that he is my father?

I hope so. I long for, wish, that somewhere in the infinite cosmos, where destinies are being stirred with people and every person touches the possibility of being any other person for a moment, there will be such a moment in which he will be my father (relieving the everlasting burden of the mysterious coincidence dictating that I must be his father, and not the other way around). I especially want everything to be over, ended, to be tucked into his bosom and to cuddle and mingle our flesh, ashes to ashes. I pray for it to be so, to be, in that same time, just another person like him, for him, who tried—a person who was in the world but, for one moment, burst and twitched in the space of life—

I think: Maybe then, in the arbitration or the indifference of his old age, and also in the wisdom that he will gain, probably through the years of his fatherhood with the children he will have—would he wish to choose me again? What do you think, would he choose me?

Speak to me.

Sometimes it's so hard to wait two or three days for a reply, because it hurts *now*.

After I fantasized about my little honeysuckle Ya'ara, you said that you're certain that I am also a very giving father to Ido, that I give more perhaps than many parents can give a child, and that I am probably not just "sucking him dry." Thank you for trying to release me from that torment. I'm just terrified to tell you how much I do suck him dry, I am Yair-Sucking, I leave him a husk, even if I don't intend it, by the very fact of my presence. But someday, in the year 2065, he will smile at me, with bald gums and glazed-over eyes, and tell me that it's all right, he too understands now the instability of the verdicts imposed in our penal colony—that one time you are Franz Kafka—and another time you're his father, Hermann . . .

Sometimes I picture it to the very details. How he will summon my spirit, hold me between his fingers, and examine me against the yellow afternoon light, like a man holding some kind of unwanted, but harmless, object in his hands. And then I will cautiously move my fingers over his body, and over mine, like passing a finger over a Möbius strip, when the finger can't distinguish whether it is passing from the inside to the outside.

I think it is time for a commercial break.

June 24

It delights me that you like my "City Stories" so much. I was already thinking that, because of you, I am experiencing a lot more of those "moments" (really: the city speaks to me as it never did).

Accept a fresh, fresh one: This very morning, in Ben Yehuda Street, near Atara Café, there was a clown who was also a magician, maybe you've seen him: a huge man, Rasputin-like, who performs a funny show with a guillotine. I know him, and it's been a while since I've stopped to watch, but today I decided to look, maybe because you came back to the word "guillotine" in your long last letter, when you were depressed and exploded.

The magician asked for a volunteer, and one guy from the audience, an American tourist, came and placed his head on the block. The magician made a fuss about measuring the hole for his neck, and cut a single hair of his on the blade, and placed a wicker basket in front of him, and everyone around was laughing. And then, when the magician raised the blade high, the guy suddenly sent both of his hands through the holes of the stocks and, without even thinking, in a very touching and instinctual way, pulled the basket toward him so his head "would fall" exactly into it.

Everybody laughed, but I was so moved, as if you were there with me and I was showing you something of *mine* that I can't explain in words.

June 28

I'm sending you a photograph that might make you happy.

I found it (and not by chance) in an old scrapbook of *The Weekly Word*, your distant cousin Alexander. Excuse me, but I can certainly understand your parents' hysteria—not only because he was six years older than you; there was something in his eyes, a wolfish expression . . .

Look at his figure on the winner's stand, for example. That smile (I do have to admit that he seems quite impressive, even with the silly swim cap and medal—a kosher alpha male. Those shoulders! That chest! Those biceps!).

Terrible, isn't it? To see all this strength and arrogance, and think he doesn't know that in five years he will be lying dead on streetcar tracks.

I am trying to find any similarities between the two of you—this photo was taken that very same week—and I can't find you in his face. So what do I find? What does it tell me? That your mother was right? In any case, I think I can see the surprising tenderness around his mouth and lower lip. So maybe even an experienced Casanova softens a little because it was your first kiss, and the only one with him?

But there is another matter that stands out as slightly peculiar. I also checked the newspapers from the following Maccabiah Games three years later and found that he participated again with the Belgian contingent (but didn't win any medals this time). According to my calculations, you were then sixteen and a half, meaning, not exactly an age at which you could be locked up at home or forbidden to meet him, or prevented in any possible way from participating in taboo behavior (and he surely came to visit you at home to bring news from the family . . .). And I've been wondering how it is possible that after the great storm you described experiencing over him, the burning oaths you swore, the full year of dreams about him and the perfumed letters, and all that—how could you completely give up the chance of a reunion with him?

I think—even though you were three years older, and must have understood by then that it had been just a momentary amusement for him, that he was not exactly the man of your dreams—but still, was there no spark of curiosity? Or the desire to come to him and say, Look at me now, see how I've grown, I'm not your little cousin anymore . . .

(I don't know why the thought of his final visit makes me so sad.)

Speaking of kisses: send warm greetings to the beauty mark you said goodbye to when you started maturing . . . I will never forget that quickie of yours—it was overwhelming. Maybe someday, in another incarnation, I'll kiss it as well.

June 30

What beautiful weather, Louise, what a bright sun! All my blinds are shut; I'm writing to you in the dark.

This is how Flaubert wrote to Louise Colet. I stumbled upon it today, and in spite of that stinger (do I really quote other people constantly?), I saw a private sign of us in it.

In the last two days I did a lot of thinking about your suggestion, your weird suggestion—ten years late, to my mind—to "go steady." You made me return to a time not particularly loved by me. I'm not sure that I found a story to be an exact "mate" to yours, certainly not to the girl you were, the sober, clear-minded girl who assessed situations and took action, so it appears to me, decisively and without remorse . . . And to tell you the truth, Miriam, I am not quite convinced that that girl would have been interested in this boy as a boyfriend.

I was around thirteen years old. I won't describe what I looked like to you—it will make you angry, and why should I provoke forces greater than mine? But I guess I managed to draw some attention to myself after a retarded girl living in our neighborhood kidnapped me and performed surgery on me without anesthesia. Now, you'll say that I am, as usual, describing everything in a dramatic, larger-than-life way, but this is exactly what she did to me. I don't know how old she was, she couldn't even speak, instead she kind of grunted, this masculine, hard, bullish girl, this miserable retarded girl I always made fun of. I used to ambush her and her father when he took her down from the house on their daily walk (he walked with a stick to protect himself from her in case she attacked, imagine that). And for several years I was the neighborhood leader of our organized mockery of her, I invented the most evil tortures for her and her poor father—writing slogans and drawing caricatures of her on the sidewalk—

And you will ask, and justly so, why I made fun of her. Why, in spite of my own cowardice, did I draw everyone's attention to her and only to her? The way I laughed at her—the amount of wit and poison I invested in it—don't ask. Well, one day she managed to escape from her house. Her father fainted on the stairs. All the neighbors and their kids were called together to search for her, and the police showed up, and basically, it was a complete mess.

I slipped from the crowd and walked to the end of the block, to an empty lot on which now stands a big hotel. There, in one of the most neglected corners, stood a heap of garbage, years of old mattresses and ovens piled up. And a small broken refrigerator, and other such detritus of the neighborhood. Behind it, by the fence, was a mess of bushes that created a small dark hideaway. I thought only I knew of it, and liked to go there to isolate myself from the world.

I had a feeling she would be there, that her animal instincts would lead her to that place which no sane man would enter. And, I swear, the moment I passed the line of light into the darkness, she leaped on me. In that same moment I also realized, with some kind of strange acceptance, that she was simply waiting for me.

You know, I can't remember when you asked me this—perhaps when you spoke of the lightning rod—if I have, ever in my life, properly cried for *HELP!* In a way that practically tears the throat apart, forces the eyes to bulge with terror and despair (hey, why did you ask me that?). Maybe I should have yelled like that, at that time when she dragged me in—but I was silent. This, Miriam, is what my story is about.

She pushed me to the ground, lay on top of me, and, without wasting a moment, started rubbing her body on mine with a horrible strength. We were two flints striking together, over and over. I couldn't move—it was as if I had lost consciousness—but I saw and heard everything. She was serious—and also feverish with the crazy idea raging inside her, the false idea that only I, of all people, could understand her exactly—and it wasn't even a sexual thing; I mean, not sexual in the common, passionate way. It was a lot more complicated, dank, and dark than that. How can I put it—it was as if she were trying to crumble and mash into dust the materials from which we both were made—

Should I go into more detail?

I mean, all the materials, all her ores and mine. What for? I don't know (I do know, I do know). To create us both, all over again—more precisely: to balance us out—or somehow to scrape away all her excess—and mine, too—and what was missing as well, in both of our bodies and souls, together (can you actually understand such a sentence? Does it make sense outside of my mind?). Simply to create us anew from the dust from which we were made. I swear to you, this is what was pecking about in her twisted mind—and only I understood it. Which is why I didn't even yell for help. It was a matter between me and her. I can't believe I'm even telling you about this.

So what do you say now—could he have been, in his way, a "mate" to the girl you were? To that philosophical, opinionated lass?

I remember she took my left palm in her rough hand, and ten, and twenty, and fifty times over, she shoved her fingers between my fingers.

And then she did it with the right hand—shoulder to shoulder—chest to chest—stomach to stomach—systematically, in the most specific, meticulous manner—and her dead eyes were shining with her one grand idea. She didn't even notice *me*, that was the amazing thing that completely hypnotized me. She had a score to settle with what I was, not with who. And the enlightened world would have found nothing logical in it—but in the dark I knew and felt that she was aiming with all her strength at my well-being as well. It was as if she was trying to shuffle the cards in our decks, hers and mine, hard, in order to—let's say—deal them all over again, in a more just way, for *both of us*. Do you understand? She of all people could grasp, with some kind of genius, animal sense, how unhappy I was with what I had received from the taunting lottery of life, and that I too was desperately in need of mending. Are you still with me, Miriam? Just if you can give something like that to someone, and hope he will truly understand—tell me if a man can tell this to someone and hope she will truly understand, tell me if a man can tell this to a woman he is wooing, and if a husband could, one day, tell this to his wife over coffee.

Y.

July 5

    I went. I bought. I returned.

    A three-day jump, Amsterdam-Paris-Switzerland. Business. The successful pursuit of two rare collector's items that were in hysterical demand in Zurich. Man of the world, boom boom.

    When the airplane took off from Lod, I felt an unexpected pang, and I discovered an umbilical cord between us that hurts when it is stretched.

    And what did I bring you from sparkling Paris? A sensational perfume? Jewels? Coy, tantalizing panties?

My most terrible waking nightmare when I am in large European cities is the sight of little children of beggar women.

    Do you know what I'm talking about? Those Indian or Turkish women sitting on the streets and in the underground train stations who always carry a baby or a small child on their knees.

    Because I noticed, a long time ago, that the children are almost always asleep. In London, in Berlin, in Rome. And I have a suspicion that the women put them to sleep on purpose, drug them, because a sleeping child looks more miserable and is hence "better for business"...

Once, in front of my regular hotel in Paris, a Turkish woman set up shop with such a child, and the next day I simply moved to another hotel.

It isn't only the cruelty that depresses me; mainly, it is the thought that these children are spending their lives asleep. To think of only one child (and there are hundreds of them) who lives for years, perhaps for his entire childhood, in London, or in wonderful Florence, almost without seeing it—and only in his sleep does he hear the footsteps of people, the noise of the cars, the pulse of the big city—and when he awakes, he is, again, only in the miserable hole where he lives.

When I pass by such a woman in the street, I always give her something—and while doing so, I whistle a pleasant, happy tune with all my strength.

I'm back.

July 7

Good morning, two letters of yours arrived today! I've been waiting so long for this moment when you couldn't hold yourself back—and the minute you closed an envelope, ideas for another letter gathered inside you, instantly. One arrived in the morning, and the other with the afternoon delivery (the pleasures of a mailbox owner!). And they are both jolly and excited, one from home and the second—I guess your house got hot and stuffy—from your secret valley near Ein Karem. It was wonderful to finally meet you in completely new words (and a new skirt!), like breathing a stream of clear air . . . and to hear the surprise in your voice when you said you've been happy lately. That's the first time the word has appeared in your letters—I immediately sent it to the lab for tests, and they verified its happiness (I'm just trying to figure out why it is that your happiness still seems so sad to me), and perhaps because of this word, something is happening to me as well today. An internal tide turning, I don't know, perhaps because I've finally succeeded in making you happy.

Because summer broke open inside me as well, you see. It's as if only now your magic spell of words allowed me, as well, to leave the dark and

windy cave we dug out together, with all our complexity and heaviness—
"happy"—and as if you permitted me something, the summer broke
open inside me—it's already July, imagine that, and I am only now waking up to summer, with its life forces and the shining, its natural rough-
ness and the excitement of wanting so much so desperately—everything
you described (how is it that you are still afraid of going back to painting
in color? A person who can write like that . . .). Look at me, me as well,
touch me, I am suddenly so alive, burning and sending tendrils into the
body of this summer, as if I myself were one of its "beating veins" you described—and I'm also focused on you today, like a laser beam—watch
out! I'm not responsible for my actions today, don't even know what's
happening to me—do you have any idea?

How about this: perhaps I will completely stop working and living in
the outside world, in their so-called existence, and only write, and write,
and write to you. I will describe how you look in every state and what it
does to me when I look at you in every state, and I will sap myself of my
essences, pour them into you until I am completely drained. A hanged
man ejaculates in his last moment. I read about it once, and it has excited
me ever since, a last will and testament of the body and soul together; this
is exactly the kind of conversation I want between us, because we will *die*
on each other in a few months—you refuse to even listen to me about
this, the "guillotine" turning your guts—but, to me, it is the heart and
soul of our relationship, maybe because what is happening between us
would never happen during the complete life of an ordinary couple—
we can have the nectar of Queen's Honey and the blood of our rawest
essence together at the same time—you are starting to feel it now, but I
knew it from the beginning.

I thought the story of the retarded girl would put you off—but you,
as usual, come and touch me, without gloves. So what, then? You, in no
way, would ever want to redeal your cards and mine, but rather the opposite? Is that what truly attracts you to me, the fact that I don't have a
full deck?

Well, fine, good—but touch me only in writing, leave me written—
and I hope we both can have the power to fight off the barbed temptations of reality a little longer. Sex, not religion, is the opiate of the masses;
and when we meet—because eventually, we will surrender——I'm feeling a bit fragile today—the heat is melting my most firm resolve. I hope

we won't—but perhaps in two or three weeks, if not tonight, we can—this predatory attack inflaming me here——It's that skirt you bought. You slipped it on, and had a body, your body, that body I almost succeeded in forgetting was resurrected in a blink, your legs moved inside your skirt, pretty and fresh—don't say, even as a joke, that "I forgot I even had legs"—and I remembered the curves of your ankles and finally grasped the secret conspiracy between the shape of a woman's ankles and the back of her neck . . .

It's clear to you, isn't it? We will eventually surrender. When the sad, thick, heavy sweetness, the nectar of autumn, falls in layers in our hearts—Yair has begun to poetize, the nectar of summer is quite active in me today as well. Oh well, how long can you continue turning come into ink alone—and it is only your black-framed glasses that keep me from writing exactly what is going on in my head at this moment, now—and at what precise times I do picture you, and how—dressed, undressed, in the orange skirt with the side slit, the orange T-shirt that clings and caresses you when you are standing up, lying down, wildly, sweetly, in my car, your thin ankles clasped like a necklace around my back—I am dying for such a miracle to happen, for you to pop up in front of me in the street by chance——

Where were we?

I have no idea how to get up from my desk in front of my secretary, a nice little Beit Ya'akov Orthodox School graduate. You are probably asking yourself, What the hell does he want from me? Why is he driving me and himself crazy in this way—I have no idea. I just want it so much right now that it hurts. On the other hand, I'm so convinced that we shouldn't dip even one toe into reality—everything will melt and evaporate into a cliché—all the delicate, transparent webs from which we have woven ourselves, all this ephemeral beauty will be ground into flesh all of a sudden, and will be lost, one-two-three! Believe me. You can tell that I know whereof I speak—and I'm telling you, we will exist only in limbo, the space between us—even though, in your opinion, we have nothing to hide, not even from your loving husband. I can absolutely not understand that part. Why hurt him? Why the humiliation? He has already been betrayed and cheated in every possible way by everything we have together—without his knowledge, he has already been betrayed, robbed by the law of the preservation of joy in nature—I have to stop here again. A shipment has arrived. Ah, all the times life has to pass through a coffee spout. I'll continue this evening. I do actually want to continue to talk about this—

July 10

I cannot believe it. I am sitting here simply refusing to believe what you have done to me.

What are you, a psychic? Do you have X-ray vision? What if that was the most wonderful letter I ever wrote to you? And aren't you curious in the slightest? Have you no simple feminine curiosity? How could you withstand the temptation? (Or is it no temptation to you at all—me, that is?)

I am trying to understand exactly what happened, how, exactly, your gears work: you received the morning letter, full of excitement over the summer and your new happiness, the one you read. But the letter I sent you later in the evening continuing the conversation—and it was, by the way, a tremendously funny letter, hilarious, even—you decided, for some reason, to return to me closed and sealed. Why? Because of what? The heat of the pages you felt through the envelope? The angle by which I wrote your name on the outside? And if I had sent you my soul, wrapped up in there, what then? Would you have sent that back as well?

Your arrogance exasperates me. You're terribly tough, have I ever told you that? Tough in a way that is unpleasant, even unfeminine! You know, I could tell from your first letters—but at that point your totality and the extreme seriousness with which you responded to everything I said and what was going on between us—I actually liked it. Then. And now it is as if the water level has sunk, revealing the rock beneath.

And your inflexible clinging to principles! "Even a whisper from that place hurts me, pains me like betrayal, and I have to protect myself from it . . ." Betrayal, nothing less! One could think that we had signed some kind of mutual pact committing us to life and death, and not simply corresponded!

Listen—what you've done is not so simple. And the more I think about it, the more I feel that it is you who have betrayed me. You, who amused herself for a few months with the harmless clown twitching near you; my letters were nothing more than a petit bourgeois turn-on for you, the secret flirtations of a decent housewife—but when it got too close, too hot, when you suddenly started to feel any emotion, a living, existing thump, you got scared and started screaming help! I am reading the little spermicidal note you attached to my sealed envelope, and simply cannot believe: now, after three months, it occurs to you to accuse me of always flirting, not with you, really, but with some "permanent temptation of dishonesty" that is in me. An "internal Don Juan complex"?! You, in general, use such anachro-puritan expressions I could die. I'm shocked you didn't write "*Le* Don *du* Juan"!

And how! And with what confidence you allowed yourself to determine that even if I wanted to get rid of my (*automatic!*) yielding to temptation, it probably wouldn't let go of me, and that I take a constant mutated pleasure in mocking and making ugly everything truly precious and pure around me.

Is it because of what I wrote toward the end of the first letter? It is, isn't it? That remark about your husband, right? I imagine so. You clenched in front of me in that moment—I could feel myself stepping into your allergic regions. Fine. I'm sorry. Watch me—look, I'm apologizing! I'll write a testimonial: your husband is not humiliated, not betrayed, robbed, or in any way hurt by the Law of the Preservation of Happiness in Nature. There it is, there you have it, signed over to you with the print of my criminal finger.

And it's true—what do I really know about him? What, in fact, do I know about the both of you and what you are to each other? And you're right (in general, Miriam, you are completely in the right), because what do I know about *relationships* that do not operate according to the normal laws of territorial battle and war over each millimeter of the other's soul, to solely constantly surrender or be surrendered?

And what do you know—about Pegasus and mermaids and the common unicorn?

No, I have to hear from you: can you stand the pain of meeting the amateur Don Juan that I am? Is he not one of the "shuffled cards"? Is he not in need of "compassion" or "mending"? Sometimes I think, Perhaps you should have met only him. Perhaps he was the only one who could make you tremble with laughter and pleasure and breach the hardware of your principality.

Perhaps it is this you find so hard to accept. That I truly, innocently, in every line I wrote you, never offered you a clichéd love affair, or a—excuse me—fuck! Maybe this was the unforgivable insult that lit the spark and suddenly aroused that exemplary girl, the good queen of the class, who never let herself run wild and burn through all her polite fire?

She is the one who is so very offended right now, because again (as it was then, maybe?), the "boy" shows that he's interested in her only as a "friend," to talk with and to consult with, or to whisper in her ears his love and passion—none of which is for her! For someone else—for the shameless, lemony beauty of the summer? For the evil queen?

What do you know, Miriam, perhaps the present boy, twenty-something years later, began to suspect a kind of hollow sound in that proud statement of yours, that you do not, do not get scared by true passion in your feelings and relationships. That, on the contrary, on the contrary, this passion is the flesh of your heart, the heart of your life . . .

Whom are you cheating?

July 11–12

This might be my last letter. Read it carefully: it's half past three, the middle of the night, and I am in my car, and everything has already happened—don't ask me what I did. If this doesn't help melt your hard heart, I'll simply throw my hands up in the air and renounce you. And myself as well. I know, it's a shame. *SHAME!!!*

Could you hear that? You have no idea how close I am to you now. I mean, close. Outside your house. I've spent this entire night no more than twenty meters from you, approaching and retreating, and I was like the tiger who prowled around you in wide circles in your dream, but I am a tiger losing his mind from the despair of *not* devouring you in the one way he is used to.

Miriam—I ran around you tonight.

That's it. Seven times around your house, on that little road surrounding your group of houses.

Your success in releasing me from my own mind in this way (you will soon hear how).

Cigarette. My head is like a hive. The car stinks. Smoke sticks in arabesques to the windshield. Just thinking that I am so close to your kitchen, from which you write to me, so close to the fluorescent light that trembles a little, the wooden owl on which you write all your "to-dos" and immediately forget. Even to your gecko, Bruria, who comes down to do her work exactly at midnight.

I am here. The whole world is sleeping—shh, rapists snuggling, murderers cuddling in their beds, and only me in the whole night, around you. I'm scared to tell you what else I did. Just tell me, are you starting to feel something? Are you turning and tossing in your sleep, incapable of understanding what is flowing up within you? It's me—my madness is starting to affect you, foaming in waves around you; I practiced a pure religious ritual around you tonight, I circled Jericho seven times tonight, how did you not hear me gasping for breath? I hadn't run like that in years, not since military training; my flaccid muscles, my body, which understood long ago that great pleasures wouldn't come to it from our association. But I wanted it to suffer—hear me, I ran around you, I saw your house from all four sides, including the rusty gate and the bicycle that is leaning on the big tree in the yard and the bougainvillea shade. Your house is very small, it looks like a cabin covered in stone, a little run-down. The garden is almost bare, Miriam, there is one window broken in the back. Everything is very different from how you described it, and suddenly I think—what was it you said about your little family most likely not expanding?

And at one point a light turned on in your house, and my soul almost left my body in fear and hope that it was you, how I prayed it was you standing in the window, looking out into the darkness—Who is running like this—my God, I can't believe it, I must be dreaming—and you would suddenly understand, in one look, you would see everything I am, Don Juan, a stranger, a man walking a tightrope, and that confused soul writing to you; you would look into me and say, Come, Froggy, come, all of you.

Luckily for me, you didn't come out. You would have fainted if you had seen me this way, in my special condition. You would have thought it was just a pervert, a normal poor old pervert, surrenderingly paying his taxes to the bureaucratic gears of his glands. You would call the police, or even worse, your husband, who would beat the hell out of me, a man like that could eat three of me for breakfast.

You probably can't read my handwriting, it is even more disturbed than usual. By the way, I've asked my mother and you were right, they really did force me to write with my right hand instead of the left. How did you know? How do you know me better than I know myself? Look at me. Sitting in the car and shivering, and knowing that I have never done anything so complete for anyone. I don't know what else to do, to make you believe that what I offered you I have never offered anyone else, no one. And I knew, from the first moment, that I didn't want a little story on the side with you, I wanted a story. Perhaps you know what it is in scientific literature—the name for such a clear, burning will, the strange perversion, this need a person has to tell his story to one particular person and no one else. This is so strong in me, toward you. A section of my brain came back to life because of you—at the back, on the left side, behind my ear—it stretches and opens when I think: Miriam. And it is the same location of the reveries and dreams I had as a child. I spent most of my childhood there, underneath the ice. It has been years since I've been able to go there—I had even forgotten the way. What did you call it? The "memory-shredders." Exactly. But I could remember just one thing—no stranger was ever allowed inside there, under no circumstances could anyone know I had such a section in my brain—don't forget, I am a person born to parents—who, until the age of eighteen, lived in a family, family as principle and family as death camp—

I'm scattered, this isn't what I wanted.

I am cold. Even though it is July—cold. When I ran, my whole skin crystallized with frost from the cold. And it was, by the way, completely different from the dance in the Mt. Carmel forest. There, everything was light and heat—and here, I was diving into a deep darkness, my skin couldn't hold everything raging inside me. Tonight, I felt myself crossing my borders. I know what's going through your mind right now: the watershed of darkness. True. A language already is being born, it's good, but look how my emotions toward you make me fall apart, and that is exactly the opposite of what I have with Maya, so why should I have it at all?

Especially in the last three laps, when I suddenly understood what I needed to do and why I really came here tonight. Don't think I didn't have a moment of hesitation—but it lasted no more than a moment, and I said, To hell with it, what are you worth if you won't do this for her? You've decided to give everything that was created in you because of her to her, and I tried to argue with it, save myself—What if someone passes by and sees me like this, and calls the police, who arrest me? Then I laughed at myself—I've been a prisoner all my life, so why be afraid now? And so I sat in the car and took my clothes off, one piece after the other, and the shoes and the socks, and then I was already a different person. It happened to me in the space of a few seconds, such a short border to cross—one moment you're dressed, and the next: flesh, animal, less than an animal, as if the skin had peeled off you with your clothes, the epidermis, and the entire pile of skin underneath it. I left the car and felt how, all of a sudden, the entire night was attracted to me, came to me from the far ends of the valley, like to new prey, a new kind of prey you don't even have to skin. It practically surrounded me, the night, clinging to me with violence, to every part of my body—I have never felt anything like this in my life, this abnormal fear, mixed with pleasure, and a little embarrassment, because it invaded each and every hole, this bastard night. It bit and chewed up pieces of me and went away with them, into the dark. And suddenly three dogs appeared, huge, as if from some Scottish folk song. I thought I was having a stroke. The kind of dogs used to lead the blind, I think; they stood and barked at me, angry, scolding barks. They shamed me, can you imagine it, I was ashamed in front of them, not as a person—as an animal; I was ashamed in front of them, like an inferior dog. Can you understand that? Could you tell anyone this? That when I started running, they were suddenly silent; even worse, they began to retreat, move away from me whimpering quietly, and disappeared into the darkness, and I was left completely alone. Only me, with myself. And it wasn't very pleasant company. I was probably the most alone I have ever been. Do you know what I did then? I smelled my armpit, and found the smell of writing you, and I thought I was probably making the right mistake for myself for once. And I started running.

Here, I'm telling you everything: I was running slowly, so that anybody who wished to catch me could, because I got excited—somehow, nobody can catch me anymore! Even if somebody caught my body, I would remain free. I made three complete circles around you this way, and I discovered that when you run naked, the coldest places of all are behind your ears, around your neck, at your waist, and behind your knees. And the whole time I was running, I was thinking in my heart, Here I am before you, Miriam, here I am before you. Perhaps you heard something in your dreams—it was my nudity shouting, it was my body, screaming with panic at what I was doing to it. If you had come outside, you would have seen how I led myself, how my soul, suddenly freed, was, for the first time, walking my body. Leading it in front of your window, showing you how pathetic and unnecessary and meaningless it is in the story we are. And how wholesale it is, my body, the cheapest part of me, the thing I don't want to pollute you with.

Already, in the first few naked steps, I felt it happen—I am finally freed, suddenly I am just my soul, flying free and thin and glowing—it returned, and I saw my body running after me, graceless and foolish and alien, running, stumbling after me, choking with anger, trying to jump forward and catch me every once in a while, reel me back in, but I am elusive, wily—even my own body cannot catch me, and with every step it became clearer who I am, and what it is: just a slave. Then it was a monkey, and then a clump of earth, no more than that, which rose up on two legs and growled, and I condemned it in front of your window, and presented it as a sacrifice in exchange for the lies and the pollution with which I sometimes infect you, the opaque wave rising every time—there is a bag full of bitter liquid deep down in my throat expressly for that purpose. And it splits open when you're good to me. I don't know why it is this way. I hope I never write any more letters like that one. I can't promise you that yet—as I was writing it, I knew it was not a good letter, that it would cut you where you are the most sensitive. You were right not to open it. It is a good thing you have such a sixth sense about me. But you should know that I wrote it in this way also on purpose, to hurt you, scratch you, splash around in it in front of your eyes, and to *prove* to you—that's it, Miriam, that's the bitter, shitty seed—to *prove* to you, for instance, that I am still free of you, yes, that I am still capable of quickly returning to who I was before you, the person who has not yet been diluted by a single drop of you—to take revenge on you a little for my own traitorousness.

And also, because of this mad reversal, that I continuously feel as if you are somehow more loyal to me than I am.

It's starting to grow light. I am already back at home (don't worry—dressed). Sitting in my car and writing. Can't stop. I will soon go inside, and prepare a grand breakfast for everyone, with omelets and cornflakes and a salad I will cut from the remains of my conscience. You have no idea what kind of story I had to invent so as not to be at home for a whole night.

And to think I did it—

I hope I don't sound cheerful or proud of my daring to you, I don't even know what I'm feeling. Only that, at this moment, the healthiest thing for me is not to know anything, not to think about running as I did, that it was me, running there at night, that stain.

Yair.

Just one more minute. Yesterday, before I left, I read *Tales from Moomin-valley* to Ido as I was putting him to sleep. I don't know if you know it— I read him the part where Moomintroll, one of the creatures, hides in a big hat that completely transforms his shape. All his friends playing with him run away in fear. Then Moomintroll's mother enters the room—she looks at him and asks him, Who are you? He begs her with his look to recognize him, because if she doesn't know him, how will he live? Then she looks at this creature, who doesn't at all resemble her beloved child, and she says quietly, "It's my Moomintroll." All of a sudden, a miracle— the way he looks changes, the stranger peels off and drops away from him, and he returns to being himself.

Now it's all up to you—I am leaving the matter in your hands.

July 16
Miriam,

At first I had no idea what I was reading: I was searching, of course, for some response to my night run (I was, specifically, looking for exclamation points after words like "enough," "crazy," and "go away"), and in the meantime, my eyes became trapped in loops and buttons and hooks and embroidery and trim and other props of feminine ritual, some of which—I didn't even know their names (what is organza? what is voile?). But I immediately surrendered and began mumbling after you . . . cashmere wool vest, purple blouse with bellflowers, the white one with square wooden buttons . . .

You can probably guess what I said to myself while I was reading it— that it's impossible, a woman would never do such a thing, no woman I know would do such a thing. But you know that, don't you?

And the plain dresses and the fancy ones, those that cover you and those that reveal you (I can't help but chew on this for longer, it gives me so much pleasure), and the classically cut one with the open back, and the femme fatale, and the purple with the round collar—I figured out that purple is generally your color—the one that feels like silk but is not silk, very airy, and clings only to your chest, and the rest of it touches you but is not quite touching (don't disturb me, we're focusing here!)—and the other purple with a boatneck open from shoulder to shoulder that falls this way on your bottom and thighs . . .

I'm reading this and laughing because, for me, clothes are the fastest way to hide myself, and I truly feel that, for you, clothing is another living layer of your being. Even though you are incapable of giving up some noises of complaint—somewhat artificial, if you ask me. It seems there are still some conventions you're committed to, the posh grousing over your fat thighs, the search for one perfect dress that will draw attention to your chest and obscure your hips (I have no idea what you're complaining about, lady, from a frankly exploring look, your ass looks wonderful to me, two cheeks of soft, glowing moons—do me a favor and leave this business to the experts).

Can I hold you and caress you a little longer?

There was a moment I thought you were mocking me—I'm always on guard for that possibility—but I was not tempted by the thought—and immediately I return, sinking into cataloguing magic. What little bird revealed that I am completely helpless in the face of the magic of Bureaucracy—unconscious, smiling stupidly to myself, I cocooned myself in all the silk webs surrounding your skin—silk and cotton and wool and lace and embroidery and satin and muslin—the one you made for your high school graduation dance, with the shining trim embroidered in DMC thread (how can you remember such things? I can't remember what I wore yesterday!), and it's impossible, I'm telling you again—no normal woman would, in this manner, in this state of pure fetal innocence, give up all her little secrets. No normal woman would serve up to me, with such an amused practicality, her bras (leave two of those for me, the ones with lace on the top, for my next life); they, by the way, delighted me in their complete simplicity, a little anachronistic alongside the temptations of our current market—oh, my girl with the fifties face, it won't help you one bit.

But best of all, I liked the smile you wore when you wrote this (did you notice it?), it's a new smile between us, that of a woman occupied with some private, intimate feminine craft—and even though the action itself doesn't excite her especially, she already knows the pleasure it will bring her and her man when they come together, because of her little preparations, this kind of private purification.

It suddenly occurs to me—
You wrote the entire letter completely naked.

Yair

July 16 (evening)
Here I am in front of you, you said.
Yes.
You know, I'm slow sometimes to get it.

Upon my first reading, I thought you were offering me your clothes to cover up my nudity—but this kind of logic doesn't suit you. On the contrary. After that, I thought it was a very original invitation to temptation, odd, a little funny, a little clumsy. A verbal striptease. But even if that was how you started writing the letter, the tone of your voice slowly changed.

Here is nudity, you say (at least this is how I'm reading it right now), nudity which is not like a knife and not like a wound. Exposed nudity, vulnerable, a little ashamed and merciful. Like yours exactly, the imperfect nudity of a woman my age. Look, you tell me my nudity is a little unsure of itself, my body is being assisted along by all kinds of little tricks to conceal its defects—but is willing to immediately give up those tricks for whoever wishes to look upon it with an appreciative eye.

Here is nudity that uses clothes (you keep saying?), blouses, dresses, bras, belts, in the same way people use words, "their" words, but you can come and touch, feel it; here is nudity that can also heal.

Miriam, twenty times a day I tell myself, She really, truly wants to help you. It's a wonder to me, because deep in my heart I still don't know what you see in me, it is hard for me to believe that this is happening to me, you and me. Us. Tell me, just once, what am I capable of giving you?

What do I give you? And what about me arouses you in this way—to me? Sometimes I actually argue with myself, shouting to myself: At least help her to help you! Come and stand in front of her as you are, in the open. Without all your games and your guillotines. What are you so afraid of, read what she is writing, it is so clear . . .

And more than that. Even when I only try—right now—to think of that place in my brain without you, without your eyes reading me—it immediately seals off to me, cools down, shrivels up. This is exactly what happened when you returned my letter to me, sealed, without reading it. I froze. I thought to myself, This is it, you're doomed. You wrote to me, not long ago, that if anyone either refuses or rejects a strong emotion of yours, you feel as if he is nullifying you, practically killing you; at that moment, the expression struck me as overwrought—but when you returned my letter, and I thought you didn't want me anymore, didn't want the feelings of me, of me-to-you, I understood the precise meaning of your "nullifying": I had a few hours in which I actually ran around inside the hollow of my head and couldn't find that place, or the way to it, and knew that it was starting to die again, and I was afraid that if you didn't want to be there with me, I could never find the way alone.

I know I'm babbling here, but I also know you understand. Who, if not you? You told me a bit about the bad years, the years of internal Siberia from your first marriage. I don't know exactly what happened to you there, but you described how you felt your very existence sucking all the flavor out of your "private ore" because there was no demand for it in the world, no one even knew it was possible to ask it of you . . . You wrote three or four sentences like that. And you then, all of a sudden, gave me a name. You named the ore that I am; only by touching me, you catalyzed the process of it, my ore started changing color and temperature and density, and the contrast of its molecular structure, noble, elevated—with what had been its baseness—what else can I say?

You revealed to me so courageously, openly and courageously, that if you weren't so sure I would eventually return to you, you would have already broken things off with me. I know, but deep inside, I am also scared that you won't make it, I want to help you terribly and am incapable of doing so. Understand this, I am incapable by law, my screwed-up law system—something lame there in the white empty spot in the center of being, somebody is lying very dead. I am allowed only to watch your heroic attempts at resuscitation, like a helpless spectator, no more, and pray that you won't give up.

July 17

Just a scribble on a café table. Mainly for the pleasure of sending you something from Tel Aviv. I had some business here today in the North around Bet Lessin, and I finished early, and instead of going straight back home, I walked around a little and thought how much fun it would be if you were here with me.

Not to do anything particularly daring—just to walk with you, hand in hand, and sit together in a café—I even ordered two coffees, black.

It's nice to relax with you this way. You sometimes complain that I am pushing too hard, as if there is some kind of "goal" I am desperate to reach with you ("You're alert, you're always on the verge of readiness").

Apple cake? With cream and to-hell-with-the-diet? All right, one plate, two forks. The waitress smiles and people are looking, let them look, you put your hand on mine and we talk delightful nonsense. You pull your dress up a little and show me your shoes under the table, and you ask me whether to buy another pair like these in a dark orange—sporty, aren't they? I feel like splurging on shoes, you say, and I swallow your long, fair legs with my eyes and say, Why not? They'll suit you—will you let me pay for them? You're smiling at me, asking me if I still hate your glasses so much, and I consider them, thoroughly, for just a moment—

(My heart simply burned to a cinder this instant, when I recognized the trap that awaits me in your face between those glasses and those lips—but still, they're too big and too serious . . .)

You're letting me blather on, and you stroke my hand. And I ask—and you say no. And I ask you again, and you tell me that you already told me twice. Told me what? I sass back at you, and you sigh and tell me again how you succeeded in finding that Chinese girl you knew years ago at university, and how she helped you locate the address of the newspaper in Shanghai. And I'm looking at you and swallowing every word from your beautiful lips—how is it that I didn't come up with such a wonderful idea? I should have thought of something like that.

You have no idea how much your explanation pleases me—that only the two of us, out of a billion Israelis, will receive this newspaper once a week. And I am reciting you, soundlessly, with my lips: "Why, even 'four billion Chinese' require double-checking," and we both laugh about you and about me, Mir Yam and Ya Ir.

Listen to this—a little girl asked her father a moment ago to make his lowest sound. He produced this kind of "baaa," strong, like a bull—and immediately, from all ends of the café, rose the similar voices of all the men trying theirs . . .

What do you think? Of course I did it, too.

Do you, by any chance, know the name of those trees with red blossoms? And who was Bet Lessin named after? First, tell me how you used to play with Anna when you were a teenager. *But I already told you all about that as well.* So, why do you mind telling me about it again? *Actually—right now, I can't remember if I already told you about our trips to Haifa, to visit Bayer's Note Shop on Herzl Street in Beit ha-Kranot?* (You did, but I remain silent.) *I did write to you about the beautiful book of music we bought there, though—with Chopin's Impromptus and Schubert's Military Marches—I just can't remember if I was playing the melody or the harmony—but hold on, that's enough, I know I told you all that!* Well, yes, you did, but you never told me about it in Tel Aviv, and not while wearing that purple dress (with a very tight bodice, almost see-through, and the skirt made of—hold me back, the voile!). And besides, I like hearing you say "mew-ssic," until you I always pronounced the word "muzic." *Really, I didn't notice.* Sure; you also pronounce "Parisian" "Parician"—or a "physsical thing." (I have the evidence—it's all written down!) *Oh, Yair, you can't imagine what a physsical thing I am saying now . . .*

Or maybe Anna will appear, by chance, passing by in one of her dazzling straw hats, and we will invite her to sit with us. She'll sit down, her legs will barely reach the ground, and she'll appraise us with that sassy look, shifting her eyes from you to me, and will understand everything. Not one word will be said, but everything that ought to be known will be, and I will feel as if I've been accepted into some small, selective club. Perhaps I won't even be afraid that we have a partner in our secret, because—as you keep telling me—you can trust Anna. (But don't tell her yet.)

I envy you for having such a friend, a soul mate.

Me? Do I? The same kind of friend as Anna is to you? I wish. There are all sorts of substitutes, from the army, work; if you combine all of them, they might amount to something near it.

There used to be one. It's over. It's a shame.

(What a sun, Miriam, what a wonderful sun, I'm closing my eyes in front of it, trying to see you.)

July 19

A letter still has not arrived. I went to the box again, on my way home, and there wasn't any. I don't know what's with me today, I've been running restlessly since morning, as if some part of me, an internal organ, is wandering alone in the world and I have no clue what's going on with it.

It's the middle of the night and I am completely awake. I've been enjoying a little sleep disorder for a few weeks now. Maya bought me sleeping pills, and I throw them down the toilet and tell her nothing helps. Want to sleep. Want not to sleep. As you said, the nights are our time together.

(And I'm being asked why I am so awake at night, and what I am writing all the time. My explanation isn't so very far from the truth—I'm telling her that, for the first time, I'm trying to write a story.)

The day before yesterday, in the coffeehouse in Tel Aviv, just in that moment of glamour and sunshine, a kind of dark, elemental thought that has been wandering through me for a while now suddenly rephrased itself—that I am some kind of "black twin." I mean (do you understand? Should I elaborate?)—one who killed his twin in the womb. I know you're not laughing at this thought—it has always been with me, ever since my very early childhood, like a shadow—that I am a little cracked in my being, I was damaged and wounded beyond repair because I strangled my twin in the womb. Who was he? I don't know. Why must I have killed him? I don't know. The thought itself always remains fetal for me. He was only a very tiny, shiny little body; I see him surrounded with a yellow or golden glow, some kind of little enwombed body, yet divine and glowing. I mean, a quiet, continuous, uninterrupted, beaming light emanated from him. And I killed him.

It depresses me, now that I wrote it down here.

Sometimes I'm sorry that you and I didn't meet in some other way, a simpler way; we could have started with some magnetic flirtation and then, only afterward, slowly begun to discover all the rest. Imagine that.

I wish we could be together in a simple place now, I don't care where—in an everyday place, a healthy place where people just meet. In the street. In an office. In a public park, wherever you like, wherever your breath is full: just to be, without uttering a single word, even if it is just a vegetable market, as you once mocked me by saying.

Do you know what I do sometimes? I press down on my eyeballs with my fists and watch the sparkles. You once told me that this is how you comforted yourself when you were a child, in your Josephan pit. You produced light from yourself. I don't feel abandoned right now, not at all, but I do feel as if I'm missing a part.

Here's the store, you see? A little vegetable market, like there used to be in the old days, cardboard and wooden boxes, old scales and black iron weights.

And there you are, how good of you to be here. Standing with your back to me. Your head is bent a little over something, and I see your fair neck, with its long, delicate gradation of bones. You're standing by the sweet potatoes. As simple as can be. You're holding something in your hands. What is it? A very large potato, with a little dirt stuck to it. And you're staring at it as if you were hypnotized. What happens next? I haven't a clue. Whatever will be written back to me.

I'm passing by you, behind you, once, again, approaching and retreating, approaching again, attracted to you. I can't understand why you are so enthralled by a potato.

You're standing in the middle of the little store, you don't see the other customers, you don't hear the buses rumbling in the street, farting black smoke. All alone, focused so deeply on yourself. What is going on there, inside you? What do you have there, inside you? Take me with you, please—hide me in there as well. And I, left on the outside, jealous of the yams. I rudely peek into your hands and can see that it looks a little bit like a human face, the apple of the earth.

And now what? I don't have a clue, I'm just floating toward you.

You notice I'm looking at you and smile with embarrassment; your painful smile, which I can feel even through your words. Always. As if every time, again, it needs to tear its way through your nerves.

Smiling, and shrugging your shoulders in an apology, with the expression of someone caught doing something inappropriate, forgetting that it is everything around you that is inappropriate. With a wave of your hand, you motion to the others in the box, as if suggesting that I should choose one, too. I bow, and find myself in front of a pile of strange, ugly, twisted faces that at once, with no explanation, break my heart.

Suddenly filth starts peeling off me, thick scabs of it falling off my body. How much of an animal I had become, Miriam, how rough, how filthy. How I was polluted.

We're both silent. At this point, not a single word has passed between us. People are crowding all around us—we're blocking the aisle and they grumble. Never mind, we have a right to it, you said it at the beginning of all this—actually, it happened when you decided that this thing between you and me has a right to exist. I was so moved by that, when you gave yourself permission to be completely free with your feelings toward me.

You look at me, surprised that I'm not hurrying to pick up a potato from the pile. I stand and look at you a little. And then, as if you suddenly recognized something in my gaze, something I myself don't see, truly don't see it—you reach out both of your hands and deliver the potato unto mine. I touch it lightly, not more than that, it's still warm from your touch, it's as warm as if it were human, and I make myself look straight into its mongoloid angel's face, with its two wide, blemished cheeks, its eyes deep and black. Deep in a blind dream. It's a burden.

Why did you choose it? Why are you delivering it to me? I want to wake up, but not to lose you. And if I wake, I won't be with you in this way any longer. I look straight into your hands. I see.

Strange, Miriam, but this is what has written itself, from me to you. I'm not certain where it came from and why I am suddenly so depressed. As if I had just received some bad news. It's completely senseless. I'm thinking about how much I wanted to make you laugh. And look what happens to me, I eventually create—this.

I'm not sure I like it, this Law of Communicating Vessels which keeps all our waters level with one another.

Shall we begin to correspond?

July 24

My darling,

Just to let you know that I'm sitting behind your pages in complete silence, listening to you, and there is no way you are too heavy for me. Nor are you a burden. And certainly not too heavy to contain.

Because I'm already inside you, Miriam—I'm finally inside your story.

You, from the first moment, were more right than I was—the facts and details of your every day are your life, not "a mob."

I can't stop thinking about what you said, that you have spent your entire life trying to turn what I call the "sweating mob" into something that is more. Because if you give up this struggle for even one hour, you yourself will immediately be transformed into a mob.

How do you do it?

I have the strong feeling that you are awake right now as well. Perhaps your dogs are jostling each other around you, nervous, asking each other, Why is she awake at such an hour? A decent woman should be asleep at such an hour. Not running back and forth between the balcony and the kitchen in the middle of the night. Did you really sniff their fur for traces of my scent? I told you, my soul almost left my body forever out of fear of them.

Don't notice me. Mumbling, napping on your shoulder, half dreaming. After these insane days I have the right to a little sleepy chat.

I close my eyes and see a woman sitting by a table, writing. Night, and the fluorescent light in her kitchen buzzes above her. She turns it off and turns on a little lamp. Her face dips into the light as she leans forward, I can see only her strong jawline, her living, fragile mouth, her yearning mouth; and of course her messy hair, which she constantly tries to tame with rubber bands and combs and pins that always fall out. An open letter is lying on the table. She glances at it every once in a while, and goes back to writing, quickly, agitatedly; the excitement licks her like tongues of fire rising around her—and for a moment, it probably frightened her, because she tries to make a joke and save herself—Tell me, where have you seen any woman with the time to stand in a vegetable market these days concentrating profoundly on a potato?! But her lips are starting to tremble. She writes something—and erases it with all her strength, she has never erased anything so violently in all her other letters, and she stands up, and sits back down, announces that she has to go outside now and take a little walk. She stays. She tries to recruit a few more of the troops of her artificial anger, so she can distance herself from the page; she actually incites herself into a fiery rage—and you should know, it is very important that you know that a woman in a vegetable market, at least *this* woman, is always one big ball of anger when she goes shopping!

And while writing those words, she bursts into tears that wet the page, and she writes me her story, fifteen pages, almost without lifting her pen once, and only by the end can she breathe again, even laugh a little, circle one tearstain—"Look, like a nineteenth-century romance novel."

Hey, Miriam.

Remember how—right at the beginning of this—when you were experiencing a moment of complete exhaustion from me, you asked, Are you always like this? A flaming, revolving sword? Even in your everyday life? With everyone? And you were asking me how I could live like that within a family, and if Maya has a similar rhythm, or perhaps I need somebody who is completely the opposite of me to calm me down.

This is exactly what I would ask you now: Are you always like this? How do all these attacks find room in your tiny house? And how were you able to hold all this back until now? I'm thinking about the woman I saw that evening in the schoolyard, and about the one who has been shaking me up for four months now, and I can only laugh at myself and at my own stupidity.

I have nothing to add right now. I only wanted you to know that I understand now, and I am experiencing something I didn't believe in when you told me about it—the feeling of joy and sorrow together, and exactly from the same place, just as you promised. You asked me what I see in you now that I know everything. I would have to write ten letters to describe everything I see . . . I will probably write them slowly; but now, I mean, at sixteen minutes to two—I only see one who, at the end of a long night of writing, rests her forehead against mine, with a terrible fatigue that has collected in her, over years, probably—she looks into my eyes and tells me that, with that potato, I touched her with a direct, correct touch, in the place inside her where she is completely mute.

I too will be quiet now. Good night.

Yair

July 25

I have been telling myself, constantly, how good it was that I never asked anyone about you! Because when you asked me at the beginning to hear all the stories about you only from you, that no story about you that I hear should be, or turn into, "gossip," I pretty much smiled to myself (what kinds of dirty stories can this one have to hide from me?).

And I still insist on being pleased that I succeeded in persuading you not to meet in the flesh—body to body and ashes to ashes—because I have no doubt that if we had met, we never could have known each other in *this* way. Because I would have had to seduce you immediately, to know you through my usual ignorant path to knowledge, a merchant bartering for perfumes and spices. Think what we would have lost, and what we would never have known.

I'm not talking about the facts. I would have discovered those facts, the real, the everyday, even if we had a short but intense flirtation. You would have told me. You would have had to. Even as a part of the bureaucracy of adultery, I would have had to know them. But then I would never have known this sadness I am feeling right now, which I have been living with and holding on to for a couple of days now (mixed with a kind of longing, which I can't quite understand).

It isn't only sadness. Everything about you, every emotion you arouse in me, caresses me day and night, fresh and new, and presses itself to me with its entire surface, and with the fullness of its breasts.

When I told you about the private language I wanted to share with Ido, you responded that you want every piece of earth, every drop of water in the sea or flickering moment of a candle to have a private name of its own. I liked you so much in that moment. Maybe because it was the first time I saw how capable you were of drifting into your imagination: why, in the middle of the sentence, you began daydreaming about a world in which all the people in it would spend their days busily naming, naming, naming all the animals, vegetables, and minerals; naming would become the true essence of humanity. And you pulled me after you, hand in hand through your garden, from a single stalk of a weed to a single grain of soil, to a water drop and a beetle, as you gave each a funny private name—but I couldn't understand what you were really saying to me then (How little I understood of you), and only can now, now that I know something about the years during which you prayed that every tree would be called only "Tree" and every flower—"Flower." The years in which "to feel" was, for you, the same as "to live above your means." I think I'm grasping what you are actually telling me—that perhaps you are finally starting to heal.

I don't know what my connection is to all this, and if I have contributed anything to this recovery. But it moves me to think that I am close to you as it is happening, because I think it has been a long time, a very, very long time, since someone was living through something so good when I was around.

Y.

I forgot the most important thing: in the name of whomever you want to make me swear to (with a festive seriousness that I think only exists in treaties between countries or pacts between children), in the name of your actually buying those dark orange sneakers (!), in the name of Amir Gilboah's *I Will Send You like a Doe*, which you bought yourself as a gift from me—and especially in the name of your going and ordering new glasses—I swear to guard you as a friend.

July 26
I thought that in Hebrew—
No, this is too formal.
This morning, in the garage—maybe because you use the word so often—the thought came to my mind that motherhood, *imahut*, sounds like *i-mahut*, nonexistent, as in "i-mmaterial" or "i-rregular." I can imagine that there are more than a few mothers who feel that their child empties them of themselves, sucks out their insides. But between you and Yokhai—
Hey . . . that was the first time I wrote his name. His name is spreading through the whole of my mouth and my brain like the first moment

after tasting honey (with an added bitter sting). I could actually see him. And you with him. This wonder child, who is so full of the joy of living that people fall in love with him everywhere he goes—

I'm reading what you're telling me about him, and I can feel *your* motherhood in my body, like a warm spring rising and flooding from me to him, milky, pouring out. And how you wrap him up, surround him with infinite love. I swear, I was watching it through a magnifying glass and couldn't find even a trace of bitterness inside you about what happened to him, nor any anger at him.

When we were in the middle of our quickies, you once asked how it is possible for a person to start his life over and over again, just as a reply to another person's call. I understood that question, as I reread you the day before yesterday. Not just "understood": something deep inside my body moved a little, deep inside, beat in my body to you. (And then I remembered, of course, what Anna said; how, during her pregnancy, her heart moved to the pulse in her womb.)

Waiting for your letter,

Yair

July 30

Yes, that is what I wrote. I am sorry, I wasn't thinking (but if I explain myself, it might hurt even more).

First of all, you are right—it really does make you think, doesn't it, how this combination of words could come out of me—accidentally—as something that doesn't even demand proof or an explanation—"anger at him," as if it were some natural law.

Perhaps it is because I can easily imagine parents who would have been angry at their child even under much less extreme circumstances. Whom else are you going to blame—whom else is there, really, to be angry with? (No, I can't even condemn them.)

You are writing that the most difficult thing by far is to see such a child, who doesn't even realize what he is missing out on, who will never have a family of his own. Who will not love, who cannot express emotions. But I know, if it were me, in some corner of my heart, there would also be anger at him. Perhaps not? Perhaps I too have this noble side that would be revealed only at a time of great testing? I'm afraid not. Still, perhaps? I don't know. How can you know? You yourself said that you never imagined how hard it could be to stand in front of his isolation. The hopelessness—and the amount of strength—you found in yourself that you never knew about.

I'm hurting you with my words, and probably also shaming myself in your eyes. Lightning rod . . . But we do have an agreement, don't we? Everything. What's the point of this if we don't? And maybe, eventually, I will understand—and then, eventually, it will be possible for me to breathe there, in that lung . . .

I experimented a little with your letter. I copied it out, changing the names of the bodies from female to male. Do you understand? I dressed myself with your story, and I tried to tell you about my son, Yokhai.

After a page and a half, I couldn't. Because of his attacks of rage. His fits. They broke me, and I couldn't continue. When he becomes strange and scary, when suddenly a wild and crazy child takes over his body, a child who can shatter and demolish everything in the house. I know I could never stand that alienation. When there is no possible way to reach him, when he becomes a blind force—I could never stand it. And you also need a lot of physical strength to stop him and hold him when he gets like that, don't you? Where are you hiding all those muscles of yours?

If I could have, I would have bought you a big house, large enough for your entire soul. I would fill it with all your big and little and hungry dreams, carpets and paintings and books and objets d'art in every size, from all around the world. I would have brought you sculptures of birds, and big vases of blue glass from Hebron, and huge pickle jars, and decorated mirrors, and lamps from China, and filigreed pillows. And I would have built the house with many windows, open and full of light, with stained glass in every color, without bars and nets.

Because it is horrible to think of you in that empty house.

I am slowly starting to roll through everything you have said to me, from the first letter. It will take me a while to grasp it, your story in its entirety. Listen: I was reading you too quickly, too urgently, too secretly. I'm afraid that too many things were lost en route. I'm thinking about heavy hints you dropped for me along the way that I, blocked off and indifferent and in my usual rush, completely missed. When you told me that "reality" constantly dripped into every one of your cells, and that you had almost no way to avoid it, not even in your imagination, or your dreams at night—

No imagination. No dreams. And if you could let yourself get carried away, it would only be through artistic creations: painting, poetry, music, of course—but even then "reality" would soon come upon you and stab you, like a slave trying to escape (and with stolen fire in your hands). So what have you left for you, tell me, where have you been living?

Yair

And he has already counted to three?

Cheesecake with raisins for every two, and a huge backrub for every three?

(When you lick his wrist again and again, until he calms down—how did you discover that this is what brings him out of the fit—is that also something you discover naturally?)

My regards to your three gloomy Labradors. Regards to the palm tree. To the jasmine. The bougainvillea. The big cypress tree on which your husband's bike—Amos's bike—leans. Regards to all the private names.

August 1

I met Yokhai. I remember now. About a year ago I was accompanying Ido's kindergarten class on a trip to Kibbutz Tzuba. We visited the chicken coop, and when we passed through the rows, one of the chickens by chance had laid an egg without a shell—and the woman working there—I have no idea why—took the egg and put it in my hand. My hand, of all the ones there.

I don't know if you ever held such a naked egg. It was still warm, and soft, and full of motion within the film that was wrapping it. I didn't dare move. I was standing with my arm outstretched, my palm slightly cupped, and felt as if some exposed secret of my life was in my hand. I didn't know then that it was a premonition of Yokhai.

August 2

Something keeps nagging at me. I still haven't written to you how I felt when I understood, last week, what that letter had really been, the one in which you described your noisy crowded house for the first time, that house you now have suddenly erased.

You know I don't keep your letters, but I remember that house well. You wouldn't believe the number of times I saw you in it, walked through it with you. Those weren't just words to me (it suddenly occurs to me that you didn't understand something important). Almost every word you wrote had a body and color and smell and sound. I am very serious with your words—perhaps you thought this has just been some sort of amusement for me, a word game?

It really isn't a simple thing for the Avraham Ofek painting of the woman and the cow to now disappear off the wall by the library—because from the moment you told me about it, I brought it into my *life*. (I mean exactly what I'm saying.) I looked it up and found it in a book, and I dove inside it, was absorbed by it. And I thought and thought, and didn't give up until I figured out why you had hung it across from Yosef Hirsch's *Sadness*. I don't know a lot about paintings, but there is some conversation going on between those two—I think I was starting to hear it—and now they're both gone. And Kandinsky's little red ring is gone as well, as is Matisse's *Open Window*, which excited you so much. I can imagine the photographs in the hallway are gone, too, because they were covered with fragile glass, Virginia Woolf's portrait, for instance, and what about the Stieglitz man sweeping the street in the rain (I found that one, too, not long ago, in the catalogue from the Paris exhibition). Or Man Ray's *Half Beard* photographs . . . Did you fantasize all that? Even the piano you play every night?

At least you left the painted tiles in the kitchen.

Look—this may seem ridiculous to you—you're the one living in a rough desert of a house, and I'm the one complaining that you took away words you had given me, just words, and I'm bargaining over them like a beggar.

But there is another matter at hand here.

I'm thinking about your symphony of colors. You, who for years have not dared to paint, certainly not in color—you painted in a symphony with colors—I wasn't even sure of how these colors looked until you. You spoke of indigo and ocher and sapphire blue, the words themselves were so colorful—you wrote about silk curtains and angora wool, and you definitely wrote about wool from Astrakhan (!)—when you wrote that, I truly thought for a moment that you were just playing with me, painting a palace of dreams for yourself . . . but I can't resist a woman who can say "Astrakhan wool." I don't even know what this wool looks like, but you have no idea what these two words did to me . . . And not just these—almost every sentence you wrote sent me on a little journey of discovery, learning, feeling, smelling. Go ahead, laugh, but this is my limited, silly way of touching your excitement, the yearning that you exposed in that letter. I couldn't understand what it was, then I thought it was heat, you were aflame—I was happy, even, for the crippled imagination we began sharing . . .

But I think this is something completely different between you and me, which upsets me.

I felt a pinch of sorrow and, yes, disappointment when I realized that you are open to the option of pretense as well.

Do you understand? Your surprising flexibility in blurring reality and invention, quite a trick . . . It surprises me to discover, only now, how capable you are of living in your imagination, your internal power of persuasion (actually made from the same materials of which lies are made).

Of course I don't feel cheated (it was absurd for you to ask my forgiveness). You haven't done anything forbidden. On the contrary. That was the tale you wanted to tell me about yourself. You probably also wanted to believe in it, very much, to see it written, alive, in words. Perhaps you also liked that it existed so fully in my own thoughts, that it had an existence in this world—and I believed in it—because that was the first rule of our constitution, do you remember?

It occasionally gives me adolescent growing pains—but in the joints of my soul. And the strange feeling that I am learning something new and unexpected about you in every letter of yours—but I am also being separated from something else that I had thought or imagined about you. And there are days when I feel that I am perhaps still very far from knowing you as I wanted to. And it is already August.

Yair

Anyway, it is important to me that you know—what you described in that overflowing letter is still alive, it still exists for me. I don't know how, but the piano, the books covering all your walls, the pregnant pot, the huge mobile brought from Venice . . . I only have to close my eyes and I immediately see what is and isn't there at the same time.

By the way, did you really bring the bird sculptures from the Kalahari, or did you just covet them and not buy them? And have you been to the Kalahari at all? I mean, did you really go there with Anna twenty years ago on your first trip abroad (what, even before the Mona Lisa and the Eiffel Tower and Big Ben?). To see the "grand velvetia plants" you had heard of only from reading your children's encyclopedia?

Is there an Anna at all?

August 5

No introductions, just a very urgent request for you to continue immediately, without pity, and without delay—

You can't imagine what you did when you wrote to him, when you simply skipped over me and went directly to him, because nobody had ever spoken to him in this way—and it's not just what you wrote but how—because that child knew about worry and even softness and maternity; he's had plenty of that, sometimes too much—but he has so little contact with that rare pleasure of being understood.

And the relief I felt, of a suit of armor that suddenly realizes there is, still, a little knight inside after all.

Listen—you've read the situation exactly: a very skinny little boy, with a small, bitter face. A boy who is always alert, and nervous as an old man, restless, and terribly passionate. Always moving through his life as if he has to prove something to somebody, always struggling for nothing less than his life. How did you know? How could a person actually know another person? And, you wrote, a partisan who still behaves as a family member, in a house. Yes, yes! Even those horrible words you wrote about his loneliness, which was unlike the usual loneliness of children. Every word of yours fell right into the place which has been preparing for them, waiting for years—not the usual loneliness of a child—instead, a loneliness that, perhaps, is felt by someone very sick, sick with a *shameful* disease (how weren't you afraid to say the Holy Name?), correct, correct again! A boy who carefully resists the weakness of the illusion that he might actually give himself to someone, that the possibility of complete surrender exists, somewhere . . .

It is as if you had come and tucked a note inside the cocoon I am, addressed to my true name. I was a soft, permeable container, a little bagpipe, and the entire world was playing me. I only write these words and I immediately feel the urgent need to smash someone's face in. The world flooded over me like an ocean, retreated in waves and returned and filled and retreated. That was how it felt to be a child—this soft, infinite, stormy wave motion, all at the same time. Have you ever known such huge motion inside you? Maybe when you were pregnant, when you gave birth—and I was *always* like that. Always. A constant manquake, a walking seismic disturbance.

I am laughing right now (hysterically, like a hyena): how awful it is that all this is already over—and how awful that I can be so happy that it is over . . . because life is so much more tolerable now, it is easier to pass from moment to moment, and with time you even forget the fear of stepping on cracks, where an abyss of crocodiles no longer waits.

You do understand, don't you? You can decipher my internal mutterings—it was you who wrote to the "filament child," you who guessed that it might be possible to discover a red coil feverishly transmitting light through transparent skin; and you probably know well, perhaps from your everyday experience, how oppressive this "bizarre rebel's light" is when it burns inside a little boy.

Yes. It drives me crazy, teases me, arouses all kinds of murderous urges to blow hard on him so as to put that light out, once and for all! Not like you—not like your last lines—you cupped your hand around him and blew softly, cautiously, even a little hopefully—to see just what would happen if, just once, they let him try to be fire.

Just don't stop now—not in the middle of this mouth-to-mouth.

Yair

August 6

Look at his photo. It took me a whole day to find it. (Because of something that was in your letter.) I took it in London five years ago, and it comes with a little tale: I was there for business for a week, and one evening when I returned to my hotel, I saw a tiny crow that looked very sick ("a little crow, its feathers raised . . ."). He was huddled on the sidewalk, inside a white chalk line that had been almost entirely erased—probably the remains of some children's game—his beak opening and closing as if he was speaking, and not just speaking—you should have seen him; as if proclaiming something with deep sorrow and umbrage, or giving some kind of incriminating testimony to an invisible authority . . .

It could have been amusing as well—but I stepped out of the stream of people and leaned on a wall to the side, looked at it, and couldn't continue walking. I was tired, perhaps slightly dizzy with hunger—and I couldn't walk away from it. I thought I had to buy bread and feed it, but I was afraid of people looking at me. I walked away a few steps and felt him calling me back, it was piercing through me, and I returned and stood there. I felt it might be dangerous for me to stare at him, because I would slowly be sucked into him, get trapped and simply cease to exist. I have no idea how long it continued, perhaps only a few moments. He was standing in the middle of the sidewalk, in between the legs of the people passing by, his feathers swollen with cold, and his bitter sad face, and his head—you see?—tucked into his side in complaint . . . People passed him carelessly, with that English gait measuring their steps. Most of them didn't even look at him. And I, crouched by the wall, knew, with some strange acceptance, that in a moment I would collapse onto the ground and remain there.

I forgot to mention that I was returning from an important meeting. I had just closed a huge deal, lots of money, man of the world, boom boom, wearing my fancy work costume. I knew it wouldn't help me— nothing could help me—because the specter coming over me was much stronger. And it was right for me—for the black twin. And in the last moment of this hold, with my last remaining strength (I'm not exaggerating this time), I reached a hand into my bag, brought out my camera, and took his picture. It was an instinctive impulse that I still, to this day, cannot explain—it probably saved me, and I don't know how—as if it gave me an electric shock right on the spot, as if that treacherous self-being of mine had found some crack through which it could suddenly evaporate.

I have no copy of it. It's yours.

August 8

Do you really want a laugh? Last night, after I finished reading your letter (for the fifth time, perhaps), I was locking up the front door before going to sleep—and for a moment I thought I saw something or someone standing inside one of the bushes in the yard. Little, very bright even in the dark. And in the first instant I was afraid it was Ido, and what was he doing there instead of being in bed? I went into a complete mad red alert, and then one second later I felt like a beanpod after somone has pulled its string and split it in half. Because I realized it was *him*. Do you understand? The child you saw in your imagination. The filament child—

The kid who used to be—I've never told you—well, come along, make yourself at home. The kid who, at the age of eight, approximately, tried to kill himself in the shed. To commit suicide, as it is called, using the thin, all-purpose belt belonging to his father. And since no one had ever explained to him exactly how people die, he, with all his strength, stretched the belt tightly around his heart, ha ha. And lay on the floor, quietly awaiting his death. All of this because he saw how one neighbor, one Surkis from around the corner, standing in an undershirt, with his hairy back and cigarette in his mouth, drowned two kittens in a tin pail, just like that, shoving his hand under the water, talking to the kid's father out of the corner of his mouth while the bubbles rose. And after a very long time on the garage floor, the most eternal time he ever felt, when he saw he wasn't dying, he got up and went back home, and sat quietly, exhausted, at dinner with his parents and his sister. He heard them talking and performed all the movements of an eight-year-old child, and vaguely understood, and still understands, that even if he had died, they would never have discovered it.

And this is the same kid who, at the age of ten, read *Zorba the Greek*. Because there was one teacher he loved who spoke of the book with such reverence, and tears shone in her eyes, and he had never seen such tears, not from another kid and certainly never from an adult. She had tears of longing, though he didn't know that word (and would never have dared write it if you hadn't written it first). And there were no books in his house—books collect dust, books are dirty, that's what the school library is for, books—and he stole money from his father's wallet, from the Holy Wallet, and went and bought a book from a bookstore for the first time in his life. He read it, and didn't understand much, didn't understand anything, really, only that it was too beautiful to contain, it was simply roaring with life, calling out his name. And with his huge overwhelming, he swallowed the whole book in about a year, and finished it exactly on his eleventh birthday. A little secret gift to himself.

Not very pleasant, hm? Discreetly, at the cost of terrible stomachaches that conquered all medicines, every dose of cod-liver oil, finishing a page, shredding it into little pieces, chewing with dedication, and swallowing. A page a day, with three-hour breaks between the doses—a whole detailed bureaucracy ruling the ritual. Do you remember those books from Am Oved Press? With the discount for the labor unions of civilian army workers? The mustard-covered—the red-trim-bound—the somewhat—bitter? Three hundred and something pulpless pages. He gnawed this way for a year out of his verbal passion of the flesh. But, oh, Miriam, you should always be a little suspicious of him—he had already learned that behind every action lies more than one motive, and behind every noble idea peeps a rat's tail. Because perhaps he ate *Zorba* also so that the house security would not discover, in their searches through the bottoms of his desk drawers, a new book with no satisfactory explanation for its presence there. For example, a book without the school library stamp?

I mean—I tried to fake one, sure I tried (I'm not stupid): I drew—on the white page at the end of the book, I drew a big stamp that looked like a miserable fake—and tore the page out and couldn't throw it into the trash—certainly not into the toilet, how can you throw a page of *Zorba* into the toilet? So, almost without thinking about it, I put it in my mouth and started chewing (I can remember it still: a strange, unpleasant, dusty taste, pages of hard labor). And I tried to write a dedication to myself from a friend, and couldn't fake strange handwriting, and swallowed that page, too. And in this manner, totally by accident, I came up with this poetigastronomical idea . . .

(I tried for a moment to read it with your eyes.)

Oh, the effort that went into this deception, and how terrified I was, while reading it, that they would discover my ruse and the theft from the wallet. It was complete nonsense to think that they would give any thought to it, but just the knowledge that it was within the limits of the possible, within the limits of my family's repertoire—

I'm not going to tell you about my parents, no way. No parents. You've told me barely a thing about yours, and rightfully so: they have nothing to do with us, we were freed from their clutches long ago, at least I was (oh well, how many years can one drag out these wars?), and besides that—there's hardly anything to tell. My parents are the most ordinary, even the most likable, couple of people you can imagine. They are reality incarnate. Mr. Brown Belt and Mrs. Rubber Gloves. There is no mystery to them—all their actions and thoughts are completely transparent, to the bone. And in general, they are no longer relevant to me. I think I told you—my father has, for the past two years, been hospitalized in a vegetable patch for his kind in Ra'Anana. My mother has taken charge of his care with the full authority of an army general. She transports pots of nutrition for him in buses and spends eight hours, daily, with him in complete silence, as she tirelessly washes and scrubs and shaves and trims him, and massages and the kneading and the feeding. She really blossoms in that environment. (Perhaps he does as well. I haven't a clue. I haven't seen him in a year and a half—what's the point?)

This week she announced to me with a shy, conspiratorial smile that she has decided to let him grow a mustache.

And you would probably ask why I didn't stand in front of them, yelling at them and demanding my own *Zorba*, because I needed it, let's say, like air for breath, like medicine. Oh, no way. Me making demands this way? Not for me—no, for me there is theft, in wide circles, approaching, retreating—and I also became introduced to a new kind of pleasure, the Coveting Crookedness, as we will so cleverly call it (it's like the name of a new tea, made with the almond essence of my bile, isn't it?). Listen, I'm talking about that pleasant pain, the bitter sweetness that dissolves deep in your guts, twisting you and everything you are, knotting you up like intestines with an infected open ulcer sucking everything out of you from the inside. With all the usual piercing pain and humiliation. You already know how to meet these feelings inside you—and afterward you learn how to reproduce them within you—your poorest but most private property, to which you keep returning—and for what else? The taste of home. The smell of home. And here it comes again—unsheathed, stabbing, ready to use at any moment—feel it, get acquainted: this is *me*. This is my body and my soul, recognizing each other once again; I can actually hear the whisper of the internal password (srsrsrsr . . .). I think perhaps you should wear thick gloves when you hold these pages.

It is so easy to infect with this filth. I was infected so easily. Have you experienced the ritual of complete excommunication concealed in the statement "I hope you have children like you!"? Yes, you have. How did you put it—those certain looks with those twisted lips, silences that negate you, turn you into dust and ashes, and how little it takes to damage a person for good . . .

Apparently you know it, at least as I do: "Miriam (did she pronounce your name the wrong way?), Miriam, just don't be whatever people are saying about you" . . .

I'm not surprised. Sometimes I think that maybe it was this wound that so attracted me to you from the first moment. Your election campaign, public smile. Your mouth at that moment (I haven't written it to you yet)—the edges of your mouth, like two hungry fledglings scurrying into the shelter of their mother's wings, or into their guess of the shadow of their mother's wings. But you—and I don't understand how—you were probably saved from this fate, you somehow escaped or reinvented yourself all over again. Successfully, more or less. Perhaps this is why you are so afraid, like a fear of death, to return there, even for a moment, for the length of a single piece of paper, for me?

August 8–9

Maybe it has been too long since I let myself get angry about it, how they came to me at night and weeded my brain so they could plant their seeds for self-inspection gears. Imagine what it must be like to read *Zorba* in terror—and how can you believe that such miserable terror is capable of clouding the eye of the Zorbic sun? Do you remember when you danced the sirtaki with me and Anthony Quinn in your living room? But where were you when I was a child?

There was no one.

I used to read only when they weren't at home (this is final: I will not tell you about them. I had a mother and I had a father—but the child I was had no parents—you guessed right: my parents bore an orphan).

I'm surprised by the freshness of those memories and the emotions that well up thinking about them. Cigarette?

No, I know, I remember. But I did laugh when I read in the beginning of our letters that without even thinking you connected the smell of smoke from my pages to the passion burning and rising from me.

Sometimes I am amazed how willing you are to believe in the fantasy that I am.

Perhaps, instead of all these heavy matters, we'll talk a little bit about the fantasy you are to me?

Whenever you tell me some new detail about yourself—that prior to Amos you were married for five (Siberian) years to that sadistic genius;

that you always blush only on your left cheek; that you have refused to drive a car for years; or that Amos has a son from a previous marriage— or anything else, important or incidental, that I didn't know about you and never imagined—I feel a little spiritual effort in my soul, as if I have to "push" that little detail inside, to fit it into your image, like pushing a book onto a shelf that's already very crowded. But the moment it's done, all the other details, all my knowledge of you I have gathered so meticulously from the beginning, rearranges itself around that change.

And because we are already on the topic of new, surprising knowledge, then let me take off my many-faceted joker's hat in your honor. There is really nothing for me to say—it was truly a fatal, elegant knockout: I never imagined that the man with you, that titan putz in the sweater, wasn't your husband. (So who was he? Because he was guarding you jealously, at least like a headguard, if not a bodyguard. The way husbands do.)

You completely confounded me. The tranquillity with which you described all the other men in your life, one by one. The one with whom you go swimming; and the painter from Beit Zayit, who sounds to me as if he's terribly in love with you; and the blind guy with whom you correspond in Braille (did you learn it especially for him?). And how do you have time for all of them in your busy week? And you actually forgot to mention the three yeshiva students who study with you, in secret, once a week . . . Just tell me, write me a description of what your husband looks like. I mean, which shadow with a knife between its teeth do I have to beware of now?

Well, fine, fine, don't be angry, just a little sting of remonstration because my small mistake had given you "a tiny, tickling, theatrical pleasure," and you didn't even feel like correcting me . . .

You asked me again if I feel cheated by you, and I tried to understand how I truly feel about you, with all your twists and turns. It's not a simple question, Miriam, and the answer itself is changing, and turning and twisting in me, and still hasn't cooled and coalesced into an opinion.

But because you are asking me now, I thought that perhaps, instead of an answer, you could go and look at *The Family of Man* (which I like a lot, too). There are two photographs in there, two facing pages I like to look at: on one side you see students listening to a lecturer in some university. He is not in the photo—their look is pointed, focused on him, and it seems that whatever he is teaching is certainly interesting to them. But on the opposite page you see people from an African tribe, listening to an old man telling them a story. Children and grown-ups sit among the crowd, they are naked and so is he; his hands are moving in front of them, and they all have the same expression: they are bewitched.

(There is no such hour)

I want to make a deal with you.

It's a strange one—and embarrassing even to explain. But you're the only person I can share this with.

It's about Yokhai and the operation he's going to have in January. I want to give you half of my luck for the surgery. Don't laugh—don't say anything! I know it sounds false and idiotic—and in exchange, please treat it like a good-luck charm, a superstition, but please, please don't reject my proposal (if it doesn't help, it certainly can't hurt).

And it's not that I'm exceptionally lucky, but my life has been managing itself more or less well. And with everything that has been happening at work (annoying in itself), I think that in the past few years, Fortune's kept a little twisted smile toward me. I also have to confess that I have made this "deal" twice: once with a woman who was facing a risky surgery and once with a woman who couldn't get pregnant. And in both cases, everything worked out. By the way, the two women didn't know I made the particular pact in question. They were, in their own ways, very close to me; but not close enough for me to tell them what I was doing.

This transaction is not without its own bureaucratic procedures—I have to know ahead of time the exact day and time you will be needing my luck, and then I begin to practice aiming it at you (actually, at Yokhai). And on the day of the operation itself, I will actually free myself from all my obligations, "strip" myself of my luck, and "project" it to him with all the power of my will (you will only have to write me how long after the surgery he will need this transmission of mine).

And please don't worry about me during this time period—it is true that on the certain day that I "strip" away my luck and, less so for two or three days after, little incidents of misfortune occur in unreasonable quantities (it is quite amazing to see how they draw themselves up and attack from every possible direction), but so far, it has all added up to only a few lost keys, a flat tire, and a surprise tax audit. And luck begins to grow again very shortly afterward (I swear!). In my opinion, shaving it from time to time is good for its growth.

Don't respond. Don't say yes or no. I said it—you heard me.

August 10

Only to report that the child has probably returned to roost.

It must be my nightmares—or because of our correspondence. Perhaps it was because of that night around your house—something in me hasn't been able to calm down since then. I hesitated over whether I should even tell you about it, about giving him the right to exist by writing to you about him. But almost every night I am filled with some kind of darkness, torn, a length of fabric swaying in the void. And now he's standing there again. It has been three or four nights at this point, and he is standing there, right now, at this very moment, insistent and shivering among the bushes; there is actually a child's shape lurking in the darkness there. And I'm going to tell you something—I have never written anything so insane, so ludicrous.

He and I have fallen into a little nightly bedtime ceremony. Even though, immediately after his debut, I cut that confusing bush down with the decisiveness of a Soviet censor. But he has returned, night after night, and plants himself by the door. It's a pity you are not here—I would show him to you.

A skinny boy, slightly hunched over, a slumped, shy flatterer. Only I know how exposed he is, know that his soul is constantly being mercilessly stirred up; how passionately he wants to give of himself and surrender. But as you said—if only he believed that he could, and that if he did, someone would be there to receive him.

Let's be honest here—he's a slightly effeminate boy, soft, a blabberer and a braggart—I look at him now and immediately remember the experience of being him—the constant nervous buzz, the quick sequences of surprises causing his heart to beat uncontrollably fast; you were right—you can see his heart through his peeled skin, sensitive as a parpur's, beating and beating.

His presence disgusts me (are you surprised?). I'm taken by a strong impulse to turn him over to the hands of the authorities of the private education system in which I studied. Because my personal tutors were grand masters in their field. Do you know what I'm talking about? What do you know, anyway? Well, a little at this point. Enough. These tutors knew the correct gait, posture, and speech—what you are allowed to say and what you should shut up about. What is better not to say, to avoid getting laughed at; how to always pick up your shoulders so you will appear wider, to close your mouth so you won't look like a complete idiot. Like a fragile ethrog swaddled in tissue paper all year long, I was educated by two peerless pedagogues, the best—my parents, may their memories be blessed, who never missed or overlooked a single sorrowful defect of mine! With the dedication of years of hard work, they succeeded in improving me, sanding me down, until I could be presented to society without too much embarrassment. These days, it doesn't even involve much effort on my part: I'm quite good at imitating most of the moves and sounds of a mature male, an elder in the community—and you can certainly say that the plaster mold of the death mask has more or less already dissolved and sunk in through my skin, into my body, my cells, as it was supposed to.

Until, suddenly, right by my front door—an infected and inferior organ of mine escaped from my body and started leaping in the dance of fools, the donkey jig.

And there is one moment—

(Why not, I've already spilled my guts.)

There is a moment when he suddenly bangs at the door for me, when I immediately work myself into a high panic. Please don't tell me it is only childish imagination, of course it is, it is exactly the imagination of my childhood—it hits me, leaving me altogether paralyzed, it gets my blood pumping crazily for a few seconds, and I can't fight it. I have to see him, to produce him emerging from the darkness, approaching me; he's running to me, barreling down to my front door, so I can—

Do you like these little private games of mine?

What would you have done in my place, anyway? Well, you are much more generous than I am. You even agreed to allow me inside you. I'm not that noble—I'm terrified. I just slam the door in his face, night after night, with all my strength and with all my locks, and hurry to the bedroom. And Maya had better be there, just so I can look at her for a moment, acknowledge her again, the presence of her full, warm body, the absolute validity of her surprisingly small feet. To gaze upon them and calm myself down—to immediately panic again—such a narrow base for two adults and a child to hold on to.

Oh well, I have to go to sleep. You don't have to respond to this scribbled nonsense. By the way, I read something in Ido's kids' magazine that I thought would interest you: you have a dinosaur's footprint in Beit Zayit. Did you know that? A dinosaur passed by your place a million years ago and left a huge footprint. Interesting, don't you think? I also tried your tze-tze recipe tonight before trying to sleep. But I think I put too much liquor in it. (It doesn't matter. If I get a letter from you in the afternoon, the night is already lost.) Enough, good night!

Y.

(Well, I lay down for almost an hour out of politeness, but I'm afraid I did not explain myself fully)— You know what? I will allow him to enter my house, once, on purpose; I'll force him to enter, so I can take him and walk him by the ear and show him, without mercy: refrigerator; dishwasher; a living room with a highly decorative set of armchairs. Here's a bedroom with a queen-size Ha-Zore'a bed. Here we have a woman. A full, soft woman with round, beautiful breasts, taking her clothes off right now—for me! And then, when his eyes already start to burn with the held-back tears of loneliness and abandonment, I will lay the final, fatal blow: drag him by the scruff of the neck to the little room at the end of the hall and yell, Well, look at what we have here! Surprise! A child! I made a child in this world! Look closely, so you can understand that you have already lost the fight between us, honey: I have a child! I escaped from you and I made something that exists, independently, in the outside world! Check my trademark, stamped on the shape of his fingers, his eyes and hair! And if you don't find the rest familiar— you know why? It doesn't belong to you! I swear, I feel like pushing his head, hard, into Ido's bed, the way you drown a kitten—Look closely, you can even touch him—why not? Touch him, feel him: a child who has been created from another's matter as well. Who is not me—and not you! Because I, with my initiative, succeeded in escaping the fate you had laid out for me. I allied myself with another chromosome pool, free from my matter, and especially from yours—and this is how. I have managed to create one thing from good, strong, healthy matter in this world, with a warranty that's been good for almost five years now, get it, baby?

What the hell am I saying?

As if Ido proves anything about me.

I have no peace. What a scorcher outside. The air wraps itself around you and sticks to you like rubber.

August 11

... and just as I was about to send you a letter this morning, I got your note from the university library. It delights me just to think of you sitting in the Judaica Reading Room, writing those wild, excited sentences while you slide in a graceful slalom to copy sentences from *History of the People of Israel in Ancient Times*—in the same breath!—every time a fellow teacher passes by you. I was thinking for the thousandth time just what fun it is that we found each other in the huge pile of peas. How lucky we are to be from the same country, and the same language, and the same Paporish and Douvshani schoolbooks . . . By the way, about the quotation you couldn't remember (when I tried to "dress myself" with the letter in which you told me about Yokhai)—

I admit it, it took me a while to get to it, but tomorrow at dawn I will send out my speedy messengers to look it up—and in seven days (no more than twenty-four hours by the clock) I will have the full quotation with the exact reference. I promise.

When I was writing you yesterday, I again felt how peculiar this whole letters business is: by the time you open a letter of mine and accept its truth, I am already somewhere else. When I read your letters, I am actually inside a moment of yours that has passed; I am with you inside a time you are no longer inhabiting. This works out to each of us being faithful to each other's abandoned moments . . . What do you think? Perhaps this is the source of the sadness aroused in me by almost every one of your letters, with no connection to its context—even your funny, wonderful note from the university. Life is passing by.

August 11–12

Immediately go and scold your three silken students for their ignorance: Rabbi Nakhman of Breslev is the source for the forgotten quotation!

In the Moharan Collection, in the chapter "Impregnation of Barren Women," he discusses "human beings who sleep through their days." Either because of works of pettiness, or because of passions and bad deeds, or because they have eaten spiritual food that reduced their minds to a state of sleep . . .

Apparently you have to revive the heart of those sleeping and awaken them, but with caution, like waking a sleepwalker. And because of this, as soon as such a person wakes, you must "dress him with the face taken away from him whilst he slept." And how do you think Rabbi Nakhman recommends you go about it?—". . . as you would heal the blind. You must close him in so that he will not suddenly see the light, and you should reduce the light for him, so what he suddenly sees will not harm him. Also, for the one who has been asleep and in the dark for a long time, when you wish to show him his face and awaken him, you must dress his face with tales . . ."

Do you know what time it is? And who has to get up tomorrow at half-past six? And who will sleep away his day tomorrow with twelve straight hours of petty works?

Yair

Did you see that? As I was sealing up this letter, a shooting star flew across the skies! So quickly, quickly, what should I ask for (I don't have a wish ready—have you any ideas)?

What you wrote once—"Let us help each other be whatever and whoever we truly are."

August 13

Oops—these days I've been so busy and tense and, mainly, tired—I almost forgot about our date! I remembered it just a minute ago (it's today, right? You said Wednesday at half past four). So forgive me the unsatisfying conditions; not exactly in line with your plans, but at least I'm here on time. I mean, the second I remembered, I stopped the car with a loud screech on the side of the road between Tel Aviv and Jerusalem (yes, in that very spot where you can see the whole forest, with all its possible shades of green on the right). Cars are flying by me, rocking the car, so my writing is a bit hiccupy. And instead of coffee and some rich cake, I'll drink warm Coke out of the can with crumbs of Ido's Bamba snack that I will gather from the backseat. What can you do? I am one of those horrible people, you know, who, in spite of his inconsiderateness, still listens to the tape of Verdi's *Requiem* sent to him by his soul mate in his car's fucked-up player (and by the way, thank you!).

Come, let's steal a few moments together. You made an interesting remark at the end of your last letter . . . I mean, your "now I will put my woman costume on for a little while"—the quick course in makeup you surprised me with before going to the lecture at the Cultural Center. Flip-flopping between the rose-pink lipstick and the more daring brown (did it match the angora?). Actually, I never imagined you wearing makeup. Somehow I thought you—never mind. I enjoyed it. It was a bit like with your clothes. You have an ironic, special grace when you squeeze into other women's words. Strange women. Strange words— The soft eyeshadow and lip liner, and I'm lying on the bed behind you, watching you, with my hands crossed behind my head in the position of the ultimate self-satisfied chauvinist (yes, yes, I read you: that macho guy, that *gever* who is so sure his wife undresses only for him).

My eyes get a little shifty when I say the word *gever*; since you told me, I am constantly checking (but until you told me, I never noticed that I always preferred to use *ish* when I say "man"). But why do I feel, more and more, that the word "woman" is not so simple for you either, in your internal dictionary?

And why do I ask? Because I know exactly what kind of *mother* you are. I told you, your motherhood rises from you like hot steam each time you mention Yokhai. Or any other child. Yet those times when, here and there, you have said—and not a few times, by the way—"the woman that I am"—almost always, my bat ears pick up some light echo, a tiny, hollow space between you and the word—

Enough. This is getting too heavy for a daytime rendezvous. Do you know what I really like best about your letters? The little things. More than anything. The coffee stain you decided to leave on the paper, for example. You wrote that it was a "stain of existence." And it was through this stain that I was privileged to learn how you drink coffee—how you always start each cup when it is too hot. And then there are a few brief moments when it is exactly right—and then it cools down, bit by bit, but you stick with the cup you poured all the way to the end . . .

Please, drink, drink.

To think that, at this very moment, you too are sitting somewhere, present with me. Where did you choose to sit? In which café did you think I would be?

Or the smell of your pages, I haven't told you about that yet—it's always the same, a thin scent of mint. Or the photograph you sent me of Anna, taken from behind. With her huge straw hat. And how, with these odd yearnings (toward a woman I don't know!), I keep turning the photograph around, over and over, looking for her intriguing, birdlike face, the laughing sparkle in her eyes, and now and then kissing her gently on her split lip.

You see, you truly succeeded (in bringing me into your reality without piercing our hallucination). But the moment it was the hardest to keep myself from flying to be by your side was when you asked me, What, you'll never eat my soup?

August 14

Well, what do you know!

What shocks me most is that I myself never noticed it. I thought it was only the chalk traces, the remains of an English children's game, hopscotch left on the sidewalk . . .

I don't know why it makes me so blue—I feel some kind of muddy sorrow for myself, for my shortsightedness. I mean, I was there, wasn't I? I was there, and you weren't. And again, my recurring realization that I always miss the point. Right now, as I am writing this, your question—the one you asked after the master's black monkey—returns to me: Why is it that I allow myself to be satisfied with crumbs from under the table of a great feast ("saving for yourself only the role of the handyman to a great love. That's all you allow yourself")—so, there it is. This too is now wrapped around my soul.

And it was a glance—you just looked, the way you look at everything. You looked and saw it at once. You didn't tell me whether you had already noticed it in the original photograph, or only after enlarging it—meaning, I wonder if that was why you decided to get the photograph enlarged. Sometimes, after a letter of yours, I tell myself that from this moment on, I will begin to live differently. I will slow down, read more slowly, listen more carefully to people's words, so I will be able to remember them a year later. To linger. I don't have to tell you how long I hold on to that resolve.

Now I have to tell myself the story all over again, don't I? To write about how I collapsed there, by the wall, and I couldn't move—the man of the world, boom boom was turned to stone—not only because of the crow, but because of that chalk line that today, only today, goddamnit, five years late, I deciphered as a police sketch of a small, human figure. A child, probably. (It is a child, isn't it? Don't answer—it frightens me too much to know.) One hand lifted up, twisted in resistance—and the other rests by his side, already peaceful.

Oh well. My internal struggle over my criminal neglect will be performed separately, and alone. It certainly justifies a committee investigation. But now I wish I could give you something—a gift equal in value, in return for this discovery. You complain that I am a cheap suitor who doesn't give gifts. I will not give you little gifts. I'm sorry, you know that if I could, I would give you plenty. At least once a day I have to resist the urge to buy you something. And still, ask me for something. What can I do for you? What can I give you?

August 16

May I interrupt?

I want to talk.

I went out earlier (it's almost three in the morning and soon I will begin to glide silently over the night skies and hunt little rodents). I stood and smoked. He wasn't there anymore. Perhaps he despaired of me. I did try to produce him, but the only thing running through me were words. He crumbled into the words I used to write about him; how did you put it—the cruel choice between keeping muteness alive and vital and verbalizing it?

I'm afraid it is no longer my choice.

I thought about what would have happened if, in some fantastical way, he could have known Ido. And I also wondered whether Ido would have liked to be friends with the child I was. To my surprise, I answered that yes, they'd get along quite well together, that perhaps there aren't another two as well suited as Ido and the self I used to be (so why are he and I now so poorly matched?).

Hey, can we talk about the kids? Shall we start a special advice section for matters of parenting and education, Don Juan's Column on Children?

Before we do, please know that I am the best father in the world. Really. Everyone who knows me thinks so. And until this past year, when my business started flourishing, I would spend a lot of time with Ido, every free moment I had. And I still take care of him with motherly dedication today. I feed him and dress him, breast-feed, and even at this very moment I feel my eyes tear up when I think about his glowing beauty. And I am endlessly destroying him. Oh, Miriam, what are we going to do? The delicate, exposed line of his chin, the way he remains lonely in every group of children, his fragile, loose smile? I molded him with my own bare cruelties—oh, really, what are we going to do? I used to know his every thought. My private language began with him; of course, we were using *their* words, but they were ours because I pulled them out of the core of my soul. I think almost every new word he learned until he was three was from me. I used to say, "There's a bird, say it after me, 'Bird,' " and he would look up at me, charmed, and say "Bird." And only after he had repeated that word, spoken it aloud, was it truly his. As if I had chewed up the word and put it in his mouth. That was our ritual for every new word. There were even a few sounds I wanted him to pronounce in a certain way: a full *sh*, not a little whistly, like mine. Or a manly, throaty *r* (like Moshe Dayan's—do you remember it?) . . . Don't laugh at my nonsense—it was because of it that I felt as if I was serving him the first Lego bricks with which to build his world; that I was leaking myself into him, branding more of him with my identity, existing in him as I probably don't exist anywhere else in the world. Do you understand? I suddenly sent out roots.

What haven't I done to exist in him? I used to stand by his bed while he slept, passing my hands over his face, finger-painting his dreams. I would whisper happy words into his ears, so they would penetrate into his dream-laboratory and, if needed, help to change his dream for the better. There was nothing I would not have done to make him laugh. And how we would laugh together . . .

But that's over. Finished. Go complain to the rank forces of life. I'm not complaining: it's the way of nature, yes sir! But lately, he has been clotting over, closing off to me; and if I ever sent roots into him, they were torn out of me like the stinger of a male wasp. Now the whole world comes and pours words and names into him, and he has thoughts that I do not know about—and it is 100 percent fine by me, that's the way of the world—and I should be happy that everything is normal, as it should be—but I no longer have ants in the palm of my hand, dancing out pictures over his face at night. I am, again, left with only myself. Do you mind my telling you about this? You wanted reality, didn't you? Please accept reality then, tossed with chunks of specifics: he now fights with me—over everything. You would think that fighting me is his raison d'être these days—and what he fights about! What to wear in the morning, and what to eat at noon, and when to go to bed, and what TV show to watch—anything I offer him he rejects, and then insists on the opposite. And you have no idea how stubborn he is (considering that, until about six years ago, he was being stored in two separate locations)!

And the more stubborn he is, the more decisive I get—it drives me absolutely crazy that such a little boy suddenly decided he knows better than his parents. So I barrage him with all my strength, with yells and insults. I'm like an insane rhinoceros; I attack this tiny child to force his surrender, run him over, squash him, humiliate him—it's terrible, no? So I explain to myself, with iron-clad logic, that during the exercises of humiliating him and squashing his spirit, I am actually educating him to become more familiar with the most basic concepts of leading a proper life, blah blah blah. So the essence of the education is that I pass on to him the knowledge that you eventually must surrender to strength and stupidity, power and narrow-mindedness. Because this is the way of the world, and there is no other. And it is terribly important for him to learn this at a young age, so the world won't break him when the stakes are much more painful.

(How did you put it?—"Those are just your venom glands talking.")

Because what I want to teach him is exactly the opposite—I want him to fly high, spread his wings above me, and piss on the fears and the shame—and be himself and do exactly what his heart tells him to do. But this fucked-up hand has got me by the throat—my mother's hand, my father's fist, the long military arm of my family. I cannot believe what comes out of my own mouth during our fights. Things that, as a child, I swore I would never repeat—and I still can't hold them back, citing the passages of heritage with a frozen tongue—I could smash my own face in—why am I fighting my own child? Tell me, why can't I let one child in this crappy dynasty grow up as he is, as I was, as I almost succeeded in being—fragile and delicate and daydreaming and without skin? Full of such a spectrum of ways of being? Why did I yell at him the time he was sobbing because we threw the old armchair out? Why do I make him eat meat when meat disgusts him? Why does it make me explode when he refuses to assume his proper place in the food chain, to accept the law of convention that "chicken" is not "dead bird"?! And I shove it into his tiny mouth with my fingers, the way my father did to me, every day!

Say "Bird": "Bird"!

Maybe I'll continue this tomorrow.

No. Tomorrow the rain will come upon us and erase everything, and it's flowing out of me in a flood now. I spare you most of the things that happen to me in my everyday life. My shell somehow functions—that's the exact word for it—but the child watching me in my recent, sleepless nights had an aura of warmth—it shivered in a haze around his thin skin. It horrifies me to now understand what he was really like—how he never had a chance (like you said—a little china cup in an elephant's cage). How vapors still steam off him from the terrible need to nestle close with another person, to really combine souls without hiding anything. He wants to give of himself—pour everything flickering there in the darkness of his imagination—not to let any parpurian emotion finish off his life over there, in the mass grave of the unknown idea. And you have no idea how many misunderstandings, how much rage and destruction of the good order these tendencies cause—such perversions the constitution of the tribe—

His first years—how wonderful they were (I'm talking about Ido now). I gave him all of myself—and the more I gave, the more and more filled I was, a river of inventions and stories and the joy of living. I used to wake up at night and feel my heart well up with the warmth of loving him, and think, I had forgotten how much love existed under our skins. I had forgotten that specific feeling of a soul rising to the banks of the body, licking the landscape from the inside. Because I was a child full of love—but see how that thought never crossed my mind with such simplicity. I never knew how to say that to myself, in that way, round, like a gift. I always thought of myself as a very hard child, a complicated, bad child, and—as they often explained to me, with a deep sigh, determining that sorrowful fact you have to somehow live through: I was a child who wasn't quite—normal. Certainly not the one they had been praying for. A child forced to pity his parents every day, for their being obligated to raise such a strange creature who so shamed them—

Enough.

Listen, this letter brings me to— I mean, I really didn't think this is where it would end up. I wanted to write to you about you, to guess you as you guessed me. To guess you as nothing less than a woman—not as a little girl (this is starting to look like a date between two pedophiles). And I, apparently, can't do it yet. I can't!

August 17

Just reporting that I fulfilled my end of the bargain this morning (regarding the return of the chalk line around the crow I promised you). And I read the story you asked me to read, and in a beautiful place, just as you wanted me to.

I took the story to the dam. I found the old car seat, your usual chair—I identified a crab-apple tree (or is it a cane apple?). I called it by its name and we embraced emotionally. I crushed some sage, and a *rotem* or a *lotem* or a totem.

I hope you are not upset at my little invasion into your territory. You have "taken me" here so many times to read my letters aloud, having soul-deep conversations with the dam and the empty dell—and after you decided to "officially" introduce me to your kin here, I figured it was about time to come and stand before them, pay my respects like a *gever*, like an *ish*.

This place is beautiful in the winter—like a Norwegian fjord in the middle of the Jerusalem mountains? Really? It's a little hard to try and picture that now; the huge dam cuts the valley in two, like a scar of surgery across a belly. The dam and the valley look pretty fake right now, in this dryness (but perhaps, as you said, they come true in the winter).

Listen, I read the whole story, I even read it aloud. No wonder you haven't gone back to read it in years—the only comfort I can offer you is that it hurt me, too, but today it hurt in an entirely new way.

You asked me to write it exactly, to report it without mercy. So.

Do you remember the moment when Gregor's mother sees him for the first time (after he has become an insect)? She looks at him, and he at her; she yells, "Help, for God's sake, help!" and backs away, until she bumps into a table and sits on it (confused, half conscious).

Before, when I read this story—the hardest part, in my opinion, was Gregor's drawn-out, long, tortured death. But this morning, when I got to her repulsion, and " 'Mother, Mother,' said Gregor in a low voice, and he looked up at her . . ."

Because there is always that small chance that if she hadn't been so repulsed, she might have been able to save him from his tragedy.

Yes, I know, if she had "recognized" him (or in your words, "approved"), it wouldn't have been Kafka's story anymore but a children's story, like, say, that Moomintroll story.

A hug. I left you a note somewhere in the area of the dam—let's see if you can find it.

August 17 (12:15 p.m. by the dam)
M.

In your last letter, you didn't smile, not once. I could see you holding something against me (?). That maybe, because of me, the old, open insult of your childhood has been resurrected in you with a painful sharpness.

Maybe it is because of me. I don't know. Maybe it was that thing you said, right at the beginning of all this, about there being something in me you had been forced to hide all your life.

(But what was that thing you didn't say?)

August 20

You still insist? You want to meet me, "the whole me"? A complete meeting? Or at the very least—without deciding ahead of time what will transpire at such a meeting? Without canceling out any possibilities in advance? "In the whole me," meaning, my soul *and* my body? Oh well!

116

A Turkish pimp with moist eyes and a drooping mustache slips in like a mongoose and flashes a pack of oily, naked photos of me in stimulating positions in front of your eyes. But don't believe it! It's only a photomontage, you better check that merchandise very well. And I believe that now comes the time when I lay my cards (the shuffled half deck, of course) on the table, so you can reconsider your proposal, weigh it carefully in this matter—because I have a body and a face that are not *mine*. Some ridiculous, terrible mistake must have been made in the mischievous lottery of life—they planted me in a body and face that my soul has been rejecting for years—

Come, Miriam, please, you will have to move back a few feet and put your fingers in your ears, because, God, for once I have to let this pass through those glands of venom in my throat. I had the soul of a volcano as a child—fire and lava and flying scalding stones, and Picasso and King David and Meir Harziyon, and Maciste and Zorba all together. But my face and body—well, you already know what I think about them. And all nine of my souls were going wild, like tongues of fire in me—and the most important thing is that I was full of joy—because I still didn't know what I looked like. Do you understand? I hadn't yet been phrased and identified and defined from every possible angle (why don't they make people get a license to use certain words, the way you have to get licensed for a handgun?). Nothing could stand in my way then—the only question was what to choose—espionage, art, commando missions, travel, crime, love—of course, love, from the moment I was born, don't even ask me what kind of shame I caused my parents—by the time I reached kindergarten! I was a four-year-old peanut, but since that point I have never stopped trying to bestow my affections on whoever didn't run away fast enough. Don't be too impressed, now: most of my beloveds didn't even know I existed. Why, to this very day I have to forcibly invade a woman's field of vision if I am interested in getting her attention. As you know very well. But in my thoughts, in my imagination—no limit, no limit! I knew with an insane confidence throughout my childhood that what was happening to me in the meanwhile was only a preface. It was only a hard test, only a tough preparatory exam for the moment life would finally begin—and suddenly I would hatch out of this worm, Jacob out of the pale Yid from the shtetl, and be Tarzan and the lion all at once. I would glow with the full spectrum of the colored fires burning within me . . . Oh, the fantasies I had—I could scream from my yearning for them. Huge red and yellow tongues, dancing and teasing one another—

But in the meantime, you have to lower your head and suffer quietly. For instance, my father would speak to me, for months at a time, in the female gender: Yaira come and Yaira go. Why? Because he saw me fighting with a kid from our neighborhood on the sidewalk in front of the house. I actually knocked this kid down right away—a miracle occurred, they were pulling for me in heaven and sent me one who was actually weaker. Unfortunately, after knocking him down, I immediately stood up and walked away, leaving him lying there, whining on the sidewalk—and I didn't break his bones like a *gever*, and didn't tear his balls off, and didn't do any of the things my father, watching through a closed window, wanted me to do, terribly. I raised my head for a moment when we were fighting and saw his face: my father's face, behind the glass, twisting, turning purple, and crumpling and warped as if it were melting in a fire. Without even knowing what he was doing, he stuck his two fists deep against his mouth, and I saw how his teeth sank into the knuckles, a blend of bloodthirstiness and the terror of an abandoned puppy. My poor father.

When I returned home, he was already waiting for me, the thin brown one in hand, which he could, in one whistling pull, whip out from his belt loops. He beat me instinctively, mechanically. The thin brown one worked overtime. To this day, this is how we joke about such moments in my family. How Yeery made Father mad, and the thin brown one worked overtime, and we all laugh until we're in tears. It doesn't matter. He was whipping me, and when that didn't provide him the necessary satisfaction, he attacked me with his fists, beating me with his fists, which he had bitten until they bled, and his little soft body fluttered and shook. He raged with blood-red eyes—this man, whom I had never seen fight, not in his life. He always became gentle and considerate and flattering if someone pushed in front of us in line at the movies. When his car was blocked in the parking lot by the general-deputy, his boss, you should have seen him bowing and scraping. And in front of the general-deputy's child, for that matter. And once, when that stinking corpse of a neighbor, that Surkis the murderer, slapped me on the street for shouting between two and four in the afternoon, my father immediately withdrew from the balcony into the apartment, so he wouldn't see it. But I saw *him*. He hit me—and I shrank, reminding myself the entire time, It's fine, it has to happen this way, fathers hit children, what do you expect, that it works the other way around? His beatings were just part of the great test—this is what I thought.

But what was I saying?

You, wanting to meet me, "the whole me," asking to meet the child I was as well and reconcile the two of us, so I'll look at him differently, differently than how he was looked at in my parents' house. I remember every word you wrote. In the margin, you wrote in pencil that "under no circumstances will we meet like two pedophiles, that's *their* language, Yair. We'll meet like two children." You see, I remember it exactly—you wouldn't believe how many phrases and sentences I remember by heart, your words and tune together: "I can't go on like this anymore; this distance from you with this vagueness, because what is happening between us is too vast for me to contain. I need your touch terribly, your touch, please, enough of this, come to me, in your body, in the whole of you, in the materials with which you were made, the unbroken and the defective, the torn or the double, but come, with open arms, as if you were giving a gift. And if you find it hard, tell yourself that Miriam wants to meet the child that you were; give me that pleasure, because in spite of all of your slurs, I am sure he was a beautiful child . . ."

And again, Miriam, time after time, you approach me and unlock my most secret doors with sacred keys that only you have—how do you have such a sixth sense about me? Just hear this story.

(No. It has to be a separate letter, in a separate envelope, as it was.)

August 20

Once upon a time, at the age of twelve, more or less, it was evening, and he returned home from a movie he saw with Shai, who was his best friend until they entered the service. They said their goodbyes in front of Shai's building, and the boy continued on his way home, alone; you-already-know-who was expecting him there. So do you wonder that he walked so slowly?

Look at him, walking alone on a side street, trying to preserve the sweetness of the movie that had been lost to him while riding the bus, because of the scorn and laughter, focused solely on him, from three little thugs (who, at that time, were called hoodlums). Shai, his white legs shaking in his pants, was sitting next to him. Now the notorious wits of these two, which struck such terror into the hearts of students and even teachers, exploded and splattered all over their faces like an overambitious gum bubble.

He walked through the silent, empty streets, trying with all his might to forget what he felt when Shai looked the other way, and sat blind and deaf, making himself absent from the situation. He knew he would have behaved in the exact same way if the situations were reversed, and he almost wept, cursing his weakness and vowing that, by God, from this day forward he would stop stealing money from the Holy Wallet to buy books. From now on, he would steal money only so he could buy dumbbells and practice pumping his muscles all day and night, like an animal. He knew it wouldn't help him either, because he didn't have *that thing* within him that immediately connects dreams to muscles in one decisive motion. That can transform the internal Tarzan roaring in your heart into a fist cracking a hooligan's jaw on the bus. That mysterious thing that probably makes an *ish* into a *gever*. He also knew that even if he was able to hit someone, sometime, everyone would be able to tell that it didn't really come naturally to him; and while he was walking, deep in thought, two women approached him in the street, one young and one old—well, not really old. A grown-up. And they were strolling along peacefully, talking between themselves with silent voices, their arms linked together, glowing with some kind of warmth that he immediately woke to and was alive to.

And as he passed them (dressed in his good pants that Father made him wear before going out, hair carefully combed with a side part), he thought he heard one of them, he couldn't tell which one, whisper to the other, "What a beautiful boy."

Oh well. I've already started this, so I don't really have a choice, do I?

He continued walking, and had made it a few steps farther, when those words penetrated him and stopped him. He was ashamed to be standing like that in the middle of the street and dragged himself into one of the apartment building entrances, and stood there in the darkness, shivering, sucking on those four words—

Within sixty seconds, of course, he started tormenting himself with doubts. Had he heard correctly? Was one of them actually looking at him and still saying what he thought he heard? And if she did say it, was it the young one or the older—and I hoped it was the young one, because he was already vaguely aware of the fact that old women have a bit more compassion for children who look like him—if it was the younger one, the pretty one, the *modern* one, then his situation might not be all that bad. Because she was speaking purely objectively with regard to him— she doesn't know him, never saw him in her life, but when she did see him, it was as if she *had* to say those words, before she could even think about it, thus giving an almost scientific validity to her statement.

But did she really say it? He wasn't completely sure; maybe they had been discussing a film they saw, quoting lines from it—or they could have said, "What a dutiful goy," or "Cuts are disputable joys," or maybe they were thinking about some *other* boy that they both know who really fit that description?

It's a bit silly to stretch it out, don't you think? But that's the thing— those words never saw light—only wave after wave of endless darkness.

So what did he do? He stood in that dark entrance, practically shaking from his distress and confusion—maybe he should run after them and explain, in his most weighty, measured voice, "Excuse me, but when I was passing by you before, one of you made a remark regarding some specific boy—an insignificant remark, true—but due to a rare coincidence that comment has a marked importance—fatal, actually—yes, a matter of life and death that is difficult to lay out in detail at the moment, a matter of national security, actually—so could you please, even if it sounds a bit odd, would you mind repeating what you so briefly mentioned when I passed you?"

So he started running after them, slowly—then sprinting; and then he stopped again, confused and defeated, immediately turned around, and returned to the dark entrance, where he stood in front of the wall, heart fluttering in his throat, and felt like prey, still half-alive. He no longer cared if someone passed by and saw him—but those four words he might have heard, he wished he had heard, began to glide in mad joy, like four birds in a frozen garden—

Well, what would you have done in his place?

He knew that even if he caught up to those women, he wouldn't dare to ask; because whoever asks a question like that aloud condemns himself to an eternal life of disgrace; and even if, let's say, the two of them (the young one, too) tell him that indeed, their reference to a beautiful boy was to him, he would never be able to truly believe them, because if they are given enough time to really look at him while he explains such an odd request, they will understand everything, it's impossible to look at him without understanding his situation, and they will pity him and lie. Do you think that I wouldn't run after them today, pleading with them to say it in a thousand and one ways; I am still running. I'm running after them to-day— Why, not a single day has really passed since that happened.

Hey, you're sticking around, aren't you?

I became so tired all of a sudden.

It makes me happy that you like my private name. I never thought of it like that—that Yair, meaning, "will shine," is a name that faces the future, or is "almost a promise." I was also relieved that you are no longer worrying about whether Wind is my real surname. As long as my name shines on you.

It took me months to discern the transparent streams of your humor—it's just like that, passing through the lines, with its hands in its pockets, whistling lightly . . .

Tell me—can you feel that I've been trying to hide a sudden, unjustifiable happiness for a whole minute now? Tears taste the same, but it's as if the taps were switched . . . This treacherous, warm wellspring of joy that has no explanation, no justification from what I've just told you, except for the astonishing fact that I told you: Warning! All units at attention! Happiness leak! I will locate the source immediately! No—actually, no. All units—pay no attention. I want it to drip into me until I am swept away by it. And I don't care that dogs are barking behind me, that the electric fence bears the writing "Family Will Make You Free!" Listen to me—I will still try to escape. I don't think I'll make it, but this time I have outside help—someone is waiting for me on the illuminated side. These are the kinds of gifts you give me. I'm not afraid of anything. I'm ready to shout with all the strength I have that I believe in the possibility of you and me coming out, toward each other, and actually meeting in the middle of the road. I believe in such wonders.

I need to be alone with myself. Goodbye, Miriam.

                                                                    Yair

(Now quickly—look inside yourself, see what it looks like when venom is injected in your blood, watch the live broadcast at the moment of the crime: It's a white room, four walls, no windows, no pictures—one tiny open eye is in each wall: four gaping eyes, no lids, no lashes, no breaks to blink—and each pair of eyes has one look, just one stable, permanent, frozen look in it; and enclosed by the walls, a blind rat runs along the floor.)

August 21

Don't panic, this is not another scrawl. Just a good-night kiss.

You once teased me, told me my letters are like balls of yarn—I know, I got so knotted up in myself that by now it might be impossible to un-tangle me. I'm not asking you to try: hold the ball of yarn in your hand, tucked between your two palms, just for a moment, for as long as you can, for one more month. It's a big request, I know—but you are now at a perfect distance from me—the perfect distance of closeness and for-eignness, and between my ignominy and my pride (you're no longer a stranger). Don't take that from me. How could I look Maya in the eye if I allowed her into the blind rat's room? She's my woman, I'm her *gever*. When she and I are together, my pupils never get shifty when I say *gever*.

Yair

August 23

Thank you so much for your quick reply—you must have felt just what has been going through me since the last letter—

And today, I want only to caress you, to comfort and be comforted . . . You practically ran to me with your writing. You gave me so much of yourself as a girl, of your mother, and especially your father—at last, someone in your childhood was gentle and loving (I found I completely misguessed him—I had imagined him stern and nosy and bitter, proba-bly because I only knew of his "Why aren't you happy, Miriam?"). But maybe he was too gentle for the difficult job he needed to do, to protect you from her.

It amazes me that even though our homes were so different from each other's, in a thousand small and large ways, both of us still "felt at home" in each other's house. And when you described your loneliness, and at the same time how crowded it was, how you had to struggle for any privacy, I thought of how much it pleases me that only the two of us, out of all the millions living here in this country, know what the winner of the Chang Shui County Milking Contest looks like . . .

Because whoever didn't grow up in such a house might think that there is a complete contradiction between "loneliness" and "a struggle for privacy," right? Only the person who grew up in that kind of house can know that feeling exactly, when that contradiction tears you apart.

Just nod.

How could you take it? (I actually want to shout, What have you got to do with such a woman, and how is it possible that you, *you*, came out of her!) And the efforts you have made, all these years, to try to be close to her to make her like you; in my opinion, it was very noble of you that you could, in that way, at such a young age, try and calm her anxiety about you . . . And what about the healing that you always talk about? Has it not happened between the two of you—not even once?

I also recognized your feeling that you are betraying her by talking to me about her; *oy*, I know, *oy*, Miriam, *oy*, the *oy*-ness of life. You always ask the hardest questions, and you've already seen that I have no answer except to sit and mourn together. And to bring up that question with you again—why does it have to happen this way, that you probably never learn to mine out the ore that you need most from your own insides?

And how are you so good at giving what you never got?

I have to leave soon (a parents' meeting for the kindergarten class!), but there is so much more to say. You're probably right that a meeting "in the middle of the road," like the one I offered, would no longer be satisfying. That a true meeting between us can happen only if both of us walk the whole way to the other. I wish I could say that with the same certainty as you; I want to, more than I've ever wanted anything—but I don't think I have ever walked such a long path.

Slowly, all right?

I'm reading your letter, thinking how simple and banal my story is compared to yours (though perhaps I tell it a bit more dramatically . . .); and afterward, I see that in the kernel of it, that bitter, crappy kernel— they are still very much alike. Then I think how many tens or maybe hundreds of times I have sold my story to impress someone (usually a woman). My Gloomy History. My Tapes. In recent years I've even stopped feeling nauseated when I do it. The one thing I haven't stopped feeling, though, is that I tell it in order to escape, in the same way a lizard abandons its tail, to keep myself from being caught. And I want to give you my soul, because this is our pact: a soul for a soul. Perhaps, someday, when I finally grow up, I'll be able to give you the gift you keep hoping to receive from me. And I will dress your face with that story.

August 26

I'm sorry, I'm sorry, I'm sorry. You're right, and I have nothing to say in my defense. Crazy days. Working and running around from morning to night. I hardly find the time to eat. I remember us, and I am with us (don't worry), and I will write a real letter soon. Actually, I don't really exist right now—hold up the bridge on your side (you're probably more capable of it than I am anyway), and just let me remind you, even in the great moments of my modesty, I remained egocentric. I'm referring of course to that fantasy of yours, describing how we met on the street, you and I and your mother, that night I was returning home from the movies, remember?

Y.

By the way, regarding your question at the end, written in large letters (and why does this question occur to you now?)—there are a few answers.

First (to the public): I started with it for no real reason, but because it was convenient during my military reserve service one winter, and it has stayed ever since.

Second (should be printed in the *Hedha-Khinhukh Teacher's Magazine*): Look, Miriam, of course I understand, *lo-gi-cal-ly*, what you were getting at in your excited little speech full of good intentions. And I wish I could reconcile with myself and look at myself with a favorable eye. Really, why not? Why, I too have at least "one person on the outside" who looks upon me with loving eyes, just like you, she even looks at me through rose-tinted glasses. She has been trying for years, with all her strength, and with all the love in her eyes, and still can't do it. It's a fact: she cannot make me shut those damning eyes in myself and convince me to see what she (probably) sees in me.

Third (just for you): You do understand, don't you? Because you were the child and the teenager who used to "switch uglinesses" in herself, moving them from the tip of her nose all the way down to her thighs . . .

and you also wrote about the kind of physical discomfort that almost "seeps out of you," so that you think everyone can see it. I'm familiar with that, too. And the feeling that some *stain* is hiding inside you, right? That's my private name for it; and it has a full range of motion, this little stain, which is mine and not mine—it was implanted in me, but my body took to it admirably well. Where it chooses to be in any particular moment is exactly the same location as the encounter I once wrote to you about—when my body and soul meet in an internal whisper of a password . . .

And isn't it true that, in that particular moment, the entire rest of your body ceases to exist? All your nerves are stretching to that place of encounter, all your blood rushes to that location (what you described, how, as a girl, you felt so tall that every time you walked into a room full of people, you immediately tried to fall)?

So, this is another answer to your question (asked in a slightly disagreeable nasal tone) "Why the beard all of a sudden?"

Y.

September 1

Do you realize yet what you've done!

Has she called you yet?

But how could such a thing happen to you? Is it the pressure of the beginning of the school year, or what?

I'm scared just to ask you what was written in the letter that was meant for me (has she received it yet . . . ?).

On the one hand, you know, it's all my worst fears coming true. On the other hand, it is almost amusing, the thought that if you are going to travel back a hundred years and have a love affair in letters, you have to expect a nineteenth-century mistake like this to happen.

And from another way of looking at it, yes, from a third side . . . it brings me pleasure, for some reason—as if we now exist in an "objective" place. There is one witness from the outside—a living witness, existing, complete. Real. For what we are.

I'm dying to know what she said—how did she react? She can keep a secret, can't she? I know, I know—you can trust Anna, I know.

But why didn't you tell me she had gone away? Only the other day you quoted an entire conversation you had with Anna about the crazy love affair of those two (Vita Sackville-West and Violet?), and you said you had read her complete passages from the book. And I even remember what Anna said, that she has been looking for the power of such a crazy love all her life—and she spoke about the courage of being honest about the pain of matters involving emotion.

But you didn't even hint during the letter that the whole discussion was happening over a transatlantic connection—and it sounded so close, as if you were in the same room and could touch! Where exactly is she flying to in the world, and for how long? The way you miss her—you would think she's been gone for years, just like that; does a woman go alone on a long journey across the world—and with a small child?

The shock of the first moment—that suddenly you address me as a woman, inquiring as to how I've been feeling and if I'm terribly lonely, and if I miss you as much as you miss me . . .

I felt such a strange shiver when you spoke to me this way—as if you had found a forbidden, hidden string and plucked it.

I was, of course, smiling to myself over the differences between what you tell me (about Yokhai, for instance) and what you tell her. For example, you would never write to me about how much he weighs, and his height, and how many pairs of shoes you bought him for the winter.

And you have never sent me a photo of him (may I keep it?).

I understand Anna is very close to Amos as well. Apparently they are soul mates. From your letter, one would think that for a moment both of you know him with the exact same closeness and intimacy—I see the two of you almost clinging to him at the same time. (Did you notice?) Read the draft—I think you'll find it interesting.

It's strange to legitimately peek this way into your other intimacies, formerly unreal to me. It is also a pleasure to eavesdrop on the private humor the two of you share. I only knew it as your humor before—thin and a bit sad—and it suddenly made sense—you have a partner. You can feel how it began to spring up between you from childhood, and grow, and become more and more intricate. Big Miriam and tiny Anna . . . And in general, you two are a huge sound box together (you're probably not conscious of it). For example, you visited her parents this week, and her father was playing the piano, and Yokhai suddenly burst out crying—and I remembered how you cried at the Bronfman concert years ago, sitting next to Anna—and I suddenly read that when Anna gave birth to her son, Amos played her that Rachmaninoff concerto over earphones, and then everybody there cried—I couldn't understand why—the doctors and the midwife and the baby, and you and Amos as well, all that crying and laughter and music flowing for all of you together.

Tell me, am I jealous?

(Because it occurred to me that this is actually the first love letter I have ever received from you.)

Yair

September 3

About Emma Kirkby and your description of what her voice evokes in you, a "braiding together" of the most profound sadness and joy, a rising fullness, that "reassuring heartbreak" you mentioned.

When I heard how you speak to Anna—I mean, when I could isolate that thing in your written voice, I thought—

Sometimes, when I hear your voice, in words, I feel a kind of whimper rising up in me, making its way through me—an internal voice heretofore unfamiliar to me: until you, I didn't know it.

Reassuring heartbreak? I don't know. In my opinion, the voice takes me apart. It's an unhappy voice, like slightly hysterical sobbing, like the whimper of a dog that hears a flute and goes mad. It stretches out from within me, against my will (the way the eye is drawn to a disaster); it nags and burdens me until sometimes I rage at you. When you wrote to the boy I was, for instance.

Add this, too, to the "tuning of the instruments."

September 8

No, I don't know how I feel right now. And I'm irritated by the pitying, concerned (self-righteous) tone you assumed after dealing such a blow. A similar feeling to the one I experienced after you took your house away—and with one wave erased everything you had ever given to me with it as well. But of course, there is no comparison.

It's hard for me even to write to you right now. I don't understand you, Miriam, and at this moment I don't even want to understand you. Tell me how you can, without warning, punch me in the stomach this way?

It's the first time since we've started this correspondence that I'm almost appalled by you. Not from what you told me—what you told me seems like a bad dream to me. I might not write to you for a few days. I need some time.

Please don't write to me either.

September 9

I can't be with it by myself.

Once, in the army, during a guard shift—I was sneaking a read, all the while terrified that I would be caught with *To the Lighthouse*—and I remember how, contrary to all my rules of caution, I yelled as if I had just been burned. From the pain, of course, but mainly—I had just started the second part of the book—because of my rage at Virginia Woolf for, with a snap of her fingers, and in parentheses, letting me know that the wonderful Mrs. Ramsay, the love of my soul, had "died rather suddenly the night before."

That was nothing compared to what I felt with your letter in my hand. I was lucky to be alone in my car, in a parking lot, when I read it.

What do you expect me to say? That you've amazed me again? That I was furious with you because you just don't do that in matters such as this? I don't know. Because, on the other hand, as the hours passed, I could also see that you stood by our crazy agreement far more loyally than I did—through all these months you were telling me your dreams and believing in them with all your heart, you were *living* them with passion and dedication and devotion, far beyond what I thought was possible or allowed. Far more than what I ever dared, in spite of all of my water-sprinkler games.

But it hurts. It hurts like a fist in the stomach. And it doesn't stop hurting. And every time I reread that letter that was supposedly "switched"—

What more will you tell me in this way of yours?

September 10

I can't stop thinking about how you continue to speak to her. Soul conversations and little daily chats. You quoted her to me in the first letter you wrote—and you took her on almost every trip of yours. She has been dead for ten years, and you still resurrect her, each and every day.

How many years did you have together? I mean, ever since she approached you in Lushka Kindergarten and swore that you two would be friends forever, until her forever ended. Twenty? Twenty-five?

And what about the child—was it born? Did he, at least, come out alive from the birth? (Is there a father in the story?)

I don't even quite understand my reaction, the depth of my shock—because I never knew her in life, only in your stories. A certain sequence of words. A tiny woman, witty and funny, and brave, who wore her heart on her sleeve (and a huge straw hat, and had a harelip, and was all bright flames of fire).

You pictured her as a bird almost every time you wrote of her.

I can now grasp how lonely you are. Yes, even with all those friends of yours, and the group of men you keep around you, and your girlfriends from the village and from work. And Amos. But the kind of friendship you had with Anna, this twinness, is something you receive perhaps once in a lifetime.

It would be stupid to comfort you now; frankly, I feel as if I am the one in need of comforting, because I found out about it only yesterday. I haven't felt this way in years—as if a very close friend of mine had died. I'm holding you tightly to me.

Yair

September 10–11

Maybe I don't understand you at all. Maybe you're completely different than I thought. Because I am, after all, only peeking at you through cracks. Composing stories that could be complete fantasies. (What isn't imaginary? What my body is telling you right now.)

And that feeling as well, that everything you tell me about yourself—even what might seem to me, in the first look, like a complete contradiction in your personality; even what strikes me with a cruelty that doesn't become you—I already know that when I look back on it, I will see how true and loyal it is to who you are, and how, in your depths, it ties together and becomes a law.

Is this how I seem to you? (I think not.)

Don't go away. I need you with me now. There is so much more to talk about. We've only just started, each letter makes me realize how much we've only just started; I think even if we spoke for thirty years, I

130

would always feel we had only just started. By the way, I was surprised when you invited me to come to the Ta'amon Café on Thursday nights to watch Amos play chess. I will not go, of course. I will be satisfied with your description. Sometimes I see someone who looks like him on the street, not young and not old, not tall and not short, with a little potbelly and a neat little beard, with gray hair, messy and wild under a beret.

But I can never be sure: either he is not wearing the gray jacket with the elbow patches (in the summer, too?) or he doesn't have the cap or he doesn't have those unmistakable eyes—the bluest, clearest eyes you have ever seen in an adult.

You write about him so beautifully, with warmth and softness, and with love; but I also feel a thin sadness spreading over your words. How can it be so easy for you to tell me that I would undoubtedly find you two quite an odd couple, that even the people closest to you don't always understand what you are doing together? And it actually makes you happy that only the two of you know.

But my heart felt the most pinched when you wrote me that when he made his living singing folk songs in Scotland thirty years ago—those must have been his happiest days. If Maya's happiest years weren't with me, I would feel a terrible loss. Truly defeated.

But actually, Maya is not really very happy right now. She has been this way for a few months. She says it might be her work—because how sunny can your mood be when you're researching the human immune system—but we both know it isn't just that. She's sad—she can't concentrate—she's floating in a bubble of depression. And I can't help her right now, because I don't understand myself. Wait for me a little longer, Maya.

I just had a flash while I was—

I'm eight years old, taking the morning bus to school. They are interviewing Arthur Rubinstein on the radio (it was the first time I heard his name). It was his birthday, and the interviewer was asking him how he saw his life. And he answered, "I am the happiest man I have ever known." I remember looking around me in amazement, almost panicked: I'm sure you know what people on the 7 a.m. bus look like—and he dared use that word, in that way, so freely . . .

It was sometime around New Year's—every New Year's they would announce how many people were now in Israel—and I remember thinking so passionately that out of three million, there must be at least one happy person—and I want to be that person! (And a week later, I was lying in my parents' garage with a belt around my heart . . .)

I just reread *To the Lighthouse* again on a confused impulse, so I could mix the sadnesses together. Perhaps to be comforted a little. It's not comforting. It's the opposite of comforting. And the hardest part is having no one to share the feeling with. I bought Rachmaninoff's Second Concerto and listened to it over and over. Music does me good right now; "if they shouted loud enough, Mrs. Ramsay would return. 'Mrs. Ramsay!' she said aloud, 'Mrs. Ramsay!' The tears ran down her face."

Y.

Just one more thing, all right?

Years ago I devised a special sight test for every woman I liked. To determine which one would be the "One Woman of My Life." I thought we would look into each other's eyes, and slowly bring our eyes closer, closer and closer, and even closer, until my eye touched hers—not the lashes, really touched—the eyelids, the eye itself, the pupils and moistures would touch. Tears will immediately come, of course, that's how the body works. But we will not give up or surrender to the rules of reflex, to the body's bureaucracy; until we rise, out of the tears and pain into the fragments of the vaguest, most ancient pictures of our two souls and float into our bodies. We will see the broken forms in each other. This is what I want, right now. That we will see the darkness in each other. Why not? Why compromise, Miriam? Why not, for once in our lives, ask to cry with another's tears?

September 14
Hello,

That's all. Hello.

It's no good, only being able to write you when I'm dead tired (this life—who the hell wrote these rules?). I'm pretty much starting to get sick of running around. It isn't just me—Maya, too. Almost everyone I meet. Especially people our age—work, the kids, there's no time for anything. Even you, yes you, yes, the Great Lingerer . . . a while ago I wrote out your schedule for each day of the week for myself, including work and afternoon meetings, Yokhai's treatments and visits to your mother, and Alexander Technique lessons, and dinner and dishwashing, and everything else I know. And I was amazed by how little spare time you have for yourself—just a few moments in a day. At least your nights are free.

And I was thinking that this activity doesn't suit you—it's as if some foreign body were drowned into your softness (if I am allowed to quote back to you what you said about my sense of humor).

So what is he really thinking about us, your man from Mars who's watching?

What you asked me to tell you—it's a bit late tonight to start such a tale (have you heard about the wise Chinese man who said, "I don't have the time to write a short letter, so I will write a long one"?); perhaps, on the other hand, it is good that I tell a story like this when I'm tired.

The truth is, I don't like to remember my friendship with him. The more I miss him, the more appalled I am by the friendship we had then, how distant and unapproachable it seems. We were both smart, weak little kids, unpopular (as the verdict is pronounced among Ido's generation). We were mocked and ostracized by the other kids—and we ostracized ourselves a little as well. I think we enjoyed being special and cursed. We invented, for instance, a private language of hand gestures—we were very adept and could chat with it during class. We were laughed at for this as well, of course—can you imagine what it must have looked like, he and I and our finger signs?

We had secret nicknames for our classmates, and would compose mocking songs about them, about the teachers. You can already guess, I'm sure, that we both (yes, he as well) were familiar, from personal experience, and thanks to the superb education we received at home, with the basic article of the constitution stating that each person possesses one quality deserving mockery. And we passed that knowledge on . . .

So we advanced our image as a double-headed creature with a multi-hemisphered brain—we developed the arrogant, bold speaking patterns of a couple—we used very manly language, that is, and used to hold public contests in writing "simultaneous poetry" in the style of the Dada poets. We swallowed Hegel and Marx without understanding a thing (we only learned about the golden era of radical sixties Matzpen socialism from the adults, and heard about it with terrible envy—I can't recall whether your name was ever mentioned). We also had a sense of something like a style—and, of course, we truly felt (without ever saying it aloud) a bit like two English boys who were meant to be sent to a boarding school and got stuck instead in the public school of a working-class neighborhood.

At the age of fifteen, we wrote our own "Modest Proposal" about producing electricity from inferior human beings; this is how we defined it, crippled, stupids, retarded, and so on (I'm sorry, I know, and still: me, everything). "The Family Cookbook" came a year later, and established and dishonored our names at school for all eternity: it was a collection of Jewish recipes, easy to prepare (and cheap, too, because the ingredients were always at home). From the menu I recommend to my gourmet friends Mother's Stomach-Lining Soup, and Cheek Dumplings à la Papa, stuffed with bitter bile . . .

It is important that I stress in this disgraceful yet inconsequential report that the more power we accumulated the more popular we became with the girls. This was a refreshing development for us: by the time we reached sixteen, we were already surrounded by a small but excited circle of groupies. We would make them read moldy books we'd borrowed from the YMCA library, and then test them, and give them hell, until they earned our good graces. There was a time we would woo girls with a plan predetermined by a secret code—one by one, we would go after girls, so that the first letters of their first names, put together, would actually spell out the name of the girl we really loved, one Khamutal, over whom we didn't even dare masturbate out of sheer love.

It continued in this way until we went into the service. Six years. Six witty years, Shai would say. Six gritty, shitty years, I would immediately respond. We were obsessed with word games. We could destroy a person's very foundations within five minutes, through a simple Ping-Pong game with his name. (I'm writing to you and thinking, If everything had ended differently, if we had succeeded in remaining together into our adult lives—after the wild irresponsibility of youth and cowardly cruelty—what a good friend I could have had.)

All right, boys, enough sentiment. We were recruited on the same day, and although we believed in pacifism and demonstrated against the occupation and all that, we were overjoyed when the draft cards arrived. I think both of us could sense the poison in our friendship. The fact that the rough army decided we were fit material was a sign that, in spite of everything, and underneath all the affected rot, we were actually just like everybody else.

In short, the long arm of the IDF separated us. Shai served in the Golani infantry brigade and I—underweight—was assigned to be a clerk. Each of us, for the first time in years, stood alone in front of our peers; we sobered up very quickly, or more accurately, we were forced into sobriety. We buried all our cleverness deep in our kit bags. And we learned to speak in those other languages—but mainly we learned to shut up. And then, in one of the glorious campaigns of our forces in Lebanon, Shai was severely wounded. His mother called me from the hospital, before she even called his grandparents. And I told her that, of course, on my first weekend off, I would go see him.

After a few, horrible, soul-filthy weeks—I have no other words to describe what happened inside me each and every day I did not go to see him. I didn't even go home on my days off, just so I wouldn't have to see him. It was impossible to keep it up, so I forced myself go to Tel Hashomer.

What do I remember? I remember the long corridor, and the geranium plants hanging from the ceilings. And the crippled guys flying by me on their wheelchairs with special skill—you can imagine how I felt walking in that hallway, so permit me to be brief. Someone was getting up for me at the end of the corridor. A thin body, with a shaved head, only one good eye wide open in his face, with no eyebrow above it. And there was also a horrible mouth, slightly pulled to the side in some kind of permanent skeleton's giggle. He was leaning on crutches; one of his legs had been amputated above the knee.

I approached him cautiously. We stood and looked each other in the eyes. In the eye. We thought, An eye for an eye; we thought, Seeing eye to eye; we thought, Beauty is in the eye of the beholder, we thought, The eyes have it—all our poisoned brilliances were running between us, and died on the edge of his naked eyelid. He started to laugh—or cry; to this very day, I don't know, with that mouth—and I was possessed by hysterical laughter and pretended to be crying.

I have nothing to say in my defense. I simply couldn't get over it. That's a longtime habit with me, huh? Also the fact that our friendship and our uniqueness was always at the exact point of the tip of the syringe of mockery.

Dear Miriam, after the donkey-foal letter, you said you wanted to hug me. How can you hug me? I couldn't hug him. I couldn't lie and tell him he was a beautiful boy. We both stood, with our faces turned aside and our shoulders shaking; all the years of our friendship, with its truly beautiful moments and our silent knowledge of each other, and mainly with the notion that our meeting at the age of twelve might have been a rare gift that our crappy luck had smuggled into our lives to us—it was all erased.

That's the story.

What was I thinking yesterday?

That it's a pity you and I can't be friends. Just friends, like the good friendship between two men. Honestly, why aren't you a man?! That would have solved so many problems: meeting every two or three weeks in some coffeeshop or steakhouse, throwing back beers, talking about fucking, business, politics; going to a soccer game in Gan Sacher on Friday afternoons; taking family trips together on Saturdays. Easy.

I remember how he lifted the remains of his face and looked up at the ceiling—there is no language that has words to describe the expression on his face, as if, in that moment, he accepted, surrendered with some horrible intellectual integrity to the verdict we both pronounced when we were friends—that if you're fucked up in some way, it's probably your fault. If you were punished, you deserved it. You deserve everything you are; you are an exact punishment for yourself, no more, no less.

His face shook in front of me—he no longer had the facial features to express everything going on inside him. After that, he turned around and we went our separate ways, without even a goodbye. It was many years ago—I know he went through a lot of surgery and physical therapy and looks pretty okay. I also heard that he got married, had one child, and they're expecting a second.

He truly was an unusually intelligent and bitter child. Hardly a week passes when I don't think about him, and still—do you see? I cut him out of my life, too. (Look at me—a hybrid of the Scorched Earth Strategy and the Salami System.)

Y.

September 17

Come to the kitchen, come to my kitchen. I already know yours well. It's the evening, and I had a somewhat happier day, the first one since you told me about Anna. I want you here with me for a moment, I think we're allowed that after five months and seventeen days exactly since we met (today!).

I'm in our yard, a square meter of grass with a water sprinkler. Surrounded by an obedient ring of chrysanthemums. This should be an autumn evening according to the calendar. But the air is warm, thick, clotted, and close. Doesn't it feel as though winter is refusing to arrive this year? (I don't care.) I am lounging here on a comfortable Keter lawn chair, under the guise of writing a reply to an angry customer to whom I mistakenly sold the wrong story—and feel you around me. I have a feeling, somehow, that today you won't fight me over this bold invitation into the depths of my house. That is, at least, what I am hoping for. Because with you I never know when the scolding will come . . .

(For example: "Sometimes you suddenly belch in front of me this way after you write a terrible, horrible thing—a salami belch, and really, I feel like simply killing you!")

Okay, I took my scolding for my hit-and-run treachery, my insistence on disguising myself as a primitive for you . . . undoubtedly I earn this scolding, and also the torch you turn on my innocent and momentary wish that we had a boy's friendship—a man's.

Hey, you shouldn't work yourself up over my nonsense—they are just words. I swear, I am not constantly trying to detach "that fact of your being a woman" from our relationship. And God forbid you should castrate yourself (!?) just so you can "truly fulfill this wish" of mine. Come, enough fighting. I like saying it to you, come; immediately a small, warm wave washes over my heart. You know, I can now think about you in every room of my house, not only in the shower; it's as if I have finally found, in the past few weeks, the place where you can exist without invading any other territory. Where do you think of me?

Consider such an hour in the evening. Our kitchen is busy now, and Ido is sitting in his royal chair, with all the treasures of Ali Baba and Ali Mama spread out in front of him. Containers of yogurt and milk and cottage cheese and chocolate spread and spaghetti and sliced apples with cinnamon sprinkled on top—of course, just the way you prepare them for Yokhai (and thank you for the idea!). Maya is at the stove, cooking something or grilling chicken wings for tomorrow. Our kitchen is so sweet in these moments—this is what I always think to myself, always, with the same amazement of discovering Eden. Sometimes I say it to myself,

under my breath, so Maya won't hear me; she laughs at my sentimentality, but I have to say it, because, in the same moment, I am there but also
not there. You know this feeling, you said it yourself—you are always, always standing outside the house at the same time you are in it, resting
your hands against the windowsill and looking in.

Then I look inside—and miss, in advance, what will, at some point,
surely be destroyed and demolished—torn apart—things are always getting torn. Especially because of me, may my name be erased. (I once read
that in ancient Chinese, the word "family" is written this way: painting a
"house" with a pig standing inside it.)

But today, everything is dipped in goodness. Peek inside, see how
merry the overcrowded table of plenty is, with the glorious detritus of
life—the crusts I cut from Ido's bread slices, the egg stains on his lips and
cheeks (and on the floor all around him), the rings of chocolate on the
tablecloth, and the olive pits and the basket of large, beautiful fruits, so
full of tropical passion, in our house; our house, in the suburbs. Our forks
and our spoons and our knives—the cup with the broken handle, the cup
with the crack—the "Number 1 Mom" mug next to the "Number 1 Girlfriend" mug—and the ugly yellow teacup, the only one left from a set of
twelve we received for our wedding . . . only he remains and refuses to
break. Maya and I have a deal—during a really bad fight, we are allowed
to break one of these cups—but this one has survived for over three years.
It is even surviving this recent period. What does that actually mean?

The colorful spice rack, and the bread box, slightly open, like the
mouth of a dreaming grandfather—that's how I wish I could be, immediately! And the notes; and the news articles I cut out and stick on the
fridge for Maya, instructions for the Heimlich maneuver and reports
about infants swallowing detergents and updated statistics about common accidents that occur in the house—and disasters that occur outside—from going too fast, eating too much, immoderate living. And
Maya smiles in front of me, her simple and beautiful face lights up. Her
beloved, homey body, which I love a lot more than my own, wrapped up
in a sweatsuit, the twin of my blue one, an anniversary gift her parents
gave us years ago. Her parents, who love me as their own son. If—God
forbid—we ever broke up, we would continue to pretend to be together,
so we wouldn't break their hearts. And she passes me the pressure cooker
and the fat Polish pot, placing the orange plastic Tupperware with rice
leftovers from yesterday on the marble counter; deftly pouring the soup

from the day before yesterday into the Polish pot after she empties out the cabbage which is now in the little cracked one—and what was in the little cracked one? Goulash leftovers, let's say, which she pours into the pot we bought on our honeymoon in Italy. We once cooked soup in it on the banks of the Arno (and don't confuse it with the pot we bought on our trip to France!). While all the containers calm themselves down after the hectic activity, we reorganized the refrigerator together, moving the fresh dairy products to the back. I lean over her, she twists to slide through the space under my arm—our kitchen dance—not to be confused with the jig of the donkey foal. Over our years together, we have combined with each other into one—I sometimes feel as if we both had a sex change into a third sex—the married sex. And once these two bodies had already mixed and blended and dissolved into each other, they became the starting point, origin of passion—and not the means for its satisfaction. We did become one flesh. It's really terrible.

You have no idea how filled with joy I was when we were both teaching Ido how to tie his shoelaces and discovered that each of us ties his laces differently.

By the way, thank you for your advice about Shai—but it's a lost cause. It is true that we have both grown up since then—but it still wouldn't work. He and I know, with our shared, internal, crippled logic (you'll be annoyed by this, but still), that our separation, forced and unnecessary, is also a well-deserved punishment—and the continuation of our relationship, in a very private way. No one understands this better than Shai.

Now, shall we return to the kitchen?

After we took the cracked pot out of there and put in the little potissimo, a good space became available—so Maya rescues a plastic container from the freezer marked *Potato Burekas*, with the date they were made, and puts it on that middle shelf in the refrigerator. That shelf is almost empty, and a bit loose. I fixed it. That's why you can't put any heavy stuff on it—that's how Maya will explain it someday to her second husband, the wrestler, the blacksmith, the talented refrigerator technician. And we both stand there a moment, taking a break from this exhausting activity—and filled with a quiet, harsh satisfaction I find hard to describe in words—it is so rough, so deep, it fills the whole of me so completely, to the tips of my nerves—and Maya's. Those nerves, as if they were bent, rounded by the combined internal heat flowing through us—those nerves might look like scorpion tails in a mating dance, or a devouring dance, and both swell and pulse together in idiotic pride for this modest specialty of ours that we develop day by day to the perfection and purity of the essence of Togetherness. So, Miriam, this is the situation: and it is only now so clear to me, in writing this, that my life with Maya, our love, is so stable and defined that it is impossible to add a new element that is too large (like myself, for instance).

Isn't that the way it goes? Two people loving each other for better or worse, corked up in the jar of marriage. And every deep breath of mine takes something from her in the petty, unwilling accounting that goes on with the person you love the most. Eventually, everything turns into an account, a balance sheet, believe me (even though you refuse to). Not only who earns how much, and who works harder at home and on the outside, and who takes more initiative in bed. Even the genes you donate to the family piggy bank are being counted somewhere. Who the kid resembles more, and which of you is aging faster, and who's lagging behind and not participating.

Even—who's the first to end a kiss.

So hold me tight, now (now!)! Lay your head on my shoulder—do you know about the one spot I dream to kiss on you—apart from the hidden beauty mark: the hollow of your shoulder, by your neck. I want to feel your heat, and your soft velvet skin—the vein that beats there, thus: the quiet, continuing beat of life springing up in you.

Come. Come under my wing, don't say a word—just agree with me in your heart that you can paint a marriage this way as well: two people, watching each other, facing each other in a very long, terribly slow ritual—the execution ritual of your deeply loved one. And now I'm being called to come in for dinner—my fried egg, over easy, just how I like it, is ready. By the way, you wrote something that really amazed me—that Amos is the only person in the world with whom you would like to share what you are able to feel now thanks to our correspondence (!).

Sorry: I don't believe you. It does sound pretty, but it's impossible.

Not just pretty—it sounds great coming out of your mouth—so generous it could make you jealous: ". . . I am certain Amos would understand precisely what excites me again, every time—that a strange man saw something in me that moved him so much he had to come and put his soul in my hand . . ."

It's not that I can't imagine it. What a joy it would be if we lived in such a mended world, in which I could call out to Maya right now, Just a minute, My, I'm just finishing up a letter to Miriam! And she would ask, Miriam? Who is Miriam? And I would finish writing you, taking my sweet time, and sit down in my home, cut into my fried egg, and say that Miriam is a woman I have been corresponding with for almost half a year. She makes me happy. And Maya would smile at me, pleased that I am finally showing signs of happiness (thus destroying years of my carefully constructed reputation). And she would toss the salad with the big tongs and ask me to tell her more. What kind of happiness is it? How is it different from the happiness she brings me? And I would think a little, and then tell her that when I'm writing you, I feel something in me becoming alive, returning to life, reviving—do you understand, Maya? Even though, at times, I write her things that make me despise myself— I am living now, through her, with something that only she could manage to resurrect in me; that, if not for her, would simply be dead. You wouldn't want anything to die in me, would you, My? This is what I would say while I cut thin slices of Swiss cheese and tomato and wrap them up together. And Maya would ask me to tell her more, and I would tell her, for example, that you collect teapots, and all your friends bring you teapots from around the world. They are all kept in the garage, however, in storage—and Maya would think about it for a moment, whether we have a unique teapot to give you. And I would have continued to tell her about you, and Maya's eyes would glow at me with love and innocence, the way they did in the old days. She would lay her elbow on the table and rest her cheek in her palm, like a girl listening to a fairy tale— and I would continue to tell her—

Yair

(But then—she would have to tell me a new story about herself—something I don't know.)

September 20

Hey, Miriam . . .

You have no idea what you have just given me.

Where do I begin? So many emotions are fighting inside me to be the first . . . When I was very young, I vowed to read all the books in the school library that no one else read; and truly, for one year I read only books whose checkout cards were empty (I became acquainted with some hidden treasures that way); or the time I wanted to teach myself how to control my dreams, so I could receive orders and requests from people to meet all their dear ones who had died and wish them well as I slept; or the time I wanted to train a dog who would, each night, accompany one lonely man who wants to wander the streets for no reason—

You can't imagine how often I am occupied with such nonsense, to this very day. I'm telling it to you in exchange for the tale you invented for me—the fantasy of how you were kind to me on the street that night, a night you were walking with your mother in a rare moment of grace you two had—in a flash flood, it brought me back to a forgotten passion to be kind, to give without keeping count. The desire to flood the streets with golden coins from my carriage—but have those coins made from myself, my flesh and blood—with no substitutions, right? To feel my soul spreading out with this generosity, how I give myself away, and nourish, and win over the principle of strangeness and miserliness of the soul and everything we already decided to call the Kremlin. I realized just how much our connection has made me be good—desire to give you only good; and even when I, here and there, get filthy in front of you, you only have to remember that it somehow still belongs to the same weird will burning my throat with the need to do you good, or just to do good. To wipe away all the mud and resentment collecting in the tunnels, come-comecomecomecome . . .

September 21

But what if I don't deserve such a generous gift?

What if I lied?

Those two women, and what they said—or didn't say—on the street that night—that was undeniably true; what if I wasn't returning from a movie or an evening out with Shai? I mean, I told them at home that I was going out with Shai, always just with Shai. My father despised Shai, his ironic glance—called him "faggot" and sometimes also "the Fluorescent One" (Shai did have a kind of deathlike pallor spread out on his face), and he used to do impressions of his voice and his gesture of flipping a curl off his forehead, out of his eyes. Shai, Shai (you already know the story, but it feels so good to write his name down after all these years).

You should also know that I was already dating girls by this time—but I didn't tell my parents, of course. Why? Just because. Maybe I already felt the need to fight for any privacy with all my strength—maybe because I started feeling some anxiety, thin as a lace curtain around me, about myself and exactly what I am. Nothing was ever verbalized or explained, of course, but there was some kind of nervousness fluttering about me, a doubt that used to freeze their hearts. Perhaps you have experienced it—when every sentence out of your mouth is stretched under the light to search for traces. Of what? It wasn't made terribly clear, not then, and I didn't understand it, nor did I want to tell myself those things about myself so explicitly. I suspected myself of it (who doesn't at that age?), but along the way I started to feel the pleasure of frightening them—and would start scattering various insinuations, demolishing their world with vague hints. I would tell them, for instance, about a mature, mysterious friend I met at the library with whom I had long conversations about art. Or float the idea of Shai and me renting an apartment together in Tel Aviv after the army . . . and Mrs. Rubber Gloves would flash a medieval look at Mr. Brown Belt and hum that Shai is already a big enough loser in proportion to his size—and why does he still not have a girlfriend? And why can't I ever hang out with someone just a little more normal, instead of spending all my time just with Shai, each of us in the other's ass? So she would say, and having been silenced by terror, I would bleat out with childish innocence that girls don't interest us at all—what really interests both of us right now, actually, is quitting school and joining an amateur theater company abroad. You should have seen the effect of those words on *their* ears—and never, ever in a million years, not under torture, would I ever tell them that I had been dating girls for a while now, normal females . . . because I started messing around with girls when I was very young, tiny Lolito that I was. I remember myself at the age of twelve—I would approach the girl—any girl, I was never too choosy—and, mustering a terrified self-confidence, would ask her out. Meaning, I would order her, in my limp way, to come with me to a movie. And after the movie I would, using my endless wiles of flattery and begging and self-humiliation, get her to make out with me. Why? Just because I wanted to, because I had to. It belonged to some bargain that she had almost no part in—in which she was only currency—or, worse yet, a receipt.

You'd be surprised if you knew how many girls agreed to be the soft, sweet-smelling cannon fodder for the frightened tyrant I was. I have no explanation. You can imagine for yourself what I was like then, what I looked like—but still, there was always some girl or other who agreed to participate as a walk-on in my internal, bloody drama. Maybe they wanted to practice on me so they'd be prepared when they met the real thing. I sometimes, to this day, wonder: maybe they felt an attraction to his strangeness, above all. I wonder why it depresses me now, again, just to think about it—so many years have passed, and that boy grew and survived—but the thought that it really was my great dark secret that created a black magic gravitational pull (because who can resist the temptation to peek into another's hell?)—

I went to a movie that evening, not with Shai, but with a girl whose name I don't remember. After we said our goodbyes, I went home. But instead of transferring at Jaffa Street and taking the bus back to my neighborhood, I entered Bahari Alley through the closed stands of the roasted-seed sellers and through the prostitutes.

Miriam, Miriam, let's see if I am capable of opening that box: I was barely twelve, I still hadn't gone further than stolen caresses and hasty kisses on lips that always sealed themselves together in front of me. I was holding 50 lirot in my hands, rolled up and sticky with my cold sweat, that I had spent several months dedicatedly stealing from the Holy Wallet, because for no small period of time had I planned, in cold blood, to do this. I would sit in class, studying language and the Bible, and see myself doing it. I would eat my Shabbat suppers with my family and see only this . . .

Shall we take a break?

Your story excited me so much, the true parts—the nightmare of your weeklong vacation in Jerusalem (how old were you? fifteen? sixteen?), as well as the imaginary meeting you hallucinated for me at the end. Little details—how ashamed you were, looking at your big shoes resting next to her tiny ones in the room at the pension; how you tried to separate the two pairs and she would constantly try to put them close together again. I'm thinking about the fruits budding in you then, late bloomer that you were, that seemed to her a final "proof" of your true promiscuous nature . . .

And more than anything, well, it's clear . . . what she whispered to you that night before you returned home, that sentence has been gnawing at me constantly with its inner defeated music (like a line from a funeral dirge)—when Father asks us, we'll say we had a wonderful time; when Father asks us, we'll say we had a wonderful time . . .

It allowed me to suddenly grasp something I never thought of in this way, until now: how miserable my parents were because of me. Perhaps as miserable as I was. It never once crossed my mind how I humiliated them, how helpless they were. How did you put it?—raising your own orphan child is also terrible.

Miriam, you once told me you have this little game with me—each day you draw one letter of mine out of a bag and read it to discover what has changed in you and in me since the last time you read it.

So, I want to send you the rest of this story in a separate letter. Do you mind?

Y.

September 21

Are you still there?

I don't know where I got the guts to do it. My whole body was shaking—why, courage itself was already a kind of betrayal. How is it possible for one child to dare to escape the gravity of his particular family and go all the way *there*. But maybe the most amazing treachery of all was that this twelve-year-old peanut stood up and allowed himself to feel such a strong emotion: lust. It's called lust. *Black lust of daybreak, we drink it at nightfall.*

In that moment, who could feel true lust? What lust?! Perhaps the only real, true lust I have ever known (the lust of guilt eternally searching for an available sin to mate with). I swear, I could compose a complete book of their positions, all the possible variations those two can get into. Only a natural continuation to "The Family Cookbook"; oh, Shai, where are you?!

Old men and young men were standing around; they all looked like the characters in cops-and-robber movies, just like the ones they would cut out of huge sheets of cardboard and place on the roof of the Orgil Cinema. I passed between them with my eyes to the ground, with the festive, frozen terror of a man sentenced to death. I thought, None of them could be Ashkenazi. I thought, This is my burial place. Someone slapped the back of my head and laughed that he would tell my yeshiva in Mea

Shearim. Pay attention, Miriam, this was the child you wanted to grace with your glance, to promise him he was a beautiful boy . . . At the end of the alley was a large back yard; men entered and left it hastily, their faces lowered. We would fantasize with choked whispers about what must be going on in there during class. Eli Ben Zikri was the only one who ever dared to actually run through the alley, and was considered a big hero because of it. And I *entered* it. The smell of urine and gutter stood thick in the air, and I felt how polluted I was with every breath. Another boy, not much older than I, turned me with a push toward one of the walls. By that wall stood a big square woman in a very short, very shiny black skirt, probably a leather skirt, but I only remember the shine next to her exposed, and very thick, thighs. But not her face, because I did not dare look at her. Can you imagine it? Until the transaction was completed, I did not dare to raise my head, even once, to look at her.

I asked, How much? And she said thirty. And I, paralyzed, handed her all the bills rolled up in my hand and heard my father's voice as he blew up about how terrible a merchant is the son he raised. Miriam—you're allowed to skip the next chapter of this tale, but I have to tell it to you. I want to be clean.

Tall buildings surrounded the yard, the walls covered with huge tar stains, long tongues of tar—and in the dark garden itself in the back, I remember piles of old wood planks from construction sites, piles of garbage, and, here and there the red glow of cigarettes. From every corner crept whistles and breathing and the indifferent voices of the prostitutes talking among themselves as they did it. I remember how she pulled her skirt up in one rough motion, and I, who at the time saw the peak of my achievements as learning to flick open a bra strap with one hand—my sister Aviva's bra, which I would stretch for practice on the old armchair—suddenly saw, in front of my eyes, the very thing. I got cold and sick, and I felt my soul shrinking, felt myself losing it for good, and I was thinking, That's it—just see how low you have sunk.

(No, I was a much more dramatic boy than that—I remember these very words echoing in my heart: Now you are truly outside human society . . .)

She asked me why I didn't take it out, and reached a brute's hand to my little dick, which was trying to escape, screaming and retreating into the depths of my underwear. She pulled it and shook it with all her strength, she rubbed and moved and squeezed it in her unpleasantly tough palm, and sadly, I left my body and watched myself from above and thought, It is impossible. You will never be mended.

Just a moment. Cigarette. I have to breathe. Why am I making such a big deal out of a visit to a whore? The whole thing was 50 lirot, big deal! Where were we?

We were with her, and she got angry and asked through her gum how long I thought she was going to wait for me, and then—listen to this—the rude geek asked her in a shaking voice if he would be allowed to kiss her once, there, on her breast . . . Skip it, Miriam, skip it, because it's going to contaminate you now. Why am I even bringing you into this? Why do I have to pollute you with this? "He wanted to sin with another of his kind, to force another being to sin with him and to exult with her in sin." But I hadn't the luck of the young Stephen Dedalus. How I envied him when I read that her lips "pressed upon his brain as upon his lips." Mine only made some kind of contemptuous snort and pulled her bra down a little. I didn't see anything—I felt warm, sweaty flesh being pushed in my face—my tongue was looking around and searching the surface of it—I remember how amazed I was when I felt a big, soft nipple, which I immediately clung to with all my being. A surge of warm love washed over me—because in that entire yard, full of hookers, I found one thing that deserved love, that was all love and purity, to which I couldn't resist surrendering the whole of me . . .

Yes, I know. It's really funny. I sucked it, hailing it in my breath and moaning with gratitude—that amazing softness filling my mouth—even now, in this moment, I can remember how it felt, and how, in a half-faint, I imagined the nipple was like a little, round, juicy woman who had nothing to do with the prostitute. Just a soft, mature, solid little woman who may be, by occupation, a prostitute but initiates boys like myself in the mysteries of sex in a pleasant, homey way—and then the shock, when that pleasant lady suddenly hardened and shrank in my mouth like a piece of rough rubber, like a little night watchman, closed off and protected from everything around (you may laugh at me). The repulsion, and the complete despair—because if even this becomes closed off and clots and becomes a stranger—what is left to believe in? . . . And by then, slaps and fists were descending on me from above, and I will never forget her surprised shout of pain, echoing all around that enclosed, stinking world: Did you see the little asshole? Do you think I'm your mother?!

When I walked out of that alley, no one would have been able to guess what I had just gone through. If they had attached me to a polygraph test, it would have written out "Best Boy in Jerusalem," as if some sharp surgeon's scalpel had in one wave cut the filth of that moment out of me, the cruel kick that someone—probably the pimp—gave me from behind, who grabbed me by my shoulders and then threw me out as choked laughter crawled after me from every corner of the dark yard. I stumbled away from there, running, falling, stained. But five minutes later I was sitting on the bus home, under the lights of the city, among people who could not guess what had happened so close to them, how heavy the fee was that I had left there. I wore my face again, I was myself again, to the point of exaggeration and ridiculousness. I dressed my face with the tale everybody knows—I must have also blinked a lot, so my eyes would look myopic and helpless. So people would look at me and mock me in their hearts—and, in that way, things would go back to what they used to be, to the normal course of events between the world and me. That child popped out at me again a week ago, when I shaved off my beard. I shaved just to meet him—don't ask. From the silly yearnings for him you aroused in me—I almost exploded from the insult of the weak face I saw staring back at me from the mirror. Still, I will make myself stay loyal to you. Not to myself: to you. And I promise never to cover it again with a hairy layer of epidermis.

When I reached my neighborhood, I was already, of course, concentrating intensely on the beautiful, reconciling things flooding my vision. I remember, for example, thinking that I would be a sailor someday and sail to distant lands, blue and green and full of light—and I would see only beautiful landscapes—and there wouldn't be anything around me, just the wide expanse of the sea, wide and clear. And while I was deep in my hallucination, two women passed by me, one young, one old. And they said what they said, that I wasn't sure they said. Perhaps they only mumbled, "What a villainous boy." I don't know.

And it wasn't you, Miriam. Not you, and not your mother. Thank you for your tremendous efforts, for reliving that horrible week with her for my sake, without your father to protect you and separate her from you. I know how difficult it was for you to go back there. I was with you during those endless nights, in the double bed in the pension. You were crying on one side of the bed—she was silent on the other—and incapable of offering even a hand to comfort you.

Without your even saying it, I know you brought me, in the last night of your story, to the only moment, probably, in those years, when the sky actually opened up for you. I am amazed again—how could you be so generous and wise and unreserved at such a young age? How did you understand exactly how miserable and humiliated she was to have to make such a request to you? When Father asks—and how much strength did it take you to reach your hand out to her, over the mountains of darkness, and to tell her, "Mother, let's go."

The movie of this keeps playing in my mind: you and she, in that empty street in the middle of the night, your arms linked (I only now grasp—that hand, the pregnancy, paralysis, her right arm . . .)—terrified by the sudden intimacy, and excited and mute and appalled, clutching each other's arm and shaking all over.

What touched me more than anything—in the middle of that storm of emotions that shook you as you wrote, you remembered how important it was to me that it will be the young one, "the modern one," who tells me (what she might not have said in the first place).

But no—you would have given me one look and known exactly where I was returning from in that moment, and how lost I already was. Just explain it to me—because I don't completely understand—how is it possible that I was such a child?

I feel terribly murky inside myself right now.

Y.

September 22

Did you happen to watch TV this evening?

I saw a program I really thought was made for you. It was the kind of show you like to watch. And it also reminded me of my "wide expanse of the sea." They showed a tribe living on an island in the Pacific—and all the nouns in their language are divided, not into male and female, but into "that which comes from the air" and "that which comes from the *yam*, sea."

(And I was thinking about another island, where words also are divided into "that which comes from Y-air" and "that coming from Mir-yam.")

September 24

You turned the kaleidoscope only slightly—and the whole picture rotated. But the mighty force it takes for just this slight turn!

Your letter arrived on a hard, annoying day. The horrible, despairing news combined with some ambiguous internal bad mood. Anyone who passed by me irritated me. In the middle of the day, I left everything. I raced to the post office and prayed for your white envelope in my box. And then, all of a sudden—how did you describe it, when you were telling me about falling in love with Amos—"For me, the sunshine was healed."

What? So, you didn't save me that night on the street—exactly the opposite? I saved you? How? With what? What, in my miserable state, did I have to give you? . . .

How do you do that? How do you know how to give such grace, and with such delicacy and secret words. I read it over and over—and this wave from within nearly takes me apart. I apparently forgot, completely, even between me and myself; I didn't let myself remember that the power of lusting, wanting this way—the power that twisted in me to the extent that it drove me to a prostitute—it is not a mutation, and it isn't shameful. You're right. It's passion and heat and creation and life . . .

You came down into my Josephan pit, you turned the pit, like a kaleidoscope, with ten sentences, no more—and deposited a little, fluttering ignominy of yours into my hand. You close my five fingers around it and say, Take care of it And it is suddenly you, not me, who was the weak one there on the street, who betrayed himself. You who agreed not to notice that exactly in this particular week he will return to the country, the beautiful Alexander—and you allowed them to smuggle you quickly out of Tel Aviv, bribe you with a weeklong vacation in Jerusalem?

Well, I can imagine it was still a great temptation. Your first time in a real hotel, and the first vacation in your life with your mother, just the two of you, and everything you were hoping would finally happen between the two of you. Perhaps you are, as usual, too hard on yourself (what could have possibly developed between you and him?)—but when you wrote of the disgust that welled up in you, when you allowed yourself to understand for what price you sold your passion—and how passionate you really were to have to make that deal—I thought, Maybe now we can seriously consider your proposal for the girl you were and the boy I was to "go steady."

And if I had to choose only one moment from all your letters, I would pick the little word sketch you wrote at the bottom—how we passed each other in the street, one by the other, like a brother and sister chained in two lines of prisoners marching in opposite directions. And how you sucked and vacuumed into yourself, from that distance, that one power of mine: the power to lust. So you could have it for along the way, and for the whole life to come; and that because of it, I was, to you, a beautiful boy.

Yair

Don't be frightened by the stain (it's embarrassing, but sometimes happiness can burst out of my body in the form of a sudden nosebleed).

September 25

Miriam, I had a dream . . .

I swear I did—not just a fragment or vague memory—a complete, intricate dream. It has been years since I've been able to remember a dream!

Do you want to hear it? You have no choice: you've described at least four to me in complete detail. You once said the best gift you can give yourself is an interesting dream. And also that, since Yokhai, you have stopped dreaming (whereas they have now returned to me).

This is how it went: I'm standing with three others in an open field—a woman and a man, very old, and another woman, younger than they. Perhaps my parents and my sister, but their faces remain blurry.

There are a few more people around us, people I don't know, dressed in thick clothes. Farmer's clothes. They walk the four of us to some kind of bathhouse or big shower (as I write this, it occurs to me to tell you; I mean, don't be scared—this is not a Holocaust dream. I know how sensitive you are to that).

The "shower" is located, for some reason, in an open field, a little green pasture. The strangers start a stream of water, water starts pouring down from four tall taps over our heads—the water is very hot, steaming—immediately the whole field is full of steam. And these people bow strangely to us and disappear, leaving us alone.

We take off our clothes, each one of us in a different corner of the field; we move slowly, calmly, without shame about undressing in front of one another (and without a will to watch as well). We lay our clothes neatly on small wooden chairs, like chairs for first-graders, and then march together and stand under the taps.

It always horrifies me when I read about how the Nazis made complete families strip together. I think not about the huge, horrible death that came a few minutes afterward but about the embarrassment and shame of these people who were forced to take off their clothes together: men and women who didn't know one another, fathers in front of their children's eyes, and adults in front of their parents' eyes. (Or what you said about Kafka and the Holocaust. Lucky indeed. Just imagine a man like him there. It's unbearable to even think about.)

So, just to tell you how it ended: We shower in tranquillity, with pleasure, it lasts a long time. We soap ourselves down in a serious manner, with long, graceful motions and some respect for this ritual.

That's the whole dream.

After writing it down, I'm a little disappointed. I probably forgot most of it. What is this, compared to your stormy, complicated dream panels? You understand, though—I really felt that I was in that shower all night. I wonder how long a dream like that could last, anyway.

Still, I'm yearning to return and be in that dream. It was as if we weren't human beings in that dream, or at least, not "human beings" in the normal sense of the word: we had a kind of nobility, like, let's say, four beautiful horses bathing in a stream. Each one concentrated only on his own cleanliness.

Should I send this? Or shouldn't I?

Y.

I'm glad I waited—tonight's harvest looks of higher quality:

I'm walking with my father in the Mamila area of Jerusalem, in front of the cement wall that stood there until '67. In the dream, it is still standing, but you could probably already pass through it into the Old City. It really doesn't matter, though. My father and I are traveling down a curvy, complex path and arrive at the Italian hospital. There, my father tells me that we have to say goodbye. It seems like a regular old everyday goodbye. I don't know if he's very sick and about to enter the hospital or if he's going to continue on his way, but a sudden, heavy burden comes between us. My father walks away from me. He turns around suddenly—as if he had just remembered something important—and he stretches his hand out toward me. He is actually holding a hand out to me. Even from far away it is a gesture of love and tenderness.

I rush to him, take his hand. I want to hold it a moment longer. But he pulls his hand away quickly and says apologetically, Look at what your pen did to me, and sucks blood from his finger. I'm eaten up with remorse for hurting him and start to mumble an apology—but he's already far away. Gone.

It was strange (strange is not the word)—

It was exciting to meet my father again in the dream. I haven't seen him in a long time. His walk, his face ... and there was something embarrassed and helpless in his stance before me ...

September 27

Greetings, my dear Anna,

We've never met, but I have a feeling we can address each other as friends. I feel as if I've known you a long time.

When I began corresponding with Miriam, she once asked me, with a smile, if I had already heard "all the stories about her." She asked me to promise to believe only what she told me about herself. So that we would never have gossip between us.

She seemed so innocent and domestic to me (I know, she certainly is also that) that the very idea that there were "stories" floating around about her amused me.

But something just happened that— Yesterday afternoon, after I put my daily letter into the school mailbox, I had to drive someone home. "Had to" because I very much wanted to be alone after that particular letter. But I had no choice: I know this woman who works at the school, vaguely (we have kids in the same kindergarten). She is a small and vital woman. And very decisive. We drove. We got stuck in traffic. She, for some reason, was very eager to talk; for a moment I even had the strange feeling that she was actually rolling the conversation along a very specific path. Because—I don't understand how this happened—she mentioned Miriam and Amos, and then your name came up as well, of course. As did the whole mess.

To be more precise: I discovered that "the entire city of Jerusalem was talking about you" and that "the whole mess stank to high heaven." (The story was passionately accompanied by hand gestures and clichéd euphemisms.) I also learned that a few parents and someone from the Ministry of Education demanded that Miriam be dismissed from the school because of the "scandal," and only the furious protests of students and other parents kept her from being fired.

Can you imagine how I felt? I could barely keep driving. I didn't know anything about it. I've been corresponding with Miriam for half a year and she didn't tell me. Perhaps she feared I wouldn't understand, or that I would be shocked by her (?).

My dear Anna, when I was a little boy and my mother or father began to sizzle and fume around me, I had a patented trick: I used to seal myself up from the outside world. And then I would start to tell myself a story. It was always the same story, about a creature named Angelus. Only I could create him, by turning my little wristwatch to the sun (or any other source of light)—and he was there, a little round stain of light dancing on the wall. Storms would bluster outside me, around me; and I would secretly make Angelus move across the walls, and talk to him inside me; I would roll him over the grimacing faces in front of me, and on their bodies, too, and on their foreheads, building annexes of light in them; and the entire time my heart spoke to him, using large, beautiful words that used to bring me a real feeling of elevation in the midst of their poison.

Yesterday he returned. In a moment's brilliance, he arrived to rescue me—I strolled with him along the car's roof, on the woman's dress, on her ignorant face. She blathered on, and with all my strength I focused myself and told Angelus about you, Anna. That you lived with Amos and loved him with all your heart—and he loved you. How can you not love Anna?—Miriam has said to me more than once. Angelus was sauntering along in his light—it has been perhaps twenty years since we met like this; I've been through so many wristwatches since we were first together—but he has remained exactly the same. I explained to him that at one particular moment—if you can measure such events in time—it so happened that your Amos and your Miriam fell in love with each other.

Maybe it happened when Miriam went to Parice—no, to Paris, to save that Yehoshua who was so dear to her. You know how once in a while she likes to feel like a knight-errant, saving someone in distress. Once she arrived there, she discovered he didn't need any saving. On the contrary, Yehoshua was living the wild life. She apparently broke down a little at that, and you commanded Amos to go and bring her back.

Maybe it happened when you met the Dutch U.N. officer, who borrowed books from the British consul library, and lived with him in a small hut near the Cremisan Monastery for half a year (as you can see, I've been thoroughly brought up-to-date), leaving Amos alone at home in Jerusalem.

But I'd rather think that it happened during the most ordinary moment. A vegetable market moment. When she was at your house, for example, preparing supper with you as usual. You were making strawberries and cream; and they were cutting vegetables together for a salad. And Miriam began to talk about something that had happened that day in class, or enthusiastically describing how light falls on the poplar leaves. Or maybe she was standing silent for a moment, not moving, diving into herself. And Amos looked at her and felt his heart expanding and melting away.

I was covered in sweat when my unwanted hitchhiker left the car, so great was the effort to be only with Angelus.

A triangle is a rather stable form, Miriam once told me. And satisfying. And even enriching. On the condition that all sides know that they are sides in a triangle, she added.

Anna, I need you to help me. I have no clue about how it really was among you three. Did the three of you live together, or did Amos shuttle back and forth between the two of you; what did you know? What didn't you know? When did they tell you? And how did you feel then—and weren't you even slightly jealous of your best friend?

Miriam said that if I refused to believe in the possibility of such "poetic geometry" (a name I gave it) in this world, then I would never feel everything I am capable of feeling. She didn't mention a specific case, she was just responding to my thesis regarding the "usual system of law" of men's and women's relationships.

I am starting to see how much I will need to explain and interpret and translate for you—even as close as you are to Miriam—so you will understand exactly what we said, she and I.

She also, at that point, slapped me with sparks—you know her, fire bursts out of her sometimes—informing me that I am brave with words and cowardly in my life, and that, to her, true courage is surrender to whatever your soul brings to you.

And Amos is a very brave man, the bravest and the most honest she has ever met.

A whole day and half a night has passed since this discovery. A lot of coffee has been flowing through the channels of my body. I still have to know—what did you really feel? Because you must have seen it start to bud between the two people you loved most. How did you handle the pain of what must have been an implicit slur on you? How do you continue to love them both without dying a hundred times a day from pain and jealousy? I know how Miriam would have answered me—that, on the contrary, despite all the inevitable pain, you loved them both even more.

But how can you?

You can. (Believe, believe, believe.)

I don't know if she told you about this, but I made a small, painful bargain with her: I have to give up one word in my mother tongue for every new word she teaches me. She wants to tell me a story, you see. The new words are so I will understand it. And she keeps telling me that it is the story I need to hear the most—the story of complete self-abandonment and entry into another person. What do you think, Anna? Is it possible? Will I be able to?

October 1

Here. At this moment, you are there—on your balcony, facing Jerusalem's forest. Under the bougainvillea shade. Your almost empty house is behind you—you are sitting with your face pointed to beauty. Floating in the twilight, in your most beloved hour of the day, which is the hardest hour for you to bear. And still, it is your most beloved. Soon Yokhai will return, and you will be absorbed in his care, from now until the medication puts him to sleep. Sometimes, when I'm at home alone, putting Ido to bed, I fantasize that you and I, together, are putting the kids to bed, in the comfort of our home and our habits.

I think about you and Amos often: what you have to go through every day, and the profound friendship you share. The place belonging only to the two of you, that only he, of all men, can understand the language of. I feel like a stranger, and a bit like a child, beside your intimacy.

Your togetherness and our togetherness, Maya's and mine, don't have too much in common. I think more life and passion exist between us than between you. But who knows? Perhaps you two have something I can't begin to imagine.

Today, almost every hour, I looked at the light through the blue stone you sent me. It really is a wonder; in it, in the twilight, for example, you can see two girls playing the piano using a book of duets. Your hands are soaring; you are full of life through the blue stone.

I have, in the past week, adopted a little habit—to, every evening, at this hour, stop moving. Like right now. And to be with you in complete silence for just a few moments (I noticed a long time ago how you rise up within me in every moment I have to myself). After my third letter or thereabouts, you asked how we would ever manage to meet—not in one place, but at one time—because I am so edgy and impatient (and hasty, tsk tsk, you added); and you wondered if I really would ever be able to linger for even one moment in another person's time, if I wouldn't just feel claustrophobic in another person's time.

You see, I'm practicing.

I'm discovering, for example, that in this hour the odors of the whole day hatch at once . . . as if they had to hide during the rest of the hours, compromise themselves, give up; there was always just one triumphant tyrant's smell, and now—the grass, and the earth, the asphalt and the smell of laundry, and I've learned to recognize the scents of jasmine and *ya'ara*—in combination and each by itself, as one can smell them only at this hour.

And each leaf has at least two shadows.

I'm starting to write like you . . .

You said that whenever I "decide" or "know," it is coming from a tough, strange knowledge choked in my throat—and you feel in it something branded in me by force and violence. You also said that I'm smart, but especially about the things I don't know.

Here, then—at this moment I have no idea what a pleasure it is to be wrapped up with you in the twilight.

Hey, Miriam,

Me

October 2

And here's some late-breaking news—

I've left home.

Don't get too excited, it's only for a week and came about quite suddenly—but I wanted to announce a temporary address change and inform you of the possible difficulties of correspondence. A slightly complicated matter that would be tragic if it wasn't so funny (and vice versa). The matter comes down to three words: saving my life. In six: the routine saving of my life. Do you have a minute?

The truth is, I'm pretty tense about this. "This" began at about ten this morning. When work is at the peak of its insanity and I am under the most pressure—telephones and people around me, and every second someone else comes to me, to ask a question or consult or reveal his most private shameful secrets through a choked throat and sometimes with tears as well. A telephone call drops a bomb in the middle of this chaos— Ido's kindergarten teacher, who asks me to come pick him up immediately. He has a high fever and is very swollen behind the ears, and the wheel of madness around me slowly . . . stops . . . I sit down, put my head in my hands, because what I have feared more than anything has come true—and what the hell do I do now? And Maya is in Safed, this is her day at the laboratory in Safed. A calculated plan of action crystallizes within me in a blink: I will run away. I will not pick him up. Let him stay in kindergarten until he grows old, or at least until Maya returns. She's already had it, and anyway, it isn't as dangerous in women. I remember now, with terror, the little bottle of vaccine I bought two years ago during one of the more recent epidemics and promised Maya to go to a nurse so she could inject me—but that bottle stayed in the refrigerator, and over time was pushed back to the notorious mustard region . . .

Okay—so I leave the last instructions to my staff, spit out a panicked last will and testament, gotta run, my boy is burning with fever, my little child is incubating his virus. Maybe he's already contaminated me—and I suddenly feel that he's been clinging to me more than usual since yesterday, and with more purpose—the kiss this morning when I dropped him off at kindergarten, the wild hug last night at bedtime—who knows what clever scheming instinct is acting in him, trying to eliminate any competing heirs, any rival mouths. I'm lucky to have had at least one child, thus paying off, with interest, my genetic debt to a tortured humanity—but what about the rest of my modest joys?

This is how my day started, and who knows what fruit it will bear (at least the *day* will bear fruit). Maya listened to me in silence, ignoring my panicked howls over the phone, and immediately enlisted her eminent self-control: she ordered me to take him to the doctor, she will cancel everything she planned to do today and come home on the next bus—and until then I'll have at least three quality hours with the little Well Poisoner. Can you grasp the severity of the situation?

I sank down in my chair, shrinking around the presumed area of disaster. Ami S., who works for me, encouragingly and helpfully informs me that if I am infected, it will be the most efficient method of birth control. I hope he suffocates. I hope he suffocates and is castrated. Ami S., who has four kids, boys and girls, and had the mumps when he was three years old, like every normal child except for me. Why, all my life I've been nervously prepared for exactly such an announcement. And now for the bitter truth (it is bitter, after all, even though you insist that not every truth has to be!): I chose this disease carefully for myself, when, at the tender age of three, I was the only one of all the nursery school children who managed to persuade the mumps germs to convert their religion and produce only scarlet fever! And since then—the interminable anticipation of a blade dropping on the source of all my happiness. There isn't a medical article on the topic I haven't read—there isn't one pediatrician I haven't pestered and interrogated on the dangers awaiting whoever didn't get it in time, as a child—or didn't force him to admit, with much prodding, that all his other colleagues were lying, and the percentage of adults who get infected and are thereafter excluded from the circle of fertility and RSA (routine sexual activity) in general is a lot larger than what those quacks publish in the *New England Journal of Medicine*.

Does it sound like I'm laughing? Does this seem like a smile to you? It's a twitch of frozen terror; my guts simply turn when I think, What if . . .

But by the time you read this, I will be in Tel Aviv. (I just popped into work to tighten some final screws and write to you. I will immediately flee the infected city.) A room awaits me there, not too bad, in a small, homey family hotel by the sea. I come there once a year for a week. They've gotten used to me. There is a pleasant side to my well-rehearsed terror of the mumps. And as you can see, I wisely choose to take advantage of them. In short—all the above was to tell you that if you write me this week, I will not receive the letter. It will have to wait until I return. It was also to torture myself more from the curiosity over what you couldn't tell me about the last letter (I understand it is somehow connected to Yokhai, but what? What happened? And why did you become difficult and depressed all of a sudden? Please tell me). And I promise that if I have a free moment there, I will do my best to scribble some hot thoughts from Sin City!

I will be leaving shortly. I am sitting down for the first moment today, and it is difficult for me to get up. I also simply enjoy writing you, so I can laugh at myself a little over this crazy day. (There is something else— a new feeling, I'm not quite sure what it is—freedom? Becoming myself again? Something like that.)

Maya arrived home at two in the afternoon to find Ido screaming in pain and me breathing through wads of cotton dipped in aftershave as a disinfectant. I know she was thinking about the vaccination bottle growing slowly moldy in the refrigerator. The first mantra of married life ("I told you so!") was already sparkling in her eyes. But I have explained to her before, and did again, that sometimes—in rare cases, but being the bitter exception is not uncommon for me—the vaccination itself might cause infection, and no sane man would, of his own free will, go out of his way so a doctor can inject him with germs of impotence. Weakened, indeed—but how can you know who exactly and by what they determine the standards?

Maya didn't smile. Maya doesn't smile at my jokes much anymore. (You aren't exactly rolling around on the floor screaming with uncontrollable laughter either, are you? Why is it that women always scowl when I'm even a little jolly?) But I long ago lost the competition against the earth's gravity for control over the edges of Maya's lips. Where did my happy, laughing girl go? Where is she?

Where were we?

I'm writing this and thinking, If only I could send this letter to her.

She sat down at the kitchen table with Ido on her lap and asked me where I intended to go. I said that, as usual, I would go to my hotel in Tel Aviv, because I would not stay in Jerusalem as long as he was contagious. She took a deep breath and asked me how long I planned to stay away from home. I said that, as usual, at least until the swelling behind his ears went down. Meaning about four or five days, a week. As usual.

It has somehow become an institution between us, my annual vacation from the epidemic. Nobody asks too many questions—but Maya's eyes fade in front of me a little.

Anyway, she helped me pack, and reminded me not to forget certain things, and by the time we reached the door, we were soft and buttery with each other again. She caressed me and asked me if it wouldn't be so difficult for me to be alone this way, if I'm sure I have to run away so far again, because I haven't caught it all these years, maybe I'm naturally immune to it (which I certainly might be). And I told her that it would be very hard for me to be alone, and invested a lot of emotion in my "very"—I swore it to her with all my heart, shit-heel that I am. We hugged again, and we felt true sorrow and even a little fear, because who knows whether, etc., and all the complications that go along with it. I've lived in deadly fear of these complications my entire life, and now I have managed to infect even Maya with the same fears. Despite her immunological education. She knows these complications are mainly in my head, but on the other hand, this year is the first time that Ido has really caught it—so isn't that an interesting development.

I said, Come on, why are you making such a big deal out of it, as if I were leaving for good (but every separation between us, even the most routine, always seems like an eternal goodbye for us). And I also mentioned that I would be back in a few days (and every meeting of ours has some of the awkwardness of a first date). And for a moment I almost stayed. But no, I left, I left, determinedly, feeling, deep in my heart, that I wouldn't return the same man. Something is about to happen. Maya felt it, too—she can immediately feel it when wind is blowing in the sails of my manhood (and if she had, only once, said that she knows, she knows me—that we don't even have to talk about it, let's just start all over again, with a clean slate, and let each of us finally give everything we can to the other, because we have grown so much since)—

Well, as you can see, I have very little trouble writing and writing and writing and passing the entire week in this manner—and perhaps that isn't such a bad idea.

A moment before I fly: I just made a little arrangement with the post office: they will transfer any letters in my mailbox to my hotel in exile (just don't write your name on the envelope). So please, don't abandon the one who was sent away!

(Four in the afternoon, already on the boardwalk!)

But . . .

Even before going to the hotel, I went to the boardwalk, sat down on a white chair, and closed my eyes to the sun in front of me—and began to wonder what a person in my situation should do with such a week, such an ultimate week. To whom will he say goodbye with a gloomy moan of mourning—and whom will he meet, in the sore howl of heat? Should he jump on a fast airplane and fly to Frankfurt? Yes, yes, corrupt Frankfurt, above all! And no one will ever know he disappeared—who will know? A marvelous week—a secret niche in time. At the Frankfurt Airport is a huge hotel for travelers wishing to stay the night in the middle of long flights. It is there that a person in my situation could live, incognito, as a sexual exile for a whole week: each night he will come down to the crowded bar and will entertain one female passenger according to his predetermined game plan, as follows: On the first day, it will be a lady intending to depart for America the next morning; on the second day, let's say a shapely lecturer from Melbourne University; on the third, he will celebrate with an Israeli who is returning to her country and homeland the next day; the night after, with a curvy black woman from the Ivory Coast. And he will continue in this manner, night after night—and if possible, in the mornings as well, because we mustn't neglect, for example, the Indian subcontinent, Latin America (and Atlantis)—your servant travels the face of the globe's soft curves with his rough stick until he spreads his sperm throughout all the continents, among all races—and will then be able to lie peacefully with his ancestors.

And while I was deep in thought, a herd of shameless women rose up from the waves and knocked on my closed eyelids with their knuckles— Open up for us, open up! And I laughed at them from underneath my eyelids: What's with this burning, I only just arrived! Yair hasn't started distributing himself today, you'll have to come back . . .

Listen, I can already tell that I'm having a hard time sitting still for even fifteen minutes—spikes, spikes. It's not going to be an easy week for me. Hey, what do you say—perhaps instead of heading off to the hotel— I really don't feel like being trapped in four walls—I will drop this infant into the mailbox over there on which someone spray-painted in huge letters SIVAN, WRITE ME ALREADY! And if you promise to join me without interfering, I will make a short cut from here straight to—

6:30 p.m.

Dizengoff! (Where else did you think a tourist from Jerusalem like myself would go?) Dizengoff Street—with exceptional generosity and warmth—for an hour, full of charms and the soft haze of twilight. And you know what was so strange about it, Miriam? There weren't any men there. At all! Only me, with a thousand women. I staggered, drunk and dizzy, and was, in each moment, baptized into another religion with the cloud of perfume of each woman who passed me. Certain perfumes drive me crazy, on the spot. I can see the complete sexual histories of every woman there passing before my eyes. And I'm also certain that each one of them could hear the drumming beat of my heart's groin—it happens, you know, in the fraction of a second between when you glance at a woman and when her scent hits you—between the lightning and the thunder. You should have seen me, shuttling between those women like a truck from the sperm bank. I hope my little enthusiasms are not making you angry. And you aren't offended by it or taking it personally in any way—it has nothing to do with you. It's just a vacation for myself. Perhaps even from us. From the immense heaviness we have created in these few months together. Just, please, don't be angry (and don't return this letter to me sealed!). Indulge me this week. You went to the Galilee for a week—you took a vacation, too—as I remember.

See, I'm starting to feel murky again. Again, the arguments I was hoping we had already freed ourselves from. I was enjoying myself so much (until this moment). I'm going back to the boardwalk, to fuel up on a ray or two of the sunset, and the smells of the sea, and the burnished skin. You can join me, if you so desire.

October 3
Miriam, hello.

I don't know if you have already received the letter I've sent you from here. To tell you the truth (bitter, of course), I hope you didn't, that yesterday's triple punch somehow evaporated en route from Tel Aviv to Jerusalem.

Everything seemed a bit more delightful yesterday, somehow. The situation is that, once a year, when Ido gets anything resembling the symptoms, I escape to a particular hotel by the sea. As I have told you. A small hotel, owned by two elderly Viennese who keep it neat and clean, a kind of place in the style we used to enjoy in the days of his majesty Franz Joseph.

All right. I'll tell you everything in order. The moment I entered the building last night, I could see that something had changed tremendously. Behind the counter, instead of Mrs. Meier, stood a skinny fellow with the eyes of a thief and oily, slicked-back hair. One look and I realized that my oasis by the sea had changed owners. And, apparently, destinies as well (excuse me for using that word in this context).

I already wanted to turn around, to leave without even touching the door—and suddenly I heard myself say, "Okay, I'll have a room for a week." And Thief-Eyes started laughing and said, "For a week? What are you going to do here that will take a week?" And idiot that I am, I was offended and drew myself up and said, "What? Do you rent only by the hour here?" He nodded slowly, inspecting me as if, of the two of us, I was the shady character. Or I was underage or something. He said, "So, do we want to pay by the hour, Doctor?" I saw that I was already getting myself into trouble and, in a mad attempt to save my honor, bargained with him, told him I would pay only by the day. So at least he would know that I'm no one's sucker. To which he responded, "Oooh, he wants to rent by the *day*," immediately took out a calculator, and calculated and rounded up and asked for the entire bill in advance. I said, "What, do you think I'll sneak out in the middle of my stay?" and he smiled and told me there are many kinds of fish in the sea. And I, just because of his foul smile, took out my wallet and weighed on his palm one month's worth minimum wage, and even justified it in some wild self-persuasion: What, I'm going to go out now and look for another room? He smiled and sniggered, and I, as I always do when I see that someone is cheating me, began to give in to it, more and more—I got swindled on purpose and derived some little stinking pleasure out of it. You aren't familiar with that pleasure (but people do love a clown to laugh at, don't they?).

Oh well. Spilt milk, etc. I went up to my room and found it to be tiny, stuffy—and instead of the lovely sight of the sea, my view is of the back yard of a pool bar. There's only a tiny dresser and a huge bed that nearly fills the whole room—and a door that doesn't really lock, and you can see the corridor through the crack in the door. I must have been very tired, because I crawled into bed and tucked my knees into my chest and slept for three solid hours, just the way I used to in the army when they sent me to some godforsaken base in the middle of nowhere. The first thing I would do was find an empty bed and curl up. It also reminds me of how Ido looked just after he was born, when we brought him home from the hospital. He looked like a little ball of yarn, rolled around himself in an unfamiliar place. He slept in despair, insistent and lonely—

Listen, it's really stuffy in here and the light is terribly weak. I'm going out to breathe.

I have been walking for ten straight hours today, maybe more, since half-past five in the morning. Just so I would not have to go back there. I haven't walked this much since my military training. Through the streets by the water, on the shore, on the wave breakers, walking slowly with no direction or purpose. Down the beach, and back up again—evaporating. Entering a café or pizzeria for a little cold synthetic fuel and returning.

It's terribly hot—those last hot days of autumn—the sun is focused on me through a magnifying glass and the wind doesn't stop. People are bending at the waist, walking headfirst into this wind—it's hard to swallow, and hard to breathe, and it cuts your throat going down. Sand flies into your face like grains of glass.

I don't really have any stories to tell you. I just saw a mailbox and thought, Why not? Last night was horrible. I thought I was stronger than that. I don't know if I can pass another night like this. The voices were the worst (every time I succeeded in falling asleep, a scream woke me up. As if they were waiting for me to nod off to scream). It's strange that there are more screams of pain than of pleasure in a place like this.

What else? How are you? Has the meeting with the educational administration already happened? Did you succeed in arguing down the principal without your voice shaking?

I really don't know what the point is of sending you this piece of paper. There is none. Just staying in touch. Perhaps tomorrow I will write again. Take care of yourself.

No exciting news. Nothing has changed in the past two hours—except that when I stopped by the hotel to get my sunglasses, the manager jumped out from behind the counter, practically blocking my way, with the excuse "They're cleaning in there right now." And I realized that while I'm out, he is doubling profits on my account! I thought about yelling at him. But I kept silent. I didn't argue. I felt myself becoming hollow, weak, a child, in the face of such filth. I turned around and went back to the street without saying a word. Maybe I should look for a new hotel (but he will never give me my money back). I don't have too much time left here anyway. I have decided to approach this as an adventure. At least I'll have a good story to tell the kids someday (if I have any more).

It's clear that, even at this very moment, he is renting out my bed again and I better not return until night. I could have purchased the entire Hilton chain with what I paid him.

Today is Abu-Gosh Day, isn't it? Have fun. Raise a cup of coffee to me.

I finished my round. An hour and ten minutes. I have found one sympathetic mailbox. In front of a little café that I like to sit in.

Do you know what I was thinking about earlier? For no good reason? In the "Cleaning Lady Who Lasted One Day" letter—do you remember it? You were describing Anna's pregnancy in detail, all the anxieties associated with it, the fear that her delicate body couldn't handle it—and every other moment the girl would come in to ask you where the bleach was, or the window spray—and your letter became more and more tortured, tense—and you will *not* let her spoil this letter, you *will not* get up from the table for her—and she's already told you she doesn't like ironing. Oh, really then, what does she like? She likes to wash the floor, that's the best—but how much floor do we have in this house?!

I was sitting down, reading it and completely entering into the pregnancy with you. It was an amazing letter. It was—by the way—as if you needed to relive each and every stage of her pregnancy all over again in writing—and her slightest mood swings. I remembered thinking that I had never read such an exciting, intimate, personal description of pregnancy, not in any book. But I couldn't help smiling at the parallel scene developing between you and your cleaning lady. "Don't you dare laugh!" you shouted at me all of a sudden—you got really angry—"What are you laughing at? What do you know? How can you? I'm paying her a fortune so I can put aside a little time for myself to do things that are important to me, that are crucial to my life!" And then the wind was knocked out of you—as if your body ran out of the substance that it needed to maintain any pretense of calm. You were so real to me, lost and sinking. You asked me, When do you think I will finally grow up? When will I learn to give orders to my cleaning lady without feeling guilty or ashamed over being a fraud of a mother and a housewife and a woman . . .

Your mother had laid into you right away, of course—she never missed a trick, or the chance to make that kind of crack—

Are you surprised at the fluidity of my memory? Have you started suspecting that I have been playing against my own rules and stopped destroying the evidence of you?

You see, every spy has his moment of weakness (how did you put it? That you keep my letters in spite of the "Sanctity of the Bond," because it helps you find a little sanctity in the bond). My moment was—I don't remember when. When you told me about the watch Yokhai smashed—the see-through one Anna gave you. You were in tears when you asked me what kind of watch I have. I laughed it off as an unimportant detail—you immediately wrote back to me: "But everything is important. How can you still not understand that everything you say is important, is precious to me, all your 'details.' " . . .

It was then that I asked myself, What am I worth if I am able to rip up all your pages, with all your "details"?

Once I made the decision—they suddenly rose out of the darkness, from all sorts of strange hiding places that would probably stir up both your mockery and compassion—if not disgust—more and more of your pages appeared from more ancient eras. I couldn't even imagine how many letters of yours I simply couldn't tear up.

Which is why I have some superb reading material here with me—and not a little of it. Actually, there's quite a lot. Tens, maybe hundreds of your pages, your words. I took hardly any clothing with me, only a bagful of your letters. Folded, squashed, used—most of them a little blue from the back pocket of my jeans.

And there are so many precious details: the coffee that you, you and that girl, drank together after a big fight over the ironing—and you made peace and concluded that it wasn't going to work out—but said your goodbyes as friends. And two hours went by until you got back to me—exhausted by wiping counters and cleaning windows, your pants rolled up to your knees and a red handkerchief on your head—to tell me that twenty years ago, whenever you would ask Anna what her dream was, she would answer, " 'My dream? To be a frustrated housewife!' And look at me now, making her dream come true . . ."

I'm softening up, huh? Licking every word of yours. Hup, let's move out and put our shoulder to the day.

Past the Dolphinarium on the beach, I find a little sewer stream. I walk alongside it and see, floating on the surface of the murky water, a strange white string—and think I am looking at a man's sperm. Sailing along slowly. Changing its shape with the coursing of the water, with the blowing wind, looking like a long bird in flight for a moment—then like a question mark—like a woman's profile—like a sword . . . I traveled with it all along its curves, all the way to the sea—and it never stopped changing its shape, even for a moment.

I was pickpocketed. I don't know how, because no one has touched me since I got here. The sons of bitches took everything—certificates, licenses, money, credit cards (I was lucky that they didn't touch the letter I took along for my morning shift—the one in which you told me about Yokhai). I was sitting there for two hours, calling all the authorities, nullifying every official layer of my existence.

Except Maya. I haven't spoken to her since I got here. Our little games of revenge. Because she could have called me, too, right?

The thing is, because of paying the hotel in advance, I was left with—

A meager 71 shekels and 40 agorot (if I had asked you, would you have sent me money?). I don't know why it all amuses me so, the mess I'm in. You see it in movies sometimes—someone walks down the wrong steps, takes a certain turn as opposed to another, opens a door, and comes face to face with the wrong man—and is suddenly sucked into a nightmare.

So I'm playing this hero (the poor, lonely hero) with myself a little. (Because some beauty always comes to rescue him eventually.)

You don't even realize how much this world is full of hints of you.

Like the *Magical Moments* radio show I'm listening to here over the beach restaurants' speakers at two o'clock ("*Io sono il vento*" by Aurelio Pierro was on today. I immediately saw your father howling along to it in his taxi, to the surprise of his passengers). Or your hidden beauty mark, hopping with impudent cheer onto a girl's shoulder, onto a soldier's cleavage, onto the cheek of an old woman.

Just like that. A lottery stand. I go up to it and buy a ticket with the little money I have. A woman sits there, her face sealed off to the world, stone—and I look straight into her eyes and say, *You're wrong. You aren't lucky. You, for the most part, are a series of coincidences—Fortuna is only the other face of that same Kremlin, and I will not accept half of your luck!*

And the woman doesn't move a muscle and asks in a completely hollow voice, "Another ticket?" And I take out a few more shekels and buy the right to freely mutter out loud, *Because the world considers me to be completely luckless. Look at my life and say it, look at me through my mother's eyes and you will know immediately. And I still feel myself to be very lucky. And I am offering you all of it!*

(I won some pennies.)

I sometimes pass with you through a few of the stops you made here growing up, trying to make you stand out in the middle of all the people and the scenery, like the children's puzzles where you have to connect the dots with a single line, revealing a shape: in the window of a flower store, a huge sunflower, tall, graceful, and generous to the other flowers, a touch self-righteous . . . and in the next moment—how did you say it, "Even reality sometimes has the density of a dream"—In Ben Yehuda Street an old woman, hunched over and almost bald, is pushing an old man in a wheelchair. He mumbles constantly through his contorted face, as if he is cursing her in his heart. She bites her lip, stops again and again, patiently stroking his neck and head, looking at him with compassion. For three years the other Miriam with the dead legs and clumsy crutches sat next to you, and from fourth grade until the end of sixth grade she tormented you—and you wouldn't tattle on her, hiding from everyone the blue bruises she gave you.

As I write you, let me guess something else—I am positive you make secret deals with destiny, too—perhaps you felt it passing into you through her pinches—but you knew how strong you were, you knew you could absorb her paralysis without really getting hurt. Isn't that right?

Speak to me, I'm listening.

I don't know if you have started getting my letters from here, and I don't know if you answered. I was hoping something from you would reach me—it wouldn't hurt. I already know the letters I brought with me by heart. I can almost write them back to you.

I wandered outside for a few hours. In the middle of the night as well—I had to escape—my head was pounding in there (they are destroying my beauty sleep for good). At around three in the morning I was standing by a traffic light in the central station area and knocked on a car window to ask for the way I lost. A fancy, well-accessorized man opened his window, made a sour face, and gave me one shekel. And out of an unfinished building some guy comes rushing out, shaking a little, rocking back and forth, yelling at me that this is his turf. Well, I wasn't about to give up the money I earned fair and square! He cursed me and pushed me, and after a few seconds we were in the middle of a fight—but not really fighting. We hardly touched. Just a lot of kicking and punching the air. Most of my scratches are from the asphalt and myself. His hands were as weak as butter, and as the moments passed, I felt myself weakening along with him. What happened to me? I could have knocked him down flat, he was so completely stoned. All my life I have dreamed about how, once in my life, I would take someone like this apart—and when the opportunity presented itself, I felt his weakness sucking me in.

So there we are: he and I, falling over from the swing of our own punches that never land or make contact in any way. We're actually backing away from each other, gradually—but we never stop striking the air. Hardly any cars passed us by—no people. One boy, around ten years old, stood and watched us with interest and smoked. The entire time I saw the contortions of the man's face in the yellow flickering of the traffic light— his eyes were hardly open. He was actually fighting for his life against me—who the hell he thought I was is anyone's guess. Then I guess I touched a wound—he made a terrible howl of pain, like a puppy whining. I have never heard such a cry from a grown man. And he fell, huddled up in pain. I left immediately, and in the back of an apartment building I puked until my soul came up. I spent the night terrified that he had died.

I went back there this morning, right after the sunrise. He wasn't there, I stood there for a few moments—and seemed to myself like a cat standing and sniffing at a spot where another cat got run over.

Miriam—

Nothing.

There are comforts, too: this morning, in Ben Yehuda, a young woman ran after a bus. She managed to jump inside the back as the driver was closing the doors. But one of her shoes fell off into the road . . . One guy passing by picked up the shoe and without hesitating for a single moment started running, full-throttle, after the bus. I stood there, giddy from the sight—and then pulled myself together, stopped a taxi (didn't even think about the money I barely have), and yelled at the driver to follow the guy—who, by the way, was running like a predator, like someone fighting for his life, pushing through the crowds, holding the shoe up high above his head, a shiny black shoe—and only after a few long minutes did we manage to catch up to him—I yelled to him to jump inside—he instantly got the picture, hopped in as we were driving, and we hurried after the bus for a few more minutes. He sat next to me without even looking at me—the shoe filled the entire taxi. The driver started playing the game as well—and we weaved and sped, risking our lives—we were in the middle of a chase from the movies—until the bus stopped at the station by Atarim Square and we managed to catch up. The guy jumped out and ran onto the bus, and I saw him walking through the passengers, and saw how he delivered her shoe to her—and the bus drove away.

After about fifty times, hearing people fucking not a meter away from me doesn't excite me anymore. In the beginning it did, yes, even against my will and conscience—the moans alone did it—and they echo from every corner of this building twenty-four hours a day. Sometimes I think I keep hearing them even after whoever has been silent for a while. (Like the way Ido would sob and yell when I dropped him off at kindergarten—I would keep hearing it all day.)

But—no longer. I guess I've grown used to it. I'm training myself to think of it more positively: for two and a half days I have been living in a huge engine room, with the noise and regular rhythms of increasingly louder piston squeaks. And the usual steam being expelled. And after a minute, everything begins all over again in another room. Sometimes I think all the rooms above and around me are trembling together—everything is shaking, vibrating—the beds squeak, the men moan, and the girls, each one in turn, let out their fake shouts—

What I find strange is that, apart from the hotel owner, I haven't yet seen a living soul here. Every time I leave my room, the place looks empty and abandoned.

If we ever sleep together, we will make love slowly, as if we were doing it in our sleep—I can see it now—like two embryos searching for each other, in slow motion, our eyes closed . . .

Miriam, I worked through the night. I felt as if I had to fight for myself a little bit (or at least honorably represent you in the battle over me). You can't surrender to this without a battle. The voices around me were starting to drive me out of my mind. I taped all your letters on the walls. Hard labor. I never realized how much you wrote to me. I wonder what emotions would pass through you, if you were here.

I'm exhausted and dizzy, I'm dying to get some sleep—but can't wipe this idiotic grin off my face.

(Dream about sleeping.) Of all things. I am suddenly sizzling, full of energy—feeling that the walls are murmuring your words.

The room is confusing and full of motion right now. It makes me dizzy to look at. It was like composing a huge crossword puzzle (meant to define its composer). In the beginning I made sure to keep every family of pages together—I couldn't—I despaired over the mess—everything was flying out of my hands and getting mixed up. In the last hour of doing it, I just taped up whatever came into my hands first. I created hybrids—blind dates—doesn't matter. You have a natural sequence about you—somehow everything you wrote is coded with it, continues in an unending flow of conversation. Hey, now I can make up my own new game of chance. I walk on my bed with closed eyes, open them, and the first sentence that jumps out—". . . and until now, I could remember the physical feeling of terror that used to creep in and fill me, turn into stone in the place where I kept my joy of living; oh, the terror that anything good in me will not be given to anyone—and will go unwanted forever. Then why should I exist?"

(I did another round, and drew the very same page!)

". . . and I have begun to suspect that 'that thing' might not even be given from no person to no person, and that all the others have known this for a long time, and that maybe this is the big secret that makes it possible for them to live. I mean, 'to live' and to 'find mates' and to paint a house with a roof and a chimney together. To be the wise lovers from Natan Zakh's poem:

A visitor won't come on such a night
And if he comes—don't open the door. It's late,
And only cold is blowing in the world.

"But I never forget how lucky I was to have met a couple of unwise lovers, who, on such a night, opened the door for me."

Yair?
Yair, wake up, it's me . . .
Yair, don't fall asleep again . . .
This is how I keep myself awake, saying my name with your mouth, in your tune—and each time my heart beats to my name in your mouth.

I'm beginning to be afraid of sleep. I know that as soon as I succeed in sinking into it, for a moment, forgetting where I am, I'll hear a shout out-side, or a moan, or bedsprings, and I can't— It's been like this for three nights.

The end of your letter with your "theory," after you told me I should try to write stories, you wrote:

Yair—

Yair Yair—

Shine on

But where am I? And where is the Yair who shines?

It's night again. Where did the days go?

I am becoming more empty, and you are becoming real.

Your pacing through the house, from the kitchen through the hall-way to the balcony; the shade of the bougainvillea falling in embroidery on your arms; the scent of your hand lotion rising all around me from your pages—it wraps me up in the feeling of a home here.

You are created in me again and again. We are not alive, remember? But everything you wrote is alive. Your life is alive to me. Your face—go-ing over every line, painting it all in my head, dressing you, stripping you slowly, slowly, one piece of clothing after another—talking to myself in your precise speech, in your written voice, with the delicate sorrow around the edges.

"It's no longer a secret," you say (precise, exact reference? Two fingers over to the right from the door), "that these surprising likenesses run be-tween us. I can sometimes feel them flowing through these letters like lines of electricity, with the tension, the constant trembling, and the dan-ger. But, of course, you know that this likeness extends to what you call 'the murky twists and turns of the soul' as well, among other things—but in these 'twists and turns,' more than in anything—exists a power like I have never known. So maybe you can understand why I so want to be close to the one who echoes back to me the least favorite parts of myself."

I don't know. I don't know much in general. It's not easy for me to discover, as you are spread out all around me, that your questions are al-ways far more profound than my answers. As for that question—you had

174

better answer it for yourself, first—here, what you wrote, when we were sister and brother for a moment, prisoners in a chain gang, shuffling in opposite directions, moving farther and farther apart: ". . . I want to submerge myself in all the channels of your emotions and passions, your exposed and most secret, and the wave-crashes and the twisting, because the place from which they spring, all of them, even the one that led you to the prostitute, is for me a place of genesis, a living, precious spring, which I am searching for . . ."

Night inside night inside night. This man no longer thinks about anything anymore, he doesn't even think about the mumps or his poor balls—this man only wants to sleep, sleep until the nightmare ends, and then forget everything. This man sliced the telephone line in his room with a knife, the trouble being that he almost called you to ask you to come to me.

You just missed a great moment: the landlord burst in without knocking on the door—or maybe he did knock and I didn't hear it (I have wads of toilet paper rolled up in my ears to try and shut out some of the noise)—and he caught me standing on the bed reading from the wall. This is how I occupy most of my days here. He saw the pages plastered over every inch of the walls. He wanted to say something, but didn't dare. He went mute—and I just went with the full brilliance of that moment and started reading aloud—". . . overcome, and aroused, as I am, by a mad passion in me to play your strange game, after all. To meet with you, yes, only in words, as you suggested. To become wild on the page—to be mixed up in your imagination, and see how far you can sweep me away."

You should have seen his face—a rare, complex expression, the combination of amazement and horror—perhaps he thought I was inventing, in this modest little room, some new perversion that even he hasn't encountered as yet. I lifted one hand in the air and focused my eyes on the wall: "It has become quite clear to me that you play this game terribly well—with a little whispering feminine intuition that in matters of words and imagination, you are 'the best.' Certainly better than in anything you do in life. And why shouldn't I meet you at your best?"

He left, slowly closing the door behind him with the kind of respect you have for the truly insane. I am, undoubtedly, beginning to acquire a status here.

Still night. No rest, writing while lying down, twisted around myself, the unending murmurs of your words and your thoughts and memories covering me, from all sides, at all times, flowing through me, leaving and entering my body like water. Anna's cheerful, crowded house—with her three brothers and her parents and their funny Dutch Hebrew—and her father's free piano lessons—"And now, after ze Brahms, ve vill play Edelveiss Glide of Vanderbeck for ze plain joy of a coffeehouse." Your mother was constantly envious, she tried to keep you from spending every free moment over there—with her twitching, pursed smile, which always seemed as if it were hurrying away to sweep any traces it might have left in the world. I don't dare imagine what she said, and what black essence she spit out when it turned out there was something wrong with Yokhai.

Yokhai. A lot of Yokhai.

You know, ever since you told me about his fits, his rages, I look at anything beautiful twice. Once for me—and once for you. To make it up to you in my own limited way—for the beauty you can't surround yourself with in your own home, that beauty I know you need like air for breath. Whenever I do, I feel, again, how blind I am—indifferent and hasty—and am afraid, again, that I've lost the first natural passion for beauty for good.

Your name. I haven't told you. I say "Miriam" to myself more and more, replacing so many other words—Miriam is understand—come—accept me—I feel good—I feel bad—secret—to grow—silence—your breasts—your heart—to breathe—clemency.

Still, didn't you want another child? Were you scared? Are you trying at all, or do you want to give the whole of yourself only to Yokhai? You are so silent about these matters, still holding your clenched hands close to your sides.

You were right in your decision not to write down the "formal" name of his disease—so that the name won't gradually replace his. Until what age will you be able to keep him at home (and how? How have you been able to not put him into an institution until now?).

He'll start growing up soon, and the difficulties will grow with him—I'm not telling you anything new. He will also be a lot stronger, physically, than you are—and then what? How will you control him during his seizures? How will you prevent him from running into the street?

". . . I already know that it will be especially hard on me when his voice changes." And in another letter you almost casually mentioned that his voice is the most beautiful part of him.

(I put these two sentences together only just now.)

Just a small thought: a pint-sized dime-store philosophical thought.

Perhaps, in that moment, in my fantasy of pupils rubbing together—the tears that burst out will be completely different from those familiar to regular users. I mean—maybe those tears will be sweeter than honey—they will drip drop drip and drip from some reservoir of hidden tear ducts that we never knew of—the sole bodily organ created in the knowledge that there will never be any use for it, throughout the entirety of life. God's sad, private joke—because He knew ahead of time just whom He was dealing with. Because you may overcome gravity, but you can never overcome the repulsion, the rejection from a soul suddenly finding itself in front of another soul that's gaping open—and immediately blinking—the blink, an instinctive border patrol.

I need you so much right now, Miriam. Come to me, sit with me on the bed, ignore all the voices, the smells—focus only on me, concentrate on me, *make* me concentrate on you, stroke my face quietly, not sexually—say "Yair"—

Open up a window, open it wide. If you open it, the scenery will be different—if you open it, the pool club below will disappear—the towels and used sheets on the laundry lines, the trash cans, the pipes, the rats running though the alleys will disappear. Even the Lysol will evaporate with the air you will bring from afar, from Beit Zayit. Perhaps you will even try to make me laugh a little—why not? I haven't even smiled in the past few days. Say, "Oh, Yair, Yair, where do I start?" Scold me a little—but this time, do it gently, please. *You're talking about Yokhai, and* asking me if I don't want another child—and in the same breath, you're asking me to make you laugh? I know, I know, but still, tell me something light right now—it doesn't matter what . . .

But you would be surprised—even Yokhai is funny sometimes. What are you talking about? Yes, truly he is, even though he doesn't really have "a sense of humor" in the usual sense of the phrase. Sometimes I even comfort myself by pretending that his humor actually belongs to another world. But sometimes, like when he wants another piece of candy and knows we won't give it to him. He'll pretend to go to his room—and then turn and run to the kitchen with this squirrely, almost mischievous expression on his face . . . And then we can enjoy a kind illusion that his secret, other humor has met ours for one moment.

*Or his problem with shoes—*what was his problem with shoes? *Don't you remember?* I don't. *But I told you about it!* But you never told me about it in Tel Aviv, and never when I was on this bed with bubble gum stuck to it—tell me. *Well, he always, always goes barefoot in the house, in the summer and winter, because the moment you put shoes on his feet, he immediately leaps up, decisively, to go outside. If Amos or I get confused and put his shoes on before he is completely dressed, then he shoots himself outside, sometimes half naked, like a programmed missile. And that, you know, is why I always call him the boy with the thousand-league boots—*

But you need a different kind of laughter right now, don't you? Perhaps I'll amuse you with a little nonsense—why not? You write such nonsense sometimes that it gives me goose bumps . . . But come, let us laugh together—about me. Did you know that I have all sorts of complicated tests for the world? For instance: if the first person in this place at this time who approaches me is a man, your next letter will disappoint me a little. If it is a woman . . .

Look at me, playing make-believe. But I still feel it healing me a little, I don't understand how—just channeling your voice numbs the pain, reassures me—like medicine flowing through my body, percolating you through my blood—don't stop, don't ever stop.

I have also developed a sensitivity (a bit heightened, I think) to all kinds of events and people crossing my path—even words, the simplest words that come to me in the everyday stream, grab my attention, make me alert, ready . . . entirely innocent words . . . "light," "sprinklers," "there's a hole in the fence," "intimate," "camels," "night" . . . *Or the sudden hug I gave Yokhai yesterday, a bit frightened.*

I am writing to you from that place in my brain I described—I am aiming all my energy, with all my strength, to that spot—where you spring from—for those words kept only for one particular woman, not for any other.

Or I turn on the transistor radio, trying to hear the message that's been sent to only me: sometimes a line in a song that sounds to me as if it belongs to us— sometimes a meaningless sentence appears and I tell myself then, Here, everything between us is an empty illusion.

Listen, I am going to buy cigarettes. I finished my carton, and this is going to be a long day. Don't move—you're just right—just like that—

(But I have to quote you from the wall as a farewell kiss): " . . . I feel more and more that the stories you tell me are your way, the most natural and possible way for you, to somehow enter into the world, enter the earth, hit roots."

A terrible thing happened. I saw Maya.

Just now. On the boardwalk. She probably couldn't stand my silence—or felt, perhaps, that something was wrong and came to look for me. She didn't see me—and I didn't go to her, imagine that (so what do you think about me now?).

I should probably not write about that. She traveled along my entire daily trek twice, from the square to the Dolphinarium, entered the same exact restaurants and pizzerias I went to when I was still eating—she guessed my moves with such precision—I told you she has a sixth sense, a sense for me, and you didn't believe me. I felt your doubt the entire time. Don't mistake her, Miriam, don't mistake us: we have a bond, she and I; I don't even have the words to describe it. It is a wordless bond, it is all body, all touch, it lives in the senses, under the skin. (And what the hell do you know about us anyway?) Listen, I walked behind her, only a few steps behind her the entire time, what torture—as if something was choking me, wouldn't let me talk to her. What have I done?

I saw her, I saw everything. What she is when she is like any other woman on the street. How men look at her. The way she has matured in this last year. That she is suddenly terribly lovely. It is as if, without me paying any attention, her face, all her features, found the right places; still, I could also see that only I, of all the men on the street, truly knew how to discern her beauty, yes, and she keeps herself only for me. She doesn't have that damned thing—do you understand? That—*hunger*—is not in her. That thing in me and you is not in her. She is clean, she is pure. What will happen now? I walked after her, watched how she became heavy, despaired of me, was defeated. And then—she went to Mrs. Meiers's hotel. I once showed it to her in its glamorous heyday. She walked in and asked Thief-Eyes something—I don't know what he told her. She walked out immediately, didn't touch the door handle.

Then she took one last walk along the boardwalk. She didn't look for me anymore. She walked like a madwoman, half-running, stamping with rage on every step. People were looking. I have never seen her this way, letting herself understand it so completely—and then she sat down, fell into one of those plastic beach chairs, and closed her eyes. I stood maybe ten steps behind her, completely exposed—if she had turned around, she would have seen me in my nakedness—up to my neck in the most putrid swamp of my ignominies. We stayed still for almost a quarter of an hour—we didn't move, not a hair. I was so exhausted, I screamed to her soundlessly, and with all my strength. If she had turned around for a moment, if she had only seen me and said my name, I would have gone home with her.

How could such a thing have happened between us? I felt myself in the throes of some seizure after she disappeared—all my muscles, even my jaw, contracted. But what could I have told her? How do you start to explain in my state?—I haven't spoken to another human being in four or five days.

Only with you. I've spoken only with you. Enough. Let me sleep.

Middle of the night. Three sanitation workers from the health department knock on the door. They seize Maya quickly, pull her away, and throw a net over my side of the bed. Maya's hand hovers over her lips as is customary in these cases: "Please, don't take him away!" "We're not taking him away," laughs one of them. "We're shooting him on the spot."

Then they discover that I can't be killed. I'm eternal, like nothing.

I didn't tell you—when I was on the way back—maybe because of what happened, or because I hadn't seen a human face in days—suddenly, all of a sudden, it all became clear to me.

Okay, hold on—slow down—okay.

I found a neglected coffeehouse. My mind was knotted up like intestines. I sat there for an hour and thought that somewhere in the universe there must be that other world we once talked about—a world of light. A worthy world. Where each person finds the one intended for him and each love is true love; and, as an added bonus, you live there for all eternity. I (you know me) immediately wondered about who would be incapable of living even there, so unfit for such generous and bountiful goodness, these damned ones who commit suicide there.

There I sat, gazing at the people walking by, occupied by different ideas about what the sentence for suicide would be in that world. How would I punish them? And, Miriam, it doesn't matter where you are right now; lift up your eyes (I guess my fantasies of you always show you deep in thought, like the one time I saw you) and say, Could that be the reason? I mean, for the ugliness and strangeness and temporality, the cowardice and the interminable burdens, and the rest of our true Esperanto alphabet?

What I mean is, is here, where we are—is *this* is the penal colony of that other world?—and has each person you see around you—man or woman, it doesn't matter, old or young—at some point already committed suicide?

Look at the first man coming toward you now, right now, and tell me his face isn't—even in one tiny single line—hiding a confession of participation in a crime. Any crime. (It might be hiding in the nose—in his loose, fallen lips—in his forehead—and, most of all, in his eyes.) This morning every person out there who passed me had one such line on his face—I saw it even in the most beautiful people.

Even in children. There was a group of them on the shore. I stood there gazing at these six- or seven-year-old kids—and almost every one of them had on his face some possible first line of bitterness and complaint and guilt. (Mainly guilt.)

Sleep. What sleep? Who sleeps? You don't come here to this shelter of ejaculation to sleep. Half past one, the middle of the night, and this building is full of life. A door is opening or being shut somewhere at every moment. Shuffling in the corridors twenty-four hours a day. Echoes of furtive laughter. (What are they laughing so much about?) I would kill to meet one of them in the hallway and shake him until he tells me exactly where this is all happening—where are the rooms with the Jacuzzis and the mirrors on the ceilings and the round beds?! When I left the hotel this morning, I saw a pair of these "tenants" for the first time. They came down with me in the elevator. We tried not to look one another in the eye. A man and a woman. Older tourists. They seemed so very conservative and upstanding that I almost fell for it.

How long has it been for you there, still on earth?

I will not leave this room again. I guess I've already gotten used to it in here. I noticed that I am more nervous on the outside. I am no longer absorbed by thoughts of whatever is going on behind the closed doors (quite banal doings, I imagine). It's strange how it is possible to pass the time without even moving—dozing off, waking up, smoking, writing a few words to you, dozing off again—and ten hours have passed.

Thoughts—when they aren't bumping into other people's thoughts—are capable of racing to the end of the world in a flash—they can zoom out of your mind and return in a second.

But even this function has slowed down in the past few hours. Everything is slightly vague, indifferent; I'm not even hungry.

In order to read your tiny handwriting, sometimes I have to get really close to the wall. You should see me walking along and across these walls.

And if I called you, would you dare brave such a place? (My good little girl with the fifties face—I would never do that to you.)

————

I guess I fell asleep again for a moment. I woke up with my heart pounding. Three a.m. And to my right, in one of the more distant rooms, they are truly out of control (from here it sounds like big drums or pistons—a completely mechanical noise). You were with me until I fell asleep. I brought you here, I was lying down and talking to you aloud. We had a conversation (I don't remember about what). Each time I spoke from your mouth, I recovered a piece of myself. For half a night you illuminated me like a candle.

A little concentrated entity is traveling inside my body, through my bloodstream. I don't think about it most of the time, most of the time I don't think about anything, but each time it passes through my heart, it opens its eyes and says *Yair*, with your voice.

According to my calculations, I should know by tomorrow or the day after if I've been infected. What's strange is, I don't really care. I swear. Most of the time I don't even think about whatever reasons threw me in here. If someone asked me why I am here, I would have to concentrate to remember.

Why am I here?

Because I need to finish some important business.

What business?

I don't know; I'll know when it happens.

And what will you do in the meantime? Just lie like that, on that bed, for days on end?

Yes. What can I do?

I am sleeping in bed with Maya. She wakes me up and shows me that a tiny woman, the size of a nut, is lying between us, a whole, complete woman. I immediately start to make my excuses—I didn't do it! I don't even know her! And Maya says in a voice without anger and with even a little compassion, But look how closely she resembles you.

Maybe I will write a diary to pass the time in my remaining days. Not so long ago you called me "My dear diary."

If I feel at all better tonight, I'll go out. I deserve a little vacation from the monastery, don't you think? (Why do I care so much about what you think?!)

At times I feel like an idiot for not really using this week. I do not understand what's keeping me from going wild. Do I owe anything to anybody here?

On the other hand, even getting up for a piss is a major operation.

If I am actually infected—

What should I do, do you think, to save a part of myself in the few days I have left? What would you do if you knew you had only one week before you caught a disease with these *particular* complications?

I mean—(just a thought—the intellectual amusement of a potentially impotent man)—could one hope for a sudden new love to save me from the claws of disease? Or, at the very least, make it retreat a little?

No, it's not in you. I probably won't fall in love with you—that's quite clear to me. What kind of love could we have? I mean, what we already have between us is too weighty to be love, isn't it? I don't think poorly of it, but over the last few days, I've had a feeling that we are somehow too densely packed to push ourselves into that single word "love." Correct me if I'm wrong.

Correct me.

Those two on the other side of the wall are really molesting each other. I'm sure those are whipping noises. It's been like that for a few hours now. No human voices—it's as if they are whipping and getting whipped in complete silence—and I am the only one who shrinks at every blow. I can't get used to it—it is as if every hit is the first. What were we talking about? The last page I wrote to you fell onto the floor. Good luck finding a needle in this haystack. I've eaten hardly anything since coming here. Previous years—huge feasts. It was part of the pleasure. Food is a man's best friend, too. It surprises me—I am really not hungry at all—only a little weak, floating along in this way. It feels kind of nice—but if I stand up too quickly, I get dizzy. So I try not to stand up. Actually, I've been in bed most of the time since yesterday (or the day before?)—a pad of paper, a pen, waking up, writing a few lines down, falling asleep. In between times, someone might as well be performing an operation on me with full anesthesia—oh well, let it be.

In the window across from mine, above the pool bar—a guy and a girl, Japanese, very young—with no curtains. With open windows. They've been making love for a whole hour now. It is so beautiful, it isn't even sexy.

I lie here, in the dark, watching. They are very much in love—and there isn't a spot on their skin they don't kiss. I desperately hope they continue on this way—because all the surrounding noises have stopped.

Terribly urgent—I suddenly remembered it. I want to give you one picture, a flicker of my memory—don't ask questions—a picture of one sweet little child, with very short hair; you can see only his mobile, expressive face; and he is jumping around, talking, waving his hands, a bit monkeyish in his sweetness. He's about five in the picture. A woman's delicate hand is resting on his head. Ignore it.

It's a very precious moment to me—it doesn't matter why—simply accept it from me. A boy walking with his mother on the sidewalk, back from kindergarten. She is a young woman, tiny and slender, with short curly hair and a gorgeous smile—shy and bold and full of love. And her hand is on his head, presenting him to me with a small show of pride—this is her boy.

I know one doesn't do such a thing, giving as a gift a picture that has been cut up, or half a photograph—but believe me, you are getting the prettiest part, and also the most beautiful moment I had with those two. There's no point in enlarging the angle of the shot and seeing all the extraneous details—that, for example, another boy is walking by their side. He isn't even part of the story, he is just another boy she is picking up from kindergarten that day, her son's friend (why can't I remove him from this picture?).

And why would you want to see the man with the birdlike face, sitting in the Subaru, the one that had been in the sprinklers, from whose trunk I took out the towel to dry your hair? The man is me. And the other boy accidentally looked up and saw what was in my face, which was apparently entirely exposed, full of joy pouring out to her and her boy. An ugly story, really, another usual scene from my film noir. Why am I telling you this?

My story with her, with that woman, was actually longer than the usual. I think I loved her. The boy's name was G. His full name doesn't matter, his sweet, serious name. She wasn't married, and didn't want to get married either—she had definite opinions in her opposition to marriage—but she had a little boy, and I (pathetic, self-deceiving in such affairs) enjoyed feeling a bit like his father from afar. Do you understand? I felt that this was the kind of boy she and I could have had. Don't forget, he was my ideal child—a living child I could transport into my imaginary world.

I mainly loved the combination of those two—and how she raised him with wisdom, with courage. It's not simple to raise a child alone—and until I met her, I always, with the sacred fury of marriage on my side, railed against women like her, who dared to produce a child by themselves, only to satisfy their maternal instincts, etc. She taught me how much greatness could be contained in such a situation. I was constantly amazed at how she alone was making a person in the world, with what totality and cleverness. Their pride in belonging to each other—the private language that was so completely theirs—a mutual sense of humor—and some kind of guarantee for each other. I felt as if I had a little secret family there, even though I had never seen the child, only in pictures.

Truly, why am I telling you this?

Because of how hard it is to break a habit? Or because I believe you will keep it better than I can?

One day she proposed that I meet him. We had just spent a great morning together, and she said, Why don't you stay a little longer once and meet G.? And I said, Why not? What's the worst that could happen? But, on the other hand, as you well know, my security officer was alerted: Why do I need him to see me? Who needs such a witness? So I suggested that I watch him from afar, without him seeing me. And N. looked at me and said, "You don't have to, you know."

Later I appeased her a little, and she agreed with my rationale—and we both started to get excited about that moment. I stayed a little longer than usual that day, and we had lunch together, and everything was great. And when it was time, I went down to the car and waited, while N. picked G. up from kindergarten.

I saw her coming around the corner, slender, independent, standing out in sharp detail against the street, with her short curly hair and laughing eyes, wearing a thin gray sweater. She was walking with two kids, as I told you. For a moment I couldn't tell which one was hers. Neither of them really resembled the pictures. The kids were walking and describing something to her enthusiastically. One of them bounced around her like a lamb. She smiled at me from the end of the street, walking toward me—smiling and shining in all her slenderness—and I had to take off my sunglasses and ask, with my eyes, Which one is yours? She laid a palm on the head of the child bouncing along at her side and made a face that said, "What kind of question is that?"

Please, accept this picture from me: a child, small for his age, alert and full of joy, full of life and wisdom, talking with large hand gestures. A child so funny and sweet—her hand resting gently on his head. My eyes sank into hers, into her pride and her complete happiness.

(The strange part was that of all of them, the other child, the stranger, noticed something—and stopped for a moment, following my gaze and hers. I could see him trying to understand, and some kind of cloud forming on his innocent forehead.)

If I had to choose one single moment, out of all the fucking, the lovemaking, the flirtations—

I'm sorry to drop this story onto you—but, again—who could I tell, if not you?

I have gotten used to talking to you aloud (have I already told you?), mumbling to you as if you were here. Talking in small, simple fragments . . . Would you like a pillow? Give me some more blanket, scratch my back—no, higher—yes.

You ask, Why don't we go for a walk? Breathe some different air? Look at this mess—at least let's throw away those empty beer cans—come on, you can help yourself out of this, just a little.

And I tell you: It's strange, I miss you more than I miss my family. And the girl in the room next to mine is really sobbing—you can't decipher her words—or even tell what language she's speaking in—but there is some kind of constant whimper—if I concentrate, I think I hear her begging him not to burn her with cigarettes. What hell.

I finally couldn't take it anymore—I went out and looked for where the voices were coming from. It turned out they weren't from the room next to mine—they weren't even on my floor. Acoustic illusions were bouncing throughout the building. I got ambitious—I ran through all four floors, listening shamelessly by every door—I didn't care about getting caught. I didn't have a clue as to what I would do if I ran into somebody—but, why, people here were actually paying for things like that! I started thinking, It's a ghost hotel, until, on the fourth floor, I heard very clear voices coming from one of the rooms—and nerve-racked as I was, I pushed the doorknob and entered. I saw the naked back of a man watching television—surrounded by maybe twenty empty beer cans scattered on the floor. The room looked exactly like mine—and the man didn't hear me and didn't move (the room smelled like maybe he was dead). When I returned to my room, so did the voices.

There's something else. If I don't tell you, you will never know, to the far reaches of my being, exactly whom you are dealing with. (What am I worth if I tell you? What am I worth if I don't?) This kind of event pays you back—with high interest—for all the slime you scattered behind you in the world. Listen, forget it—have this written inside you:

I was at home with Maya, about two years ago. We were eating supper in the kitchen. With Ido. It was a nice, quiet evening, just the way I like it. The phone jangles—I walk down the hall to pick it up—and hear the voice of a woman telling me her name is T. and she is a friend of N.'s. I immediately remember who she is, and the pit of my stomach clenches a little. T. was the only witness to our affair—and why is she calling my home? She tells me in a tense voice that N. died yesterday.

I'm silent. Maya and Ido are laughing behind me. He was learning how to whistle then (by sucking air inward), and Maya was trying to learn how from him—and on the telephone T. is asking me if I heard what she said. I say yes, and pulling together a slightly formal voice, I tell her that we don't want a children's encyclopedia.

Now she is silent. I remember that, in the remains of my mind's clarity, I was wondering what would happen to G., he must have been seven or eight. Since I had broken up with N., she and I had kept no contact. She promised not to call or write and, of course, kept her promise. It's terrible to say it now—but on my part, I mean, I practically wiped her out of me after we ended things.

Please understand—T., the woman on the phone, accused me of adultery and dishonesty throughout the entire course of our affair. She never told me directly, but I understood exactly how T. felt about me from a few disapproving silences. And even though I never met her, I felt that I always had to justify myself to her. (I was not a little occupied with what her opinion of me must be.)

And she says, I understand I must have called at an inconvenient time.

Maya calls out from the kitchen, Who is it? We always report our callers to each other—we don't even have to report it at this point—most of the time we can tell who it is from the other's "Hello."

I say aloud, You know what—it wouldn't hurt if you gave me a few details on this new encyclopedia.

And Maya in the kitchen says, "By the time he learns to read, it will already be out of date."

I make a "let's hear him out" gesture. Ido tries to say, "En-cy-clo-pe-di-a," and they both laugh—and the kitchen sails away from me.

T., who waited through this cozy conversation patiently, said quickly, with disgust, that N. had passed away yesterday at Hadassah Hospital after having been very ill for half a year. I didn't even know she had gotten sick. She had died twenty minutes away from me. I didn't feel anything—and there had been hours when my soul had touched her soul.

I also thought about how faithfully she had kept her promise—she didn't call me even once, even when she got sick—she didn't even write. She was so strong, so faithful to me—and I was such a jerk for giving her up as I did. And I actually knew so little about her.

I could have never told you this story, couldn't I? Couldn't I? I have this stupid belief that if I tell you, nothing like it will ever happen to me again, in my life.

I wanted to know what had happened to her during those years—what would happen to her child now. I asked a few more empty questions, verbal dung for the satisfaction of my listeners. T. ignored it, quickly gave me the details about the funeral, and hung up. And I hung up the phone because we weren't interested in buying encyclopedias. I returned to the kitchen, and M. asked me if I had fallen for another one.

I. showed me his whistle. And I? I sat down to my supper, and talked and laughed and whistled inward and outward, and felt like those Nazis who would come home to their families after work.

My hand hurts from writing. The blinds are shut, so I can forget, for a moment, if it is day or night. I don't know how you will feel about this story. But look at it this way—you were gracious to me—you were the pit in the ground into which I could, once, yell out this secret. I've never even told myself about it since it happened.

Listen, I've probably been looking for you for years, and in my search I wasted so much, constantly making too many mistakes by following the paths of too many coincidences. It's becoming clearer to me that I've been looking for you for a long time—like a man in a smoke-filled room looking for a window. I guess everything was upside down. I've always thought coincidence was my original sin—and also my most recurring sin—because my most important decisions have been made without any strong intentions—and certainly without this "lingering" of yours. In the past few days, though, I am starting to realize that perhaps it is the other way around: Coincidence is not my sin but my punishment.

It's a rather horrible punishment. You know what? It is the most horrible punishment. It proliferates, it spreads everywhere. A person, for example, thinking about a child—it even doesn't matter whose child—it could be his own son—and he suddenly asks himself, How can it be possible? That a child, a wonder of creation, is born of an encounter that is not fated—and is preventable—between two

(Does it ever occur for you—you write a sentence that, a moment earlier, you had no knowledge of? Not in this way, never to that extent—suddenly a short, terse verdict is laid in front of you—with no possibility of appeal.)

Miriam,

A few minutes ago (it's now seven in the morning)—I heard a noise. I jumped out of bed (I guess I had fallen asleep for a little bit)—I was convinced that they had come to rob me, or rape me (anything is possible here), and saw that someone had pushed some paper under the door.

Your letter.

Finally, from light-years away—I think it came in the mail a couple of days ago and has lain on the check-in counter since (the envelope is covered with scribbles and doodles and phone numbers in many different handwritings). It's a shame it didn't reach me earlier—it would have helped me a lot, saved me. I haven't opened it yet. I can't. I'm afraid I will not be able to stand such joy in my present condition. I'm also a little afraid of what is inside, that thing you were wondering about telling me. I don't think myself capable of handling anything too heavy right now. Maybe I'll take a small nap and later—

But I'm already feeling different—completely different (as if they returned my ID card to me).

One more moment—I want to suck all the sweetness from the moment before.

A new yearning for home has awakened within me. I phoned Maya and we talked. Everything is fine—Ido has already recovered. He hasn't had a fever for a few days now and is just a bit swollen. I ironed out my soul a little, and hers—I heard the noises of home in the background. She told me she had come to Tel Aviv to look for me. I didn't say anything. Neither did she. Suddenly we sighed together—at least that was something good, our joined sigh. I was filled with affection for her—we are good friends. I might not have given her her due in these letters. It is still hard to talk about her to you—too many voices mixing together. But in life, in reality, she is my best friend—you know that, don't you? She is the light and the heat, the bloodstream and the tissue of my life. She truly is my daily joy. It is all so complicated.

I told her I couldn't come back yet. She was silent again. I told her that something was happening to me here, it got a little convoluted, I went somewhere I didn't mean to go—and now I have to continue to untangle the mess. I made it clear to her that it was something with myself. She said, Take your time. I told her it wouldn't take long, just a few more days. She said that if it was important to me, she would manage. I thought about how generous she is, and how horrible I would have been to her, and how much I would have argued with her had our positions been reversed.

After that, I dialed your number, and hung up before you could pick

up the phone. But even the ringing was enough to make me feel better—
that I was still capable of creating a sound you would hear.

I'm going to read your letter.

Just a moment.

Hey, Miriam . . .

Too heavy to contain, too dense to contain, too tense to contain—and
yet, still—look at what a huge space you have cleared for me inside yourself—me with all my elbow angles poking you.

I wanted to simply jump into a taxi now, at this moment, at ten at
night, to fly to you and hold you close, with all my strength, to stroke
your face, comfort you. I wanted to lie with you, so I could be as close as
possible to the story, to the place of that story, of you and Amos and
Anna. And Yokhai.

You can probably guess the nausea I feel over some of the things I
wrote to you over the past months unintentionally, innocently, rudeness,
stupidity—without paying attention, with the cruelty of a baby crushing
a chick—they all rise up in my throat.

My spoiled nonsense about the mumps—and what would *you* do if
you had a disease with such complications . . . How the hell could you
stand me?

I wish you could feel how much I am with you now, in body and soul,
more than ever—practically reigniting a huge engine inside me. I'm
coming back, Miriam. I don't want to remember where I have been these
past few days, to what depths I sank. I want to wake up to life, to give
you all my genetic material, what I am, for better or for worse, with my
words. The microscopic double helix of my DNA spiraling through
every sentence of mine to you. I'm writing wretched nonsense, I know,
because now I want to bring you even my stupidity, and my enthusiasm,
my cowardice, and my treachery—and the miserliness of my heart. But I
also have two or three good things in me that could mix with all of your
goodness. Let my fears mate with yours, our disappointments and failures—only yesterday I wrote how insulting it is to think of a child being
born by the non-fatal combination of a man and a woman. And you
never, not once, told me how many times that similar combination of
words had floated in your mind—when a child was not born. Why

didn't you tell me? You hid such a thing from me for six months—what were you afraid of?

Maybe you didn't trust me—didn't feel I could be a lightning rod for your sorrow and pain—or thought I wasn't worthy. Is that it? I was unworthy to hear such a story of yours? That's it, isn't it? I'm reading between your lines, and it insults me and stings me to the edge of despair—until now you weren't sure whether you should tell me. Perhaps you were frightened that I would pollute such an amazing tale of purity. You hesitated so much over whether I could be trustworthy—

Miriam, if you have any feeling left toward me, a shred of goodwill, help me—don't make it easy on me—now—*now*—be my knife. Ask me how it is possible that still, even now, I have to suppress a miserable urge to run immediately from the disaster area each time you expose another one of your wounds in front of me. I, of course, will deny it—and tell you that, on the contrary, your mothering of Yokhai is even more wonderful to me now that you've told me; and that ever since you told me, I have felt the new enormous power you possess, and it pulses in three different places in my body—deep in my mind, on the left side—in the fireball under my heart—and in the root of my dick—and if you draw a line connecting the three, you will have a precise portrait of me at in this moment—

This is what I will say. And you will yell, Enough, enough! Because you know already that when I write this way, this enthusiastically, I am lying; I am again intimate only at shouting distance. Save me from myself, please. Look straight into my eyes and ask me again, as you did in the letter, if the muscles in the back of my soul are not arching away right now—if you aren't suddenly becoming too heavy for my amorphous delusions to hold. Ask me more than that. Ask me if I understand what I truly feel when you pull your stitches out in front of me like this. Don't make it easy on me—defend me from my black twin, because I can't do it alone. I can't defeat him. Demand that I understand what I feel when this wound of yours gapes in front of me, mercilessly, sucking me in and closing over me—ask me if I even know how to feel another person's pain. And do I know where it is supposed to hurt—the hurt he feels—do I understand in what part of the body it hurts? Do I really believe, in the depths of my heart, that it is possible to ache with another's pain, or is it, in my eyes, just a social convention, a shared lie, an empty cliché. Another person's pain. I repeat the word "pain" the way Yokhai repeats words he doesn't understand—you said that in this particular way of stepping into puddles he is trying to bring this thing he is not certain of into his own existence, into existence outside himself. Pain, pain, pain.

I have to go out, buy—something. I've been living on yogurt and beer for almost a week—and finished the yogurt this morning. I will not survive another night without solid food, and they'll be closing the night grocery store on Ben Yehuda in fifteen minutes. You know what really makes me feel despair? You told me something so serious, so difficult, and I am still incapable of being who you really need—a man who knows you as you are with yourself, between you and yourself. I haven't reached the secret you are. Please, don't go easy on me, please tell me—

Yair, Yair, come and feel my body, right now, all of it; make me overcome the embarrassment of little words that are giggling like girls, tell me to become rounder, become fuller; *feel how I spread in you into the farthest reaches that don't exist in your flesh, that are only possibilities in you*—whisper to me to feel your breasts, their roundness and softness, at the exact point of gravity that pulls them downward and to the sides, the part of the breast that's always highlighted in paintings. Ask me to loosen my shoulders and smile—*Loosen them. Even though mine are pretty tense as well, ten years of Alexander and they're still tense.* Go on, keep going, all the time, for eternity, tell me again and again—*Loosen up, loosen up, feel how your face slowly becomes soft and round; be delicate, don't be afraid of that word. Perhaps you could have been a happier man if you had dared to be a bit more delicate, allowed yourself to be filled with your own delicacy—it is in you, it's right for you, it's your hidden spring, don't shut it down with stones.* And tell me, *Come and flow into my body; inscribe words into my veins throughout the length of my body, down my legs and between them—so I can feel, for once, what it feels like when it is yours, not only what you desire. But you are so tense. Yair, maybe it is because I am tense now, as if preparing for pain, because . . . now, my belly . . . I am asking you to fill my belly, my soft, empty . . .*

Don't stop. You mustn't protect me, not in this place we are in—that's our contract, isn't it, Yair? We're hand in hand, and tonight we write everything.

Words of truth. (How do you like to say in your high-flown language "*Kosht Imrei Emet*"—a sheaf of truths?) *Write, write whatever comes to your mind, and my mind . . . fill my belly from within, search in me for that spot, my blind spot, that you once named without even noticing—"my body and my soul, recognizing each other once again, I can actually hear the whisper of the internal password (srsrsrsrsr . . .)." Imagine for a moment how my hopes collect there, in a puddle, from month to month, that then transforms into a dagger of sorrow and despair, gloom of the soul and gloom of the body.*

Remember then how you saw me for the first time on that evening; now that you finally understand why I was so miserable, what I was despairing over at the moment you looked at me—the private, sad visit I received that day.

The void of "almost."

Don't leave the room—be with us. My words are coming out of your mouth, it is so strange . . . Your will excites me, and embarrasses me in an indescribable way—but don't you remember, this is the exact one and only story I wanted to tell you: the story of a complete entering into the other, not to get lost in him, and certainly not to give up yourself, but in order to experience, just once, a stranger, I mean, another in you . . .

I can now, with all my body and soul, feel your desire for it, Yair—and your fear as well. They are both raging within you, as they always, always do with you. You touch my pain with your bare hands for a moment, and I can feel how precious it is to you and that you truly do not want me to be alone in it. And the moment after, you ricochet to the farthest reaches . . . Just don't come out of me, because if you leave me now, you will never return. You will run to the ends of the earth, and you will never want to remember what is starting inside you now, with me . . . your soul, slowly, painfully opening up this way to another person. Just don't stop writing—hold on to your pen with all your remaining strength. You're shaking with tension, but as you write, you hit more roots in me . . . Don't be afraid, not even from that thought you had once, a million years ago, or was it two days—you wanted to wake up without your memory, after an accident, or an operation, and start remembering our story, step by step, and tell it to yourself from the beginning, without knowing for even one moment whether you were the man or the woman in the story.

I also wish you could remember yourself as a woman—or as not-man and not-woman—the you before everything, before definitions and genders and words and the sexes; perhaps, in this way, you will also arrive—as if by coincidence—at my initial potential, at the possibility of being me.

If you reach it, you will truly know how I am standing in front of you now; bent over a little, tense. You were so amazed by my motherliness—from the first moment, you practically sucked my maternity out of me—and the more you sucked, the more I flowed, and the more I flowed, the thirstier I was for it—and I never knew, never tried, and never dared to tell myself this tale with such intensity.

You can guess how I feel, now that you know the reality of the situation, the cold facts. But what can I do, Yair? I am probably not the most rational person when discussing this matter, my nonexistent motherhood.

And Darwin is not saluting me from his grave.

And you are right. It is very, very difficult to create something from two people.

But you are so truly a mother to me! This is not something that could ever change—it is your being, Miriam; and I could never think of you without feeling it (I all of a sudden understand—"Amos has a child from his first marriage." I never made the connection . . .) I can't stop thinking about those moments in the delivery room when she felt that something had gone very wrong in her body, and you promised her, immediately promised, you both promised—such a promise.

And how you are counting to a million with him. All the way to a million.

You know, perhaps there was such a moment in the spaces of time and entities, a fraction of a second when you could have been me, my possibility . . . What do you say? Can you believe there is truly such a place, can one ask such a wish from your Kremlin? No, don't turn on the light, the light here is too red . . . write in the dark. Your handwriting was very shaky in the last moments, a weeping hand. Do you remember how hurt I was when you never asked me what is my Luz? Time and time again I asked you to guess it, and you completely ignored me (you certainly know how to ignore certain questions), and eventually I gave up, and then I hadn't continued to ask even myself, and I lost the question.

   But now, write, tell me:
   More and more, I think that my Luz is my yearning.
   And what is yours?

Do you really want to know? No, you don't.

   You're silent. You're suddenly refusing to be written. The magic is gone. I know what you're thinking, it's written all over your face: ". . . and how is it that a person who so hungers for the love and love's nectar that it practically shouts out from his every word—how is it that he insists on stuffing himself with snacks . . ." I read it, I read it. It was an especially unnecessary section of your last letter. Let's leave it for now— it's a pity to spoil this. Don't try to change everything about me—and don't take that, in particular, away from me, because, in spite of your misgivings, it is certainly *a* Luz.

Don't leave, Yair, don't drop your pen; play your false game for me just one minute more, even though the muscles in the back of your soul are twisting away in you until the pain is unbearable. I know it well, you have made me feel things I almost couldn't endure, too. But now, as you sit with yourself in that room, perhaps lonelier than you have ever dared to allow yourself to be, I want you to write it once, for your eyes only—why you are doing this to yourself—and how it is that you are willing to allow strangers to enter your most wounded place.

Enough. I'm sick of being buried here, masturbating with words. Why, in this manner I could have you say anything I liked—and this infantile game has been going on for far too long. Two in the morning, and I've been writing for more than five hours straight. I'm completely muzzy-headed, and want something substantial, alive, warm, arching in my hands; and here I am instead, whipping myself over and over with thoughts of you. We're back to whipping me! I won't send you these; there is a point at which you and I begin speaking in different languages. And what the hell do you understand about this kind of wonder, anyway, when a person who was a complete stranger becomes the living center of all of your emotions and thoughts and imagination? What do you know about being inflamed? About heat between strangers? Complete strangers are the best of all, those familiar with all the amendments of the constitution, for whom it is clear that after the storm, they will go away and be alone. Alone. Do you want to hear something? Do you want to know how it really works, what everyone is thinking, everyone, behind their beautiful words and veiled looks?

So this is how it happened. After you came—after I did—we lay relaxed, breathing together, gurgling in our satiety—and after a few more minutes I yawned the Prelude Yawn of the "Well, Back to Our Lives" song and dance. You caught me in both your strong hands and said, *Don't go.*

I smiled into your neck, because the strange excitement in your voice made me laugh. And I stayed for a moment or two more, even dozed off for a bit—and then wanted to pull out, because how long could you stay like that anyway?—taken over by the need to straighten up our skins, like re-establishing the front lines after a big battle. A masculine voice was already buzzing with a sore throat inside me, What am I doing here with this strange body in the first place? So, because of that first step back—and because of my usual dishonesty in such a moment—I purred like an exceptionally satisfied cat that I would be willing to stay like this with you forever, and you said, quickly, *Then stay.* And I asked you, with a smile, Forever? And you said, *Yes. For eternity. For today. Don't go.* I laughed into your naked, warm shoulder that it would be simpler to cut it off for you and you could use it whenever you liked—because I still had a few errands to run that day—and you said with that strange urgency, *No, please, stay a little longer, as long as you can, as long as we both can—you're in no hurry to go anywhere today.*

You weren't speaking with your usual satisfied, wrung-out sex voice, but instead in a slightly frightened, pleading tone; I heard something new in your voice—not a momentary whim but a profound will—for a moment I thought I understood what you wanted to happen between us. I was almost tempted by it; I relaxed the muscles in my back and shoulders so you wouldn't feel the rebellion inside me, curling over to protect himself, so you wouldn't hear him inside me complaining, Hey, what's with her? What more does she want? She got hers already. And you, as if you heard, whispered, *Even though you want to pull out, don't, don't go—come on, get over it, stay with me just a little longer,* and I said, with a quarter of annoyed laughter, What is this? Some kind of human experiment? You didn't answer, just pressed your warm, soft chest to me, as if speaking with it, you spoke the language of the breast to me—I felt your breath close to my ear and was a bit confused, and didn't want to hurt you, because I felt you falling into one of your feminine moods, which have always been a bit too profound for me. My dick was shrunken and folded up in itself—as it always is during a moment of transcendent thought—but you didn't let it come out of you. Don't forget, I was a bit hungry, as I always am afterward. I lay there, uneasy, as if I had been forced to deposit my destiny in the hands of a stranger—it's odd you became so strange to me after such an intense intimacy—and the way you were sticking to me was just a shade too intimate for the moment—I wondered when you would tire of this game, when you would finish making this request with your heart, because I could feel around my dick how intently your eyes were closed—my hand had fallen numb behind your back, and my watch strap got caught and tangled in your hair—and I prayed to simply fall asleep, so that he—the recently deceased—would simply fall out and we could smile and forget—and you whispered to me in that voice, *No. Help me keep it in.* And I started to think that you could read my mind.

A bitter gob of ancient essences balled up in my throat, a low and hairy "ahem," and you felt it, of course—and didn't stop whispering in my ear, like a prayer, to be with you, and not with him: *Be with me, with me,* and I told myself to remember that I was planning to start doing back exercises again tomorrow, and tried to occupy myself with the lists of tasks awaiting me at work, I'd been neglecting things over there for too long. You whispered something into my ear—but you were too close, I couldn't hear you—and you passed your tongue delicately over it—we both contracted, together, my fish's tail fluttered for a moment, your sea rose toward it, and in my heart I thought, Well, all right, maybe it won't be too bad—it's been a long time since I've trembled twice without pulling out in between, I wonder how long I can last. You stretched your body out in front of me, and I passed my fingers down, strumming your spine, plucking your vertebrae, and licked your neck, which was a little salty. I thought to myself that the word "flesh" is a bit meaty, butchered—but if, in my heart, I say "Miriam's Flesh," it's as if a soft veil of delicacy and beauty spreads over the word, and in my heart I told myself over and over, "Her flesh, her body, her thighs." I remembered Maya then, for some reason—and the thought made me wilt at once, my spine sucked the entire thick sap back in, my head fell over heavily, and I said, Well, it's not working. You said, *But don't pull out, it doesn't matter, just don't come out.* I asked irritated, Fine, but for how long? And you whispered, as if asleep, *Until we're too scared.*

I thought to myself, This isn't scary, it's just exasperating—you have to listen to your body and know that if it wants to come out, you need to let it come out and not molest it. There is probably some biological reason connected to this need or impulse or instinct of ours; your insistence filled me with terrible unease and also a strange animosity toward you. I heard you breathing deeply, concentrating your breathing into my ear—and I remembered our little fancy that day we walked together—the one and only walk we've managed to take during our three full wild days together—that the ear looks kind of like the archaeological remains of an amphitheater—and maybe that's why they designed them like that.

But for how long are you planning for us to stay like this, I grumbled, and explained that as I am a defective human being made of flesh and blood, I have to pee every once in a while. You hugged me close and said, *Pee in me.* I thought about it for a moment, and believe me, I did try to enjoy the shred of delightful rudeness that drew me into your offer—and I asked if it wouldn't maybe be dangerous for your health or something. You mumbled that I was dangerous for your health—*and I'm not saying let's go fly together to the Land of Fire, only that we stay connected, body to body.* But what for? I was so annoyed by that point—I feel connected enough to you, I don't think there is a single place in my mind I could disconnect from you—you enter my childhood memories to meet me in them—your words nest in me and throw out my own fledglings—and I started to work myself into a rage just so I could prop myself up on my elbows and pull out of you that way—but you pulled me to you, hard and close, and said, *Does it annoy you that I enter your thoughts?* No, our meeting that night on the street was wonderful, as is the fact that I started dreaming again because of you. I can write your diary and reproduce your voice from mine more or less—it's pretty great, isn't it, great, fine, but now I wanted to pull out, definitely wanted to come out. You listened, smiled to yourself, and said, *Don't go.*

And I asked despairingly, Why? *So we will stay connected for as long as we can.* I buzzed back that any two dogs could be stuck together in this condition, so what's the matter—and you said quickly, *Don't run away, not now*—and what if I suddenly popped out, or didn't come out, or what if I did? *Listen* (you said)—*I need to pee, too.* So pee around me. *I can't, I'm too embarrassed.* So what do you suggest? *And what do you suggest? Do you know what? What?* Let's fall asleep, and then in our sleep we'll make it together like children . . .

And you laughed, because of the time I told you—or told you in my thoughts—how once, as an adult, I tried to pee in my bed and simply couldn't do it. And you knew, of course, why *I* was laughing—I was filled with pleasure at how you know everything about me, all my thoughts and the tiniest details of my stories—it suddenly so pleased me, when a moment ago it had annoyed me so much. I don't understand that. I don't understand myself with you—just as you said, in the place where I am the closest to you, I run away the most at the same time. Beware of me in that place—come to that place and I'll kick you like a horse—trust only my treachery—this is how you'll be protected. You, as if you weren't listening, said that even if we got soiled in that way, purity would be left, and we would possess it between ourselves. This time I allowed myself to be swept away by your high-flown sentimentality—you use words, I swear, that are like those community ceremonies from the fifties. I stupidly said that I believed you could purify me—and you asked excitedly, *Do you really think so?* Your left cheek blushed—and I said, If anybody can, you can. You closed your eyes and looked as if you couldn't contain it—I heard your thoughts, the clench of your flesh around me, and I knew you, again, were making a tremendous wish—but I was wrong. It was a vow. Apparently there are a few more letters of your body I still cannot read. *It is a vow between me and myself.* What is it? I asked, but I knew the answer immediately, without stopping it streamed from your body into mine. *Say it.* You vowed to sleep with me once for every time I have ever slept with a woman without love. *You're right.* Actually, you didn't say anything—I just felt your lashes down there caressing me. But I also started feeling trapped inside you, you weren't letting me breathe—you were wrapping yourself around me, holding me back in some unbearable way. You of all people should know how capable I am of having claustrophobic panic attacks, in someone else's body as well, if it locks around me suddenly. You clung to me and said, *But please, don't come out—I have to know what happens when you stay inside me this way, it has to happen with you.* And I said, I'll tell you what happens. We will rot here, together, in piss and shit, and maybe we'll even decompose and fuse together—maybe something else, something you can't even imagine, will happen to us. Some kind of mutation.

This is exactly what I hoped you would say, that perhaps something happens to two bodies that stay together in this way, in spite of everything, in spite of the natural impulses separating them eventually. I continued grumbling, again desperate—just what could happen? Your insistence became somewhat strange and burdensome—I started feeling like a child forced to kiss his aunt—explain it to me, what could happen except for another such half an hour? We'll be completely sick of each other! And you said, *But maybe we will discover something, some secret human beings mustn't find. Maybe we will travel together to reach some final, ultimate spot—and if you touch it, you will never want to separate anymore.*

But for how long! I yelled out—and you said, as if to yourself, *Until all the hairs on our bodies stand up in fear—not from embarrassment, or discomfort—I am talking about unbearable fear, combining with each other in totality—all boundaries falling apart—the absolute nakedness I thought you wanted so badly.* You weren't talking to me anymore, you were mumbling to yourself with some kind of odd decisiveness, trancelike, it didn't matter at all to you if I was listening, or comprehending you—the same way you sometimes dive into yourself in front of me. Those times, when you mumble to yourself—I truly feel that I am only a device for you, Miriam—that you actually strike a spark from me to ignite yourself to life—that this is truly a life-or-death war for you.

I don't like those games, I said—my voice sounded a little hollow, like a complaining child. You immediately responded, *This is not a game, I'm not playing with you—this is terribly serious.* You caught my face in your hands: *Look straight into my eyes,* and I backed away. I hadn't had the chance to warn you yet—these kinds of looks are dangerous to me; I suddenly start to feel my face as a network of thousands of tiny muscles, and then it's impossible to prevent them from starting to tremble and go wild, because the wonder is, all these muscles, cells, bones, nerves—they manage to stay clenched together as one entity in everyday life (these are things I mustn't even think about)—and how many thousands of muscles have to function, constantly, working so terribly hard just to hold a pair of lips together in a normal state—not to mention the strength of those tiny dams holding tear glands constantly closed—and it is so tempting to simply melt and drip into your body and be with you until you are dust. You scare me. You want to swallow me, you want me to disappear inside you. And, I whined, I'm also very hungry. *Take some grapes. They will give you strength and glucose.*

You reached a hand to the fruit bowl by the bed and pushed a grape into my mouth, saying, *This is not a grape,* anav; *this is an* anava—as if a grape could be a she-grape: the word sent a shocking wave of heat into my body—I bit into it, and juice sprayed onto your cheek and ran down. One drop hung on the corner of your lips—I licked it and passed half a she-grape from my mouth to yours—and I passed the whole of my tongue over your beautiful lips. *Come, my darling, lie inside me,* you whispered in your heart—and I was instantly filled—again, suddenly—and we entwined even closer to each other and fell into eternal time. I remember how you lifted your white legs up straight and tight in the air in one mind-blowing motion—and I tilted them so they both rested on my right shoulder—I leaned my head on them and thought, *Mew-ssic.* We both watched us, you and me, together, a player with his white cello—and this, together, pushed us even deeper into the heart of consummation—and enflamed us into fire—the smell of my sweat was as strong as it is now, as I write you—my body sticky, hot, my lips burning, my skin stinging with madness—we both came. We didn't care at all about the other's pleasure, didn't keep track of it in the way I am inclined to do—and the pleasure was so intense I had to think about something else immediately—the same way sometimes I have to read your letters through half-closed eyes—so I thought that the thin voice wailing out at that moment was my voice, and how strange it is that when I am with you, I come with a terribly squeaky voice—so I immediately made some thick basso sounds, even though I clearly know that, in your opinion, I was the most myself when I was screaming before. So, in order to put my manliness back in order, I roared out, as is customary, that the second time is always so much better and harder. For a moment you couldn't resist the light rudeness in my voice and drawled back in a deep, slightly exaggerated voice, *Oh yeah? What do you know, anyway? Poor men, who have to be satisfied with so little.* And we knew we were both only paying lip service to our sexes, that really, something was truly happening to us, because we were no longer representing them as is customary and appropriate. We managed, by some miracle, to escape from the usual political system of men and women—and because of our intimacy and our wallowing in each other, it's as if we had found a way to realize that our bodies are, after all, only a coincidence. Right? Just a few chunks of meat that happened to be stuck together in one way and not another. A man came out, or a woman—and it's true that this coincidence determines it—but just knowing that changes everything again. It's scary to write it down—as if the words themselves are capable of bewitching me—and then I would want this to last forever, the ability to move freely between sexes, to have my spirit finally fly like the bird in the oath of Bein ha-Betarim, the covenant of the flesh—

Miriam, I am still terrified of this feeling starting to rise up within me—that another step forward—I mean—if we walk another step forward—or further inward—we might both break the laws of personal possession in their most elemental sense, the sane sense, I mean. I am especially worried about you, yes, very worried—that you don't know how to keep a hold on yourself and are really capable of any insanity. There's nothing we can do—you have to acknowledge the facts. You're so exposed—your totality scares me. It is that clear to you that my feelings could never compare to yours, isn't it? Your wide range of shades and depths, and your abandon—and also your hidden demands that I be loyal to myself at least in the same way you are loyal to me, that I mourn being distinct from you—you have been broadcasting this to me this entire time, in these words, and in others— Don't even try to deny that you want to be me!

Just a minute, no—don't be easy on me—clench me with all the strength of your groin clamps, wrap your two legs around my body and whisper in my ear that this is you, and this is me, and that I won't pull out—fight me! I've been writing for hours, my words are starting to fall apart, I am in a state of exhaustion—I no longer know what to do with you—and that is the bitter truth. It's not that I am suddenly retreating, and I'm not saying that we should end things now, even before that stupid ultimatum, that guillotine finally—

Maybe we should stop this now, before it's really too late, Miriam.

October 13

Yair. It really is Yair. But I won't give you my surname.

I truly would have liked to tell you, tell you everything. What do you think? I could so easily write it down for you, here, in order—name, address, telephone number, occupation, and age—so there can at least be a clear path to the recipient of your feelings of disgust. But then, all those sweaty molecules will start sticking together into a new, epidermic story—and we will both die twice.

It really is better this way, believe me. Why do you want to know how small, how banal I am in real life?

That's it. This is where our broadcast ends, and our little hallucinations. And everything. I am in Jerusalem again, tightly screwed back into my life—you do understand that I cannot continue this after what happened. Even I have some limit to my baseness. I can't stand the thought of what you went through because of me, in those stinking places on the beach—it's only proof of how any connection with me continues to soil everything.

Miriam, Miriaaammm, oh, how I loved to roar out your name in the beginning. I'm now lying in the lowest cellar I have ever been in—I feel like a human roach. There is no punishment I deserve more than terminating my connection with you—it is the one judgment I can pronounce upon myself. I had almost written: "Who knows how long it will take until I'm myself again?"—but as you well know, who is that self, anyway, and who would even be interested in returning to it?

Because at least twice a day during my time with you, he would squeeze his hand through a crack in the door and inquire whether his nightmare was over already and whether you were gone—and I have no doubt that as soon as tomorrow rolls around— What am I talking about? Tomorrow? Tonight, now, when I seal this envelope! And I will see him sitting in my chair, legs up on the table, grinning at me: Baby, I'm home!

Enough, enough. Let's finish it. It's like the eulogy at my own funeral. In these past months you gave me the greatest gift I have ever received from anyone (I can only compare it to what Maya gave me when she agreed to have a child with me), and I've destroyed it. Oh well, I'm dedicatedly destroying what Maya gave me as well.

I can't describe in words what the thought of you getting up and leaving everything behind to come to Tel Aviv does to me. You were there for me; again, perhaps it seems only natural to you—you felt that I was in distress, and you sailed out to help—but it still moves me terribly to think that a person would do such a thing for another person—for me.

And the thought tormenting me now is that I became so absorbed in myself that I didn't see you, didn't guess that you were—that for two days we were perhaps a hundred meters away from each other—perhaps we even passed each other in touching distance—and I, what did I see? Only words.

To think of you walking between the prostitutes on the beach, approaching them and asking them—or going into the hotels that rent by the hour along Allenby and ha-Yarkon—then returning to walk there at night as well; and the "health clubs" and "massage parlors"—investigating, insisting and arguing with those loathsome characters over there—and that guy who looked at you and started following you, weren't you scared? Just imagine—a student of yours could have seen you—didn't you realize how crazy you were to do such a thing—for me?

My most terribly dear and wonderful Miriam—the horrible squeezing under my heart tells me that now is the moment I should have stood up and come to you and said, Let's try, why not, maybe we can— Your Honor, Judge, perhaps you will be lenient and order reality to loosen up its jaws just a little, so we can escape from them, for just one moment, and be two human beings who wish to be alone. Why not? Two human beings who like each other. Who will it hurt if they take shelter in each other and curl up together for two hours a week in some shitty motel, so they can watch what happens to them and find out where they can go together? Actually, Your Honor, why does it have to be a shitty motel? Go easy this time—let it go—ignore them—treat it like the rehabilitation of the outlaw I am; why can't you think of them meeting in a beautiful open space, on the seashore, in a glittering city, on the lawn of Ramat Rakhel against the desert, in the oak forest above the Kinneret . . .

You asked at the end of your letter, What will become of us now?

That's right: What will become of us?

Yair

Just another moment. I can't stop. It's as if everything will end if I stop writing.

I knew it from your response to my first letter—I knew you would take me to a very faraway place, over my horizon—and yet I still went with you—why did I go with you? After you wrote to me how thrilled you were by my letter, my first impulse was to cut it off immediately. Can you grasp what it means that this is what you wrote, at the beginning of all of this—without knowing who I was, without any games or pretense?

It is so rare—believe me, trust the expert; and even then I told myself, She is too good and innocent for your games of self-immolation—be gallant for once in your life! Let this one go—even Jack must have taken mercy and spared one woman from his ripping—mustn' he?

You will probably object to this comparison, but in some strange way your integrity now seems very close to what you called my "fuss and mirrors." It is not easily understood, your integrity—at least not by the common ruling laws of my swinish hypocrisy. It is a private integrity, made of your element alone, a battlefield created by the war of the strong forces within you that are constantly working together, mixing into one another. You touch all of it, and somehow don't die of it. On the contrary. I wish I could learn this wisdom from you—but I don't think I will ever be able to.

Does this cause me sorrow? Yes. And shame, too. Perhaps you think I don't even know what shame is. Please don't take away my right to be ashamed.

You know, all through the period of our correspondence I was faithful to you. I mean—this may sound pitiful to you, but still—I even lost the urge (well, almost) to look at each passing woman and fantasize about her or try my luck with her—and if I was momentarily tempted, I immediately felt how you (you, not Maya) shrank with pain. It is important to me that you know that there were no exceptions; this is not a simple matter with me. In this way, ten times a day, a huge surge of pride filled me for being *yours*. My pride over this, my "loyalty," probably makes you sick; truly, what right do I have to it, as we are actually talking about retreating to our rear lines of loyalty here. And still.

Miriam—this is my last letter. I will most likely not write to you again. You see? We never even reached the guillotine. We settled it on our own. If I wasn't such a fool, I could have been happy with you; it doesn't matter how—in any way the world would have allowed us to be happy. By the way, I'm looking at the date, and remember that it is your birthday this week, isn't it? You're forty years old this week. Three days ago, of course. You were probably waiting for me that day, hoping I would bring you a gift, that I would come to you as a gift; and all you got, eventually, was that heap from Tel Aviv. With the "Don't come out" letter at the end for dessert.

What should I wish for you on your birthday? Actually, I should wish you for yourself, because you are the most precious, rarest gift I can think of right now—I wish I had more courage, for your sake.

No. I want to wish for something greater. Why compromise? I want a real wish. I wish, I wish time would stop—and that this past summer could continue forever—that I could elude the goddamn grip I have on myself—and be discovered, suddenly, in another place—in front of you, for example. But new, free, naked. Even for just one day. Even for one page of a letter. One blink of absolute freedom. Why not? Really? Otherwise, what am I worth?

Yair Einhorn

(Midnight.)

(That's it? All that noise and mystery for that kind of name?)

I'm thirty-three years old. I live in Talpiyot—the address is on the envelope—in a new, crowded neighborhood of private bungalows. This is where I chose to build my home—it's a kind of nouveau riche slum. What else? I run quite a large business, it's called the Book Bunk, it's actually right on the edge of the Jerusalem Forest, not too far from your house. I sell used books and search for rare books on commission. What else? Ask me, ask me, the turnstile is open. I have a staff of ten, including a book doctor and one young genius in a wheelchair who knows almost every book ever written in Hebrew and can recognize a book by a single sentence from it (he found your "dress his face with tales"). And there are seven cavalrymen on motorcycles whom I saved from a pizza delivery business that went bankrupt and closed. I've turned them into deliverers of books and send them to customers' homes all over the country. They leave black, burning stripes on the land, delivering every book and magazine that exists in the galaxy, from how-to guides about growing orchids, to Elvis Presley biographies, to volumes of Judaica and issues of the Dutch Royal House fan magazine.

I make sure to bite a little piece of paper from every copy of *Zorba* that rolls through my hands (well, I'm not as young as I used to be). And of course, I forever tip my hat to you for successfully, and without much ado, arranging the subscriptions to the Chinese newspaper for the only two interested readers in the country.

I'm a bit winded—but I said everything, didn't I? I did it.

So what, then? Should we perhaps hum along a bit about daily affairs, to get over the embarrassment? It suddenly became uncomfortable, didn't it? Someone exhaled a breath of reality. Should I tell you about my work? Why not, we've already yielded to the little sweaty molecules—do you want to hear what my workers receive as holiday gifts?

Enough, Miriam. Give up on me. It was all fantasy—if there was any other solution, any other system at work in the world . . . I would pass almost everything I did or said through your eyes first, through your thoughts and your hungry mouth— If someone pissed me off at work or on the road, I used to think of you. I would roll your name under my tongue and immediately calm down. I never met a person into whose hands I wanted to deliver my soul in this way—nor did I ever think I would trust her to know how to put me together again, correctly. There are certain geniuses to whom you could give a jigsaw puzzle of a parrot—and they could put those pieces together to make a fish. I gave you a creep—and you made a human out of it—the same pieces, but somehow, always better.

I should perhaps tell you that in recent past weeks I thought, with my usual denseness, that if I had a purpose in life, it was you—or it has something to do with you, or that through you, I will somehow reach it. There isn't much reason behind this thinking, but this is how I felt—and you are the only person to whom I could write such words without feeling ridiculous. Now I will have to go back and look for this "purpose" in a different, and simpler, place—where it is probably easier for me to search under the light, or the Lila, the Liza, or the Lorelei. Pitful, aren't I?

It occurs to me that if, let's say, I was kidnapped—or disappeared without a trace—and a detective came here and tried to understand or figure out who I was based on what everyone around me here knows, he could never find me. This is another thing I never learned until you— that I mainly live in what I'm not.

I had hoped this profession would make me happier, and it doesn't. The details are truly unimportant. I never told you how many jobs I had already tried, how many mistakes I have wallowed in. I thought I finally found my vocation—working with books, searching to find for people the stories from their childhood that they loved. What could be more suitable for me? Apparently it isn't. I am only almost happy here. It is still a secondhand pleasure.

You have no idea how much I loathe books this minute. Why is it that none of the thousands of books that surround me can help me? And none of them tell our story.

And none of them gave me what your letters gave me.

Yair

Miriam

I trip up the very same way all over again. He ran off the school bus to me, spread his hands out by his sides, and whinnied happily . . . oh, he came home today in such a good mood. And as sometimes occurs, she was in him for a second. I saw her in him, trapped.

Why am I writing in here? I don't want to write in this notebook—a few words and I will rip this page out and leave it alone. But, just the way she was in him, she was so real today you could almost touch her. Perhaps he smiled her smile for a moment, or it was the angle of light on his face. I don't know. I don't know, I don't know why I insist on hurting myself by writing in this notebook here when the house is full of empty pages. I swore I would not open this notebook until an answer came from him, and could only hold myself back for two days. Not even two days. A day and a half. It's not much, but at least I know what condition I am in. I hoped I would be stronger; what will happen now? I think I'm a little bit scared. As if I had opened the cover of this and all his letters were roaring and bellowing and crying out to me. Enough, quiet.

He is asleep. Fell asleep, exhausted. He will sleep until morning, and I will not be able to give him the Apenotin. He screamed and cried and bled so much . . . the insult of every fall . . . I wish I could fall asleep like that, wake up some other time. His forehead now has a new, large cut—

and he'll start scratching at it tomorrow morning. I barely made it out unhurt this time. Except for the usual hurt—if, at some point, I was asked to return the deposit, how would I show my face with all his scars? If I was quicker, less clumsy, I could at least dive under him and cushion his falls. Make use of my body.

I'm just scribbling so as not to think, in order to resist the temptation of flipping back and going to meet him. You. You you. Where are you now? How could you not know of the gift awaiting you here from me? How did you not feel how I was with you for a whole week, word for word? The tens and hundreds of pages under this page . . . I feel like a nutshell on stormy waves writing you here. And now it occurs to me that maybe I should have added a foreword to the beginning of this notebook, or some kind of explanation at its end. But what would I write? What, of all things could I say? Perhaps what I told you once, that to discover a person and tell him something about himself he doesn't know—that is a great gift of love to me. The greatest.

I also was thinking of telling you that if you read your letters straight through, without mine, from first to last, you would learn many new things about yourself. Not only the "bad" things that you're sometimes so eager to discover about yourself. Perhaps you will begin to see yourself with another's eyes. Mine, for instance. But I will tell you all this only when we meet face-to-face. Now, please, don't bother me, Yair, let me go—I have to write about something else here.

He ran the length of the whole garden path to me, probably not understanding why I wasn't running toward him with a "Who's Coming to Me?" There is that little gap in the middle of the path where a brick is missing, Amos has been promising to fix it for two months and has no time. His leg caught in it, twisted, and—this is not an excuse. I usually never wait for him to reach that brick, I always get there before he does. Maybe it was because this kind of running is something that has never left him since he was two—he's always been running, happy, free; we both would gallop toward each other, cheering. Also because he is always taken aback by my hug, not understanding who this woman is (why am I writing about this?). What happened today? What happened was, I saw him; I mean, I saw him in a way I must not see him—how his body jangles loosely, his feet and the length of his face when his glasses fell off—I truly mustn't write about such things. I only thought that she was trying, trying so hard, and not succeeding at taking off—and felt a moment of uncontrollable anger. Not at him. Not at him? Yes, partly at him. Whatever inside him prevents her from shining out through him. It has been ten years and I'm still looking for codes, hints. "Anger at him" (and I attacked you for it). Yes. And anger at Amos about the brick. And anger at Anna, oh, I didn't neglect her today. All these angers still don't add up to a single answer.

I stood there, and he got out of the van and ran, and there, the missing brick, and I saw the driver looking at him from behind.

Yes.

He was about to drive away, and stopped and looked; I saw the other three boys on the van, gazing out without seeing a thing. They've been riding together every day for four years and still don't recognize Yokhai. He doesn't recognize them either. And for some reason the driver lingered today for another moment and watched him run—a new driver, probably inexperienced, and his look, more than anything else—"the way the eye is drawn to a disaster." When he tripped where the brick was missing—by that time, I think I was so absent, not with him, not wanting to be allied with him, an enemy, I didn't even move.

I will not rip out this page. It will remain in your notebook, and you will receive it, too. You've already heard harder things than this from me. But now there is a new twist: I have never written this kind of letter to myself before.

I should have ripped out the previous page. I see that it is leaving open a gap for others to follow, which is unwanted in my current condition. Some stormy weather here this afternoon; at least the house is cleaner than it has been in a long time. Then again, I'm back at this notebook, each word pulling out another after it. I wanted the only words in it to be yours, and spent a whole week copying them out, holding myself back from adding even a single word of mine, and now, look—a flood. But they aren't the words I wanted you to hear, and not in my good voice.

Because you haven't sent even one line in response to what I told you in the last letter, that precious thing I told you. Not even a short, polite rejection. How could you? You could. I can't. It terrifies me to finally understand how much I can't.

Good morning, it's a new day. Don't worry, I'm fine. I was rescued from that little whirlpool that sucked me in for a moment yesterday. You will read what I wrote in the previous pages, and we'll both laugh at me together.

Quarter past five. It will be light soon.

I finished copying out your letters three days ago, at this hour exactly. For a few minutes I sat there, feeling nothing. A little overwhelmed, a little drunk. I thought that from now on I would be able to write only with your words, and that closing this notebook was hard, almost unbearable for me. I also felt that I was waiting for my first heartbeat of sobriety, and it wasn't coming. In its place, I was privileged with a sunrise of a kind I haven't seen in years. Waves and waves of golden light streaming over Jerusalem, and I told myself it must be an omen.

Right now, here it is, the sun. A little less dramatic today, but of course. Come on, let's go for a walk.

What perfume. Smell it, it's the air you can have only at this hour, full of foggy smells and so cold! Every tree and rock is swaddled in its own cloud . . . and if I linger here another moment longer, I too will freeze and be swaddled, too. I'm taking you to the dam again, this time to show you a sight that even a slave swept away by the parted seas never saw. (Only my breath, my breath suddenly grew short, so I stopped to rest on a rock.)

Your sentences and fragments of your sentences are humming in my head, like the sound of tracks after a long train ride. I could recite them to you by heart. I would prefer that you forget some of them, of course. In general, I do not want words standing between us anymore, and would rather simply be with you, in our bodies, no matter how. To be able to touch you and breathe in the scent of your sweat, to watch you do all sorts of things—making an omelet. Anything.

Only when we meet will I tell you what happened to me since the conversation with Amos, and my whole week with your letters. How I argued with you as I copied those letters and how my heart went out to you. How many packets of Kleenex I went through, because of the painful misunderstandings and the crazy understanding— Come, let's continue, the sun will soon evaporate the clouds completely.

But now I remembered—I forgot to lock the door and Yokhai sometimes grows restless at this hour. What a shame, what a pity, I wanted to go all the way to the dam with you, because it is deep there and you can dive under the clouds and walk—but I have to return, immediately—

Nothing to worry about, I am here and he is asleep and I hadn't forgotten to lock the door. I was just worried. I worried the moment before getting there, and it infuriates me, because I so wanted you to see just how I imagine the place where they match destinies to people—and then maybe you could get lost in it with me for a time. It also smells very special when the dry, thorny plants are moist; no other time of day smells like it. If I had had three more minutes there, or even one, I could have taken you there.

At least I saw the sunrise; and so I have a secret oath with this day, someday we will go there together, when our time is more spread out.

Look at me, sitting on the steps outside, trying to catch my breath, enjoying being just a body, living tissue performing its correct functions. Completely free from words like "pity" and "but". . .

(It's already six, and I have to hurry inside. They pick up Yokhai at eight. I'll see you later.)

On the way here, I picked an early winter lemon, green and hard. The entire space of the classroom is already full of its scent. Thirty-three heads bent over examination pages; every once in a while a pair of eyes rises with difficulty and stares at me (I sometimes wonder how it must affect me, that I am gazed at for so many hours during the day) . . .

One pupil whom I'm very fond of holds up a page on which he's written, "Is rosemary season over?" in big letters.

You already know I'm a little slow, certainly compared to you, but my mind has been getting clearer and clearer since yesterday, and I understand things that seemed so complicated in a much simpler way. For example—under no circumstances would I like to turn my back on what is between you and me, and I am willing to wait as long as you need. Because "what is between us," between you and me, is worth waiting for. I feel as if there is time for us. Life is long, and even a bouquet of thirty saffron flowers is a wonderful bouquet. I also can see, Yair, that I don't think you are the person who can heal what is wounded inside me; but perhaps, at this stage of my life, I don't need a doctor as much as I need someone with the same sort of wound.

A few more moments of such thoughts and it will have turned completely ripe and yellow (when I was in eighth grade, I once received an F on an algebra test, because I wrote that a prime number can be divided only by one and itself—and for an example of such a number I wrote: the scent of a lemon. By the way, you, in many ways, are also like the scent of a lemon).

Every day, when my bus passes where you work, I pity you for having to work in such an ugly, smoky part of town. But if your window faces the street and you look out of it right now, you will see me writing through the bus window, and you will be happy. I didn't tell you that I pass by your funny sign in that industrial area at least five times a week. How did it never occur to me? At no moment did I sense that this was the location from which your webs were being spun.

And what would happen if I came to visit you? (Don't worry, I would never come to you without an invitation.) To ask you to find one particular story for me? I will tell you that I can remember only one sentence from it, maybe "It is heartbreaking, the thought that you can see into a grown-up person that way" or "Who can resist the temptation to peek into another's hell?" and immediately, your seven cavalrymen will leap onto their steeds, storming to the ends of the land, and begin to circle us in smaller and smaller arcs, until they finally stand with the their headlights facing us, point their fingers at us, and say, "You're the story."

I immediately cradle myself with thoughts of us in those few, quiet, in-between moments. Could it be that you went abroad again? What will you bring back this time?

I do envy you this—your freedom of movement through the world (it's impossible for Amos and me to travel together, and I can't go alone because of the very thought of a hotel room at night).

On your next business trip to Paris, please go to the Rodin Museum; there is a sculpture there: *The Poet and the Muse*. Look at it. Twice. Then go to the museum shop and check to see if they are still selling the postcard of that sculpture. They once added a quotation under the photo of the sculpture (you know you are absolutely forbidden to count on me for exact quotations and who said what, but I think it's Baudelaire): "Put down your lute, poet, and give me a kiss."

Buy it for yourself, from me.

When I think about what gifts I would like to buy for you, I sometimes hear you scolding me: "And how, in your opinion, will I be able to bring this home? How will I explain it? What will I say?" Then I shrink and give up.

But really, what do I care about how you will explain it? I'll buy it, and you can do whatever you like with it.

I told you before: I will take no part in these "bureaucracies" and in the endless secretive trafficking. If you decide to come to me, then it can only be in the open, without hiding and without lies, because I don't know how to live in cracks.

(But I just had an idea of what I could buy for you that you could bring home without fear: bread, butter, cheese, milk . . .)

Maybe it's because you tried in Tel Aviv, and without much success in my opinion, to write my "diary." I'm having difficulties writing down my own thoughts, those that pass between me and myself; it is as if an echo has been added to each word, and I can't decide: Does it feel good? Does it not feel good? (Ood ood ood . . . ?) You are the food that is good.

Bambi, William, and Kedem lie around me. They've grown lately, swallowed up the space—there's hardly any room for the humans in the house. Want a dog? You'll see how happy it makes Ido.

I told you why Amos bought them for me. But it's becoming more and more apparent that they've remained poor orphans as they've grown up, and I always pity them a little for having gotten me as a moth—

You have to hear what just happened: We had a blackout. Pitch-black—listening to the commotion outside, I think there must be a blackout through the whole village. But this morning I lit a candle in my father's memory (it's strange: this is the first time the anniversary of his death hasn't been marked by rain); the remains of his candle now light up the house for me ... Jessye Norman stopped in the middle of *Dido and Aeneas*. The refrigerator stopped. The clock. The heater. All the little comforts—and only my father's candle lingers.

I haven't told you that he was the electrician of the house—he had golden hands (he used to tell me: "You don't need brains to be an electrician—you need luck"). When I was at the university in Jerusalem, he used to make special trips from Tel Aviv to fix things in my apartment, he wouldn't even let me change a lightbulb by myself. I guess he didn't have much faith in my luck.

I can't remember the last time I wrote by candlelight—it instantly changes everything, makes you feel like writing in other words, using a quill and ink.

My precious Yair,

Do you remember when, in Tel Aviv, you wrote the letter in which I asked you to dive with me all the way to the place where you could have been an initial possibility of me?

Do you know what I really want?

Not for you to be me, not at all; but rather, for you to linger in that place of potential, not for too long, just one moment, before "deciding" who you really are, who, of the the two of us, you are going to be.

So then, when you decide to be you, as of course you will, what will the point be if you aren't exactly who you are (I am enough of myself already)?

Just that you hesitate one moment before you become distinguished from me, at those imaginary crossroads between us.

That hesitation—do you understand? It's a whole world.

And I have another wish (you're allowed three): I hope, I pray, that we will always mourn the fact that each one of us chose to be exactly he himself, mourn it together in a tiny corner of our souls.

(There, my father's candle flickered a bit. Even he is confirming it.)

... later, when the lights came back on, in the middle of doing the dishes, I felt some kind of "transmission" approaching. I started to walk, confused, around the house; I looked out every window and didn't see anyone. I turned on the radio and heard an educational program about astronomy; some expert said, "The probability of an event occurring diminishes the more information it contains."

I immediately wrote it down, wet hands and all. Not that I understood it—but I could tell that something important is coded in it!

It will be fine. I am certain of it.

I don't know why, I'm not searching for a reason. It will be fine. It will all work out for the best; maybe because of the smell of rain in the air that just passed by; the three dogs raised their heads and I felt the garden whistling and murmuring . . . A few weeks ago you said that you feel me in "three different places in the body." I now feel you in a few more places (let's say five, by my last count).

The wonder is how I feel you in a place I thought was already completely dead in me, closed off by a scar.

(To "sober" myself up a little, I immediately went back and reread a few choice passages from Tel Aviv.)

So then? We had only three days together, on the "one and only walk we've managed to take on our three days together"? Cheap. Terribly cheap.

Why can we not be spoiled with wide, relaxed time, spreading out over forever? Why couldn't you dare to imagine a completely fantastical situation in which we are, for example, living together, even for a short time, in the same house? One ordinary and banal supper in our kitchen?

The fiery heat of the revolving sword—I already told you: it's you. You. The heat, and the sword, and the constant revolving. And you positioned yourself in front of every possible entrance to the Garden, so you would never be able to go back. I really wish I knew what it was, the horrible, shameful sin for which you were expelled. Was it something you did? Something you were? Were you too little, or too much?

Too little and too much at the same time, but never exactly at the same time? That is probably your huge "betrayal" of them: you couldn't match their "exactly."

I believe, with all my heart, that there is a place, perhaps not Eden, but a place we can be together. A place which is no larger than a pinhead, in reality, because of all the inevitable limitations—but which will be wide and open between us, and in it you can be you and everything you are.

There is only one thing about which I am not yet sure, and this is what loosens up my hands . . . that, perhaps, you are not at all capable of believing that somewhere in this world exists a place where you can be yourself, and where you will be loved.

(If this is so, you will never, ever, believe that someone is capable of truly loving you.)

I'm not such a hero either. It only takes writing "our kitchen" to scare me, to make me have to walk around with a nervous stomach, as I have for a few hours now, as if I had signed my name to some blasphemy.

I am, however, also incapable of going along with you, with how you are now castrating your imagination when you think of me (or write about me, or have fantasies about me). Because our imaginations created us for each other, so how is it that you (you!) fail to understand the extent to which it is our earth, our Luz . . .

Perhaps during those three days we went to the Galilee?

And slept in a little cabin in Metula?

We made love the whole night and didn't speak at all.

Only silly talk.

I told you that you give me shivers all down my spine, and you said, shreckles, like shivering in a forest of freckles. Then you kissed me between my eyebrows, and I massaged your entire body with only my eyelashes, and wrote words to you on your forehead with my fingers (but I wrote them backward so that you would be able to read them from the inside).

In the beginning, we touched each other only as total strangers.

Then we touched each other as others had taught us.

Only afterward did we dare touch like you and me.

I thought that when you are with me in this way, you are part of my home, as the word would be pronounced in my most internal language.

I thought, the root of my soul, the root of your soul.

It gave us so much pleasure . . .

At midnight, in the middle of our sleep, you fluffed up the pillow under my head, and I mumbled that it didn't matter, and you said, "But it does matter. Pillows are important, Miriam. The most important thing is for the pillow to be in the exact right place . . ."

(And every time I write my name with your mouth, I understand something new.)

And inside my confusion and my fear (of your silence not being just temporary or due to a sudden long journey, or just a horrible postal malfunction; that, perhaps, something is developing here that I never imagined possible between us)—

I am still comforted, inside all this, by the thought that I received the "gospel" from Amos, because no one, no one knows better than he how to give the gift of love and how to accept it, as well.

I am convinced that I can finally feel the emotion Amos named for me only because you stepped forward and gave yourself to me, with your full name (the most beautiful gift I received for my fortieth birthday). You understand, don't you? If you hadn't given me your name, I could never have felt that emotion, even if I heard its precise name one hundred times.

I didn't even tell you—I meant to tell you when we met, and not until then, when I would give you this notebook (I'm writing in it now, as if I have already given up on the possibility that we will ever meet)—

Well, what?

That I knew your name before you revealed it to me.

Sarah, our secretary, was handing out the mail as usual and, when she came up to me, spat out nastily, "I don't think he's sent you anything today." I was confused for a moment and asked, "Who?" And she said your name, your full name, the real one, adding that, by the way, she didn't know we were so close and told me that you and she have kids in the same kindergarten class (yes, it is she, the vital lady). You must understand, Sarah is always terribly alert to any kind of "dramas" that might be brewing in the teachers' lounge, and I think she is particularly sensitive to me, trying to understand what exactly is going on there in my private life that apparently refuses to allow her to squeeze it into any kind of category.

In short: she must have seen you, more than once, when you dropped off your letters, you perfect spy.

When I blushed (all over my body, in a perfectly reasonable fashion for a sixteen-year-old girl), she started flowing over like a spring with gossip about you. I was probably too overwhelmed to silence her immediately, as she deserved; and it so happened that, against my will, and perhaps—a little—because I couldn't withstand the temptation, I heard, in one moment, quite a few "stories."

Sarah, as you well know, has a big mouth. (Srsrsrsrsr . . .) And I eventually had to practically stand up and walk away for her to be quiet. I don't want to hear about you from strangers!

Talk, Yair.

Come to me, be here with me. Let's make up, we had such a fight this afternoon, and it is so hard for me to fight with you, it's unbearable, especially with you gone. And it's even worse to be alone with my anger at you, with Sarah's whispers. I don't want to write the details down in this notebook, what came over me, what I became in a blink—I don't want to go there again. Not without you.

I cleaned myself up and calmed down a little.

I'm in the bath. I mean, Yokhai is in the bathtub and I am watching him, sitting on the toilet seat and writing to you. I hope you don't mind. Isn't it a bit late for him? you ask. Your voice always softens when you speak of him. Yes, it's late. It's late for me too, I can barely keep my eyes open. But he wet the bed again, and after I finished wiping him off, I thought, He can't stay like that the whole night. You wouldn't leave Ido that way. So even though I had given him his bath an hour ago, I brought him back here.

To tell you the truth, I thought we'd only have a short shower and then back to bed. But he had other plans, and the moment I finished giving him his shower, he decisively sat in the bathtub and made happy splashing motions in the air, and looked so sweet and flashed me such a sassy smile that I couldn't refuse him.

So come, sit, join us. I don't know how long we'll stay here, because lingering in the bathtub is an adventure demanding absolute precision and courtesy to all of the tiniest details—where to sit, making the water fall exactly on the middle of his back—where to place the two soaps, and the comb, the boat, and a few other toys—but in the meantime, it seems everything is well, because he is smiling his most melting smile, slowly running water through his fingers, his eyes almost closed. If you were here right now, you would see what solid pleasure is.

Nilly also comes in, with her tail straight up in the air, to watch. This cat is utterly human—and also utterly pregnant, as I am only now noticing. So is this the reason for your recent aggressiveness toward the dogs? And who's the father this time, the tiger-striped or the yellow? Probably both of them. Will you refuse to nurse again, your little protest against nature's enslavement of females? Oh, Nilly, Nilly, you free soul, tell me, can you be free without being cruel?

It's eleven at night. Total silence. The room is filled with the peach scent of the bath foam, Yokhai is sending his hands to roam the hills, above the two rings his fat brown knees make sticking out of the water. Nilly has curled up on the little bathmat and fallen asleep. And outside, the wind is blowing, and the poplar behind the house bends and rustles. You thought of me just now.

Yair, I am not ignoring your last letter—your farewell words were clear and sharp. Nor does your long silence leave any room for doubt. But what can I do? I feel it, I feel every time you address me with a word or thought. Like right now, at this minute. You sometimes wake me in the middle of the night. That's when I know you dreamed of me. I cannot explain it, it is only that my mind and my heart suddenly leap to the peak of the mountain; if I am to believe in these leaps, then you haven't stopped speaking to me in the past few weeks, in the daytime and at night, in the city and the country, in the kitchen and in the bathtub— wait one minute.

That's it, that's done. There is always one moment when his head starts to droop and his eyes flutter and my heart stops in my chest—but he was only brought down by fatigue today, thank God.

Should I tell you everything? Should I? Would you go through each of my daily routines with me?

It's strange, we never spoke of such things.

First of all, you have to take him out of the tub. Easy enough to say. But it's as if his body has absorbed all the water and my tiredness as well. I lift him out and dry him off, and he keeps slumping over onto me, he's already completely asleep, Yokhai with his peachy smell. I carry him to his room. He's very heavy; he's thin, but has a special heaviness to him, the density of his insides, I think. I diaper him, because I don't have the energy to give him another bath tonight. Wait—

When I went outside to hang the basket of fresh laundry, the air was full of fog again; my garden transformed into a silent ghost's ball, and I couldn't leave, in spite of the cold. I drank in the air and danced around the cypress tree with a moist pillowcase and one manly pajama. Tell me (have you noticed what a wonderful couple we are? I always say "Tell me" and you always say "Listen"), how is this strange weather affecting you? This long drought—do you feel it, too, this cosmic, private restlessness? Every day I walk with this constricting, ever-present feeling of coming chaos—a gigantic mistake growing . . . and how long can this last before—?

But, as I read in the papers this morning, the rabbis have already charged us to fast for rain—so it might still be so good as to grace us with its presence (even though I just hung the laundry).

Can you hear that? It's the neighbor's new baby, I told you about her. She is still crying day and night. Huge eyes and lips like cherries—and what crying! She's already a month and a half old, and the saga of her name continues. I sometimes think that's why she cries so much. Every day or two they stop by to consult with me—as what, a baby expert or an expert on names?—bringing a new list. I listen, and give them my opinion, and they get excited—and then some grandmother or aunt is always unsatisfied. It is truly beginning to upset me. Not their requests for advice, but the fact that there is a little girl in the world living nameless for so long. It's not right (perhaps this is why the rain hasn't come yet?).

. . . All this chatter—it's only fatigue. I'm already sitting with the last cup of tea of the day. I almost poured you a cup by mistake. I'm wrapping myself around the steaming cup. For some reason, over the past few days I can't stand the taste of coffee. You are probably enough caffeine for me right now. I had so many little and big things to tell you today. Even now, my hand is drawn to my pad of paper and my envelopes, but I can't write you a letter. I made a decision, Yair, I will not write you until you reply to my last letter. You are requested to help me maintain my pride in this respect.

Some decisive, impatient soul immediately asks me, Why should I not write these things to myself, between me and myself? Why does it seem

so false to me? (And egocentric? And like some lady in a Victorian salon?) Why shouldn't I start writing some kind of "diary" like this, kept
between myself and me, so I can at least ease the burden of your silence,
the burden of my own expectations? What, don't I deserve that? Am I
not, myself, an address?

My heart shrinks even considering it; the pain of giving up my old
hopes, the promise I made you of wanting to give what you have awakened within me to you and only you. This is how it tastes. Here, finally,
Amos's car.

On certain days, even swimming is not enough to cleanse me. I had to
stop and get out after five laps, I felt as if someone had tied weights to my
ankles and wrists. I walked home from the pool, through the strange season occurring here, between big wheels of dry tumbleweed and trees that
seem more and more hollow, desperate. The smell, as usual, affects me
more than anything, a dry bitterness rising from the ground. The big
snails should already be out at this time of day. Where are they now? My
heart is aching for the narcissus that has only just bloomed and is dim-
ming and fading away. The daisies are at the peak of their bloom this
week, in places that were completely naked at this time last year; their
carpets of blooms are now almost wild, almost embarrassing, promiscuous . . . I actually have to stop for a moment to decide whether I will walk
around them or splash about through them.

I had to stop and sit in the middle of the road, it so depressed me, the
thought that perhaps I didn't dare want you with all the strength of my
being.

No (No, NO)! I wanted it very, very much. Very few times in my life
have I dared to want this way.

It's already November. Another special milestone I have marked in
my calendar has passed. Where are you? What are you doing with this
heartache? I know you don't suffer any less than I do, perhaps even
more; because now we are both allied against you. So, of course, my first
impulse is to come and help you, write you a letter of comfort, be a
mother and a sister to you . . .

But I have already played this part too many times in my life, and I
dared to want something different with you, you know.

Do you know? Did you even understand? My heart sinks——did you

understand my will, my hunger? The passion of my yearning for someone, a man above all, who would not only dare to strip me of my clothes,
but would look at what is there within me, so we could see, together,
what I am made of.

There, I am not just naked. I am completely bare in my nakedness.

Strange. The hardest thing for me to give up now is this will. It
screams out of every mouth of my body.

. . . They changed the area codes in Jerusalem, too, and alongside the
usual mess is my own private sorrow that the "bureaucracy" tipped some
aesthetic balance in my previous number.

I am comforted by the fact that they added a round six to you.

Half past three in the morning. What happened? Why did you wake me
up? What is the reason behind this sudden emotion?

It's lasting until now, a clear internal signal that doesn't stop even as I
write; on the contrary—it is like an alarm in my body, ticking and alert.

But . . . how can I even have any "feelings" for you, feelings like I
used to have? I was so wrong about you.

I'm still trying not to completely surrender my anger at you, my anger
as well at the insult that grows from hour to hour, even now. I have been
trying to understand why, but it is very difficult for me to believe such a
reason for your violent disappearance: was it really just because you felt
as if you were "polluting" me during my trip to Tel Aviv? My search for
you?

And what makes you think I was "polluted" on my journey? I had
more than a few good, even purifying, moments. I met people I would
never have met in any other way. And I told you about the sunset and
how the depths of the sun sparkled with green. About the fisherman with
his little kerosene stove. Even my conversation with the two prostitutes.
What are you talking about? Your disappearance from my life is polluting me so much more!

The hour I sat on the seawall—the water was so beautiful, so clear, I
could see into the horizon; and a kingfisher gliding around me—perhaps
he is a distant relative of the one in my garden? Who knows, maybe I am
being guarded by a secret network of kingfishers. I wish I had brought

my camera (I packed so hastily)—I wanted to take pictures and send you a few, so you could see where you were.

Only a few weeks have passed since then, and it seems like a year to me. I wandered around the streets by the sea for two days, walking, waiting for one special look, waiting to suddenly hear my name from one of the thousands of people passing by me, and smiling. I was smiling the entire time. I thought of what you wrote so long ago about my public smile, and I rejoiced in my new smile.

You paid no attention to where you arrived, as if by coincidence—straight into the kingdom of my childhood, my Nekhemya Street, with memories of everything mixed together.

Do you remember the letter I wrote you from a little vegetarian deli stuck between a steakhouse and a pizzeria?

Only the day before yesterday, it occurred to me—I had an epiphany: it is right in the same location as the old Café Ginati Yam.

(Well, these days even I can hardly recognize my kingdom under all the marble and hotels and Ackerstein bricks.) It truly sent thrills of pleasure through me—that was the café my father used to love to sit in, in between his taxi shifts. And once a week, in the afternoon, I would join him.

All the fine ladies, the chatterers and slatherers of makeup, would come here dressed to the nines. A little stage stood in the middle of the café, and a band played Viennese music (and Romanian, too, I think) on a cello and a violin.

My father would buy me ice cream in the summertime, they would serve huge scoops of ice cream in metal bowls. One man would pass by with a big glass box, the kind that opens from both ends (like old sewing kits, do you remember?), and from that box he sold cones of newspaper filled with nuts and seeds. My father would flag him down with a kingly wave of his hand, very unlike him, and we would spend a long time trying to decide what we wanted, and always picked the same thing: walnuts. And we cracked them together.

(And what was written here will probably never be told from my heart, by my mouth.)

Sitting in the kitchen, in darkness, in silence, and thinking thoughts of no substance, only a certain rhythm. Waves of something vague becoming stronger in me. I don't understand why I am still writing—what is this impulse that doesn't let go of me? Because I find no release in it, every time I swear to myself that I will stop for a minute, to think about it and try and understand, *before* my hand reaches for the notebook and opens it—but my hand is always quicker. I am also trying not to think about you—but you, of course, are always quicker than me.

In these hours, when you are not writing me, and not coming to me, bringing me your body, when you can leave me alone, abandoning me to everything you already know I live with, I begin to consider the possibility that you perhaps have quite a few women with whom you correspond this way, simultaneously. That you tell each one a completely different story, and with each you determine the length of your connection according to a "private sign on the general calendar." Until, let's say, the first swallow of spring, or until——until what else? The sun's eclipse? The next earthquake in China? I know that this is a stupid idea, false and repulsive and cynical; but as we both know, something in you has given rise to ideas that would never have occurred to me before.

If I had at least known what it was, the "private sign" you had intended for me, at least this—it is something the condemned woman should know, isn't it?

I remember how, about seven and a half years ago, when Yokhai's disease broke out, I used to sit nights, here in the kitchen, and write these kinds of lists. Not exactly these kinds—but there was something similar in the writing, the unsteadiness of it, and the strength with which it forced itself upon me, actually possessing me (oh well, what's the point of picking at this).

What wouldn't I give now, to read Milena's lost letters to K.? To see, for instance, with what exact words she responded to his "love is that you are my knife with which I dig deeply into myself."

I hope she immediately sent him a telegram in which she made it clear that a person must never, not ever, agree to be anyone else's knife. You mustn't even ask such a thing of someone.

On second thought, I actually don't understand Milena at all. If I were Milena, I'd have behaved completely differently. I would have left

Prague and gone to him in Vienna, and entered his home and said, "I'm here. You can't escape me any longer. I am no longer satisfied with imaginary travel. You cannot heal with words alone—you can sicken, yes, this is apparently not too hard. But comfort? Resurrect? For that you must, in some moment, see eyes in front of you, touch lips, hands—the entire body rebelling, screaming out at your infantile ideas about some 'pure' amorphousness—oh yeah? What's so pure about it? What is pure in me now?!"

Listen to what a big heroine I am. I don't dare even to call you at work.

I drew out what you said (in your kitchen) about how your life with Maya is so stable and defined that "it is impossible to add a new element that is too large (like myself, for instance)."

As I looked at this piece of paper in front of me, it became so clear, Yair, that your life is truly so stable, so defined, that you weren't able to find any room in it for me, either.

There is no room for me in your life. I should have already accepted that. Even if you had wanted me very much, you probably wouldn't have dared make room for me in your "reality."

(Perhaps this is why you let me into the only place you were ever truly free, into your childhood, with such sweeping force.)

I don't understand, I don't understand you. You hide the world of your imagination from Maya and the physical world from me. How can you navigate between all these opening and closing doors? Where do you truly live a full life? I would like to hear from you once, so you can answer me this—if we have all already committed suicide once, why repeat the mistake over and over?

I used to sit and write the entire night then, trying to document every day that passed, so I could understand it and solve it; also, so that I might not lose my mind to my fear and helplessness. During the day, I would write down Yokhai's every move—follow his tracks as he walked through the house, the repetitive, endless actions of the day, what words he had left— what he ate, how he ate. And at night I would sit here and try to crack the code, turn all of it into something legible, some method, some pattern. I had hundreds of pages, notebook upon notebook. I've kept them somewhere in our basement, and there is no rhyme or reason in them, or in keeping them. I don't have the courage to throw them away; yet I have even less courage to open them and see myself as I once was. If he ate a tomato at breakfast, he would be upset for hours. When we moved the armchair into the living room, he moved it back. We turned off the lamp and he turned it back on. If we reduced the dose of this medicine or that, he wouldn't have an attack for three days. He tore up a piece of paper, he tore up another . . . I would follow him at home, at kindergarten, and simply write him down . . . The more that was erased in him, the more I would write of him.

So what am I writing now? The documentation of my disease?

The new coat was not received with delight. We had intentionally set Saturday aside for this task, when we had time, were in no hurry—but by noon we were desperate. Even Amos gave up, so we wrapped it up again. I guess something in its texture is different from the other coat. Perhaps the edges of the sleeves or the collar. Maybe its smell. It was the closest coat I could find to his old one, and now we will have no other choice but to patch the old one up. And we better do it today, because how long will the rain wait for us as considerately as it has? The one accomplishment of the day: if we failed with the coat, we have at least succeeded with the long thermals, without even cutting off the sleeves.

I have just finished cleaning up the last traces of riot in his room, and Amos took him out to fly his kite. I am disconnecting the phone—you won't call on a Saturday—and am sitting to rest for a moment. I have been waiting so long for this moment.

On the right side, in the back, just under the bone that juts out. That is where you are, in my brain. I think it's exactly on the opposite side, for you (oh, then how will we ever truly meet?). In the past few days, coming near that place has been accompanied by pain and so much anger toward you; but now, to my surprise (and certainly to my joy), I am touched by the same precious moment I had sitting with Amos on the balcony after receiving your last letter.

Should I tell you more than I have?

Should I give up on you then, on the possibility that we— Should I give up already?

(Then who am I actually writing to here?)

You will see, there will come a day when we will be old and wise, and all these wars will have passed between us. You will hold me close and say, "How clever you were in those days, when you didn't give up, when you knew how to do the exact right thing, come to our meeting place and wait and wait, and stay there as long as I needed you."

Fine. I'm going to tell you. Here it is: It happened as we were busy with one of our house's most annoying rituals—the preparation of our monthly tax report. You're probably intimately acquainted with this particular burden of independence (because of your own business, right?). Amos has to report what he makes from private lectures; it's always so little money for so much heartache, and I have to assist him, because he is completely helpless in the face of columns and charts. Whereas I am the high priestess of practicality . . .

I really used to hate doing it. What am I? An accountant? And the complex calculations involved in finding a percentage of taxes from such minuscule income. But one time I discovered that there is something pleasant about it, too. It is another way to re-create and linger for one more moment on all kinds of little events, the highlights of family life: buying shoes in a larger size for Yokhai . . . dinner at a restaurant with a couple of friends . . . and also an unusual amount of money spent over recent months on envelopes and stamps . . .

Amos asked me what was wrong as I was typing in the numbers. I couldn't talk, simply because I was afraid that if I started, I would burst out into the kind of tears that rivers can't wash away.

My face burned. Amos saw it, of course. And we continued working in complete silence, and I pulled myself together in the meantime.

We worked in silence together for almost half an hour, until we finished up; we saw how much we would have to pay them this month (it turned out to be quite a lot).

We then moved to the balcony and sat down. It was dark; we didn't turn on the light. Usually, Amos's presence calms me down immediately, but I felt that he, too, was tense, somewhat alert . . . his tension wrapped around my body and, to tell you the truth, worried me a bit.

And then he said, with complete simplicity, You're in love, Miriam.

And I said yes. Before I even knew what I was saying. Because the moment I heard that word, I felt such a motion inside me—

That I have had no words to describe until now.

I didn't describe it well enough in my last letter. I'm beginning to think that I didn't say enough; or maybe I said too much? Because I knew that a lot would depend on the way in which I told you about the conversation.

Again, my usual fear of your "selective hearing," and more than that, your *collective* hearing.

But my chorus, too, was also constantly buzzing—Where are you living? How long will you delude yourself? You still can't grasp that he meant what he wrote? That he is truly, honestly incapable of defeating himself? You have corresponded for seven months with a person who gave you a false name—who knows what else he made up? No, truly, would you look at yourself: your husband had to discover for you that you had fallen in love with another man; you, yourself, couldn't understand it on your own. And where were you for that life lesson?

I'm uncomfortable. This is not how I wanted to meet you today.

Can you believe it, though? I never, not even one time, told myself, in that way, with those simple words, that one word a savior (only now I begin to discover how binding it is?). And I gave this emotion so many words, too many words, too many words, and a lot of names. Mainly yours.

So how is it possible that only when I heard it from Amos—

The great fugue. Oh, really, how are you not even in the least bit cautious? What did you think would happen if you abandoned your peace of mind to the hands of this fugue on such a day? Well, it's a bit much, even on regular days. And why do you listen to it now, again and again? It's like a huge net being dropped over, twisting you up, and not allowing for any rest. This moment of unison, for example—for a moment, you could imagine you could rest on it a little, huh? You thought you could be happy, rejoicing, celebrating; you thought you would immediately start dancing, and here comes the cello, tearing out your guts.

How did you come into my life, anyway? How is it that I was so unprotected? You didn't even enter through a window; you found some tiny portal, barely a crack—and entered me this way, and pierced my heart.

I bought a box of Time cigarettes this morning. I walked out of the village and smoked three, one right after another. I refused all through high school, even during the Ta'amon Café period, when everyone around me smoked. And now, at the age of forty . . . It's horrible, how my lungs burn upward, flame living inside me and licking up the edges.

Even more horrible how much the burning relieved me.

"I mainly live in what I'm not." When I read that, a shout almost escaped me: so do I! But I never dared to say it to myself in the same way, because, well, my life is more or less full of what I am (and I've even gotten used to what I'm missing). I am happy with my mate, and grateful for Yokhai, who time after time gives me joy and understanding I never would have come to any other way. I am surrounded by loving friends, my house is near a little forest, and I have as much music as I need, and my work. I love it, too. Look at the grandness of my list of "haves." My have-list is full, full; you yourself once said that it is even overflowing—

But the knowledge of what I don't have has now suddenly become so active and demanding that it is hard to contain. It's suddenly full of life—and what will become of it now? What will I do with it?

How delightful it is to write when such things happen: the young couple, our neighbors to the right of us, just left. They brought me a huge bouquet and thanked me very much, because they finally had an idea of what to name her, the little cherry-lipped girl: Miriam.

It never once crossed my mind to suggest that name to them. I am so happy. A beautiful girl named after me will be in the world; also, of course, because of the relief; my secret bargain with the rain.

Nine-thirty p.m. What a mess. Where do I start? The floor is covered with paper and toys, pots and forks and pillows and clothes and chairs thrown and scattered everywhere. And hundreds of pieces of different puzzles that will take me God knows how long to sort out. I worked all afternoon on a Winnie-the-Pooh puzzle with him. At the age of two he could finish it in a few moments. By the time he was four it took an hour and a half. And today he spent the whole afternoon trying until, eventually, he worked himself into a rage. I understood him. One more minute, and then I will start putting the house back together. I need to relax, with music and writing. Tell me, how many times a day do you feel a prick in your heart when you think, I will never write to her about this moment? Not at this moment, either.

About the child he was before the disease—this is another thing I told you very little about. I really couldn't speak about it to anyone in the world, not even Amos—the happy child with such a quick mind, and what a sense of humor and charm—whom we lost over the course of a few weeks and months. He was such a verbal child, he had so many words at his disposal, and a complete library of books for kids his age. I would read him a story in the morning, and one at noon, and two or three more in the evening (and because of that putting him to bed would sometimes take two hours). We used to have such conversations, true heart-to-heart conversations. You have never seen a two-year-old with such an open, illuminated spirit. Somewhere we have a videotape taken at his two-year birthday party. I don't dare watch it—on it, he is dancing and laughing and acting out the children's book *Raspberry Juice* with us. Not three months later, his illness was unleashed on his system in full force, and his language began to disappear. He lost word after word, and we watched it happen and couldn't help him; we couldn't, the doctors couldn't. He would search for words like a person who is certain he placed something in his pocket and it was gone. This is the first time I have been capable of writing about it in this way; I can now remember it from this distance without dying from it. I used to sit with him and recite words for him. In the evening, he would remember them—and in the morning, no longer. And once, in a fit (my own), I sat for a whole night and crossed out the damned words that had betrayed him in each and every book of his.

I remember that the few words remaining on the pages looked to me like people's faces screaming in terror from their windows at night.

When the words were gone, he still had five or six songs left, for a few months anyway. The songs were the last to go. Eventually, there was only one song left, the Lilac Song. Every word was erased from me as well. I called every kind of tree just—a tree. Every flower—flower. And when you told me about how your heart curdled when Ido learned how to say "light," and in this way lost all his other lights, I thought I would have to break it off with you right then and there, because I would not be able to endure what you were awakening in me without even knowing what you were doing. Even your most innocent mistakes. I couldn't break it off with you, of course: probably for the very same reason.

I have told you so little. I mainly wanted to hear you, I was thirsty for you. I have tried to understand it, solve it, with all my strength; I have refused to accept the biting insult mocking me that from the moment I began to want you to listen to me, to really, truly hear my story, a story that has nothing to do with you—you disappeared.

I would now write you the simplest, most elemental letter, essential and undoubtable, like a math formula or an aria by Mozart; an axiom about you and me, about the most fragile, beating, and painful places of yearning. But it is almost ten, and soon I won't be here alone, and I don't want to be seen by anybody else when I am so upset. Please, I am still trying to understand, in a reasonable fashion, what truly happened to you, how you are capable of separation after we reached such an intimacy. I don't know what to think anymore. I sometimes think you are afraid or angry about my "telling" Amos something about you. How offensive it is to think that this is truly the reason. But maybe you think I "betrayed" you.

I hope that you at least believe me about this: that the thought of exposing the content of our relationship to him did not cross my mind for a moment. You don't suspect me of that, do you?

But why do you think I couldn't have told him that which excites me even now—that a man who didn't know me saw something in me that touched his heart so deeply—

And here I am, furious, again. I already swore to myself that I wouldn't be. If you can't at least understand *this*, we will never have a chance; I mean, if there is something in me that Amos loves, it is undoubtedly the same thing that made me accept your first offer! What Amos loves in me is what led me to write you back! This is the whole of it, what's not to understand? He loves the exact same woman in me who replied to your first letter; it is that same woman who once accepted his offer as well, who accepts him again and again, and each time she discovers something in him new and even more beloved. What is there to love about me, if not her? And how can you even love me without wanting to see her flourish and bloom? She is the heart of my life.

I actually shrunk for a moment at the thought that, without even reading this, you were smiling to yourself, even chuckling.

You weren't chuckling, were you? It's impossible for someone to sneer this way, somewhere in the world at the same moment that Barbara Bonney is singing this motet. Listen, come, let's rejoice with her, can you feel it? Every note this man has written feels as if it is strumming a nerve tuned only for him. You can dance it without even moving, or move as within a dream, like the two embryos in your dream.

Don't think, by the way, that I am completely immune to the other voices telling stories about you and about Amos; the winks behind my back, and the moans of all of the good souls who are so concerned, with their certainty that some essential screw is loose in my head, the screw bolted in them so tightly.

My face is burning. Even my palms are blushing. I hope I have another moment alone, because I have to say it, finally, at least to myself (because I am also an address, can you hear me? I am the address, I am the address to which this letter is sent!).

Still . . . I stopped for a moment. I went to wash my face, it was like putting a fire out with a thimbleful of water. I thought, as I stood in front of the mirror, how afraid I am to actually see you face-to-face. Because, before anything else, immediately, you will be exposed to the less beautiful things in me. I have, for instance, a white spot, not a large one, above my left eye, a little crescent. I don't think you saw it from where you were standing. Why did you ask me, so long ago under the sprinklers, not to dye my hair? I already have so many gray hairs—my mother was already completely white at my age. I had meant to start dyeing it this year, and then your letter came. You know, I noticed that when I close my eyes in front of the mirror, I see you.

My heart is going wild. Maybe because she is singing the Hallelujah right now. I haven't told you, I've been having a little blood pressure problem lately (yes, it is my dignified age, of course, my too-real reality, my body's bureaucracy, altogether at the same time). Dr. Shapira demands that I take pills to relax my heartbeats—but I refuse to give them up. If only you could put your hand on my heart now, you would make me so very happy.

I will stop here and continue tomorrow.

No! I won't stop! Did you see that pitiful demonstration of my fear of being too heavy to contain? Of the child who is so certain she is terribly fat;

she wasn't at all fat, but tortured herself for years and years by sitting ramrod straight at the edge of her chair so no one would see the folds of flesh on her back.

So what if I'm heavy? You'd promise to hold me.

Yair, I never dared the way I dared with you. I never allowed myself such license, internal license, I mean, with no boundaries; and you know I have the most generous partner in the world, a man who tells me in countless ways, Just be you, yourself. Anything you like, Miriam, as long as you are you, yourself. But I never dared, not all the way, not to the places beyond my strength, and surely not the way I now know I want to feel. Perhaps I can't really reach that place by myself with only my own strength to see it through. Perhaps someone like me, someone who needs someone else to bring her her happiness, no, not just her happiness, her most profound confirmation, will forever be

(You see? The sentence is incomplete. But the verdict is already written here.)

Because I am probably only capable of being in that place with another. Not alone.

I suddenly remember that, from a very young age, ever since I read the Krilov fables as a teenager, I had an internal sketch of myself: I am that miser, dying of starvation on the box of coins they had given to his hands to protect; and it's a lot worse for me, because those gold coins are mine!

And I don't want you to be a lightning rod for me. Why should you capture my lightning? Just the opposite. Are you listening? Come and tell me, Be light!

It is a moment before the beginning of a new day. I have to add an apology. Not to you. I want to write here how ashamed I am for putting myself under such a strain as I wrote yesterday.

Amos arrived at eleven, just as I was finishing up my last lines. Can you imagine how I looked at that moment? You could, unquestionably, "see it on me." He asked me what was going on, if I was all right. I told him I was terribly shaken by something I was writing. He waited another minute to see if I wanted to tell him what it was and, perhaps, to whom I was writing. I don't doubt that he knew—and I said nothing. I didn't see the need to share it with him. He didn't ask, and went to take a shower. When he returned, I had already pulled myself together, more or less. We didn't talk about it. We talked about other things. And Amos will wait, without impatience and without fear, for me, for the time when I will be able to talk to him. Do you understand? There is no daily, or hourly, duty or report between us, about the strength of our emotions and what direction they are blowing in. You don't have to take flower bulbs out of the ground every moment to check what length their roots are today.

You don't understand, do you? You think that such peace is possible between us only because he must not truly love me, or love me enough, or that we no longer share true passion. Isn't that what you think? That if he doesn't immediately storm at me and take me apart to discover why I am isolating myself so suddenly and for whom, he probably doesn't love me enough.

But to me—this is love.

The middle of the night. I got up and everything is spinning around me. I'm afraid of what I will write down here. It's the rain, the first rain. He already decided in April that we will end it in the rain. Of course, the first rain, which I love so much, which he loves, too, perhaps—and this is why he chose it. I don't even need to ask him to confirm it, I know. I'm so cold, all of a sudden, shivering . . . and all the times I wrote him so innocently telling him how I was waiting for that drink, thirsty for it, how it fills me with such a feeling of bounty and hope again every year, unites me with the sequence of life and time and renewal. I don't have many unions like it . . .

I'm freezing, even in my robe and a sweater, my entire body pricked with pins of chill. He also said we would deposit the decision for our separation into the hands of an outside force, something completely indifferent to us . . . and the strange sentence in his last letter, his wish for time to stop, for the summer to continue forever—and I, like some stupid—

It doesn't matter to me anymore. I even wonder how it is that I was so surprised, couldn't guess it ahead of time.

It still makes me wilt, like no other idea of his shriveled me. It transforms him into my enemy; he never was that, but now he is. A poor, des-

perate enemy, one who actually deserves compassion—but who uses uncon-
ventional weapons. I don't want to write something in here that sounds so
completely primitive, but I know, in my most private logic, that you *don't do*
such things—you don't play around this way with someone's feelings!!!

After one day of high fever and shivers and nightmares. What an odd illness, so quick and concentrated, it left at dawn, as soon as it came (maybe
I caught it from Y.? Or caught it from his rhythms, at least). Here, I too
am already writing only the first letter of his name. Not because of the
Sanctity of the Bond. Just out of weakness.

It tears at me painfully to write about you in the third person. I try, but it
is already rebelling against me, as if it is a horrible mistake . . . The words
fade instantly, and there is none of the flush of life in them. Never mind.
I'll get used to it. I have to. But still, turn your face to me now, the face I
have still never seen.

The shock from the night before last, a complete despairing of the
possibility that we will ever . . .

I went over all your letters again. I saw all the times you didn't answer
me after I had asked if you had yet given up the guillotine. Why, I didn't
even know if you were still flirting with the idea of it for two months.
Then came the moment, and I know exactly when it was . . . when you
told me about the egg without a shell. I told myself then that I would stop
nagging you with this question, because it was unnecessary. Since then,
from letter to letter, I truly believed you had released yourself from your
internal "deal." That cruel, stupid—

Yair, I know the deal is not just "stupid." Believe me, I understand
what you need to fight in order to escape yourself at last, to come to me;
you need complete internal freedom. I also know, of course, how hard it
is to recover, even as an adult, from those diseases from childhood that
left scars.

Perhaps—it occurs to me—perhaps you are even more afraid of the
recovery. If it is so, say it, just tell me, and we can weep over it together,
about the wretched feelings planted in us, that we are, ourselves, the disease. That if we dared to rebel and recover, perhaps our life's breath
would suddenly be taken away from us. Is that it?

Always. It always is. That fear, the prophecy of the heart, that the disease or the falseness or the stain planted in us is our most basic element, our Luz . . .

Why can't you tell me something so horrible? It will bring us even closer to each other if you can simply come to me and tell me . . . and I would say yes . . . and, for a moment, perhaps we could breathe our relief together.

Because I have no other person that knows me there, in that last curve of my soul, that much. Neither do you.

But what was I thinking? What I believed would happen to me when I would be with you "there." My profound pain springs from places that have nothing to do with you, from things you and I haven't even started to discuss. We have only started the long journey . . .

I imagine a storm, a volcanic eruption from your insides and mine, something sweeping and shaking, that exposes us, forces us to live in another skin (or even better than that—with no skin at all).

I see the perfect bubble of a level rule, straight, complete, the innocence of both total knowledge and total abandon to that knowledge. A match between two. The two of us. Which neither of us can reach separately.

This is the one (and only) pain in my life that you can solve or allay: the pain of my separateness from you. It was, until you, only a vague, dull pain. Perhaps I couldn't even name it so clearly, perhaps it would erode and sink into the other burdens of life. But you came and gave it a name, and a vocabulary.

On second thought, Yair, I'm not certain that you can ease even that pain. But at least our connection can "ground" itself in us, as you once called it. I do prefer to think about us participating, together, in the same "merciful surplus of strength," full of grace, that Kafka speaks of in his diary, in the entry on September 19, 1917 (when he is wondering how he can "write to someone: I am unhappy"):

"And it is not a lie, and it does not still my pain; it is simply the merciful surplus of strength at a moment when suffering has raked me to the bottom of my being."

The one thought that does not cease: Where will the first rain catch me? At home? In the street? In front of my pupils? And where on my body will the first drop hit? My ear is alert at night for any sounds of pattering . . .

Other possibilities are open to me: to rid myself of the torture, to not cooperate, to stop rubbing the wound of expectation.

To my list of losses I am adding this morning, with a heavy heart— my internal freedom.

Another day. You're gone. I can't stop looking at the sky. How is it that you managed to transform the whole world into two huge clamps slowly tightening around me? Enough, enough, enough (but "enough" is also "Yair, speak to me"). I'm picturing you differently these days. Look: you're a clock mender. A dark, intriguing clock mender, sitting in a little suffocating alcove, full of tickings. There you are. A lonely man, burning with a tremendous urge that ebbs and flows like a wave constantly winding the gears of several clocks at once, setting them so they will sound out one after another according to some predetermined secret plan, ringing all night and all day, in the summer and winter, throughout the whole of time . . .

You have some of that clock mender in you, don't you? With the will and arrogance to set your falling in love, constant and ever-changing, so that you will always be surrounded by music (feminine?) that will ring and swing like a pendulum in you, hum inside you so there won't be a single moment of unbearable silence, of a quiet in which one might hear time itself, God forbid, passing, escaping.

Is that what we were? I was just a prop in some private ceremony (or is it a ritual?) of yours? Perhaps you change women every season of the year. This was your "Summer of Miriam." And afterward, another woman's winter will come. Perhaps, as part of your secret self-bureaucracies, you count out the time in between us with "moments" of women. I was just another clock hand, pointing out to you that another "hour," another season, had passed, another woman . . .

So then, perhaps, your conversation is not truly with us little miserable daughters of Eve, after all, but with His Majesty, Time.

Get out of my life.

Morning. I haven't written for two days. A feeling of relief that I cannot fully understand. Touching the tips of my toes into the frozen waters of being able to live with this . . .

A woman is here, crawling on the ground after being hit by a disaster. She isn't even so sure what it was . . . certain moments of the day, she feels as if everything around her was erased. After that, it becomes clear that everything exists exactly as it did before, except she doesn't. She barely moves her lips during her internal conversations. Strange how all this hardly hurts her. It's better this way.

She'll be fine. She only has to really want, with all her will (oh), to be fine. She moves through her day precisely and economically, as if a huge cork is plugging up her heart's mouth. She uses the illness from earlier this week as a good excuse for this dullness in her thoughts. Yokhai is home all of a sudden. So there are things to be busy with.

Now she is reading the lines she just wrote. You can live with it.

Bank—dry cleaners—two classes—glass mender for the latest broken window—meeting—another meeting—conversation with a physiotherapist—grocery—give my watch to the clock mender to be fixed—comforting a mourner . . . What is he thinking of today, my green man of Mars?

"Look at this woman. I guess it hurts her unbearably to touch reality."

At least the writing is still here.
    Like putting stones in a turbulent river.
    Slowly, slowly, perhaps, with hard work, a bridge can be built over which she can escape from this place.

Yokhai has been home for three days now. They've stationed a construction waste container by his school gate. There is no one to talk to about it.

I've been spending time with him, doing a little organizing, rehabilitating the skin of our home as much as Yokhai allows it.

It's hard to concentrate when he's here.

I arranged all the chairs in the house in a line for him. He is walking on them with surprising skill. It probably pleases him greatly, his organ of balance. This is how it was once scientifically explained to us . . . perhaps he is writing something in his constant movement. Perhaps there is some hidden meaning to the paper balls he rolls into the corners of rooms, to the door frames he touches . . .

Don't look for meaning.

Going and coming back, so concentrated and serious, mysterious, ever-busy, and always fascinated by his internal life. He doesn't even know I'm here . . .

(But just now, when I hugged him, he hugged me back.)

Night. Of course, small-minded people will tell me that it is a quarter past four in the morning right now; still, I had three hours of sleep. An unexpected gift! (And Anna, wherever she is, is laughing: you and your Pollyannaisms.)

A brief flash of happiness . . . Ariela called to ask about what's going on. During our conversation she told me that today she taught the part when Romeo leaves Verona for the first time and says that he had a good dream that night; one student burst in and said that he was able to sleep, he doesn't understand how horrible it is . . .

It stabbed me, as if I had betrayed something by sleeping.

I have already spent two hours on the phone to City Hall. They transfer me from clerk to clerk. The last one, the manager, was nice at first, but it turned out that the contractor who stationed the waste container didn't break any law, not one. Except for the law of one child. Then, lady, have the child come in the other gate, he shouted at me, and then he hung up on me. And Amos just called—they are renovating the building next door to the school and it will last for at least two months.

I sit down. Yokhai certainly looks happy, pacing along his path, counting to himself. What will happen? Bambi, William, and Kedem are looking at him, bored. Sometimes I think that, in the same way he doesn't perceive them at all, they too somehow don't register his existence. Perhaps this is why I have some difficulty loving them with all my heart. What will happen now? Nilly touches him a lot more, rubs her back against him, plays with him—even more than she does with her kittens. He truly responds the most to her. Why don't they make more of an effort with him? I love dogs so much, and of all of them, the ones I am least successful with are my own.

The conversation with Amos was horrible. He asked me what we were going to do, and how we would handle this for two more months, and shouted that he has just started a new group, and it is actually on the right track, and I answered that I, too, as he knows, have a job, and we buzzed back and forth, and I got angry. We both didn't raise our voices even half an octave, so as not to scare Yokhai. Here we are, the dogs have fallen asleep again. Maybe something in this house makes them fall asleep. I don't know. I don't know what I feel anymore. We hosted a couple of kids here a few weeks ago, the Herman boys. The dogs, all three of them, almost lost their minds with joy. I saw their bodies suddenly moving in new ways, heard voices I didn't recognize from them. Puppies' voices.

Walking back and forth on the chairs, as if from strings in the sky. A moment before I blow up, I tell myself, How can I burden him with the troubles of those of us who walk the ground? To the place he is probably in right now?

The thin and loose embroidery of things new to me . . . that is what I mourn above everything. With him, I finally succeeded in getting over my loathsome impulse to unstitch myself, my own black twin. I actually surprised myself, finding that I could weave more and more intricately, without immediately unstitching it. Without spoiling it for myself. A joy in living, and a love of living (and even a little love for myself!).

So what is happening to me now? What is happening is this: Y. is becoming my knife.

It happened today again. The moment he saw that orange bin he stuck his feet under the front seat and refused to allow anyone to take him out of the car. An hour and a half of efforts, of persuasion from his teachers, the principal, his favorite physiotherapist, to no avail. Temptations and threats and promises and bribes; Amos even ran to a toy shop and bought him a truck that looked a little like the container—and after that, he argued with the construction workers, threatening them and begging them—nothing. Yokhai simply refuses to recognize that this is the same school he has been studying at for four years now. I left work at eleven to be with him. I had to cancel three classes and one test.

In spite of everything, I am fortunate. I mustn't forget that, not for a moment. I'm thinking about the person with the lifeless face and fireless body sitting in front of me on the bus.

We continue to study drought in my little circle tonight. Akiva decided that this would be our modest contribution toward hastening the coming of the rain. I sat among them wondering if I wasn't forming some kind of fifth column inside this general wish for a coming downpour. Some kind of Jonah the Prophet, in his boat—except the other way around . . . Yudaleh brought in a teaching from the Zohar: Rabbi Shimon once said that there is one gazelle in the land, and He the Most High does much for her. When she screams, the Blessed One hears her pain and accepts her voice. When the world needs mercy and water, she gives her voice, and the Holy Blessed He hears her, and then pities the world, as it is written, "as a deer longs for flowing streams" (Psalm 42). When she needs to give birth, and is held in, constricted on all sides, and bows her head between her knees and screams and throws her voice, the King of the World pities her and invites one snake to come upon her, which bites her groin, tearing through and opening that one place, and she delivers her calf immediately.

I told them about the scared, trembling gazelle that almost bumped into me this morning in the fog, as I was on my way to the creek. They became excited: It is she! It is she!

A telephone call at seven in the morning. It is the contractor who owns the waste container; he launched into an attack, shouting at me, Why are you bothering my workers? Why have you been driving me crazy for a week? I'm working by the letter of the law, and if you make any more trouble for me, I'll come to your house with a bulldozer . . . As he yelled, I started speaking to him quietly, even though I knew there was not a chance he was listening (I wonder, now, why did I speak. As if I had decided to, let's say, present my case in front of some kind of mysterious court that probably passes judgment on such matters). Anyway, by the time I got to the blue gate in our garden, which we have not been able to paint for years so that he won't get confused and scared, I noticed the man was no longer shouting. I don't even know when he stopped shouting and started listening. I felt exposed and embarrassed . . . Look at what is happening to you, you gave up Yokhai's disability check for years so they wouldn't turn your boy into some "retard." And now you're using your troubles to influence a total stranger. The contractor was breathing, deep breaths. A strange silence surrounded him too. Then he told me that there is something he cannot tell me. If he spoke of it to anyone, he would have to kill himself, die by his own hands. But if I wait for him for one hour and then bring Yokhai to school, the container will be gone. And so it was.

A lunchtime treat: *Uncle Vanya*, produced by our theater program. Some of the kids weren't so great, but still, there were moments during which I loved this marvelous play even more than before.

This time my big moment was when Sonya suddenly stands up and starts delivering an enthusiastic speech about the importance of preserving the forest, because this is what her beloved is the most passionate about. In the darkness I wrote, quickly, along the whole length of my inner arm, under my sleeve: Yair, I wanted badly to tell you about yourself, your story was even more important to me than my own. And now I feel I have lost my story.

But there . . . I am looking at my arm, and my skin is moving underneath the letters; it is warm, the flesh is breathing, and my body is alive.

A thought that hasn't let go of me: What was truly there in the first moment? If I hadn't smiled that smile and hugged myself, what then . . .

To think I was so very charming without making any kind of effort.

What I gave him, that thing that spoke to him from deep inside me that, without my knowledge, revived him in this way; the thing between me and myself . . .

I know it exists. It existed before he looked at me, too. It still exists, even if there is no one to look at it now. It is the good in me, and it cannot be destroyed. And thanks to that, I cannot be destroyed.

If only I could give that to myself as well right now.

Just like that. To release it . . . watch it spring out . . .

This morning, at the bus stop by the junction into the village, an old, heavy, unkempt woman approached me. She apparently works as a cleaning lady for one of the families here. She said she has been watching me for quite some time, and that she likes my face and would like to tell me about something so as to hear my opinion about it.

Meanwhile, the bus came. We sat together. She opened up and told me about herself and her life, her illnesses, and her children, who are currently scattered around the world; and the entire time she kept asking me if I was sure she wasn't a nuisance.

She told me she came from a religious family, and that with everything happening around her in the past few years, she is beginning to think that perhaps there is no God. The thought frightens her very much, it has been destroying her life and her health. But a few months ago she saw a television program about India, and it inspired her; a new thought has gripped her and isn't letting go: how she, Rivka, with only her own strength, will force God to reveal Himself. She will use all her savings to travel to the land of India (she isn't scared, because she will be protected by her holy purpose as a sacred messenger). She will go to the temple they showed on television, where there are so many thousands of idols, and she will walk between the gods, pretending to examine them, hesitating over which one of them to choose— Maybe this one? Maybe that one? And then our God, Elohim Ha Shem, will not be able to stand the fact that even she, who has been so loyal to Him for sixty-five years, is doubting Him; that, simply out of jealousy, He will burst out and reveal Himself in front of her, and will shout from the depths of His heart: Rivka, enough! Enough of it! I am here!

It truly delighted me so much. Not just the story, but the fact that she chose to tell it to me.

What makes me even happier is that things are happening all the time in the world, and they are not just about him and me.

An exhibition of seventh-graders' work in the hall in front of the teachers' lounge. I'm walking with the other teachers, looking at the work, practically floating on my pride for their growth over the past year. But I am well practiced . . . I felt the dagger flying out there in the room and started to shrink in expectation of it.

I read the following in Avishai Riklin's biology paper: "In order for the bird to be able to fully develop its voice, it must be exposed to its kind during the first months of its life. Otherwise, its singing ability will be permanently damaged."

I am stuck there, staring at it, probably for a long time; until Ariela comes up to me and pulls me away, gently. I'm followed by curious, worried looks. My throat burns.

(Come sing with me, my kind.)

A diary is a daybook. If this is one, it should be called a nightbook.

I got up for a drink at a quarter past three and stumbled into Yokhai in the darkness. He was walking around half-asleep, completely confused and without pants. He must have come back from the bathroom and started wandering, for God knows how long, until I found him. I put on his pajamas and brought him back to bed, and he kept getting up again and again. So I agreed to walk along his track with him—I hadn't slept so well anyway—and there was something pleasant about it. He walked with me in the exact same way we walk in the street, half a step behind me, holding on to the edge of my sleeve . . . and if I am completely aware of him, which doesn't always happen on the street, our steps match in a perfect harmony of movement. We succeeded tonight, not a single motion squeaked in our rhythm, and I was prepared to go on for much longer and longer; it looked as if he was getting some pleasure from it, because he showed no signs of tiring until a quarter to four—he actually seemed to be having fun, telling me something in his own way.

I then had an idea. I walked him to the kitchen, shut the door, and turned on the heater. I took off his pajamas and wrapped him up in a big towel, and, of course, served him burekas and a whole variety of flavored yogurts. It took us a little while, but he cooperated marvelously; he didn't jump up or shout, even when I brought out the scissors. Finally, after three months of fights and scandal, he let me cut his hair.

It's unbelievable the way he sat, completely quiet. He was possessed of a stoic relaxation, even a little royal, with only his slight humming and rocking, stopping only to bite into the burekas. Every once in a while he looked up with a sassy expression, as if to say, "You see? It simply depends on my will . . ."

Even when I cut his bangs, even when a few hairs fell into his mouth (!). What is this? I don't know my own child! You could almost think for a moment that he had made the clear-minded decision to compensate for his horrible rage that afternoon, when Amos and I tried together. And perhaps it is truly so.

Every time I forget, he has a way of, gently, and without words, reminding me.

What will happen when he starts growing a mustache and a beard? How will we shave him? Maybe while he sleeps, a particularly deep sleep, like the ones he has after a fit. Well, I don't exactly have to plan for this now.

In two or three years we will have to be separated from our child for a second time; in the meantime, we have the grace of childhood. What will he look like in five years? I can't even imagine it, not in this moment. Anna had a thin, sexy fuzz, but then Anna was dark; Amos is quite dark as well. It seems as if Yokhai inherited his very soft, fair hair from me (and his clumsiness, and his lack of confidence, and we shouldn't forget his feeling of utter strangeness in the world . . .).

And what will happen in ten years? In twenty? Strange rooms, strange people, and itchy wool blankets.

When he ran out of patience, he stood up with his hair half-cut, but didn't run away even then. He continued walking, slowly, the length of the corridor and back, and didn't once object that I continued cutting his hair as he walked. Let it be while walking, while running, while dancing, while jumping! Such moments of grace don't come every day. Amos will go crazy when he wakes up.

And just as I was finishing, he hinted at wanting to go back to bed. He let me put a splash of Amos's aftershave, which he likes, on the back of his neck; and a few scattered kisses. And in this manner of sleepy reconciliation, I put him to bed.

I am waiting for the sunrise. I too must sleep, for at least one more hour, before this long day begins. The house is full of fuzzy footprints, and I can hardly hold myself back from waking Amos and telling him . . . to see the special smile he has for such news. What a pity I can't listen to music right now—the Third Quartet is certainly suitable. Will you wait for me until morning, Ludwig van? I don't know why I was so angry with you a few days ago—how could I forget you are so full of life, so optimistic?

My social life is becoming suspiciously active; I met Ariela at Atara Café this morning. It's the first time we have ever met outside the teachers' lounge to talk. Poor Ariela was a bit unnerved by me and thought I was investigating her. At one moment she said quite honestly that despite all her affection for me, she still becomes embarrassed by these intimate conversations at such an early stage of our friendship. What could I tell her? That I am probably already too used to this kind of talk? That it has suddenly become unbearable to me to *not* say everything, or at least practically everything, to a person who looks as if she might be able to understand, exactly?

I don't think my first enthusiasm was misplaced. Ariela is charming and clever (even though I can feel how she is a few years younger, and that weighs on me).

I remember especially this, from our meeting: in a moment of total honesty she confessed that if her Gideon "cheated on her once or twice" with another woman, it would cause her terrible pain, but she would eventually get over it and stay with him. But if he fell in love with someone else, she would leave immediately ("In a moment!"). I flew off the handle—because of the unbearable pain that every disappointment, or feeling of being at odds with someone close to me, causes now . . . I told her that it was exactly the other way around with me: if I knew that Amos was only playing around with someone, it would be a serious reason for me not to respect him and not to want to live with him. But if he fell in love . . . to see such a living, beloved emotion in him would only make him more beautiful to my eyes.

I saw, in her gaze, that she was distancing herself from me, her unripe eyes rose up for a moment. It was so hard for me to see. I grabbed her hand in a sudden panic. She got scared—Tell me, Miriam, are you all right?

I just found K.'s recipe for the possibility of perfect joy. Believe in the eternal thing in yourself, and do not aspire to it.

Then again, this morning I can hardly believe in that which is eternal in me. I instead aspire, probably, to the finite thing outside myself that is quickly becoming destroyed.

(As I was writing this, Nilly came up to me, and I decided to ask her as well. I said, "Nilly, do you think I will ever be happy? If so, move your left ear. And if not, the right." And what did that cat do? She moved both of them!)

Maybe she understood, long before I did, that you can never return from this place in peace. (Not just home—in general.)

Amos is in Be'er Sheva. On a two-day teachers' workshop. Oh, the pictures I've been developing in my mind over the last few hours as I've been circling the phone, hovering. I could make him come here in an instant (so I delude myself). I will make an appeal to his cheapness, pluck the one string that can always be roused to noise—I will whisper, "My husband is not home," into the phone, as in some bad movie, and he won't be able to resist the temptation.

An hour of complete insanity passed. With all the excitement in the world, I walked through the house gathering a few bunches of paper balls that Yokhai has hidden in the corners. I prepared a little exhibition of them on the kitchen table. After that, I opened each and every one of them in the order I set. I ironed them flat with my hands—and crumpled them back again into little balls. Then I scattered them once again into the corners . . . There is undoubtedly something to it, squashing up paper in this way. Reason returns to me at midnight, with the prickles of needles, like blood rushing back into a hand that fell asleep.

This morning's lottery (again!) drew the last letter from Tel Aviv: ". . . that you actually strike a spark from me to ignite yourself to life."

I'm reading it and am filled with despair. I don't understand the tone of his complaint, this thrusting of guilt onto me; it makes me so happy each time someone, anyone, a pupil, a friend, Amos "takes a spark from me."

Please, take it, I have so few takers.

I want this—each time the green man on Mars gazes down at me, he will see how sparks fly, every time I interact and connect with another person.

. . . And immediately, upon my first exit from the house after writing, "reality" responds: I sneezed hard by the traffic light at Ha-Mekasher Junction. A young man, tanned, with blond curls and a backpack, passed in front of me. He took a deep breath and laughed: "Even your germs, baby."

A stupid quarrel with A. It started with his suggestion that I take a vacation, to refresh myself. Maybe even go abroad. And I attacked him, screeched out that he probably doesn't want me by his side right now, that he can hardly stand me in the condition I've been in. It was complete nonsense, it had no basis in reality, but I was already swept away on a tide of anger. I felt as if internal streams of poisons were breaking open inside me, my guts were burning . . . I said horrible things. As an impartial observer I listened to myself . . . I sounded as if I was reciting text from some cheap melodrama—Maybe he already has someone else, and if he wants to be with her, he should look for a better, less transparent excuse. His face sank in front of me, faded away; he tried to calm me down and looked so worried for me, scared—it tore my heart, and still I wasn't able to stop. It was as if a burning, twisting spiral cord had been cut loose and scratched my insides; it was a crazy mix of pain and meaningless pleasure. Then I said something about him and Anna (something I had never thought before and will not write down now), and his face tightened as if I had slapped him. He left home, slamming the door, and came back just before dawn, after I had spent hours with my nightmares, seeing him in every possible place. I apologized and he forgave me. But how will he really be able to forgive and forget? The air in the house is constrainedly polite and burning. Yokhai, who witnessed it, sticks by Amos and refuses to let go of him; he considers me with a new kind of look, as if he finally understands, for the first time, what the story truly is.

Another fit tonight. Probably because of the tension. This time he suddenly refused to swallow the Apenotin. He raged, and broke another window, and hurt his hand. Amos couldn't stand it and went out for a walk. I struggled with him by myself for long minutes until I succeeded in calming him down (he really is a lot stronger than I am). While doing that, he again scraped open the scab on his forehead. I really don't know how to keep him from doing that again and again, he takes such a terrible pleasure in scraping and rubbing his wounds, and it drives me crazy (also because I understand it so completely). Later, when I finally managed to get him to bed, he asked me with hand signs to tie him down, something we haven't had to do for a long time now, months. Amos wasn't there, so I decided to do it alone. Again, it was amazing to see how it immediately calmed him. I rubbed his feet and sang quietly to him until he fell asleep; so perhaps we renewed our pact with each other.

I sank in front of the television, exhausted. I was so run-down, so empty, I thought that if a miracle didn't happen in a few minutes, I would simply cease to exist. With no pain.

A miracle happened, as usual. They broadcast another one of "my" programs, about the forgotten tribes that Amos suspects the BBC invents just for me. This time it was about a tribe living in the Sahara desert. Once a year they migrate to a new place to live, and they feast for a week and marry off the girls. Each girl chooses two men and spends her first night with them. One very pretty girl told the camera, "On this night I will become a woman." For a few weeks she will have sexual relations with both of them, but after that, she will marry a third . . .

They showed her after the first night, sitting with both her men, combing the hair of one of them— He laughed and told the other one, "You see? At night she loved you more, but now she loves me."

Nothing happened, but I felt that I was slowly returning from some dark place.

Why, you can, during a complete life with someone (said Amos later, in the kitchen, after we made up), travel the whole spectrum of human emotions, and I said, And animal ones as well. He closed his eyes and became silent with memories not from here, and I saw, flashing on his (already tired, already comfortable) face, what used to scare me in him, the mark of times and memories in which I have no part. This time, for some reason, it brought me joy, even relief, as if, for a moment, a polygon crystal filled with shadows had turned in front of me, and at the end of the turn again showed the well-known features; and it wasn't fake, this is his face now; each facet, together, is also the sum of all his faces. I was filled with love for him in a way I haven't felt for weeks. Love for him, because of him, himself, alone. I thought how lucky I was that I was no longer a young girl, and that he is no longer a young man; and thought how much I love his wrinkles.

I'm eight or nine years old, in the apartment on 15 Nekhemya Street; folded up into my hiding place behind the "geyser" in the bathroom, my body clinging to the hot boiler as I whisper tragic love stories to myself that I used to invent (it bursts open inside me as I write—the smell of burning wood, the lavender bottle I found on the beach and kept back there, hidden with *Life Assets,* the book that was my Bible; the way I used to search for my groom among the fallen soldiers of the *Scrolls of Fire.* My little round mirror, my treasure with the red velvet back, in front of which I would practice wild Hollywood kisses for hours, exemplary little girl that I was. I was also Eliki, and Marisol the Spanish singer—it's been thirty years since I've thought of her, and just like that, she springs out of my little finger . . .).

I am crouched there, behind the geyser; it was the only place in the house my mother couldn't get into. I'm whispering a story to myself, completely focused on it, but I suddenly feel something—deep furrows are being plowed into my back: she is on tiptoe, she has sneaked in to listen to me (the smell of the bleach from her hands slaps me in the face). Then, as if I hadn't noticed her, I begin raising my voice, speaking with elevated language, ornamented and lofty. I excite myself without shame, so that she'll understand and know exactly just how splendid and glamorous I am, so she will feel like a dry raisin in front of the harvest celebration that I am. So she knows that I will never be her.

(It now becomes clear to me that more than once, when I was writing to Yair, perhaps more than I was willing to admit, I used to write for that pair of eyes as well, that were always, always, snooping over my shoulder. Oh, the twisted temptation to once again feel how they are bulging open behind me in amazement, monstrous and shocked at what I am capable of . . .)

Not now, though. In these pages I don't feel them there at all.

No one to the left of me, no one to the right. There are none behind me, none to my side.

Over the last hour, the sky has begun to produce an unusual light within the usual twilight, almost European. I've been sitting here for even longer, hypnotized, absorbing the changing colors into my body. Only my writing hand is moving. Our kingfisher is simply going out of his mind with the beauty of it, diving again and again into the turquoise light, not to hunt for insects, or to impress a female kingfisher, either—only to add his own color to the picture. I suddenly know again that the world *exists*; it is beautiful, and even if I am not always completely available to appreciate its beauty, others can feel it, and soon I will be able to return to that, to fee

Dear God

Everything is fine. Everything is fine. Now. It's all over. I am writing mainly to keep myself from shaking. I was sitting on the balcony, writing, and Yokhai was playing in the garden. I usually lift my head every few seconds to watch him, but I guess I forgot for a moment. When I next lifted my head, he was gone and the gate was open. I ran as if my life depended on it, and the thoughts were racing through my head—that maybe I should pierce the tires of parked cars, so they wouldn't be able to go, etc., and where could he have gone, and who will find him. I asked neighbors, people in the street. No one had seen him. I ran to the center of the village like a madwoman, bursting into the grocery store, to the candy shelves, because sometimes . . . but he wasn't there. Everyone stared at me, with that look of . . . I return home (this all happened about half an hour ago), and he is not at home.

The fear. Until now, I——and all the internal judges, of course, pronouncing the verdict: they left him in my care and I didn't keep him safe. Again, I get up, run down the road into the valley, and there—finally

—I see him walking along the lower path. No. First I hear a strange, heavy, ringing noise; only then do I see him, walking, bent over. My first thought—they did something to him. I run to him and see that someone has hung a huge cowbell around his neck.

At least he isn't hurt (I have ten hands in such moments as these). I immediately check him all over his body, and he is fine. Just that bell. Who's done this? What is—and as he moves, the bell rings and the thick, rough rope scratches his delicate neck. I try to tear it off with my hands, with my teeth, and I can't. I see two giggling teenagers behind a rock; I don't know them. Perhaps they are from the nearby school. My mind is blank. I sit Yokhai down on a rock and walk up to them, without the faintest idea as to why. They back off. I hear someone explaining, out loud, in my voice, I'd better stay away from them—I start running after them, and they escape. Fifteen-year-olds, teenagers, slim like bamboo sticks, but I caught up to them by the split rock. I'm breathless, so I ask them with my eyes, with my hands, with my teeth, *Why*? They laugh at me—one of them has huge pimples on his forehead, the other is trying to grow a little beard. They are older than I thought, maybe seventeen, and they start playing with me, turning me around, making obscene gestures as they dance in front of me, poking me from behind, on my back, the back of my neck. All of it is silent, and I don't know why I don't yell for help. I just know I have to get away. But then they begin to imitate Yokhai, his walk, his blinking. I choose the larger of the two—he is a head taller than I am, and I wait for him to come close to me. And then, with the whole of my palm, I slap him. I slap him so hard I fall—but apparently he falls as well. I get up first, being at least more practiced in these situations, and the other guy backs off a little. So I pick up a thick piece of wood that had been left there and swing it in his face. The one on the ground is actually screaming in pain, holding his face and screaming. Soon the other one will scream, too. I will kill them and throw their bodies in a well. The other bends to pick up a stone, and I slam him behind his knees with all the strength I don't have. He falls for what seems like a long time and howls in pain. My mind finally starts to clear as he is lying at my feet, begging me not to hurt him. I still need to do something to the bastard—but Yokhai is alone, I left him alone again! I run to him, leaving them behind. They curse and stones fall close to me—but not a single one hits me. That's it. That's the whole story.

What's odd is that I was sure such an incident would knock Yokhai off balance for months, we would have to change medications, his whole daily schedule—but he was actually laughing. He came up to me and laughed quietly, the way he sometimes does when he sees himself in the mirror. I don't know what made him laugh now, but at least he wasn't scared: I truly would never have guessed that reaction. I hugged him to calm him down; more to calm myself down; I refused to understand that those were my legs shaking so badly down there. Fear always concentrates itself in my legs. But by then I had fully recovered my senses, and I started worrying about having left this notebook on the balcony table. (Now, as I write, I finally remember again the kingfisher's dance, how lovely it was, truly, an otherworldly beauty that was of this world, still. I have to figure out sometime why it always is that a "hard time" can last for months, yet a moment of grace is always just a moment.) What else did I want to write here? That I eventually managed to untie the rope by myself; with all my shaking, I stood there and untied it. The teenagers came closer, keeping a safe distance all the while. I don't know why, perhaps as a final slap in their face, I tied the bell to my own neck—it was heavy, and the rope cut the back of my neck. Yokhai looked up at me, too, without comprehending why, and I didn't quite understand it either, but it felt right. I took Yokhai by the hand and walked away with a broken body and a broken soul, and he was jumping with joy, and the bell was ringing.

Would you look at me? Standing in the kitchen, smeared with flour and dough and food coloring, surrounded by hundreds of colorful candies scattered out of their bags onto the floor. And I escaped my soul, finding shelter within my notebook and your beloved Schubert.

I'm trying to prepare a lion cake for Yokhai's birthday, wavy mane and all—it has to look exactly like the painting in the book . . . He has been sitting with Josie Mendelsohn's book day after day, for a year now, dreaming about this cake (or at least I like to think he is). Now everything falls on me, and I can't cut straight, and the mane looks like a wig, and I'm thinking of your tiny precise hands. I need you here, now, to hold my two left hands.

If you were here right now, you would know exactly what I should do. I would call you now, or at four in the morning. You would understand everything just by my "Hello" and be here in fifteen minutes with a bouquet of chrysanthemums picked from one of the neighbors' gardens.

I would stand in front of you, and tell you that I have apparently stranded myself again. You would comfort me, reminding me of all the good things in my life, one by one, and all the dear moments I had this summer. You would tell me that I wasn't only stranded, I was embraced as well, there were so many moments when I was taken in. We would laugh together over the fact that I am probably the oldest orphan ever to be adopted.

By the time my tears were dried, the mane would roar, and you would ask me to tell you about one good thing, good "at this very moment." I would think a lot . . . and finally guess that my situation isn't completely to be despaired over, if I can still enjoy the smell of a fresh cucumber. If I only had you this summer, oh, how many times have I prayed to have you this summer. You would have understood so much sooner than I did what I should do. Oy, Anutchka. You embraced this slippery life so fully, much more so than I do. I discover that in all sorts of little ways, in the tiniest, most intimate roadmarks you left behind in the world, without a prick of envy. How can you envy someone who knew how to love in this way, and who in this way encouraged others to love her with complete freedom and with such purity?

But again, those thoughts rise up, the same ones that tormented my life after you left, that I promised you I would never think again. And again, I am defenseless against them, the maybes and ifs, the thoughts that nibble that it isn't fair, and even terribly illogical in so many ways, that I was left alive and not you.

It is an even more painful stab to my heart, because of Yair knowing about you. It made the burden of sorrow a bit lighter, even the burden of missing you; not that I miss you any less, but I somehow didn't die of it ten times a day. And now I don't know how I will find the strength to endure it all over again, by myself. Tomorrow, as you know, won't be an easy day. Stay by my side, hold on, and I will, too.

We went to her grave in the morning, with Omma and Oppa and her brothers; and in the afternoon we celebrated his birthday. Friends came (ours. I invited our new neighbors' kids, but it was clear, eventually, that they weren't coming). Yokhai was on cloud nine; Tammy baked him his favorite fruitcake, so he had some compensation for the lion with the sparse mane that I managed to produce. He was feeling safe and secure, surrounded by goodness, and everyone brought him lots of cheese burekas . . . There was such a good feeling in the air, people stayed and stayed, didn't want to leave. I looked out at the garden, and at the house that was suddenly so full of light, so happy, full of people, I mean, we haven't hosted this many people in maybe three years. Amos drank a bit too much, and almost fell off the roof later when he went up there to lasso the moon for Yokhai.

When the guests started leaving at nine, Yokhai panicked; he ran to them, holding on and screaming, he hit his head against the table. I understand how he felt, as if something in him was leaking, running out as they left.

He had a fit just after ten while he was taking a bath, inside a full bathtub. We barely managed to hold his head above the water as we pulled him out. The fit has been in the air for a few days now, with all the nervousness and other signals that come beforehand (I'm comforted by the fact that at least he stayed well through the party).

We held him together this time; we could hardly look each other in the eye. He gasped and stiffened between us and shook. Out of the corner of my eye I could see Amos passing his finger over his temple, right by his ear again and again, to calm him down, and I heard him whisper, "Sweetheart, honey." I thought about how at one time, years ago, I would still call God out for a harsh conversation about justice after every fit.

The fit lasted longer and was more severe than usual—time refused to pass. His body was hard as a stone between our hands, his hands clenched, frozen, against his open mouth, from which no scream emerged. I saw Amos's face twisting in front of him, as if trying to absorb the pain into himself.

Amos once said that when a man cries out, "I'm hurt," he doesn't necessarily believe that his pain can be relieved; more often than not, he just needs someone to chase away the loneliness inside his pain.

I started to breathe again only after the color had returned to his feet. We carried him to bed. He immediately tried to stand up and walk, he had no idea at all what had happened; but his legs folded under him and he lay down, exhausted. After a moment, he threw up all the burekas he had eaten. Amos kept stroking him with his good hands, and I had to go, go out to the balcony and write a little bit.

Now he's bawling, a good sign that everything has passed—but it is always my hardest moment. He probably isn't suffering anymore, not the way he did before . . . His mind is completely foggy, he is beginning to fall asleep . . . and that's when his bawling begins, bellowing up from the depths in some kind of sorrow that his body can't contain, as if his body is singing a song of mourning about itself.

I will go back in. In a minute. If only I could sit here all night and write and write. Writing like this is good for me, I can see that. Even when I write things that are hard and depressing, something in me quiets and focuses.

I want to sit here and write about the simplest things. Describe the leaf that just now fell, or the stack of chairs on the balcony . . . or the moth attracted to our lamps . . . to tell the history of one complete night, until the darkness changes with the sunrise, until the colors change. I don't mind sitting like this for days and nights, describing every blade of grass, every flower, stones in the fence, pinecones; and after that, when I feel ready, to cautiously shift to writing about myself, about my body, for instance. To start with what you can touch with it; and also to start from afar, from the distance of my toes, and slowly come closer, and write about each organ in my body and remember its senses, once and now. Memories of an ankle, perhaps, or a cheek, or my neck. Why not? Trace its history through caresses and kisses and scars, sustaining my existence through writing. It will take a long time, but there's time, and life is long, and I want to tell myself about myself, tell myself what probably no one else can tell me, tell my story without adding anything to myself, but also without taking anything away from myself. To write without wanting anything from anyone. To write solely in my own voice.

I hear Amos inside, starting to clean up. I will go, too. There will be a lot of laundry to do tonight, and we must clean the rug in Yokhai's room. This too. Everything.

December 1
Yair, hello.

It is evening. And I am at home. It is a cloudy, vague night outside, dull weather. The sky smells of a consistent, moderate cold. Not pleasant.

I make my report to you as if you were in another country. You are in another country. A month and a half has passed since the last letter I wrote you, a letter that now seems a distant dream. I have no idea if you have any interest in reading my words. Despite this, I continued writing to you, quite a lot actually, between me and myself.

Without my intending it, this notebook became sort of a diary. I discovered it sometimes helps me to alleviate my sorrow. And sometimes it sharpens my sorrow very much. I still see my desire (my need, even) to write it as a beautiful, unexpected gift I give to myself.

And you? Do you still speak to me? Do you still remember? Will you feel relieved when the rain finally comes down?

I hope I will also understand what I am feeling more by then, but I am afraid that won't be the case. I would have liked to be able to write that I wished everything would end between us and wash away completely with the first rain. But that is still the opposite of how I feel, and that is the one thing I have no doubts about, whether you reply or not. Even now.

Why am I writing to you? I'm not even sure if I know. Maybe because the clouds are thickening more than usual—or because, for the first time since your disappearance, I feel able, again, to address you, speak to you. I am slowly coming to think that perhaps I am approaching the place at which I will be able to separate myself from you, or at least from the painful constant expectation of your arrival at my door. And I will be able to do so without giving up a single emotion or sense that you aroused in me. Not one.

You know, I've been thinking lately about how little we spoke about things that were outside the closed circle we were in together. I remember how, more than once, before sitting down to write to you, I would decide to tell you about at least one thing that happened to me in the "external" world since the last letter. To bring some piece of "reality" into our bubble, give it some space. I think now that I almost never succeeded, whatever I had to tell you about us was always more important, more urgent . . . But for how long, do you think, could such an exchange continue without nourishment from the outside, from everyday reality? How much time would have passed until that density would have become suffocation? Do you think people exist who could have lived complete lives like this?

(Yet now, at this moment, I feel once more that it is in just this kind of density that I could truly start breathing.)

Here, listen to this real something that you didn't know before: Every night before he goes to sleep, Yokhai comes to me and snuggles up against my heart, and I quietly sing Polish songs to him, without understanding a single word in them. They are songs my father used to sing to me. It calms him down. His body is sometimes attacked by such strong storms that he shakes, especially when he's tired, and talk doesn't help him then. Even the pills don't always help. But songs in Polish do. This language, alien to both of us.

And tomorrow is our weekly day of fun. As you know. We will go, as usual, to the junkyard by Abu-Gosh. I will drink tea with Nadji, and watch as Yokhai goes crazy with a sledgehammer on the old rusty cars. It's not easy for me to see the extent of the destructive forces and violence that are in my child. But it seems to clean him out for a whole week.

You also know that exactly one month from today he is supposed to go through surgery, to repair the little defect his heart has struggled with since birth. Truly, God was not lazy when He made him, was He? The number of surgeries this child has already undergone—well, never mind. We will slowly, slowly repair whatever didn't work naturally. I only hope that I can recover a little bit before January, so that I can endure whatever follows (I think that tomorrow I will bring one more sledgehammer to Abu-Gosh). Enough. I'm chattering on to keep from hearing what I'm feeling, to keep from hearing whether drops of rain have already started to fall. Why did you choose the rain over anything else?—you're such a bastard.

I see this letter is taking me to a place I didn't mean to go. I didn't want to fight with you, I didn't want to bargain. It's too painful. I was hoping that I had already found a way to be more balanced inside myself, in front of you. But when I address you again, and you aren't there, that insulting voice returns, with the feeling of just having missed a— I'll stop here. I am not willing to hear myself this way. (And still, to my sorrow, incapable of erasing something that comes from me to you.)

You gave me so much pleasure, and hurt me so very badly. Never in my life have I known such pleasure and pain, and so mixed in with each other. I promise not to write to you anymore, and will not try to make any attempts to contact you. I will never bother you again. With a heavy heart, I will close the gate I so gladly opened for you.

But if you decide to come to me anyway, I want you to know where I am right now. If you come, I need for you to be there completely, with your most sensitive understanding; I need for you to flow into me completely, unstintingly. I need it terribly, as one needs air to breathe.

There's no point to any of this if you can't give me all of yourself. Really. So you shouldn't come, because then I was wrong about you, clearly.

(But if you are the man who called out to me, and roared and brayed and howled, then you will understand.)

Yours,
Miriam

Yair, you have to hear what happened. I wrote my name, and then I heard you calling for me. I simply heard you calling out my name.

At first I was certain it was coming from outside the house, but the street was empty. So I automatically sat down and dialed your work number. Forgive me, I had no control over the decision—it simply wasn't given to my will. I spoke to your secretary, and heard a few voices in the background and music from the radio. I tried to pick out your voice, and the secretary was asking me to talk, already. I asked for a messenger to come and pick up a book from me. I stressed that it must be delivered directly into your hands. My voice was shaking. She said, He'll be at your home in ten minutes, ma'am. Even when she was urging me to speak, there was no mockery in her voice.

I thought, That woman who is working for you perhaps is especially perceptive to women's voices, even if she is a nice little Beit Ya'akov graduate.

So I'm sitting at my table waiting for the doorbell to ring. I truly have no idea why I so suddenly dialed your number. It went against my every intention.

Ten minutes now. What more do I have to tell you?

Perhaps—that today, there was actually a stretch of more than twenty minutes when I didn't think of you. That I didn't hear a word that reminded me of you. That I told myself that perhaps healing from you would be a quick matter, like everything else associated with you.

That in the middle of my morning class, my heart suddenly went out to you with such force that I could hardly continue speaking.

Because in that moment I remembered how they used to call you "Yeery" and thought that the nickname doesn't at all suit you; I thought of how many years you were called that, and it became so urgent for me to tell you that you shouldn't allow anyone to call you that! Don't put up with it! Not from anyone! There is too much emptiness, flimsiness, to the name that is so unlike you. Yeery, Yeery. It just doesn't fit.

(Meery)
(Nobody ever called me that.)

I am regretting calling so much. I thought I could hold myself back, but that strange, depressing matter of the rain not falling—it's beyond my strength to bear. He is probably already riding to me. And what will I give him? What book? Because of Yokhai, all the books that are precious to me are packed up in the shed.

I wish I knew how to fill this sudden silence.

This isn't anything like fall, is it? It's a new season, dry, white and cold (yes, perhaps we should try chatting about the weather) . . . It truly isn't a laughing matter; all the fields have dried up around the village, and someone in the grocery store told me that foxes and jackals have been coming out at night into the gardens to drink from the hoses. And yesterday a flock of storks (that had left two months ago!) reappeared here, as if they had gotten confused, returning during the wrong season. They hovered around the dry dam all day and seemed lost, tortured. I was horrified—the whole cycle of nature is falling apart. Perhaps they are waiting for us, for you and me; someone is stopping everything for us.

He is riding toward me—I think I can even see him, between the trees and the bends in the road; I can see almost his entire trek from here on the balcony, can follow him as he comes to me from you. I'll find a book in a minute and put this letter between the pages (I'll write "Private and Personal" on it, don't worry). How strange to think that right at this moment a person is driving from you to me. A thread.

I dreamed about Yokhai last night, that he went back to talking. A week ago he successfully counted up to four in class, and we had a big celebration. I guess I let myself have this dream because of it: He and I are walking through a huge desert. There isn't a living soul around us, and the sun beats down hard. He stumbles, and I take him in my arms, I see his lips have become dry and cracked, and he then lifts his head with one last effort and tells me, "You should know that I understood your every word the entire time. I wish to inform you that it was you who did not understand."

Listen: I'm wrapping up my cookbook for you. It isn't any old cookbook. Anna wrote it by hand, for my thirtieth birthday (she worked on it all through her pregnancy). Three hundred and sixty-five recipes. Keep it. If you won't have my soup, at least take the recipe.

The doorbell is ringing. Ten minutes, on the dot.

You really are on time. (Horrifying!)

I think she can already recognize my voice—but what do I care?

Are we agreed now? I come to you in words, and you, on a motorcycle?

Again, I couldn't hold myself back. This morning was so gray and windy. Amos brought home a huge pile of firewood; on my owl I discovered that I wrote in some moment of prescient clarity earlier this week, "Call chimney man."

On the radio they promised that it will come down in two days at the latest. The first rain. Their language became mine for the length of three words: the first rain.

I at least had the presence of mind to prepare a small package beforehand, so I would have something to give the messenger. You'll see for yourself.

What about you? Why don't you send a note with the messenger? Or simply come as a messenger yourself, for once? You will take off your helmet, and I will see that it is you and . . . you'll see how simple it can be.

What shall I tell you today?

(The truth is, I already thought about what I would tell you, and fill these horrible minutes with.)

I dreamed about you again last night. My nights are full of dreams now. We were together, in a tall building somewhere. I was close to you in the dream, I could see you and hear you beside me, but I couldn't touch you.

You were standing on top of the railing of the balcony (the word "balcony" recurs throughout the dream, again and again, like a song of mourning, "balcony," "balcony"); I suddenly see that you intend to jump, headfirst, onto the back terrace. I try to stop you, warning you that there is no water there. Even though I see everything happening in front of my eyes, you can't hear my voice (or perhaps I am incapable of making a sound).

You jump, headfirst, onto the terrace, and I hear you mumble to yourself, "I knew this is what was going to happen."

"I couldn't stop him," I tell myself, and my heart breaks.

Your fall ends—and I see you lying on the ground, your body naked; you are lying on your side, and your head is swollen, probably from the collision. You don't move, but I can hear you muttering to yourself over and over, "In spite of everything, I only broke a few teeth and have a mild concussion. That's all."

I am relieved that you are alive, but the fact that I remained on the balcony, above you, causes me terrible pain and suffering (until now).

And here he is, at the door. Perhaps this time?

Twenty-four hours have passed. It seems as if I haven't moved from my place. I mean, I did, I went through all the necessary motions. I fed others and dressed, I cooked and scheduled Yokhai's bus pickups. I played hostess when a couple of our friends who live in America paid us a surprise visit on their vacation home; I was friendly and amusing. I cannot understand how I managed to get through such a show; and now, sitting down, the pen practically floats into my hand, and I feel that I haven't stopped writing you for one moment of the whole day that has just passed. The day closed and opened, as if the outside world blinked . . . and I am still sitting in my rocking chair, waiting for Yokhai to come home from his treatment. Night falls, the rain stands still in the air, and I am writing to you. Sometimes I discover a page under my hand; but most of the time there is none.

If only I could fall asleep now and wake on a day when it doesn't hurt any longer. But I wake up night after night at three—exactly the hour you ran around me—and I cannot go back to sleep. Why? I have no baby to keep me awake at these hours.

It is the baby in me who is keeping me from sleep (no, it is the woman in me).

Strange how this spiritual mess translates into my body language. But you don't deserve to hear about my body. I don't think anyone has ever insulted it in this way, and I just can't understand how it is that when I felt more womanly than I ever had in my life, you didn't respond.

Did you hear it, Yair? Just now on the five o'clock news—they just announced that it will start raining tomorrow morning!

"We finally have good news," said the newscaster, and my heart started beating insanely fast inside me. Instead of taking a pill, I quickly dialed your Rukhama (we've already become a little friendly, you see), and I asked her to send me someone, urgently, it's an emergency.

So this is it, isn't it? Our last chance. The last words. The end of the story you began writing for us eight and something months ago. We didn't even have a full pregnancy.

My hands have started to shake; how many minutes do I have left? Ten? Nine? Is anyone manning the guillotine—has the blade fallen yet?

I didn't even get a book ready. If only I could meet your eyes now, so I could see inside you and then tell you what I see.

I see a man who is not a man. A boy who is not a boy. I see a man whose maturity and masculinity are only a scab that has hardened, sealing over a boy's wound.

You yourself once wrote it on an envelope: "Scabbing wind." (You were still Wind then.) I remember thinking that the scab had hardened directly over the point that connects man and boy in you, a place that is not alive, and at the same time not dead.

(He has yet to reach the curve into the forest, your biker. He's a little slower than usual, I think. Perhaps he's a new one. Very well. Let him drive slowly, slowly, delayed along the way . . . A large, heavy cloud is hanging above the forest.)

From letter to letter I felt something growing in me, something within my strength to do, and it is inextricably connected to you. It wasn't a coincidence that I was the woman you addressed, because with your sharp intuition, you grasped that I could melt this scab away, until the child, your enlightened twin, could be exposed. From there, perhaps you would be able to go back to being the man you are, the one you were meant to be. Who is this man? You will probably never allow me to discover him. I can only imagine him as everything together, man and boy, man and woman, alive and dead; a lot of things and people at the same time, without the violent, artificial separation you create in yourself.

To me, you are the most yourself in that place where all your souls touch one another, mix and mingle, with no separation.

When I met you there, I was instantly filled with you, my body and my soul spoke directly to you, above your words, which I didn't always like; because it was there that you truly excited me, filled me with delight, hurt me and pitied me.

When you allowed me, for those brief moments, to be there with you, I became aroused in a way I never had been by a man, yes, by a *gever*.

Did you feel it? It's happening. I suddenly got hot and cold at the same time, and can, in all my cells, truly feel you standing in front of me, so close, as if you were on the other side of my door.

No, I will not delude myself.

But it has been completely quiet outside for a few minutes now. Not a leaf moving. I am terrified to lift the pen off the page, I can feel your eyes hanging on my lips. What do you want me to say? What can I say that I haven't said already? What is there left to say in words?

There are steps outside, coming up the stairs to the balcony. Yair, if I have one wish left, I wish, I pray, I beg for all these thousands of words to now turn into a body.

With love,
Miriam

Rain

And on Thursday morning, when the clouds sank into the valley of
Beit Zayit and practically sat down on the house, and the rain didn't
come, and didn't come—on that morning, at exactly half past nine, he
called

I asked if it was she, if this was Miriam

And I knew it was him, before he even opened his mouth. I heard him
breathing heavily and almost couldn't breathe myself

Miriam, is it you?

Yes, yes, it's me, yes . . . and there was a very long silence, and our
quick breaths, and I thought he could hear my heart beating

Just a minute, what did I want to tell you

_____

And everything that was, and was not, between us. All these wild months started melting in my chest

Listen, it's not at all what you think

I'm not thinking about anything. Who could think? His voice was thick. He sounded as if he had just emerged from the forest

I just have to ask you something, something small

And was wounded by the battle he had with himself before calling

Are you home alone?

Yes, I'm alone

Look, this has nothing to do with—with that, with us, is that clear?

What, with what remaining strength I had, I asked him, What are you telling me?

It's about Ido, about him, not us, not you and me, I mean, and I started to tell her what had happened that morning

But wait, speak more slowly, please

We've been having some problems with him lately

Slow down, I can't understand you when you talk like this, explain it to me again, what happened to Ido? The name of his child on my tongue

He is outside

What do you mean? Outside where?

His voice lowered until he was almost growling. I could make out only fragments of what he was saying: earlier that morning, he and his wife had some kind of fight with the child

He isn't even five and a half, and stubborn as a mule

I wonder who he got it from, I thought

No, no, no! He is far more stubborn than I am, and certainly more so than my wife. He is stubborn in a way that is from another planet. She has a nice voice, not at all as I had imagined, it's very young. And Maya—that's my wife, Maya

Yes, I know. His wife and his son and him

Say, are you too busy, do you mind hearing this—

Mind—a mind was something I did not have at that moment

I mean, do you have the patience—

Tell me everything

You don't need everything, the details aren't important

There he goes, blowing hot and cold in the same familiar way, it's in his voice as well

She pounces on every word of mine, there was still some breathing space in between the letters, and now she practically exhales on my every inhale

It was silent between us for a moment, as if we were both completely exhausted by our short conversation

Listen. I'll keep things short. This morning he got dressed slowly again, just to drive us crazy, and Maya said she wouldn't wait for him today, she has been late to work all week because of him

He stuttered, breathing hard, and shot out a round of words that sounded completely irrelevant to me

And we had decided earlier that if he would not get dressed on time this morning, she should simply go and leave him behind, and that way we could give him a little scare, a good dose of his own medicine

My soul quickly expanded and went out to him, for the way in which he set himself up for defeat

276

because I could be late to work today, Thursdays are the days for our weekly meetings

At work? At the bookshop, the Book Bunk?

Yes, yes, with books, I was annoyed to hear my name for my business from her mouth. Her familiarity with my life irritated the hell out of me, how she clearly enjoyed showing off, oh, she knows all the dirt on me, it was so female and flustered, where was the nobility I had associated with her, why did I call her anyway

I pictured him at his office for a moment, between the thousands of books, surrounded by people coming to search for a book there; he is running around, quick, spreading out his enthusiasm, filling every pocket of air in the room

At least once a day one person rises from the stacks of books and comes over to me; you should see the smile on his face when he shows me the book he has been searching for, for years; it's almost always something he read as a child—I think it's the only thing that can bring that kind of light into someone's eyes. My private name for it is "Miriam's Light," that's what I call it, tell her, no

We were silent together

Having several conversations with her at once, I wonder whether the phone company will charge for all of them

We breathed together

To make things short, do you hear me

An unknown noise, it was the whispering sound of the cigarette he held in his mouth, he sucked on it, and it, as if it had a life of its own, kept breathing out a bit after he did

We concluded that after he gives in, apologizes, and gets dressed, I will drive him to kindergarten; today we decided to really teach him a lesson

His voice evened out for a moment, and immediately took distance from me; some noise interfered with the connection, perhaps it was because of the heavy clouds

We have some interference on the connection because I'm walking around the house with the cordless, I have to watch him—can you even hear me

I'm not sure

I'll try to talk from the kitchen

Their kitchen

What did you say?

———

I didn't say anything

How is it now?

It's good now, where are you?

Where are you?

I'm home . . .

She truly does have a surprising voice, very young, fresh and quick, not at all what I imagined, she skips over syllables

I found myself smiling, that story of his didn't sound so terribly serious, it was even a little weak as far as excuses go

So this is it, the situation: Maya left and he ran out after her, half naked, his coat open, because he suddenly realized that today we were serious about it

From the first moment of our conversation, he sounded as if he had no clue what the next sentence to come out of his mouth would be, and I used my gravest voice and asked him what the problem was now

Don't you understand? He has to learn that you can't be smart with us and he has to say he's sorry

---

His voice contracted again, the living contact with his excitement aroused me even more, and I knew he was able to excite himself so that he would believe any story he invented, and I almost yelled at him, Come, come, enough with your stories and your excuses

I shut the door in his face, can you understand me; that has never happened to us, and he was quite amazed by it, a bit shocked, I think

I tried not to make any mistakes, to play his little game with complete seriousness. So why don't you take him to kindergarten now?

No, I can't now, don't you understand, she doesn't understand anything, he wants to come inside the house without saying he's sorry

A faraway bell started ringing. I was so confused, something clenched in my stomach, in that place that always knows before I do. You're telling me your wife already left?

Yes, yes. It was as if she hadn't been listening this entire time, as if she heard only what she wanted to hear

He's outside? I mean, your son has been standing outside the door since . . . when did you say she

Since the morning, I told you, since half past seven, this is her day in Safed

But it's already after half past nine

———

Yes, this is what I've been telling you, he's very stubborn, what an id-iot I am for thinking she would immediately understand everything, without having to explain everything to her twenty times, she is so slow, I swear, he's standing by the door, but I can watch him through the kitchen blinds

Isn't he cold? It's terribly cold outside right now

Of course he's cold, you can see how the weather is outside, and the wind

And it will rain soon, I said, and my voice broke a little, slipped over the word

What the hell do I care about the rain, damn it, he should say he's sorry!

I was truly taken aback, it was a raging bark with a bite at the same time. So why don't you let him in the house and talk to him about

Because we decided, we made a decision, do you understand?

No, I don't understand . . . and I suddenly started to fear that I really didn't understand anything at all

I already told him that he would be able to come inside only after he says he is sorry!!

But sorry about what? Every time he yelled, I felt as if he was striking me

Tell me, have you not heard a word I've been saying?

This man is doing things I thought no one could do to me anymore, that I wouldn't let anyone do to me ever again. But he is a five-year-old child!

Almost five and a half, and he's very strong, he has an iron will, and I took off my shoes and my shirt as well

I don't understand. What did you do?

I don't want to have any advantage over him

He's barefoot and without a shirt?

No, I only mean it's cold outside, and we should be under totally equal conditions, but I am not going to let him win

You can't hold out this way all day—what does Maya say about this— I mean, your wife

My wife isn't here. She said "Maya." She'll be back late tonight. Could you do me a favor and leave out the excuses and explanations for one minute, because I really do have to go to work and he is still showing no signs of breaking

I suddenly stopped chasing him, perhaps because he was too far from my grasp, beyond any hope, and for a moment I had some respite and could ask myself if I really did want to reach him

I guess I finally managed to shock the great counselor of pedagogy into silence, to explain just what she is facing here

Do you want to teach him something or break him? I didn't mean to—the shout broke out of me

I remembered something and laughed aloud, so she would know exactly what I was thinking about

Don Juan's Column on Children, I thought, and how he traps me again without even noticing it, by-the-by, as if he

Listen, forget about it, the whole thing, I made a terrible mistake by calling her, thrusting her into my own foulness, so shut up, don't say another word; yes, as a matter of fact, I do believe he must be broken, once and for all, otherwise he will never learn

I don't think you need to break somebody to

Yes, you do, you have to you have to. Oh shut up, could you at least try and camouflage the shit you are, this is the only way children learn, the way she continues with this lame earnestness to argue with me, with all her decency and that honesty, instead of coming here and kicking me

You're behaving like a child yourself right now, Yair. Even his voice was thin and whiny, and I didn't know what to do, mainly I wanted to help the child because I finally realized that this situation was much more serious than I thought, the way I spoke his name, for the first time naturally

"Yair," with emphasis on the "ir," who else pronounces my name like that, like a teacher; here, listen, I'm going to give him one last chance, can't you hear, he doesn't give a damn about me

I heard silence, then steps, he is walking barefoot, I thought, his feet touching the floor, and I remembered Maya's "surprisingly small feet," and also "such a narrow base for two adults and a child to hold on to," of course, and didn't know what I was supposed to be hearing, and then high, and strained by shouting with perfect enunciation, his voice

So if someone wants to come inside the house, he should knock on the door nicely and say he is sorry, and then we will forgive him and go to kindergarten immediately, because all his friends have already been there for a while now

Another silence, and then he whispered into the phone receiver with a scared, secretive voice, it was ridiculous but also a little frightening

You see, he's not moving! He's not answering me! You should see his face! He won't even consider surrendering

Then stop it, go easy on him, I yelled. I lost control and yelled

———

I will not surrender to him, I will not surrender to such blackmail; if you surrender once, it lasts forever

He sounded hysterical, and I felt drops of sweat start to prickle on my forehead, I'm here, and both of them are there and his wife is on her way to Safed and what can you

Walking with the cordless from room to room and shouting at her and the walls, and I don't have a clue why I called her, a minute before I dialed her number I wasn't even considering it

Yair, are you listening to me? Listen to me for a minute, calm down, think about what you're doing to him

It will only do him good, he will say he is sorry like a good boy and then he'll come in and we'll make up

He'll be sick

Then he'll be sick once, so what, it's not that bad

He'll get sick and you will torment yourself over it

Twenty times a year he gets sick from germs, so now he'll be sick for a good reason, you don't die from getting a cold these days

You're being cruel to him

———

Will you please let me conduct this dispute the way I know best

And he hung up on me. I was left amazed and breathless, just like he always leaves me, and how could I let him suck me in this way, into him

I called work to let them know I would be late, so they could postpone the meeting for me, and while I was talking, I peeked through the window and saw that he was shivering, at least I think he was shivering, his shoulders shrunk and he was hopping from leg to leg. I had no choice, I took off my undershirt as well, and my socks, because this may be a long fight, but it will be a fair one

I sank into Amos's armchair, completely exhausted. I tried to calm myself down a little, but all I could think was that perhaps he will now disappear and never return, because now I saw him, in his shame and his ignominy

When I looked up again, the little idiot wasn't by the door anymore, but was standing in the middle of the little path in front of the entrance, crouched over, gazing at some black beetle that had been flipped on its back

I have to disconnect my thoughts from him right now. But the child, I thought; and suddenly became weak, swept into a strange fog of dizziness, my heart started pounding fiercely with a beat outside of the usual repertoire of reactions to him. I said it again and again, and then aloud for no reason ... The child? The child?

Just don't look at him, it only weakens my resolve in this fight, she practically started shouting at me in the last moments

———

286

I took deep breaths, I focused my thoughts: I mustn't abandon the child to his rage. My breath again caught on the words—the child

A moment after that, I returned to the window, and what do I see, what do I see? A tall old man, who looked suspicious and was wearing a long raincoat, standing by Ido

I said it again and again, "The child," and the word was different, it had a new taste in my mouth; the more I said it, the stronger I felt I was becoming, being recharged, and suddenly something struck me and I stopped breathing

Maybe that old man has already had a chance to do something to him. I heard him asking Ido if he is "little Einhorn," and Ido just stared at him, he was probably already a little cloudy-headed from the cold

It's impossible, how can it be, why now, I'm in such a different place in my life and

The old man bent down over him and asked him if Father or Mother was home, and Ido kept staring

I went to the calendar in the kitchen and counted the days. Nothing penetrated my mind. The words scattered away from me like beads from a torn necklace. I counted in my head again, and then counted on my fingers, and thought, Either way, I'm reaching the same conclusion. I sat down and started to shake

The man asked him what he was doing outside, and Ido just stared at him, and I thought that the old man probably thinks he's retarded

I stood up to call Amos, and again fell back into the armchair. I sat
there and went over my body, seeing if I felt anything, and there was
nothing, other than a very decisive physical hint telling me I wasn't
wrong

The old man sent his hand into his pocket, searching for something.
I opened the door immediately and asked, forcefully, Yes, sir, is there
a problem here?

Be calm, I told myself. Immediately they came to me in an insane
rush, all the signs my body has been sending me over the past week,
the spiritual turmoil, the changes, the strange taste of coffee . . . but
I haven't had treatment for over ten months now, it is impossible that
it could happen, just like that, after all those years of suffering and
torture

The old man was frightened of me, I looked wild and half naked and
ready to fight, and he said with a smile, Oh, nothing, sir, I was only
bringing you a letter from City Hall that was mistakenly delivered to
our house

It was then that I finally remembered Yair and the child, and knew I
couldn't lose my mind now, I would have to postpone everything until
Yair let the child back into the house

The old man handed me the letter, but instead of leaving, he started
getting interested in the situation before him, saying emphatically,
as if to Ido, that little children can catch pneumonia being outside
like this

I focused all my strength and thought about the poor child, the poor child, the poor child, being at the mercy of the heat of the sword re- volving over him at that moment; I knew how miserable he must feel, and how miserable it made Yair

I answered the old man, facing Ido as well, that as soon as the "little child" says he's sorry, and says it nicely, he will be allowed back into the house, only after all the shit he's been putting his parents through

I remember how he read stories to him when he was going to bed, and with what tenderness he wrote about him, how I always felt that he knows how to be a father better than I know how to be a mother, if only because Ido is a healthy child, yes, because he can have more points of contact with his child's soul

Ido shrunk a little because of the unfamiliar words, the "shit he's been putting his parents through," as if I had slapped him

Because I didn't know how I would be able to help them, I took off my shoes as well. It was crazy, it was foolishness, but it somehow seemed logical at that moment; I also took off my sweater, and stayed in my thin blouse, everything that touched my body felt new, every touch filled me with rejoicing, and fear, as if I was peeling open a gift that still wasn't completely mine

The old man took half a step back and chuckled warily, with no un- derstanding, and I skewered him with my eyes until he got the hell out of my yard

The house was cold, but I didn't turn on the heat. I thought I would probably get sick now. Ido and I will become ill, Ido and I, and Yair, too, we will all get sick with the same thing now

I turned quickly, went back inside, slammed the door closed, and immediately leaped to the blinds

But I have to be healthy now, healthy

I saw Ido slowly opening his hand, and saw a red candy that the old maniac had somehow managed to slip into his palm

Eventually, I dared say it aloud, for the first time in its fullness, that little thought, the whole fullness of those two marvelous, terrifying words

Damn it, where is she, where is she

I couldn't hold myself back anymore. I dialed his number, and saw how my fingers were shaking, and stopped; I understood why my ring has been cutting into my fingers so much over the past few days, and I was so relieved

Why doesn't she call *now*, when she's needed

He jumped on the phone right on the first ring and yelled "Yes!?" He really yelled. I told him it was me, and he was silent, as if he was trying to make his way through his mind to the memory of who I was at all. Me, too; for a moment I couldn't remember what it was I wanted to tell him. I said my name again, and even that sounded new to me, and full, full of life. Yair absentmindedly said, "Oh yes, it's you," and immediately started to speak quickly, complainingly

Would you just look at how he insists, he won't break, you will understand that I was right before, this is a war, and you will see, I will
bend his will this time, there won't be any more—

His voice had already mutated completely, it was thin and entangled
in the insult of his song, the rage of it. I could feel his voice moving
farther and farther away from me, drawn backward and tied to itself,
all the way to its roots; but tell me, why do you need to bend him

Why, *why*, because otherwise he will think that he has beaten me,
and he has to know that we still have two or three unshakable principles, and that the father is stronger than the child; it is important,
necessary, for him

But you are abusing him, this is really abuse . . . my temples pulse
with tension. With excitement, too. We repeated the same words
again and again, spoke the same sentences, we couldn't escape the
trap

Believe me, it's not easy on me either, but I'm not going to give up,
because I have already invested half a day of work into this, and there
is no point wasting what has already

I was so confused that I asked him—I mean, it slipped out of my
mouth so stupidly—why on earth he called me

Because I—I didn't know what to say, why did I call her, of all people;
because you understand children, and you have a child, and I just
thought I could consult with you for a moment, but also

He didn't say, Because—

—because you are a mother

Those five simple words fluttered their wings inside me, and a wave broke, and I almost started to cry. I couldn't fall apart at that moment, though, so in order to keep up my strength, I fiercely held on to my thoughts of Anna, how much I wanted her to be with me now, at this moment; and how things will change between all of us; what will Yokhai understand, and will he understand that nothing will change between us, and I thought, This has to be a healthy child, God, I need a completely healthy child, terribly; and before anything, I need to call Amos. No, you can't tell him such a thing over the telephone. I will ask him to come home, and tell him then; one minute, one minute, quiet, think

Miriam? Are you there? She suddenly disappeared on me. Miriam? Can you hear me?

I don't know where I found the strength I gathered around myself in that moment; I lowered my voice the same way I do in class, to overcome the storm of voices inside my head, and I said, Yair, open the door right now, let him in, hug him and get him dressed and make him hot chocolate

No, no, you don't understand at all, it isn't like it is with you two, with your whole system

What does he mean, "our system"? I became furious, what does he know about "our system"? I could imagine the way he saw us, to what extent our home, and what we are as a couple, must seem false and delicate and castrated to him, in comparison to all that he calls "the rules," with all the predatory battles involved, and with a last strain to my muscles, I said, You can force a boy to say that he's sorry, but it is pointless

No, no, why are you getting involved at all, who asked you to get involved and analyze the psychology of my

You called me, I yelled, and immediately regretted it

I'm really sorry about this, you're right, forget it, I didn't call at all, it was the weakness of a moment, I don't want to get you involved in this, forgive me, all right? I didn't mean for us to talk to each other at all, anyway. Forgive me as well, I thought, but did not say, for the lies I am telling you at this moment

But you can't take it back, you already got me involved, I'm a part of it now, Yair, you can't disappear now! Each time I raised my voice, I thought, It has been years since a yell has rung out in our home, and each shout dizzied me, and I thought, Perhaps everything will end right here, right now, maybe it will happen while I'm talking to him

And stop using my name all the time

Perhaps I want you to remember who you are

I don't forget that for one minute—I am completely in control of the situation right now, and will manage it exactly as the situation demands

He kept babbling to me in this mix of arrogance and panic, I couldn't escape the feeling that I am also a guilty party in some way; he was, with all his strength, rolling himself into a great void, so that he could cry out for my help from the bottom of the pit, force me to save him

I'm sick of her whining, I never imagined she would be so fragile, and while talking to her, I cut myself a thick slice of bread and wiped butter onto it. I added some tomato and sprinkled some salt and zatar on top, and settled myself down for a snack, because why should I get hungry because of him, and I patiently explained to her that it's nothing personal, I even admire his powers of endurance, because, to be frank, it was almost daunting to see the toughness in him, being, after all, only a five-and-a-half-year-old kid

And you are thirty-three, I muttered, with not much hope that it would sink in, and could already feel how he is fencing with me, alongside this war with his child, and the more I plead for the child, the more I am doing him harm, urging Yair on, more and more

But then, without intending to, I peeped out at him, and wasn't hungry anymore, I threw the slice of bread into the trash and shouted at him in my heart to just give up, give up, damn him, he should simply walk the three steps to the door and knock on the fucking door, why is he playing these games of honor with me

I thought I heard the sound of rolling thunder from afar, the air got colder, and I shivered; and I whispered to him, like an initiation, But you love your child, you love him

He fell, for the first time, at this moment. One of his legs simply collapsed under him, but he immediately stood up straight and dragged himself to a little wicker chair, a rocking chair we have in the yard

---

God, I thought, dear God, before you take care of anything else, make it so that over there, things will end well between them

He lay down across the chair, his head falling over one side and his legs draped over the other, his eyes were open, gazing at a little shrunken lemon left over from the summer

Perhaps it was because I fell silent for a moment. Without saying a word, he hung up on me again, completely matter-of-factly, as if he had completely forgotten I was there; I sank back into the armchair, and counted the days on my fingers again, and thought that I had to get things in order, and if there could just be one moment of quiet, but there was no quiet

Someone is holding a private, exclusive screening of this whole picture inside my head—Ido is outside, and I am peeping out at him, and the way everything repeats itself hopelessly, a slightly balding man bowing over the cracks of the blinds to watch his own pornography

I immediately dialed him again, before I lost my nerve and started hesitating. This is crazy, I thought, for eight months I didn't dare call him, and now, for the third time this morning

My hands started to become blue, and I knew that I had to hurry now, because I didn't have much time, I know the symptoms, all right? So I went around, opening all the windows in the house; the cold, cutting wind blew through it, and I stood up tall and allowed it to slice me as well, and after that, I ran to the windows and saw that he had gotten up and was walking, a few steps forward, and then backward, stopping then, confused

———

Rain   295

In spite of the intensity of the circumstances, I also felt a little special joy within my absurd internal confusion, as if Yair and I already had this routine of little chats in the morning

He took his little peanut in his hand, and pressed down on it, looking around to all sides, with a desperation that tore me apart

The air stretched out, became clear and alert, and the wind stopped, all of a sudden, not a leaf moved, and I thought, Here it comes

Now, he will surrender now, because of his pee-pee, he won't have any choice, ha, at least we will be done with it, finally finished, and he stepped to the front door with tight legs, stood in front of it, and did not knock. I counted to fifty to myself, opened my eyes, and he was still standing in front of the door, his head bowed down, but still not knocking, not knocking

The rain, the first

What came to my mind then? How, years ago, Maya had asked me to teach her the proper way to fold our little boy's penis into his diaper, upward or downward? Say you're sorry, I yelled, and bit into my fist with all my strength

At first, a few, hesitating drops on the leaves of the lemon tree . . . now on the honeysuckle, and the jasmine, and here, the bougainvillea is getting wet, dust is being washed off, leaf by leaf, heavy drops on the windowpane and

The marks of my teeth on my fist scared me, the blood that started dripping

It became stronger at once, became full, roared as if everything that had been stored in the skies since the beginning of autumn, the immense, held-back

I saw Ido, lifting his head, looking around, surprised, reaching his hand up to the sky, I didn't understand his motions, it was as if he was dancing a little dance; he suddenly looked happy and I thought perhaps he was going crazy

I opened the big window, and all the smells of rain hovered inside: the smell of the earth and the rain, of the grass and the rain, rainy trees; the smells of this rain, and past rains, the smell of Annaleh in the rain, smelling like breath, when we were children, through the yarn hats we wore

It's rain—just one minute—it started raining! How can I leave him in the rain

Good smells rise up from the distant chicken coops and my neighbor's stable, everything suddenly smelled of a fresh foaling, even Jerusalem Forest slowly became green in front of my eyes, washed inside the milky fog

He is standing in the running water, not making any attempts to hide, maybe he is even enjoying it, maybe now he can understand that I will have to give up

This is the moment I have been scared of for months, this is the bounty that he resists

It only penetrated my head then, that it wasn't just any rain, it is *the* rain; who imagined that this was what would become of it? Why, I planned to run in it, bathe in it, scream out her name and say goodbye to her for good, in the rain, in my tears, and instead I'm hiding from my child behind blinds

The house trembled under the strong showers; it was an unusually hard first rain, with thunder and lightning and a sudden darkness that went down on the valley and two or three sharp light beams that spread and reached across the valley like open fingers, and I thought, Everything will be all right, the rain came

His pants were already completely wet from the rain, perhaps from urine, too, and he didn't stop jumping and dancing and spreading his hands out to the sky, as if he couldn't feel how cold and wet he was, and how terrible it was to be outside in that weather; his hair was soaked with water, plastered against his face, and he was dancing

I was relieved, for no coherent reason; only my childish belief in the rain, and maybe it will end with a rainbow, a special gift for me, for how I will be by the end of this winter

I ran through the house like a madman and banged my head against the wall, hard, a few times, and the phone rang, and I knew it was her, so I didn't pick it up, what can I tell her

I was again flooded by my marvelous intuition, which had absorbed itself into my body by now, all the heaviness and grace, and I still couldn't contain it, not alongside what was happening to Yair and the child

—————

I took off my pants, too, so I really wouldn't have any advantage over him, and ran in front of the open windows only in my underwear, and thought I must be losing my mind

I let the phone ring for maybe five minutes. He didn't answer. Perhaps he had already picked his son up and taken him to kindergarten, but I knew he hadn't, I felt him continuing to call me with tingles on my flesh, the profundity of his madness prickling me across the distance

The little son of a bitch broke me. I've lost myself completely. All the gears of fatherhood have fallen apart on me, the only thing I thought I knew how to do well

The rain became terribly heavy, the few fingers of light folding together and clenching behind the clouds. The darkness of evening spread over the middle of the day, and my soul was suddenly lost in a panic. I saw the child outside, thrown down, frozen and naked. I called the taxi service in Giv'at Sha'ul, and they said it could take an hour because of the rain

I went to his room, got into his bed, and made some space for myself between his bears and monkeys and lions as if I was high on something

Don't think, I told myself, just follow your instincts. I got dressed and went out into the rain. I was soaked after a moment, I hadn't even taken the time to put on something prettier, or comb my hair, or put on lipstick, nothing; so he wouldn't think that I—so he wouldn't think

I pulled the covers over my head and shouted with all my strength for him to say he is sorry and come inside, blood from my hand stained the sheets, and I bit it again

The old Mini Minor was standing in the garage. I hesitated for a moment and thought I had better not, I haven't driven for too many years, this isn't the time to start, I don't even have a license right now, I didn't renew it this year

I thought I heard him talking outside and became worried that perhaps the old pervert had come back, or perhaps he had brought the police

I stood there, confused, torn by all my different impulses, and my new words shone in me again, amid the confusion and the burden: I'm pregnant, and an expanse of life spread itself out inside me, gradually, as if I was asking my body a question, and each time, my body answered yes, my body answered yes

He was only talking to the shriveled-up lemon, and told it that we always say he does everything "slow on purpose," and then he answered himself as the lemon—he still had the strength for make-believe—and I thought that I wished Miriam would call, and the telephone rang. I picked it up, nervous—I meant to spew out everything I had been feeling about her that had been gathering up for a long time in my stomach juices, about her, and her Amos, who's just so great, oh no, they would never come to such a pass with a child, no, they would sit down and talk quietly and reasonably and hum out some fair formula of compromise, and good for

You don't understand anything

———

But it was Maya. She had arrived in Safed and couldn't find me at work and was astonished to hear it, she couldn't believe he was still there

This really is not the time to remember how to drive, not in such a rain, not when I'm so upset, I haven't driven for seven years (and my reasons for doing so seemed so false to me, I almost forgot why— was it the fear that I might hit someone? To damage someone, so that my life would no longer be worth living, and the immense responsibility that would fall on Amos), but to start now, in my condition, in this situation—I suddenly have a "situation" . . .

So I poured out everything that had been building up in me, because she has some responsibility for what's been going on, too, why, we had decided on this together, this morning; but, no, in the end I am always the one who has to punish him, and she gets away scot-free, and he will never forget this about me, and right at that moment, I was starting to stand trial, starting to know the tremendous hate he will feel for me for this morning

I ran to the gate of the village in the rain, the terrible rain, I shouldn't run now—I vowed that the moment the matter with Yair and Ido is settled, I will start to be careful, keep myself healthy; where is Anna to tell me in Polish that I now have to be careful for two. Why haven't I called Amos yet? But no cars passed through the gate, there wasn't a living soul in sight

And on top of everything else, she's busting my balls all the way from Safed, repeating Miriam's same recital, that he mustn't be broken, he's only a child, I am the one behaving like a child

I'm standing there in the rain, and in spite of all the stress I'm also laughing, laughing at myself, something like this could happen only to me, of course, to the extent that I drive myself crazy over one thing, and to the extent that I had so given myself over to another person, I hadn't made the time to understand all the obvious signs my body has been sending me

I thought I would explode over the way they both seemed to be teaming up with each other on how to scold me, from the height of their judge's bench

I was sopping like a rag, and probably looked that way, too; I was hoping that all the excitement wouldn't harm me; I spent the entire time trying to stay clear-headed, thinking about the child over there, outside; so I pushed back my thoughts about how blind I had been, about this pregnancy that had sneaked in when I wasn't thinking about it, not at all

It's all very well and good, I cut Maya with my words, but Ido happens to be a man, and he certainly understands all the rules of this little battle, he understands maybe even more than what you might guess, because you came from a house all made of honey and cotton balls, she never even got one healthy slap from her parents, but I don't expect you to understand that, either, none of you are capable of understanding

When I saw that no one would help me get out of Beit Zayit, I returned home and stood in the garage; what am I worth if I can't do this?

While speaking with her, I ran to the window and saw that he was lying on the chair again, curled up, mumbling to himself, playing with a long branch, poking it into the streams of water running under the chair, strangely quiet, and I thought he might already be in shock from the cold

302

The old Mini started up immediately. There was even half a tank in it. Amos, Amos, you're the best, I am so lucky, a clumsy, lucky woman

I hung up on Maya and ran outside; on my way, I grabbed a blanket that was on the washing machine. I spread it over him, and he didn't even look at me. I said his name, and he didn't answer me. So I sat by his chair in the water, and looked at him, and in my heart I said again, Say it, say you're sorry

A strange thought passed through me, that now I would need both of them together, Amos and Yair, and that now Yair would have to stay with me, he wouldn't be able to deny me anymore

I want to bring you my stupidity, even, and my enthusiasm, my cowardice and my treachery—and the miserliness of my heart. But I also have two or three good things in me that could mix with all your goodness. Let my fears mate with yours, our disappointments and failures, and failing again and again—correct me if I'm wrong. Correct me.

Be with me. Revive me. Tell me: Be light

But what have I already given you? Just words, and what can words

They can probably do it at some time, perhaps there are moments of grace, when heaven opens up on the earth, as well

I slowly pushed his chair under the eaves, so he wouldn't get wetter; hard rain fell on me, and in a moment I began to freeze with the cold.

Ido was looking at me from wrapped up in the blanket, and for a moment I was afraid that his pupils had become cloudy

I drove slowly through the roundabout, praying that no one would come toward me; I decided not to think about the actions I had to do, to let my instinct guide me, because I suddenly trusted it, my instinct

I don't know if he was having a hard time recognizing me because of his cloudiness, or because of how I looked, because I was completely unrecognizable at that point, and I saw his body stiffen in front of me

How lucky that I rode past his house that night two weeks ago, to see his street and his house, the entire journey from me to him

As if he was tensing up for a blow from me, even though I have never raised a hand to him; after all, I am not my father

I was driving in waterfalls; I thought about how sometimes Yair looks like a spoon that has broken in two inside a teacup

I was hoping he couldn't see how the muscles in my face were starting to shake, as they always do when I'm cold, I mustn't be cold

Rain hit the windshield hard; I've never seen Jerusalem like this, so diagonal through the rain

He pushed himself up a little onto the chair, and saw I was only in my underwear, and then he asked me, I couldn't believe what I was hearing, if he too could be this way, without clothes

In my heart I was talking to the child, to Ido; hold on, I told him, I'm coming

So I took a deep breath, with the vestiges of my ability to think, I responded, quietly, that perhaps he hasn't been able to understand me until now, perhaps he was so stupid that he couldn't understand such simple words, but if he gets up now, I will even help him inside, and together we will go to the door and knock, we'll even say we're sorry together

The entire time I knew, with a terrible clarity, that all this would never have happened if today wasn't "the last day"

I didn't have any choice. What choice did I have? Because he wasn't at all ready to hear about saying he was sorry, and I thought I mustn't stay beside him for even one more moment, because I didn't know what I would do to him, and I got up and went inside, and leaned on the door, and I saw a little puddle gathering around my feet

But when did it begin, when could it have happened, maybe when he was writing my diary in Tel Aviv

I stood in the doorway and explained from far away that he was wrong if he thinks Mother will come to help him, because Mother is in Safed and she will return only at night, so now the only people left are him and me, without Mother

Maybe the day he told me his name? And how could "it" hold on and survive through the whole period of his silence

He didn't answer me. Perhaps he could feel how he was breaking me even more, I asked him if he understood what I was saying, if he was strong enough to walk from the chair to the door to knock on it, because all of a sudden it seemed a huge distance

Perhaps only after I started copying down his letters, and our words mixed together, or when I started writing my own diary

I slowly slid down the door and sat on the ground, and explained to him, quietly and considerately, that we has to help each other now, because something has happened here, a complication has come up; I will explain to you how such a thing can happen in life later, someday I will explain to you, someday you will understand, you will even thank me for not giving in to you

I saw a flash of myself in the rearview mirror, like a plucked chicken, wet; my nose was red like it always is when I'm cold, and I thought, What will he think of me, and I thought that he is still so very young

He got off the chair and lay at my feet on the ground, purposely laid himself down in the water, purposely turned his back on me and curled up again and didn't move, and I wasn't cold anymore, I thought it was strange how you stop feeling anything, I was left only with the hope that he wouldn't die on me, in front of my eyes

I pitied the child who is reneging on a debt he doesn't even know about, the way children usually do

As much as I tried, I couldn't grasp how such a horror was happening to our family, that no one could hear or see what was going on here, where were all the neighbors, and just people, the witnesses, where

I ran, steps going down into the yard

So strange, I could see drops hitting my body, but didn't feel them, the rain washed down and got into the house, inside blurred into outside and became one, I saw that I wasn't understanding anything, and closed my eyes and just stopped

As I ran down the steps, I saw both of them in one glance, Yair and the child, separated by maybe three steps; they were lying in that little yard, lying in water, twisted at a horrible angle to each other like two bent nails. Yair was naked and blue from the cold, his ribs were poking out and he hardly moved, his eyes were squeezed shut. Ido lay beside a wicker chair, covered with a blanket, and I remember how surprised I was to see him wrapped up, protected—rain hit the wall of the house, splashing hard on Yair, and me. I thought: We meet in water, we meet at the end as we did in the beginning, inside a story he wrote for us. He opened his eyes and looked at me for a moment, and closed them again in pain. I saw his lashes tremble, and he bawled out, a cry I have never heard from a grown-up, and he said my name again and again and again. I also remember that, before I hurried to his child, before I touched Yair, my eyes were drawn briefly to their hands, Yair's and Ido's; they were bluish, transparent from the cold, and resembled each other marvelously; they both had long, beautiful fingers, long and thin and fragile

February 1998